# PRINCES
## OF THE
## LOWER EAST SIDE

Scalisi Family Saga Book 2

# MEREDITH ALLISON

PERSNICKETY PUBLISHING

Editor: Michelle Morgan of FictionEdit.com

Proofreader: Jenny Hanson

Cover Design: Les of GermanCreative

*For my best friend, Sade, the first fan I ever had.*
*Gray Squirrel to Woodchuck, over and out until next time!*

# CONTENTS

# PART I

# CHAPTER ONE

*Catania, Sicily*
*March, 1926*

On her last night in paradise, Mia Angela Scalisi stood on the crumbling, modest balcony outside the bedroom of her cousin Carlo's small villa, overlooking the beach and the Mediterranean Sea. The sharp, angular waves, capped with foamy peaks, crashed against the craggy rocks of the shore in an orchestral roar.

The villa was a hundred years old and badly in need of repair in some places, but the view it offered—the imposing Mount Etna puffing away over the crystal sea—more than made up for it. A doting host, Carlo had offered her the bedroom he shared with his wife, the largest room in his home, but she'd turned it down for a different one. She didn't want to put them out, and she didn't need that much space. The room was cramped, but it had the balcony and the view, and she'd enjoyed it immensely every day for the last thirteen months. But now, it was finally time to say goodbye.

Mia should have returned late last summer per her contract with Hyman Goldberg, but—to her fortune—she'd received a

telegram from Mr. Goldberg in August telling her the construction of the new, exclusive nightclub where she was to perform
had been delayed to a spring opening, and that she should stay
and enjoy an extended visit with her family, if she wished.

She did wish. She was in no hurry to run back to New York
to fulfill her obligation as Hyman's new, shiny commodity. Moreover, the delay had also given her time to gather information on
what was happening back at home, since she knew Hyman
would never tell her the truth in letters. *When the cat's away…*

And it seemed there had been quite a few playful mice back
home.

The salty breeze off the sea mingled with the luscious scent
of blood orange from the villa's grove nearby wafted toward her
in the darkening sky. Mia closed her eyes, letting the aroma seep
up her nostrils where she prayed it would embed itself in her
memory forever. She might never come back, so every one of
these last moments in Catania was precious.

She thought of New York often—what was happening there,
of the life she'd put on hold, the people she'd left behind. She'd
left abruptly, and had moments of genuine regret about that. She
should have put her affairs in better order, but the promise of a
family she'd never known existed was too urgent to deny.
Nothing mattered as much as they did, these people she'd never
met when she boarded the ship that carried her to the other side
of the world.

The uncertainty of what she would return to kept her up at
night until the heavy, sweet red wine she drank before bed took
hold of her and lulled her to sleep.

It was the only thing that kept her from the nightmares.

If she did not imbibe rather heavily before bed, she would
see them in her dreams—the men she'd ordered dead on her
rampage of revenge for her brother. She would see Kiddo
Grainger, with his bloody, broken mouth as he screamed at her
for mercy. She'd see Vinnie Fiore, a bloody hole in his forehead
she'd put there herself, pointing accusingly at her and running
toward her.

And she'd see *him*, the man responsible for it all. The man she'd had murdered outside the Chicago courthouse where he'd just won a legal victory that would keep him out of prison. Salvatore Bellomo had earned his freedom from jail, but she'd made sure he never left the courthouse alive. That was the most vivid dream of all, and the worst. But there was no ghostly haunting. She simply relived that freezing winter day as she'd turned her back and stared at the heavy gray sky, the icy wind biting her cheeks as she waited for the sound—the booming echoes of three gunshots from a pistol wielded by one of Johnny Torrio's most reliable button men, and the soft, agonized groan that followed. And then the silence in the aftermath, before she'd walked away, leaving him there to stiffen in the chill.

She'd had a sense of buoyancy that day as she'd hurried from the crime scene to her waiting car. How free she'd felt, but how fleeting that feeling had been. It had quickly given way to a heaviness she'd never experienced before, an internal weight so great she sometimes needed to sit down abruptly, because her legs could not bear the pressure.

And there was also grief, finally.

Away from the oppression of the city and all its burdens, in a space where she'd been warm and welcomed and loved, the full brunt of the grief for Nick had hit her, because she'd finally allowed it to. Together with his widow, his daughter, and the family he'd never known he'd had, Mia mourned her brother intensely. The first few months had been sheer agony, but now, the pain lessened into a dull ache she instinctively knew would never leave her. And she welcomed it, because it was a delicate, gossamer tie that would keep her connected to him until she, too, died.

The breeze gusted again, and her cheeks were suddenly cold. Mia swiped her fingers over them, realizing they were cold from tears she hadn't known she'd shed.

"Mia?"

She turned from the balcony toward the voice. Her sister-in-law Gloria stepped into the small bedroom, her hand still on the knob. Sicily had done wonders for her, too. Her skin had lost its haggard, drawn appearance, and her brown eyes were soft with lingering sadness instead of haunted with anguish as they'd been before she'd left New York. Her parents still lived, so together with her family and her in-laws, she'd been as safe and cared for as Mia had been.

Gloria tilted her head. "Are you all right?"

Mia nodded. "Is Emilia packed?"

"She is. She's with her *zia*."

Carlo's younger sister, Raquel, was actually some degree of cousin to Emilia and not truly her aunt, but the little girl had begun calling her that and no one had seen fit to correct her. Raquel had taken to her immediately, and Emilia, now nearly four, loved nothing more than to follow the young woman around the beach as they collected shells, and to the orange grove where Emilia loved to snack on the sweet, succulent fruits. At twenty, with no prospects of a husband in Sicily, Raquel would be journeying to America soon to live with Mia and Gloria, nannying for Emilia and working in the shop if she liked. She reminded Mia of herself, how she'd been before Nick had died. Vivacious, witty, with a sharp sense of humor and intelligence.

Gloria leaned on the doorframe, one hand on her hip. "Don Catalano is waiting for you in the grove with that mute bulldog of a man, Paolo. He sent me to tell you."

Mia frowned at the slight to her godfather Don Catalano's most trusted enforcer. "Don't speak of him that way. He's more loyal than blood." She stepped away from the window. On her way to the door, she started when Gloria reached out and snatched her arm. She met her sister-in-law's alert, probing dark eyes.

"Yes?"

"Don Catalano calls, you go to him immediately," Gloria said softly. "No questions asked. And you change—I see it."

Mia tightened her jaw for a beat. "What of it, Gloria?"

"When you first started meeting with him after we arrived,

you said it was because he wanted to help you, help us. That he knew Nicky back in New York."

"Don Catalano has been a friend to our family since before either Nick or I were born."

Gloria narrowed her large eyes to slits. "You meet with him several times a week. Every week. How much help is he providing?"

The don had been, as a matter of fact, providing Mia with quite a bit of tutelage to retake the operation she'd left behind. He had instilled in her a belief that as Nick's sister, she should maintain her control of the liquor operation, rather than let it drift into the hands of his friends, however trusted they'd been. She'd spilled blood for her brother—the ultimate act of vengeance for a loved one's murder, and had thereby built a reputation she'd never planned to build or, frankly, wanted.

"Now," the don had asked her almost every time they'd spoken over the last year, "what you gonna do with it?"

"What are you driving at?" Mia asked Gloria quietly. "He *is* my godfather. He's as much family as Carlo is."

"He is a *Mafia chief*," Gloria hissed. Her grip on Mia's arm tightened. "He goes against the head of the government. Do you know what that could mean for us?"

"This is not my home country," Mia replied. "The head of the government is no president of mine. And besides, I'll worry about such things when he does."

Gloria's full lips thinned to a tight, white line. "Does he know…everything?"

Mia didn't answer right away. Of course Don Catalano knew everything. He'd known plenty of what had happened to her brother, and what she'd done in the aftermath, before she'd even arrived in Sicily. Over the course of the past year, she'd told him all the details about the killings and the business. But Gloria did not know everything, despite her best efforts, and Mia had decided long ago it would be best to keep it that way indefinitely.

She met Gloria's stare with an unwavering one of her own that, after an extended moment, caused her sister-in-law to drop her hand from Mia's arm, her expression stricken. Mia never intended to try to intimidate Gloria, or wanted to, but when it was clear she had, a flash of guilt ran through her.

*But she should know by now she can only push me so far.*

"If you'll excuse me," she said in a soft voice that carried all the deadly venom of a viper. "I shouldn't keep him waiting."

She brushed past Gloria and headed out into the balmy night air that carried a hint of a chill, but it didn't bother her.

In the blood orange grove, Mia plucked a large, ripe orange from a tree as she passed. It felt ready to burst through the rind as she tossed it and caught it gently in her palm. She spotted the white-haired don sitting at a large, round table with his enforcer Paolo Scarpa and another man. On the table was a bottle of red wine, accompanied by a plate of bread, cheese, olives, and salami.

As she got closer, she recognized the third man. "Johnny!"

A somewhat frail Johnny Torrio rose from his seat as she rushed toward him. She caught herself at the last moment and embraced him carefully. He lightly kissed each of her cheeks.

"Ah, Mia," he said warmly, and his voice, so Brooklyn, sounded of home. He pinched her cheeks. "Sicily agrees with you. Look at you, like a real village girl." He gestured to the airy, printed teal frock she wore, in the style of the carefree young women of the village, instead of her old, high-fashion wardrobe.

She beamed at him. "Johnny, when did you get here?"

"I docked in Italy a few days ago. Made it down from Irsina just this morning. Beautiful here, really."

She was touched he'd left his native village so soon after arriving, especially in his condition, just to make sure he saw her before she left. "It is. Don Catalano told me everything that— that happened to you."

He waved a hand. "Sit, sit. We have so much to discuss."

Mia turned smiling eyes on Don Catalano as she embraced him. "Did you set this up, Godfather?"

The tall don was clean-shaven except for an impressive salt-and-pepper moustache he groomed meticulously. His dark eyes were surrounded by crow's feet, but they were as alert as they'd ever been. His ponderous body had taken bullets and other wounds over the years, but despite a limp, he still moved with agility for a man of his size and age.

"A little goodbye surprise for you," he said in English. Mia loved to converse in Sicilian, and her mastery of the language had blossomed during her time here, but Don Catalano liked to speak in English to stay sharp in case he ever returned to New York, he said.

Paolo flicked open a knife and held his hand out for the orange. Mia handed it to him and he deftly cut it into slices and added them to the plate. The don pushed it toward her, and she took a slice.

"Johnny, how are you, really?" Mia asked, settling back into her chair. "It's so good to see you. But after hearing what happened to you and Al getting *shot* at—" The sweetness of the blood orange's juice soured on her tongue.

Johnny sighed as he accepted the cigar Don Catalano extended to him. "Well, you warned us Weiss was coming after us, didn't you? We should've listened. We got careless. Cocky. Right after you left New York, Weiss hit Al's limo. Word on the street says he threw a goddamn fit when he realized Al wasn't in the car. Then twelve days later, they got me outside my house. Made sure they hit me."

Mia shook her head, rage throbbing to life in her chest. "Why is he still breathing?"

Johnny shrugged almost dismissively, puffing his cigar to get it going. "He's Al's problem now. I survived by the grace of God, I did my time, and now I'm here. I want peace, Mia. Al can have it. I'm quitting. It's Europe for me now." He reached out and patted her hand. "I knew you'd come to Sicily, and I know you're leaving for New York tomorrow. I asked the don to set up a meeting. I couldn't contact you directly. This country has plenty of spies too, you know."

Mia glanced at her godfather. "So I've been informed."

Johnny inclined his head at Don Catalano. "I hear you've taken her under your wing."

The older man spread his hands, his stogie grasped between his forefinger and middle finger. "She's family, if not blood. I gotta watch out for her."

The don had been in New York when Mia's parents had arrived twenty-five years ago, and his father had known the man from their days in Sicily before he'd left. Nick had remembered him from their childhood, but Mia hadn't been born yet. Shortly after her family had settled onto Elizabeth Street and Mia had been born, the don returned to Sicily. He had returned to New York occasionally for visits and to check up on Nick and Mia, but she hadn't seen him when Nick had been off in France, and he'd visited only once before they'd moved to Chicago. He was currently a large importer of Italian goods to the States, but his true business was gambling. He kept a few gambling houses run by trusted associates in Manhattan, Brooklyn, and Harlem.

"I'm too old to travel with her to New York to protect her, so I teach her instead," Don Catalano went on. "I send Paolo for protection."

The silent enforcer bobbed his head.

"So how is Al?" Mia said. "I haven't wanted to write him for safety reasons. Never know who might get a hold of your letters."

Johnny nodded approvingly, then his face darkened. "I gave him total control of the Outfit, and, well…I guess you could say he's taking to leadership."

The note of derision in Johnny's voice caught Mia's attention. He sounded as though he wasn't entirely pleased with Al.

"Custom silk suits for every day of the week, a jeweled ring for every finger, gourmet meals three times a day," Johnny recited, shaking his head. "Let's just say he's a far cry from the guy you remember who cooked his own peppers and *salsicce* in the frypan and served you himself."

Mia frowned. "Oh."

"And he and the Irish gang are really going at each other," Johnny continued, tapping an ash from his cigar. "He and Weiss are both wily bastards, so it's no shock they're still alive. But you're not going back to Chicago, are you?"

"Not any time soon, but I still have unfinished business there," Mia said coolly. She was referring as much to Weiss as she was to bringing Nick's remains, buried at Mount Carmel Cemetery, back to New York.

Johnny's keen gaze narrowed. "I see."

"You hear anything in New York?" Don Catalano said. He refilled Johnny's wineglass, then poured Mia some red wine. "I hear a few things, but information takes a little while to get here."

"Al's got a friend there, Frankie Yale," Johnny said. "He manages Al's Canadian Club, but he's been helping run the Templeton up across the border, too."

"Nick's operation?" Mia said.

Johnny studied her closely. "I don't think I would call it that now. I wouldn't even call it a *Scalisi* operation anymore."

She glanced away and toyed with an orange peel. Johnny's words didn't surprise her, though they stung. "Was it ever?"

"It ought to be," Johnny said, leaning toward her. "That was your brother's brainchild. His hard work. Now you got all these vultures buzzing around, looking for whatever they can take."

Don Catalano had heavily implied the same over the past year, as he shared with her the information he'd received from New York. Information about Nick's closest friends and business partners, Charlie Lazzari and Moritz Schapiro.

"It seems your old pals Charlie and Moritz have made the business flourish, certainly, but doing business in New York ain't without its pressures," Johnny went on. "It's catching up to them. So many protection payments to avoid truck hijackings. Bad blood among gangsters means executions of good men. And while liquor's still king, heroin's the coming thing." He caught sight of the stormy look on her face and shrugged. "Sorry. It's good money, and they know it."

Though it displeased her to hear his words, she'd heard them before. And none of it was surprising. She'd been gone a long time, and men tended to get antsy. Like Moritz.

They would probably be shocked to learn how much she knew about what they'd been up to since she'd sailed away last January.

*When the cat's away...you don't know who your friends are.*

"Well, it's time for me to go back to New York and play my part in Hyman's new club," she said, plucking a piece of bread from the plate in the center of the table. "That was the price for his two-million-dollar investment in Nick's operation."

"It's also time to go home and salvage what you can of that operation," Johnny said gently. "Because he died for it. He was murdered for it."

"I know," she said bitterly.

"I know you know," he replied. He didn't seem miffed. "My point is, you'll never forget that. I'll never forget that. But...some people in your life might have."

"I suppose I'll see for myself soon enough." She reached for another slice of blood orange.

Don Catalano flicked his head at her. "I'll have a crate of those shipped home with you, if you like."

She smiled. "Thank you, Godfather. I'd like that."

"There's one other thing." Johnny hesitated. "Some detective. He came sniffing around Chicago after you had Bellomo whacked."

The ease and forthrightness with which he said it caught Mia off guard for a brief moment. She glanced at Don Catalano, but his face was impassive, as if Johnny had only mentioned a snowstorm.

"And?" Mia said.

"Thinks we had something to do with it. We got him off your scent for a while, but my cop pals tell me he's been trying to reopen the case file. You know, no one on the department was in any hurry to try to find a killer's killer. But this guy, all of a sudden, he's back at it. Last I heard, he was headed east to pursue some leads. Don't be surprised if you hear from him."

"What's his name?"

"I don't recall." Johnny lifted a shoulder and took an olive.

"Sorry. But I got eyes and ears on the streets. If it comes up, I'll let you know."

Don Catalano frowned at her. "You're already well known, but appearing at the Jew's nightclub will elevate that publicity. Are you sure it is best for you to go now?"

"I got to," Mia said. "I'm under contract."

"Yes, yes." Don Catalano sniffed and sipped his wine. "I can have the contract canceled, if you wish."

It had been a standing offer for the last year she'd been in Sicily and remade his acquaintance. He'd never said so, but Mia knew the don felt an immeasurable amount of guilt for remaining so out of touch with her and Nick since he'd returned to Sicily. He'd only heard bits and pieces of Nick's activities, he explained to her, and once word of his successes had reached Sicilian shores, the don had thought it best not to interfere. But when Nick had been killed, he'd told Mia he hadn't known how to reach her. She'd bounced between New York and Chicago, and by the time word of Sal Bellomo's murder—at her order—reached him, she was already on a ship back to Sicily.

After they'd reunited, Mia realized his treatment of her was like that of a father to a son, or even an uncle to a nephew. He respected her for avenging her brother's murder so thoroughly, and as such, did not treat her as the young woman she was, but as another person of respect. As though she were a man.

It frequently made her smile a little when she thought of it in private, though she tried not to do so around her godfather in those moments.

She shook her head. "You know what that would do to the operation. Mr. Goldberg was very clear—he'll withdraw his support, try to reclaim the business for his own. And I won't see my brother's work into the hands of someone who isn't family."

"Goldberg has earned more than his two-million investment by now," the don said, fixing her with a scornful glance.

"But he's invested three times that now over the past year," Mia said. "More trucks, more distilleries, more supplies. More men."

"So, I have him killed." The don shrugged. "No contract, no Goldberg, no problem."

The chill that should have rippled her skin at the ease with which murder was discussed never came. She placed a hand over his. "Thank you, Godfather. I know you only want the best for me. The appearances, they'll help my career. And Mr. Goldberg is…an ally. For now."

"Still," her godfather muttered. "I do not like the idea."

"I must agree with you, Don Catalano." Johnny puffed a perfect smoke ring. "She's like a goddaughter to me, too. We're both here, and she's there."

Mia smiled. "I have protection. You're sending Paolo with me."

The smaller man was in his mid-forties, and his black hair was only slightly shot through with gray. His eyes were nearly black, and he wore no moustache. Though he was mute after an attack in his youth had left him with half a tongue, his expressive face spoke volumes, and he lifted his brows at the don, as though in agreement with Mia.

At a first glance, the idea of him as an enforcer of any kind— much less a bodyguard—was laughable. But on one of her first trips to Palermo to go shopping, she'd been accosted by a trio of young, lewd men. She'd hardly opened her mouth to curse them in Sicilian when Paolo had brushed her aside to snatch one of the youths by the throat and slash the cheek of another with a blade concealed in his shirt sleeve. She'd never seen anyone move so fast. Word spread quickly after that, and she was given a wide berth whenever she left the villa, always with Paolo at her side.

The don had told her that her father had saved Paolo's life during the attack that left him without a tongue so many years ago, and then helped him find steady employment before leaving for America. It was a favor Paolo had never forgotten, and that history, combined with the knowledge that Mia had avenged the murder of her brother, had seemed to cement his loyalty to her.

"And," she added, "I have…friends." *I think.*

The word felt foreign, and echoed quietly through her mind

as she considered whether it applied to the men she'd left behind in New York.

"*Friends*," the don repeated. "Friends who put money first over loyalty. And you are a woman, Mia. They will not hold you in high esteem no matter what they say. Be very careful with these *friends* of yours. They are not blood."

It was from Don Catalano that Nick had learned this oft-repeated ideal that had become his catchphrase.

"Don't forget that," the don added.

"I won't," Mia said quietly. "Ever."

After her chat with Don Catalano and Johnny, Mia returned to her room to finish packing. Her mind always spun after talks with the don, but seeing Johnny and hearing all he had to say had left her particularly pensive now.

She hadn't been expecting her homegoing to be a particularly happy occasion, but now a feeling of dread filled her. Vultures, Johnny had called them. Vultures in the form of all the princes of the Lower East Side and Manhattan were descending on the little bit of a dream her brother had carved out for himself.

When Nick had first built the operation, all Mia had cared about was what it could mean for her. She'd wanted to be a star at the Chicago Theatre, and maybe one day, be in moving pictures. She had idolized Lillian Gish since she had first seen the young actress in *The Birth of a Nation* when she was twelve years old. The complexity of the story itself had been lost on Mia as she'd sat in the back row of the small, dark theater she'd snuck into in the Bowery, and spent three hours completely entranced by Lillian Gish's luminous doe eyes, the perfectly cut bow-shaped mouth that rivaled Clara Bow's, and the expressive face that could contort from a coy expression to one of sheer terror to heartbreak to joy.

Mia had wanted to be just like her. The Italian Lillian Gish. It had been her dream since childhood.

She'd seen Nick's deal as a way to hasten the realization of her dream. She'd seen a life of luxury, beautiful clothes, the fanciest parties. She'd seen herself as the It Girl of Chicago—the girl every woman wanted to be like, and every man wanted to be with.

Then the reality of the life Nick lived had caught up to her, to him, to all of them, and Mia had seen what was truly involved. Murder, blood, disloyalty, distrust, and betrayal. It was late nights and greased palms and lies. So many lies. Lies to enemies, lies to friends, lies to loved ones. Lies, and broken promises.

When Nick died, Mia had cared about only one thing—revenge. It was the Sicilian way, the code of honor. An eye for an eye. But it hadn't been tradition that drove her. It had been a tidal wave of rage and grief that pushed her to sniff out all those who'd been complicit in his death. Only one name remained on her list—Hymie Weiss.

But with the things she'd been hearing from New York this past year via the don, and the realization her brother's business was suffering at the hands of men he'd once trusted, she wondered if that list might grow.

No, that wasn't quite right.

The list *would* grow. What she didn't know yet was by how many.

Mia cupped her forehead and closed her eyes. This life wasn't her. She was supposed to just be a showgirl, and that was all. But it was impossible to pretend as though what she'd done last year hadn't changed her in so many ways. Some, perhaps, permanently.

"He'd get that same look," Gloria said from the doorway.

Startled, Mia lifted her head. "What?"

"Nick." Gloria walked into the room. "When something was troubling him or he had a big decision to make, he'd grip his forehead like that, too. What's troubling you? Something the don said?"

"Yes and no. I'm just thinking about all I need to do when we get home."

Gloria sighed. "This place has come to feel like home. Both our families are here. It'll be hard to leave."

"You don't *have* to leave, you know," Mia said softly, rehashing their old argument. "Emilia's happy here. Clearly, so are you. What is there to go back to?"

"You tell me." Gloria folded her hands.

"You know I've got the new show now." Mia flicked her head toward the most recent stack of letters she'd received; one had been from Mr. Goldberg. He hadn't written her much, but his latest letter had arrived nearly two weeks ago and reminded her the new venue was finally complete and would be opening inside of four weeks. She was expected back in the city for rehearsals and costume fittings.

"And there's the shop," she added. Another "gift" from Hyman, but like all his gifts and favors, they came with very long strings. "I can't leave it in Trudy's hands forever."

"Why not? She likes it."

"It's my shop. My responsibility. Besides, Raquel is eager to come and see the city."

Gloria lowered her brow. "I think we both know it's not just the shop you want to return to. It's the *business*. The real business. Nick's business."

Mia strolled to the small chest of drawers against the wall opposite the bed, where she'd been packing up her cosmetics. Gloria's unsettling ability to read her mind was unsettling and made her feel entirely exposed.

Yes, she did want to return to New York to see to the perfume and cosmetics shop that was a classy front for Hyman's illegal business dealings—liquor sales. That had been part of the bargain, and Trudy, the Irish girl who had been her maid in Chicago, did not handle that part of it, because Mia refused to put her in that position. It was too dangerous. Charlie and Moritz had been handling the distribution and the warehouse beneath the shop, but now, perhaps, it was time she took that over, too.

*My shop. My responsibility.*

"Or maybe it's not all business," Gloria said, glancing toward Mia's nightstand, where the envelope of Charlie's most recent letter rested. The letter itself had been stashed in a safe place to be kept from prying eyes—those of her suspicious sister-in-law, and those of her newly found and very curious family members, who seemed to understand that Mia was not the average young woman, that she carried some notoriety in America in the vein of the activities of the local *Mafioso*—but the envelope remained unguarded. Mia cursed herself.

Gloria picked it up. "From Charlie. He's written you every week since you've been here, hasn't he?"

"Not *every* week," she muttered. But no more than two weeks ever went by without a letter from him. And the contents of the letters were rarely business. Mia's lips burned with a low, pleasant heat, as though calling her to remember their passionate goodbye on the dock before she'd left the country. He'd been Nick's best friend, and in the wake of tragedy and Mia's determination to continue Nick's business arrangement, had been a steadfast pillar of support. He'd believed in her when no one else had. He respected her, and he'd killed for her.

He loved her.

He'd never uttered the words exactly, nor had he written them in any of his letters, but Mia knew it, as surely as she knew the sky was blue and the sand on the beach was powder soft. He loved her deeply.

In his letters, he spoke of looking forward to seeing her again, of welcoming her back to the city, and that he hoped she was safe and happy and enjoying Sicily. Not business, personal, but distantly friendly. There was an undercurrent of tenderness in the way he wrote, almost as if she could see his love for her in the ink and the marks of his letters, in his signature.

As Mia had never been in love before, she had no idea what she felt for him, beyond deeply felt gratitude for his support and his role in her life. And always, her belly dipped and fluttered when she pictured him, when she recalled their last moment on the dock before she'd walked away, never looking back. He was another reason she wanted to return home, yes.

He'd promised to wait for her, whatever that meant. Perhaps he had waited. More likely, he had not. He was a man, and men were the most disappointing, dishonest, unreliable creatures on the planet. Even Nick had let her down several times, most recently by dying and abandoning her. But perhaps Charlie was that one, rare exception.

When she glanced at Gloria again, her sister-in-law was smiling slightly. "I knew it," she said. "That's what this is really about, isn't it?"

Mia plucked the envelope from her fingers. "Go pack your things. We must be at the dock early in the morning, if you're still determined to come with me. And I hope you know, I don't think you should."

"Yes, I know, and I'm going," Gloria said, hands on her hips. "You promised my husband to watch out for me and Em, but he would want me to watch over you, too. You need someone to look after you, Mia. To care for you. Even if you don't think you need anyone."

"I have Paolo." Mia had asked him once if he'd known what she'd done in America. He understood English, so she spoke both Sicilian and English to him. Paolo had responded with a single, firm nod. And that had been the only time they had discussed it—as much of a discussion as could be had with a mute man.

When she'd announced to her family two weeks ago that she was returning to New York, there seemed an unspoken under-standing Paolo would also make that trip. Nevertheless, Don Catalano, who had made the arrangements for her, had told her in no uncertain terms the fierce Sicilian man would be accompa-nying her as her bodyguard and remaining by her side in New York.

She had come to appreciate his silent presence, his protective hovering. It was hard to understand why he had chosen her to devote himself to, but it wasn't a gift she was interested in questioning.

"I don't trust Paolo," Gloria said. "How do you trust a man who can't talk?"

"I find him the most trustworthy of men for that reason alone."

"You can't travel and live on your own with a man you're not married to," she insisted. "You're still just a young girl, after all."

"I'll be twenty-three in September."

"You are a *child*," Gloria repeated softly.

Mia smiled, a little bitterly, down at her small case of cosmetics, dropping the envelope on top. When she was a child, she'd lost both of her parents—her father to a heart attack when she was just a toddler. Her mother had died in a terrible fire at the Triangle Shirtwaist Factory, leaping from the top of the building in order to avoid being burned by the flames. Mia and Nick had been forced to hustle the streets, begging for handouts, learning poker to swindle the gangsters, stealing food, freezing nearly to death in their filthy tenement. She'd become a vaudeville performer, because young girls telling raunchy jokes to older men made money. When Nick had been drafted to the war, she'd worked a dozen hours a day for an abusive woman in a dress factory, just to keep a little food in her stomach. She'd known more about being an adult at twelve than most women her age knew now. Once she might have been proud of that, but now, it only made her sad.

Finally, she looked at Gloria. "I haven't been a child for a very long time."

# CHAPTER TWO

*New York City*
*April, 1926*

The moon was just beginning to rise in the sky on the first Wednesday after Easter when the ocean liner approached New York City. Mia stood at the railing of the ship, a blanket wrapped around her shoulders to ward off the early spring chill in the air and to watch the shadow of the Statue of Liberty as it grew larger on the horizon.

It was a sight she had never seen before, not from this angle —sailing toward Lady Liberty from a land of oppression. But her parents had. She wondered what had gone through their minds twenty-five years ago, a young couple with a two-year-old boy, a small, scared family watching the symbol of their new life grow bigger as their ship drew nearer.

Had they thought they were home? And if they'd known how their lives would unfold, and that of their children's, would they have come? Had there ever been a moment when either of them had looked at their baby boy and thought he would grow up to be a criminal and a murderer, and die at the age of twenty-five?

Had they ever looked at her when she was a baby, born inside their tiny tenement on Elizabeth Street, and thought she would grow up to be the same? Mia would be turning twenty-three in a matter of months. Would she outlive her brother? Her dead parents?

The screech of the ship's whistle pierced the air, and with Gloria, Emilia, and Paolo in tow, Mia walked down the wide ramp of the ship to the same dock on which she'd bid Charlie Lazzari farewell over a year ago. She paused, looking down first at her shoes, then up at the sky.

She was home.

The morning she had left, Carlo, his wife Isabella, their two small children, Anthony and Sofia, and his sister Raquel had lined up outside the villa to see them off. She'd embraced each of them, then held her cousin's hands in hers.

"Thank you, Carlo," she'd said earnestly. "I know I was here much longer than I planned. Thank you for everything."

"You are blood," he'd replied firmly. "Scalisi blood. What's mine is yours. Should you ever need our help, I am here. Should you ever need a home, this is yours."

"And you," Mia said. "If you ever come to America, there's nothing you won't have. I swear that to you."

He'd nodded and inclined his head at Raquel. "Take care of her."

"I'm a grown woman," Raquel had protested. "It's time I make the trip, start a new life."

"I'll look after her like she's my sister," Mia promised.

"Don't forget about us," Isabella had added tearfully.

*Never*, Mia thought now, following Paolo as he led the way toward a waiting taxi. *I will never forget about my family. My blood.*

The taximan drove them to the Murray Hill Hotel, where Mr. Goldberg had set up a two-bedroom suite for her, Gloria, and Emilia. Mia identified herself at the front counter and requested another suite for Paolo, next to her own. The flustered concierge informed her he had no rooms ready, but begged her to give him until the following morning to accommodate her. Perhaps he was aware she was on Hyman Goldberg's payroll, because he seemed almost terrified he was unable to meet her request immediately. She reassured him that would be fine. Paolo allowed the concierge to assist him with carrying up their trunks, but only to the end of the hall. Then he dismissed the man and dragged both trunks by himself.

In the meantime, she refused to let Paolo sleep out in the hallway, as he gestured. She made up the living room sofa for him with extra bedding the now very curious concierge was happy to supply.

When her sister-in-law and niece were sleeping peacefully, and sounds of Paolo's snores from the living room reached her, Mia stood at her bedroom window and stared out at the city. Her city.

The New York City skyline and all of its bright lights called to her like a siren in the darkness and she, a shipwrecked sailor. It was both dark yet beautiful, dangerous yet enticing. It was full of promise.

*And it's mine for the taking.*

Was that Nick's voice echoing in her head, or her own?

Perhaps both. Perhaps she, now, wanted the same things he had once wanted. Wanted so much, he'd been willing to risk his life for them. That he'd ultimately lost it had not been in his plans, but Nick had been smart enough to know the odds of keeping his life were likely not in his favor.

For the first time since getting off the ship, Mia drew in a deep, deep breath, clearing her mind and accepting that the last year spent in paradise was over, and had only been a respite from her reality. What that reality comprised, she had yet to find out. But the feeling of bewilderment that had clouded her brain since setting sail from Sicily began to dissipate now that she was home.

And yet, she still felt completely out to sea.

Mia opened the window. Even the small crack allowed a flood of cold air to flow into her room and around her, freezing her through her thin nightgown. From outside, sounds of loud music from establishments up and down the street filled her ears.

A Saturday night in the city. Soon, she would become the Saturday Night Special again.

She wrapped her arms around herself and thought of Charlie. She hadn't telegrammed him to let him know she was returning, had never replied to his last letter. He, like everyone else in this city, had no idea she was back or even that she was on her way. He would have wanted to be the one to greet her with open arms, but after all this time, she had no idea where they stood. She had no idea if she could still trust him. If there was *anyone* left in this city she could trust beyond the people currently in her hotel suite.

After all, she had left the relative safety of dangerous Sicily for the lion's den of New York. Sal hadn't been a big-time gangster, but by now, news of what had happened to him and why it had happened and at whose order would surely have reached the East Coast. People would know what she'd done. They'd know she was following in her brother's infamous footsteps.

Perhaps most dangerous of all were her so-called friends and allies. A year was not a long time, and yet, it could feel like a lifetime to some. People changed day by day, minute by minute. She certainly had. A little more than a year ago, she'd arrived in Sicily, frightened and unsure of herself, eager to meet her long-lost family, and ready to turn her back on everything she'd done.

A bitter smile quirked her lips. Oh, how she had changed.

Were her friends still her friends? Would they still stand by her? And if the answers to those questions were no, where would that leave her?

She leaned her elbows on the windowsill, lifting her gaze to the velvety-black sky, mists of gauzy clouds mottling it. Tonight, she would not be able to smell the salty, citrus-drenched air or listen to the calming, low roar of the ocean. She would not feel the soft powder beneath her toes on the beach, would not sit outside at night in silent reflection with a bottle of homemade wine and a ripe blood orange with only the breeze, the buzzing insects, and her thoughts to keep her company.

Catania had been paradise, a haven, and the first place she'd ever truly felt at home. New York was familiar, but strange, also. It felt like a place in which she could never let her guard down.

But the sky was familiar and comforting. It was the only thing the two locations had in common, and it was the only thing to bring her solace tonight.

She fell asleep in the easy chair she pulled to the window, resting her head on her arms.

AFTER BREAKFAST THE NEXT MORNING, MIA CALLED DOWN TO the front desk to check on Paolo's room. The hotel manager assured her the room next to hers had been evacuated of its guests and was currently being cleaned. Mia encouraged Paolo to have another cup of coffee while they waited, and within the hour, a knock came at the door to alert her the room was ready.

To her surprise, Paolo seemed rather grumpy as he toted his lone suitcase to his spacious room. Mia stood in the doorway, arms folded, watching as he set the suitcase down and walked the perimeter of the room, grunting disapprovingly under his breath. He eyed the fringed silk lampshades, the gilt-framed end tables, the decorative baubles, but did not touch any of it. He looked over his shoulder at her, his brow drawn into a deep furrow.

"Paolo, what's the matter?" Mia asked, amused. "Don't you like your room?"

He waved a hand in frustrated dismissal before grabbing a beautiful, small deco lamp that was more decoration than function and gestured impatiently as if to say, *What can I do with this?*

"You think it's too much," Mia said.

He spread his hands wide in exasperation. *Yes.*

"Well, I'm sorry, but this is yours now." Mia smiled and walked into the room toward him. She patted his shoulder. "You're an important man. You escorted me across the world safely, and the don says you're to be my bodyguard. You deserve to have a comfortable place to eat and rest your head at night. Allow me to provide that for you. All right?"

He shrugged reluctantly, but bowed his head in deference. Then he mimed driving a car, lifting his eyebrows. He made the motion again and pointed at her.

"Yes. I will want you to accompany me out today. And, we should probably look into getting our own automobile."

She'd had Nick's yellow Cadillac Phaeton transported from Chicago to New York, but it was rather ostentatious. It seemed a better idea—safer—for her to travel in something less conspicuous.

Paolo patted his chest.

"Yes, I'll leave it to you, whatever you think is best," Mia said. "I don't know anything about cars. Just get something black and simple."

"Auntee! Auntee!"

Emilia's excited voice filled the hallway, and Gloria and the little girl appeared in the doorway.

Mia smiled at them as Emilia bounded over to her. She swept her niece up in her arms. "Well, you certainly look beautiful, Emilia. Are you trying to impress Aunt Connie and Uncle Joe?"

The little girl, in a pretty sky-blue frock, nodded shyly. She was now a girl of nearly four, with pink cheeks, glowing olive skin, and huge, dark eyes that took in everything. Her black curls were combed neatly and crowned with a large, matching blue bow.

Mia smiled. "I'm certain they'll be very happy to see you." She glanced over Emilia's head at Gloria. "Are you ready?"

Gloria nodded, an eager smile lighting up her face. Though Gloria had loved spending as much time with her parents as she could in Sicily, Mia knew how much she'd missed her aunt and uncle, who had effectively raised her.

They drove south from the hotel toward Lower Manhattan. Mia's spirits lifted as the areas grew more familiar. When she'd been in New York at the end of 1924, she hadn't strayed to the old neighborhood as frequently as she would have liked, but when she had she always felt a sense of nostalgia. Though they'd been poor, she still had fond childhood memories after their parents had died and before Nick had been drafted. The tenement community had truly been like family—for many years, the only family she'd thought they had.

As they passed an alley where street vendors lined either side, she spotted a group of three young men in rather handsome, tailored suits harassing an older fruit vendor. Two of them pressed him to the side of the brick building his stall sat in front of while a third flicked a pocketknife in front of the man's face. He looked terrified. Finally, he reached into his pocket, pulled out a wad of money, and handed it to the young man with the knife. The young man flicked the knife closed and waved to his compatriots. They shoved the vendor to the ground, stole a couple of oranges, and walked away, laughing.

The taxi moved slowly enough to allow her to grab the door handle. "Stop the cab. Those men are—"

"No, miss, please," the driver begged, speeding up a little more.

Paolo leaned across her and pulled the door shut, giving her a reproving stare.

"But that vendor—"

"Nothing we can do." The driver accelerated until he'd caught up to the normal flow of traffic. "You should know that."

"I've been away," Mia said. "For a year. What the hell's going on?"

"Then I'm sorry to tell you, this neighborhood's changed a lot since the new gang's started operating here."

"New gang?" Mia leaned forward. "What new gang?"

"I'm not sure who the leader is, but the street calls him Gems. He's been promising the young men of the neighborhood they'll be rich soon if they'll work for him."

"Work for him doing *what*?"

"I'm not sure. People say the boys are peddling heroin, collecting money." The driver sighed. "This used to be such a nice place to live. Me and my wife, we liked it here. Sure, it's never been totally safe, but if you mind your potatoes, people leave you be. Now, though…" He shook his head.

Mia sat back in her seat. "Does this Gems fellow have a last name? Or a real first name?"

"I'm sure he does, but I don't know it. I try to mind my own, you understand."

She did.

The taxi delivered them to Mulberry Street. Mia stepped out of the car and waited for Gloria and Emilia to exit, glancing around and frowning. She couldn't help but notice with dismay the change in the neighborhood, as the driver had said. There seemed to be more trash and refuse in the street, damage to buildings she couldn't remember having any before, and more young hoodlums prowling about. Like the young men earlier, they also wore bespoke suits rather than the drab, worn clothes of the people who lived in the neighborhood, as though they'd just gotten a taste of money and were eager to flaunt it. They swaggered and gambled brazenly in the street, laughed loudly, and made rude remarks to the women who passed. Men passing by with cartloads of supplies seemed to cross the street to avoid them.

Mia followed Gloria and Emilia through the door of d'Abbruzzo Grocery, Paolo trailing behind at a respectful distance. There were three other customers in the store, and Uncle Joe assisted one of them, a short man with a round belly.

When the customer seemed satisfied with his information about the imported olive oil the store carried, Mia called, "Sir, we have some questions as well."

Uncle Joe turned quickly to assist her—and stopped when he saw them. A wide smile split his face, and he rushed toward them, calling for Connie.

Gloria's aunt emerged, covered in flour, from the back where she made her famous, fresh pasta and gnocchi in the kitchen. She cried out joyously and scuttled across the floor toward them.

As Mia embraced them, her gaze fell on the customer Uncle Joe had been assisting, and she stilled. The short, rotund man with the round face and thick lips was familiar to her.

It was none other than Joe "The Boss" Masseria.

He smiled at her indulgently, hands folded in front of him, as he waited for the reunited family to finish embracing.

"Ah," Uncle Joe said, clasping his hands. "It's so good to see you both."

"We missed you so much!" Gloria said, eyes shining with tears.

"How touching," Mr. Masseria said. "To see a family back together."

Gloria looked at him, then glanced quickly at Mia, confusion written in her round brown eyes.

"Don Masseria," Uncle Joe said quickly. "My family. My niece, Gloria, and her daughter, Emilia. And this—"

"Mia Scalisi." Mr. Masseria drew her name out like Sicilians said it in the Old Country. "Of course. We met in Atlantic City a few times." He shook her hand, then lightly kissed each of her cheeks. "Your brother, he was a good man."

"Thank you," Mia said. "And thank you for the wreath you sent to his funeral. And the generous gift you sent to his wife and me."

"It was the least I could do." He reached for Gloria, kissed her cheeks, then gently pinched Emilia's. "Nick always showed me respect. Always paid me a tribute, always paid protection money for the good Signor d'Abbruzzo."

His implication—that he expected these things to continue— was not lost on Mia and told her two things: he knew the deal Nick had cultivated, and he knew she was involved now.

She smiled politely. Was today a collection day?

As if reading her mind, Aunt Connie said, "Don Masseria is here to help us end the degradation of our neighborhood."

Mia frowned. "What's that?"

"Did you not see when you came here?" Aunt Connie insisted, sounding upset. "The damage, the filth, the violence? The white powder has come here. This used to be a good family neighborhood. Now it is as bad as anywhere else. Young people, even children, hooked on the powder. There's a murder every other night. A beating. Theft. Vandals."

Mia looked at her uncle. "Powder?" But she already knew.

"Heroin," Mr. Masseria said with a bland smile. "It is affecting this neighborhood."

"Don Masseria has promised to help stamp it out here," Aunt Connie went on. "He hears the cries of the women—the mothers, the grandmothers, the wives. It is ruining our young people, our men. Worse than liquor."

Gloria pressed her hands to Emilia's ears. "I'm not sure this is proper conversation for a child."

"Connie, they just got in," Uncle Joe said gently. "Tell them happy stories, not the bad ones."

"Of course," Aunt Connie replied, flustered. "Are you hungry? There's coffee in the back, and pastries."

Gloria glanced at Mia, who nodded. "Yes, please, Aunt Connie. Emilia, would you like some cookies?"

As Aunt Connie led Gloria and Emilia away, Mia turned back to Uncle Joe and Mr. Masseria. "I noticed some young men earlier. They didn't look like neighborhood men. In suits. Nice ones. They seemed to be making themselves right at home here."

Uncle Joe nodded. "They're the peddlers."

Mia looked at Mr. Masseria. "And you have a plan to tidy things up?"

He lifted a shoulder. "I know who they work for. I'll talk to him, tell him to stop letting them deal here."

"Who is it?"

He studied her. "No one you know, I'm sure," he patronized.

"Have you been affected directly, Uncle Joe?" Mia asked.

"Yes," Uncle Joe said sadly. "A couple months ago, there was a robbery. They held me up with guns, took all the money from the register, destroyed some shelves and some product. But luckily for us, Don Masseria helped us rebuild, gave us the money that was stolen from us."

*Lucky for you, or lucky for him?* Mia glanced at Mr. Masseria, who smiled at her, a bit smugly. "That was very kind of you, Don Masseria. I am grateful and indebted to you, on behalf of my family."

"Uncle Joe!" Emilia shouted imperiously, sticking her head out of the back room. "Aunt Connie says you got a quarter for me!"

Uncle Joe grinned at the child, then turned to Mia and Mr. Masseria. "Excuse me, please."

Mr. Masseria gestured toward Emilia. "There is nothing more urgent than the needs and desires of our children."

When they were alone, Mia turned toward him. "So, this business with heroin dealers in the neighborhood is true?"

Mr. Masseria nodded. "You saw what you saw."

"And they don't work for you?"

If he was surprised by her candor and her borderline disrespect, he didn't show it. "They are not mine. I conduct my heroin operation elsewhere."

"Who is, then? And don't tell me he's no one I know. I don't know plenty of people, but if I need to, I make it my business to introduce myself."

This time, Mr. Masseria indicated his surprise with a slight lift of his eyebrows. "Is that so? Well. He calls himself Gems."

"Gems," she repeated. "Second time today I've heard that name."

"A reference to the strength of his balls or perhaps the jewelry he wears, I do not know. I've heard both stories." He smirked. "He's new in town. From Jersey, but has been all over. He was in Chicago before, I believe, but after you left. Now, he's here to make a better life for himself, like so many of our people from the old country. He's a young, impressionable fellow. I will speak with him."

"I would consider that favor," Mia said. "For me, and my family."

His brows lifted higher. "Since you seem to want to be taken seriously as your brother was, I will be frank with you. It is a favor, yes, but one your uncle hardly deserves."

"What's that supposed to mean?"

"As your uncle stated, I helped him quite generously after his misfortune. Yet his protection payments have waned ever since your brother died. I did not raise the matter out of respect, but it's been over a year now since Domenico's death." Mr. Masseria's voice took on a sharp tone, and his gaze was steady and hard.

*Aha*, Mia thought. *So we come to the heart of the matter.* Out of the corner of her eye, Paolo—whom she still had not introduced—took a step in their direction at the tone of Mr. Masseria's voice. Mia subtly held out a hand to stop him.

"I'll resume the protection payments," she said. "And I'll double what you were getting paid before if you give me your word this store will not be bothered again."

"Double?" He looked impressed and amused. "A lot of money for a young lady."

"I'm involved in some lucrative endeavors."

"So I've heard."

She didn't like the way he said that.

"Well." Mr. Masseria bowed his head. "Fine. You will pay me double protection payments, and I will see to it your family's store is not bothered by the young hoodlums in the neighborhood."

"And that you'll make this Gems fellow stop his business dealings in this neighborhood."

His brow lowered. "Do you ask me, or do you *tell* me, Signorina Scalisi?"

Mia opened her pocketbook and deliberately peeled off five twenty-dollar bills from the roll she carried. "For the first month in advance, consider it another favor." She swallowed. "Please."

He blinked slowly, then took the money, folded the bills, and tucked them into his suit coat pocket. For a long moment, he studied her. "You remind me very much of your brother. I see you are as smart as he was, but you have a cooler temper, a more reasonable head. But I hear you are as ruthless."

She said nothing and waited.

"You would be surprised to know how quickly news in Chicago finds its way here," he said. "But I say this in admiration of you. Of the vengeance you took for your blood."

"Vengeance is only finished when all involved are dead," she said. Hymie Weiss still breathed, and as long as he did, Nick remained unavenged.

"In time, in time." Mr. Masseria tilted his head, observing her. "You are quite young."

"Indeed," she said. "However, I learned from my brother that age is but a number."

He chuckled, apparently pleased by that. "I hear you are working for the Jew, Hyman Goldberg."

"I am headlining his new nightclub."

"Ah. That will keep you very busy. Luckily all your partners are doing such a fine job with the liquor."

Again, the way he spoke made her hackles rise. It was as though he knew something she did not. And she did not want him to know that she did not know everything.

Her gaze flicked to his breast pocket where he'd hidden the money. "Do I have your word, Don Masseria?"

Mr. Masseria patted his chest. "You have my word that I will impress upon this young fellow that it is not in his interest to conduct his business here."

She released a breath. "Thank you."

He touched the brim of his hat. "I have enjoyed doing business with you, Signorina Scalisi. Consider the little neighborhood problem solved. I wish you well."

She watched him stride out of the shop. She'd been home for hardly a full day and had already made a dangerous friend.

Dangerous, because she wasn't sure if—or when—he'd become an enemy.

# CHAPTER THREE

They remained at the grocery for another hour before Mia stated it was time to leave. She needed to visit her shop, and would have gladly left Gloria and Emilia with Uncle Joe and Aunt Connie, but with a determined gleam in her eye, Gloria insisted on accompanying her.

After Aunt Connie made them promise to come for Mass and then Sunday dinner, Paolo drove them to Midtown and stopped in front of the elegant storefront of the shop Hyman Goldberg had unceremoniously dumped in her lap over a year ago.

The shop was open, which meant there was one person inside to tend to customers.

With a real smile of pleasure, Mia walked through the door, immediately finding the young, pretty, redheaded woman, standing on a short stepladder and neatly arranging a selection of ladies' gloves on a shelf behind the counter.

At the sound of the tinkling bell, Trudy called over her shoulder, "I'll be right with you."

"Take your time," Mia replied.

Trudy whirled, nearly toppling off the stepladder. Her blue eyes widened, lips parting to emit a surprised gasp. "Miss Scalisi!" She scurried off the ladder and rushed into Mia's open arms.

"It's wonderful to see you," Mia said, hugging her tightly. She pulled back, surprised to see tears gleaming in Trudy's eyes. "How have you been? You look very well."

Trudy's fashionable chiffon and lace bell-sleeved dress was a beautiful pale green that brought out the rosiness in her creamy skin. Her makeup was light and artfully applied, down to the deep rose lip rouge she wore.

"You cut you hair." Mia ran a hand over the short, deep-red bob.

"Oh," Trudy said, patting her hair and flushing. "No, it's a faux bob. My hair's pinned up."

"Well, it's beautiful, and so are you."

"Thank you," Trudy said. "Well, Mr. Goldberg says the girls who run the shop should be presentable for the clientele."

Mia cocked an ear. Trudy's musical Irish brogue sounded less pronounced than she remembered. Her *r*s were more fluid and less hard, and her words more enunciated. *Have I been gone so long?* "You're certainly that. You even sound a little different."

Trudy's cheeks turned a darker shade of pink and she glanced at the floor. "Mr. Goldberg also said I should take measures to not sound like a common Irish immigrant."

One of Mia's eyebrows arched slowly. "He told you that you sound *common?*"

"I've been listening to the radio and going to the theater to learn how to speak properly."

"You speak however you'd like to," Mia said stubbornly. "This is my shop, and I'm back, and I say you don't have to change how you talk. You don't have to change *anything* you don't want to."

Trudy swallowed. "But Mr. Goldberg—"

"You let me worry about Mr. Goldberg." Mia glanced over her shoulder at Gloria. "Can we have a moment?"

"Certainly." Gloria took Emilia's hand and led her toward a corner of the shop to look at hand-painted compact mirrors.

Mia turned back to Trudy. "Do you know where Mr. Gold-berg is this afternoon?"

"I believe he was to be having a meeting," Trudy said, and Mia was happy to hear her brogue again. "At the penthouse."

"A meeting with who?"

"Mr. Schapiro, Mr. Lazzari, and a new gentleman I haven't met. There's to be a delivery tonight."

Mia wrinkled her brow. "Have you been involved in those?"

Trudy shook her head. "I only know the days they're happening to make sure any inventory for the store is moved well out of the way. Some of those deliverymen can be rather ungen-tle, you see. We lost a crate of French perfume not long ago because of them."

"I never intended for you to get mixed up with all that," Mia said.

"Well, I'm no bootlegger," Trudy said slowly, lowering her voice as her eyes slid to Gloria, "but if you recall, I *did* launder blood out of Mr. Scalisi's shirts a time or two."

It was Mia's turn to flush. A time or two—more like dozens of times. She'd been so adept at getting the stains out Nick never wanted anyone else to do his laundering. And Trudy had never said a word to either of them—or anyone else, to Mia's knowl-edge—about it.

"How have you been?" Trudy asked. "It's a wonderful surprise to see you. I hadn't heard from you for a couple of months and had no idea you'd be returning now. Did you enjoy your time with your family?"

"I did, thank you," Mia said. "It was wonderful to live with them for the past year. And I apologize about not writing sooner. I didn't intend to give anyone here any warning about my return."

Trudy nodded slowly, a look of comprehension that surprised Mia stealing across her delicate, symmetrical features. "Then I reckon it's best I don't telephone Mr. Goldberg and let him know you're on your way." A tiny, sly smile perked up the corners of her mouth.

Mia gave her an appreciative nod.

Behind her, Gloria cleared her throat. "I'm Gloria," she said to Trudy. "I don't believe we've ever met, actually. I'm Mia's sister-in-law."

Trudy gave her hand a gentle shake. "How do you do. I've heard much of you, Mrs. Scalisi, as well as your darling babe." She bent down slightly to smile at Emilia, holding her mother's hand. "Aren't you a beauty? What is your name, little lamb?"

"Emilia," Mia's niece murmured.

"What a pretty name for a pretty girl!"

"What do you say?" Gloria prompted gently.

"Thank you," Emilia whispered gravely, staring at Trudy with round eyes.

Trudy fished a sweet from the pocket of her dress. "If it's all right with you, ma'am?"

Gloria smiled down at Emilia. "Emmy, look. A sweet for you from the kind lady."

"Thank you!" Emilia said with a great deal more enthusiasm as she took the candy.

Trudy straightened and smiled at Mia. "A wee precious thing, she is."

Mia put her hand on Trudy's arm. "You've done a wonderful job of taking care of this shop while I was gone. Thank you, Trudy."

"Oh, it was my pleasure, Miss Scalisi. I suppose I found it rather fun and liberating to come to work each day."

"How is your family in Brooklyn?"

"They are all well," Trudy said. "I've been able to spend lots of time with them and with my little sister. She's nearly finished with high school. She's a proper young woman now."

"That's wonderful."

Trudy shifted her weight. "I suppose I'll be taking on a new endeavor, now you're back. I've made you a list of clientele and their personal preferences, when they like to shop and what they usually buy. I've kept careful inventory logs and when each item should be ordered and how long it takes to arrive. I—"

"Trudy." Mia smiled. "How could I possibly follow in your footsteps? You know this place better than I do. I'd like you to be the general manager. If you enjoy it and want it. It comes with a raise, of course."

"Truly?"

"If you want it," Mia repeated.

"Oh." Trudy's face brightened. "Well, I'd certainly love the opportunity, Miss Scalisi."

"Then it's yours." She glanced around. "What happened to the other woman who worked here?"

"She moved out west six months ago."

"Well, let me know if you'd like more help around the place."

"Well, another girl for evenings and some weekend help would be nice."

"Then you'll have it."

Trudy beamed. "You're far too kind, Miss Scalisi."

Mia squeezed her hand. "I appreciate your loyalty."

They visited for a little longer, and Mia discreetly checked the time. She didn't want to miss out on the meeting Trudy had told her about. She hadn't been invited, but she intended to be punctual. After Trudy gave her a spare key to the shop, Mia bid her goodbye.

Outside the shop, Mia turned to Paolo. "After you drop me at Mr. Goldberg's, please take Gloria and Emilia—"

Paolo shook his head firmly.

"What?" Mia said, exasperated.

He pointed at her, then himself, then mimed driving. Then he folded his arms.

"Paolo, if we all taxi to the hotel, and then you and I go back to Mr. Goldberg's, it'll take too long," she said impatiently.

"It's fine," Gloria said. "Emilia and I will take our own cab. Apparently, you have something very important to do, don't you?"

Mia sighed. Gloria didn't look particularly happy. "It is important."

"That's clear." She took Emilia's hand. "Could I trouble you for a little cash to get home?"

"It's no trouble." Mia opened her pocketbook, but Paolo beat her to it, handing over some bills from his pocket.

Mia waited on the sidewalk until the cab showed up. Gloria helped Emilia inside, then glanced at Mia over her shoulder. "I suppose you'll be late?"

"It's not even four o'clock, Glo."

"Never can tell."

"I'll be back in time for supper," Mia said.

Gloria nodded, then gave her another long, sweeping glance. A ghost of her old smile appeared. "Keep them in line. I know you will in that dress." She climbed into the taxi and shut the door.

Mia glanced down at her new, cap-sleeved cream chiffon dress. She'd had a number of new dresses made while she'd been in Sicily, and this had been one of her favorites. The bottom of the dress was covered in a beautiful black, red, and green floral embroidery, with small black embroidered flowers covering the bodice front and back. A pair of black-velvet-trimmed white gloves and black T-strap heels completed the look.

She'd once said nothing was impossible; all a girl needed was the right dress. Though she felt a lifetime from the girl who'd said that, perhaps there was still some truth to it. She wasn't looking to do the impossible. Just find out what the men she'd trusted had been up to while she'd been away.

And find out if she still *could* trust them.

They arrived at Hyman Goldberg's Midtown penthouse five minutes later. Paolo stopped her from getting out of the car with a touch to the forearm. He jogged around to her side and opened the door. His deference never failed to surprise her. It seemed to go beyond basic gentlemanly chivalry or even common courtesy.

The driver leaned across the seat. "You want I should wait?"

Before she could respond, Paolo pointed at him and nodded. Then he walked ahead of her to open the set of thick, glass-plated doors.

As they walked across the lobby to the elevator bank, Mia glanced around. Nothing had changed since the last time she'd been here. It was familiar, almost normal. However, she'd never dropped in on Hyman unannounced, and her stomach did a little quivering dance of nerves before she steeled herself.

Paolo called the elevator for her, and when it arrived, he swept her inside ahead of him.

"Paolo," she said quietly as they rode to the top. "Thank you for coming with me. I don't just mean here. I mean to America."

He nodded.

"Do you miss it? Sicily, I mean."

The older man stared straight ahead, swallowing several times and blinking rapidly. Then he gave a slight shake of his head. He patted his chest, wincing.

"It...hurts? To be there?"

He nodded.

"I'm sorry."

Again, a nod. He met her gaze in the doors' reflection.

"If there's ever anything you want, anything I can do for you, you need only let me know."

His eyes flashed with gratitude, but he gave her a small smile, pointed to his mouth, and shrugged. *How?*

She grinned at his little joke.

They arrived at the top of the building, Hyman's penthouse. A few guards stood in the open foyer in front of his office. They all did satisfying double-takes as she walked toward them.

"He's inside?" she said before anyone else could speak.

"He's—he's—yes. He didn't mention you were coming," one of the guards stuttered.

"He never mentioned you were home," another one added.

"Well, surprise, boys," Mia said without cracking a smile. She turned for the door.

One of the guards stopped her with a hand on her forearm. "Just a min—"

Like lightning, Paolo leaped in front of her with a low growl and grabbed the guard by the neck before ramming him against a wide marble pillar. Air whooshed out of the guard's lungs, his eyes shocked and rolling as he grabbed at Paolo's hand around his throat. Before either of the other two could move a muscle, Paolo had drawn the pistol at his waist and pointed it at the forehead of one of them.

The man's speed and agility shocked her, but Mia placed a hand on his, pressing lightly to get him to lower the gun.

"It's all right, Paolo," she said softly, her calm exterior belying her thundering heart. "They're just doing their jobs."

Paolo bared his teeth as he lowered the gun and released the guard, who immediately doubled over and gasped for air.

The other two stared at them in shock.

"I'll show myself in, yeah?" Mia turned on her heel without waiting for an answer and crossed the floor to the heavy oak doors. She put her ear to the door, and picked out what sounded like a few masculine voices.

So Trudy's dope had been spot on. Mia was right on time.

She pushed open the door, and the voices grew louder and clearer, punctuated by laughter and the smack of pool balls clattering into one another. She stepped silently into the room.

Hyman leaned over the table, lining up a shot, while three men looked on. Moritz Schapiro rested a hand on the table, smirking, and Charlie Lazzari stood a few feet back, leaning on his pool cue, an amused look on his face. A third man had his back to her, but for a moment, her gaze only settled on Charlie.

Now that she was back, now that she was in the same room as him, she realized for the first time how much she'd missed him.

Then, a stern inner voice resounded through her mind. *This is business. Don't behave like some lovesick schoolgirl.*

Mia stepped forward a few more feet. No one noticed her. If she'd been someone who'd shown up with bad intentions, all three men could have been dead before they'd hit the floor.

Perhaps she'd point that out.

She cleared her throat.

Abruptly, the chatter and laughter ceased, and all four heads swiveled in her direction. After a brief moment of silence, the three faces she recognized adopted similar shocked expressions, as though they were looking at a ghost.

The unfamiliar man appeared to be around the same age as Charlie and Moritz, and was tall and quite handsome. His broad shoulders filled out his perfectly tailored suit, and his eyes matched his thick, wavy dark hair. He lifted a cigarette to full, smirking lips, his gaze going over her with lazy disrespect.

"Hello," Mia said coolly.

"Mia," Charlie murmured.

Hyman recovered first. "Miss Scalisi," he said, setting his cue across the table. "What a shocking, but happy surprise. Did you telegram me, and I missed it somehow?" He crossed the room to her, sweeping her hand into his and bending over it gallantly.

"No. I never telegrammed."

He straightened, his brow creasing ever so slightly in confusion. "No?"

"No." She smiled politely. "I thought I'd just drop in and say hello. Find out how things have been."

Moritz and Charlie walked over to her, moving almost hesitantly as though they truly believed she were an apparition. When they reached her, they both hesitated.

Mia stood still, waiting.

"It—it's good to see you," Moritz said, scooping up her hand and pressing his lips lightly to her knuckles. He laid his other hand on top when he straightened, meeting her eyes and offering her a small but sincere smile. "Truly. You look wonderful."

"Indeed," Hyman chimed in. "The Sicilian sun agrees with you tremendously, my dear."

"Thank you," Mia replied. "It's very nice to see you again, Morrie, Mr. Goldberg." She turned her head to look at Charlie.

His gaze went over every inch of her face, then her dress, and back up. She studied him in turn; there was something so different about him than she remembered, though he looked like the same man as she'd left last January, down to the errant black curl hanging over his forehead. His eyes were sterner, and his tenderly cut mouth had more of a downward turn than she recalled, but he was still Charlie. Her Charlie.

Her heart turned a double backward somersault, but she kept her poise. She wanted so much to believe Charlie was still with her, had waited as he'd promised, but there was nothing she could trust. Nothing, and no one, except her family.

"Last person I expected to walk through that door," Charlie murmured.

"Well," Mia said, her voice coming out much colder than she'd intended. "Here I am."

She wondered if he might have hugged her, but with the other men in the room, and all of their curious glances at Paolo, silent and steadfast behind her, Charlie simply took her hand but kissed it with enough pressure to let her know she'd been missed, indeed.

"When?" he asked, releasing her. Her fingers slid slowly against his as she lowered her arm back to her side, and she nearly jumped at the crackle of electricity that passed between them.

"Last night," she answered. "It was nearly a two-week trip."

"Why didn't you tell me you were coming home?"

"I thought it best to keep it to myself," she said.

Charlie's jaw flexed, an unreadable expression in his dark eyes.

"We haven't met," the strange man said, strolling over. "But I've heard quite a lot about you. I'm Jacopo Morelli." He extended his hand to her, and she noted, with a healthy dose of suspicion, the gold, bejeweled rings that adorned the last three fingers. Emerald, ruby, diamond.

She slipped her hand into his and he, too, lifted her hand to kiss it, pulling her forward a few steps to do so until she was almost against him. Mia lifted a brow as he pecked the backs of her fingers.

"You're even more beautiful than I heard," Jacopo said in an insolent tone. "Beauty, brains. Danger. Talent. Sounds like my dream girl."

*More like a nightmare.* She gently extracted her hand from his. "Charmed, I'm sure, Mr. Morelli."

"Ah, please," he said with a wide grin, placing a hand over his heart. "All my friends call me Jake."

She resisted the urge to sneer. "Since we've only just met, I'll stick to 'Mr. Morelli' for now."

"Oh, but I want us to be so much closer," he murmured, his dark eyes burning into her. "I need a dame like you in my life. And it's pretty clear to me you need a real man inside—pardon me. *Beside* you."

Charlie turned slowly to stare at him through narrow eyes.

Mia felt a spark of amusement. This man was trying to intimidate her as much as he was trying to woo her, as ridiculous as it was. He was an incredibly handsome man, and certainly, weaker women might collapse under his charm. She was certain many had.

But she was not weak.

"So, Mia, tell us, who is your quiet companion?" Hyman broke in with a polite smile, as much to save her from Mr. Morelli as to indulge all of their obvious curiosities about Paolo. "Is he a bodyguard? A counselor? Friend?"

Mia looked at Paolo, who frowned and nodded once. "Yeah," she replied.

"Oh," Mr. Goldberg said, clearly confused. "Well. Splendid."

"This is Paolo Scarpa," she clarified. "He knew my father and works for my cousin Carlo in Catania." She decided in a split-second that keeping things simple about him was the best course of action. She wasn't sure why, but some instinct advised her against sharing more.

"You're quite a long way from there," Hyman said to Paolo. "What sort of work is it that you do?"

Mia thought back to the lightning-fast, violent reaction Paolo had when Hyman's guard had merely touched her, or the unpleasant scene with the youths in Palermo. That was certainly one line of work.

Paolo, of course, said nothing and stared steadily at Hyman.

"Ah…?" Hyman lifted his brows delicately and glanced at Mia.

"He doesn't speak," she informed him.

"Why is that?"

"He has an injury."

"I…see." Hyman nodded slowly. But when it was clear as the seconds ticked by that neither Mia nor Paolo himself were going to offer more, he smiled politely at the man. "Well, any friend of Miss Scalisi's is a friend of mine, Mr. Scarpa, even the silent ones."

Charlie stepped forward and extended a hand. "Charlie Lazzari."

Paolo sniffed and looked Charlie up and down before shifting his gaze to Mia. She gave a slight flick of her head, and Paolo grasped Charlie's hand in a brief shake before releasing it and stepping back.

"Moritz Schapiro," Moritz spoke up. "Pleasure to meet you, sir."

Again, Paolo looked at Mia. She nodded, and he shook hands with Moritz.

"Charlie and Morrie are my two most trusted allies, along with Mr. Goldberg," she said to Paolo. "They all knew Domenico."

At the mention of her brother's name, Paolo bowed his head and quickly crossed himself.

"Jake Morelli," Jake added, grinning, his hand out.

Paolo glanced at Mia again, and she looked at Jake with cool appraisal, then back at Paolo. He did not shake Mr. Morelli's hand.

"What, ain't I good enough to get my hand sniffed by your dog there?" Jake said, dropping his hand.

She ignored him. "So, now that I'm here, I suppose we can talk some business," she said. "Unless your game of pool is too pressing to be further interrupted."

"No, no," Hyman said. "We were just playing for fun,

anyhow." He walked back to the pool table and scooped up a stack of cash, folded it, and tucked it into his pocket.

*Perhaps only fun for Hyman.*

"Would you gentlemen excuse us, please?" he added, smiling his bland, polite smile at Charlie, Moritz, and Jake. There was no reason to dismiss Charlie and Moritz—at least, none she could think of, unless something had drastically changed in the past year—so Mia assumed it was so Jake wouldn't take offense. And if his mere presence in Hyman Goldberg's penthouse weren't indication enough, his efforts to not offend Jake made it clear they had business.

"It's no trouble," Jake said. "Just tell me what time the delivery's gonna be tonight so I can be at the shop early with my guys."

Mia snapped her head toward him, then back to Hyman. "Delivery? Shop? My shop?"

"Liquor, dollface," Jake said. "What'd you think I meant, flowers? And yeah. That pretty little storefront with your name attached."

She ignored him and kept her gaze on Hyman, then glanced at Charlie and Moritz. "I've been wondering. How *is* the—our —operation?"

The men exchanged a three-way glance. Jake lit up another cigarette and leaned against the pool table, smirking.

"A lot's happened in a year," Charlie began.

"We needed some support," Moritz said at the same time.

Mia folded her arms. "Well, I suppose there's no need for privacy now, is there?" She wasn't angry, but she was curious— and deeply suspicious.

Hyman held up a hand to stop them. He walked toward her. "I had hoped to have this conversation with you alone," he said quietly. "But since we're all here... Come, sit." He placed a light hand on her back and guided her to the seating area beside the fireplace.

Mia sat in a high-backed chair, Paolo standing behind her at a respectful distance. Jake dropped into the chair beside her with a grin at Charlie, who had been on his way to claim the seat himself. He said nothing and took a seat on the sofa that faced the two chairs across the shiny, glass-topped coffee table. Moritz sat beside him, while Hyman opted to lean against the mantel.

"The good news is that demand is as high as it can be," Hyman said. "Your friend in Iowa, Mr. Wyatt, is pumping out whiskey in huge quantities to service all of our locations."

"And the bad news?" Mia asked.

"Well, I wouldn't call it bad, but we needed extra warehouse space in our key locations, including here in the city. And some of those locations threatened to encroach on territories already spoken for."

Jake looked over at her, flashing a wide smile. "That's where I come in."

"You don't say," Mia replied.

"I do say. And I was, of course, only too happy to partner with the great Mr. Goldberg and the fantastic Mr. Lazzari and Mr. Schapiro."

Mia noted the mocking note in his voice. He was amusing, but bold. "Only too happy, to the tune of what percentage?"

Jake lifted his brows. He glanced at the other men. "Sharp, this one."

"Miss Scalisi is more than sharp," Hyman said. "It would suit anyone to not underestimate her."

Jake reached out and lightly touched the back of her hand. She didn't move it away. "A reasonable percentage."

"I like real numbers, if you don't mind."

"Go ahead," Charlie said. "Tell her."

"A mere five percent," Jake replied.

"*Five* percent?" She looked at Charlie and Moritz, then Hyman.

"It was a fair percentage we negotiated," Hyman replied.

"Correct me if I'm wrong," Mia said, "but Mr. Dennison in Omaha receives ten percent. Mr. Wyatt receives twenty. The Outfit in Chicago gets fifteen."

"And per our agreement last year," Hyman said, "I forfeited

my percentage to take you on as my personal supplier and since I've marked up my prices, I've already recouped my initial investment." He studied her. "You once told me if I took you up on that, I'd get all my money back before I saw a second of 1925. You were nearly correct. I got all my money back by February of last year. New Year's Eve 1924 was a wonderful moneymaker."

Mia allowed herself a small but genuine smile of pleasure in return.

"So you see," Hyman continued, "there's plenty of room for a little five percent to go to Mr. Morelli."

The pleasure seeped out of her like air from a balloon. "Which leaves fifty percent for the three of us," she said. "Not even seventeen percent a head."

"Love a broad who knows numbers," Jake said, flashing a grin that was both lazy and devilish.

She stood up, tucking her hands behind her back. Paolo perked up, immediately wary as he tracked her slow steps to stand in front of Jake and look down at him.

"I'm the sister of the man who masterminded this deal, the person he trusted more than anyone else in life. These two men were his original partners. They've known one another since they were hardly young men. How do you, an outsider, figure you're entitled to a percentage, rather than a few dollars for a job well done?"

His dark eyes glinted with malevolence, but the arrogant smirk never left his face as he made a show of leaning his head back to look up at her. "'Cause I got the goods, sweetie. That's how."

"Yeah, I'm still confused about those goods," she said. "What exactly do you do that's so valuable?"

"Simple," he replied. "Connections. You wanted the ware-house space, the distribution areas that didn't belong to you, I know the fellas who control 'em. They deal with me, and they don't bother none of you or your men. I'm in the business of protection, Miss Scalisi. Among other things." Jake's gaze traveled over her. "You need protectin'? I'd do it for nothing." He eyed her again, stopping at her chest. "Well. Almost nothing."

"Sure, I need protection," she said, fixing him with an icy stare, her voice hard. "I need protection from vultures and leeches and men who think they're smarter than me."

"Mia," Moritz said quietly, "it's done."

She tore her gaze from Jake and shifted it to Moritz. "You might have written me."

He shrugged. "We thought it best to have the conversation in person."

*No. You thought it best to make decisions without me.*

Hyman cleared his throat. "Mia, I wanted to run something by you I've been germinating in my mind for some time. As you know, the club opens in less than a month. I want to have a little pre-opening-night showcase here. For my good friends. Some businessmen, some politicians. A private party in which to show off my new star."

Mia tilted her head. "Which part of that are you 'running by' me? This sounds like something else that just *is*, regardless of my opinion on the matter."

Hyman spread his hands. "You've always been the most astute person I know. What can I say? You've already got a great number of fans who are eager to see you. My friends, they're influential men. And women. They've got the pull to bring in a lot patrons."

"Have you and your partner decided on a name for the club yet?" Mia asked. "You never mentioned it."

"She came from Stems," Jake said, jerking his head toward Mia. "How about 'Legs'?"

Hyman smiled politely at him, but Mia noticed the horror in his eyes. "Clever, Mr. Morelli. No, as tempting as it is to name clubs after the limitless physical charms women possess, we decided on something a little less on the nose. The Divine."

"It has a certain ring to it, Mr. Goldberg," Moritz said.

"Better off calling it Legs," Jake muttered. "Lookit, why don't you hire me for your next venture? You could use a guy with my brains. I can guarantee you, most guys would go to a place called Legs before they'd go to a joint called The Divine. Sounds like church."

Mia had been in Hyman's company long enough to recognize the look of carefully arranged politeness on his face. At least that was something that hadn't changed in a year.

"I believe your many talents are better suited elsewhere, Mr. Morelli," he said. "Anyhow. Mia, since you're back now, why not have the party this Saturday night? A homecoming celebration for New York's biggest It Girl!"

Today was Friday. "As in, tomorrow night?"

"Oh," he said with insincere surprise. "Is that tomorrow already? Then, yes. Tomorrow. Where's your vivacious nature? Live a little! Let's celebrate."

"So soon?" she asked, startled. "Hyman, I just got back into the country. I need time to prepare."

"You're a consummate professional, aren't you?" he asked smoothly, and she knew this was a test—his test to see if she was up to snuff. "What are you worried about?"

"It—it was a long journey. Besides, don't *you* need time to prepare?"

"That's why it pays to have people on my payroll who will drop everything at my request," he said. "I just need to make some phone calls. And since you're here now, I see no reason to lose any momentum. As for tomorrow, don't fret, dear. Just sing a couple of easy songs. No dance numbers." He fetched a large envelope from his desk. "I might as well give this to you now."

"What is it?" she asked, taking the envelope from him. It was heavy with documents.

"A list of songs from the band," he replied. "Some popular songs and some original ones. You'll want to familiarize yourself with them."

"All for the showcase?" she asked, hoping she didn't sound as worried as she felt.

"Not all," he said with a smile, as though he could tell. "For when we open, mostly. Can you learn them?"

"Of course." *Do I have a choice?*

"Just the popular ones you already know for tomorrow," Hyman said. "The showcase is just meant to be a little tease, to get the city excited for you again."

"I'm already excited," Jake said.

Hyman glanced at him briefly. "Construction on the club is complete, and we're finalizing our food and beverage licenses. Just putting on the finishing touches. We could open in thirty days, or we could open in two. It's quite fluid, so I'd like to have the party now." He strolled toward her, steepling his fingers. "As for the club itself, I'd like you to begin rehearsals and gown fittings soon."

"I'd like to be a fly on the wall in that dressing room," Jake said, giving her a lascivious wink.

Mia ignored him, dismayed at the news. On the other hand, what else would she be doing with her time? She was back now, and per the contract she'd signed many months ago, she was Hyman Goldberg's to command. Besides, if all she had to do was sing a couple of songs, that was no big deal. She'd kept up with her vocal exercises in Sicily for both the enjoyment of it and with the knowledge she'd have to have her voice in shape for when she got home.

She wouldn't show Hyman she was nervous—because it *was* a test. He knew it, and so did she.

"Very well," she replied.

He raised an eyebrow. "And here I expected an argument. I suspect Sicily was very good for you, indeed."

She decided not to mention she just didn't have much fight left. "A contract is a contract, Mr. Goldberg."

He nodded, but she didn't miss the flash of triumph in his eyes. "Indeed it is, Miss Scalisi."

She turned and glanced at Paolo, who immediately crossed to her side. "As lovely as it was to visit with you all, I should be going. I promised Gloria I'd return for supper, and I don't want to get any more on her bad side than I already am by coming here."

"How are your sister-in-law and niece?" Hyman offered his elbow to escort her to the door. Moritz and Charlie trailed.

"They're well." Mia smiled. "She was sad to leave her parents, but insists I can't take care of myself. So here she is."

"She, and Mr. Scarpa," Hyman replied, acknowledging the man with a glance over his shoulder.

Paolo eyed him warily.

"Yes." At the door, Mia turned to look at the other men. "I suppose we'll see each other soon."

Jake shouldered his way forward, elbowing Moritz out of his way. "How about tonight?" He leaned an elbow against the door jamb.

She lifted a brow. "I beg your pardon?"

"Tonight. Let me take you for a drink." He grinned. "After the shipment. We can get to know each other better."

One side of her mouth curled up. She couldn't help it; the man was so outrageously arrogant, it was funny. "And what the goddamn hell makes you think I want to get to know you at all?"

"Everyone needs a shoulder to cry on." His hand drifted up to toy with one of her dangling earrings. "And I got two."

"Congratulations." Mia tilted her head back, her earring slipping through his fingers. She could practically feel the fury radiating off Paolo.

"So, is that a yes?" His eyes gleamed at her. "Will I see you tonight?"

"Sure," she said. "You'll see me. At the shop for the unloading."

"You're breaking my heart, doll."

"Give it a rest, Morelli," Charlie said sharply.

"At least I had the balls to ask, didn't I?" Jake replied.

"Gentlemen," Hyman interjected, taking Mia's arm again. "I'll see Miss Scalisi and Mr. Scarpa out, and return shortly."

He led her through the door, pulling it closed behind him, then led her a few steps out into the lobby before sighing. "I'd like to apologize to you for Mr. Morelli," he said. "He's rather...brash."

"He's certainly a character," Mia said drily.

"He is smart, though. Very ambitious."

"Who does he work for? Where'd he come from?"

"He's never stated explicitly, but word on the street is that he's aligned himself with Mr. Maranzano."

Salvatore Maranzano had emigrated from Sicily after the war and settled in New York. He'd courted Nick to join his outfit, but Nick had deemed him too "small time" to consider. Now, he'd set up shop in Brooklyn with a legitimate real estate business that fronted his bootlegging operations. He and Mr. Masseria would never be mistaken for dear friends.

"If that's true, then we may have him to contend with," Mia said.

"That may be the case, but it's too early to tell yet. Nothing for you to worry about at this time." Hyman patted her shoulder, then hesitated. "The delivery is scheduled for midnight. Are you really planning to come?"

"Is that a problem?"

He held up his hands. "Of course not. Don't get so bristly. Remember, after I signed over the shop to you, I told you it would give you the opportunity to be a part of your brother's operation. I meant it then, and I still mean it now."

Mia faced him. "I hope it *is* still considered my brother's operation, Mr. Goldberg."

"As much as it can belong to a dead man's memory, of course."

She was surprised at how much that stung. "I'll see you later."

"Enjoy your supper."

Mia walked out of the penthouse into the elevator, Paolo at her side. As they rode down to the ground floor, she said, "Bring your pistol tonight."

# CHAPTER FOUR

"Did you have a nice visit with your friends?" Gloria asked after they were seated at a private table in one of the hotel's two main dining rooms. Paolo, though invited to sit with them, opted for a small table not far from them where he could give them privacy and keep an eye on things.

As places to stay went, the Murray Hill Hotel was by and large the nicest Mia had ever been in. The dining room was all Roman columns and crystal chandeliers, and brassy gold silk and velvet drapes hanging on the elaborately frescoed walls. The tables and chairs were made of heavy, carved oak, the latter upholstered with the finest stamped leather, and all resting on plush Wilton carpeting she could have buried her toes in.

"Nice enough," Mia replied, not missing the brief look of annoyance that flashed across her sister-in-law's face. Gloria had her way of trying to sneak information out of Mia through casual, nonchalant questions, but Mia had yet to fall for it.

She smiled at Emilia, who was doing her best to sit up straight in her chair. Though still a toddler, the little girl took enormous pride in the manners her mother, aunt, and grandmother had done their best to instill in her in Sicily. Not only that, but Emilia could speak Sicilian better than she could speak

English. Gloria discouraged that, wanting her daughter to be a proper American girl, but Mia still spoke Sicilian to Emilia occasionally. Nick would have wanted her to.

"Are you happy to be home?" she asked.

Emilia shrugged. "I miss Nonna. And Auntie Raquel. And the beach. And the seashells. Can we go back?"

"One day," Mia said, reaching for her hand.

"This is our home," Gloria said with a smile. "We were just... on a holiday for a long time."

"But why can't we go on another holiday?"

"Because I had to come back for work," Mia said. "And I need you and Mama to look after me."

Emilia frowned. "But why? You're a big girl."

"Your auntie gets herself into trouble sometimes," Gloria explained. "She needs us to straighten her out."

Mia grinned. "Don't you want to help straighten me out, Em?"

"Daddy can," Emilia said brightly. "When he comes home. When's he coming home?"

With that, the glow of the evening went out of the room. Gloria and Mia exchanged a glance over Emilia's head.

A look of anguish flashed across Gloria's face. It reflected the same pain that tore at Mia's heart. Before she could say anything, Gloria interjected.

"Soon, darling," she said softly.

Mia looked at her reproachfully, but Gloria averted her gaze.

At that moment, the waiter came to take their orders. Mia sat back in her chair as Gloria ordered for them all, grateful for the interruption. From then on, the meal went smoothly—at least as far as the little girl could tell. The strain between her mother and aunt was palpable only to them.

Afterward, they retired to their large suite, where Mia helped Emilia with her letters. When it was Emilia's bedtime, Gloria helped her wash for bed while Mia rang the concierge for a pot of tea, her eyes traveling to the clock constantly. The unloading was at midnight, Hyman had said, so she and Paolo would need to leave at half past eleven.

From the bedroom Gloria shared with Emilia, Mia heard a loud, fussy shriek. "No! I don't *wanna* go to bed!"

"Oh brother," Mia said under her breath, and hurried down the short hall, Paolo on her heels.

In the room, Emilia was sitting straight up in the small bed the hotel had provided for her, arms folded tightly over her chest, and her dark curls flying madly around her head as she shook it.

"Emilia," Gloria snapped. "I'm not asking you. It's *time* for *bed*."

"No!"

"Em," Mia said, stepping into the room. "Be a good girl. Do as your mother says."

"No," Emilia repeated. "I'm not tired. I wanna hear a story."

"Only good girls get bedtime stories," Gloria said, "and you've been a very naughty girl. You will lie down, shut your eyes, and go to sleep. I am turning out this light and shutting the door, and I won't hear another word of it from you."

"No," Emilia said again, but this time she sounded so terrified that both women stared at her. "I don't *like* the dark. I don't *wanna* be in the dark!"

Gloria sighed, then went to her daughter's side. "Are you afraid of the dark, Emmy? Is that what all this fuss is about?"

The little girl nodded, dark eyes locked on Mia. "I 'member the time at the parade. The loud noises. Auntie pushing us to the ground so I couldn't breathe. The man with the bloody head."

That brought Mia up sharply. The Thanksgiving before she'd left for Sicily a year ago, a man had pulled a gun on her at the Macy's parade. Out of sheer instinct, she'd tackled Gloria and Emilia to the ground. Emilia had never spoken of it, not during all their time in Sicily. Perhaps she'd been too exhausted from long days full of frolicking in the hot sun to have nightmares before. Perhaps being in New York triggered her terror, even though she'd been too young to know exactly what had happened or remember it in detail.

*But maybe she does.* Another part of Mia's ugly life that had touched the parts she wanted to keep clean and pure and beautiful.

She stepped toward the bed. "Emilia. I will *never* let anything happen to you. Do you understand me? I would die to keep you safe. I would kill to keep you safe. Anyone who ever threatened you—I'd make sure they would never, ever hurt you." Her voice had become low and almost menacing, and her niece's eyes widened in fright.

"You're scaring her, dammit," Gloria snapped. Her gaze shifted over Mia's shoulder. "*He's* not helping, either."

Mia followed the path of her stare toward Paolo, who stood in the doorway. "He's just standing there. *He's* not doing anything."

"Just let me handle my own daughter," Gloria insisted as Emilia burst into fresh tears. "Go, Mia. You're only making this worse."

Mia blinked at her. Gloria had never spoken to her this way before, and had always encouraged the bond between her and Emilia, even when it took the form of an extra bedtime story or a cookie and milk in bed.

"Very well," she said, trying to mask the sting. "Emilia, good-night, dear. Be a good girl for your mother." She turned on her heel and strode out of the room. Paolo followed, lingering by the sofa as if to study her from a distance.

She paced for a moment, frowning at the floor. She and Gloria never fought. They'd had a few tense conversations in the past, but Gloria had never snapped at her the way she'd done a moment ago. In the past, Mia might have rushed to mend things, regardless of who was right or wrong.

She looked up at Paolo, who watched her with alert eyes. "We're going to the meeting early."

He nodded.

Mia took her coat from the coatrack and slipped it over her shoulders, made sure Nick's blackjack was in the pocket—just in case—then headed for the door and opened it. At a light touch on her arm, she turned.

Paolo gestured behind him toward Emilia's bedroom, brow creased, his silent question plain.

*Aren't you going to say goodbye?*

She never left her family without saying goodbye. She never wanted Gloria to worry about her the way she'd worried about Nick. Mia had to leave Gloria out to a certain extent, but she always wanted her to know she'd come back. Nick would have wanted her to do that.

She hesitated, looking at Emilia's closed bedroom door, the clear boundary between *her* and *them*.

Then a chilly wind swept through her heart.

"They'll be fine," Mia said shortly, and walked out the door.

IT WAS ONLY A QUARTER AFTER TEN WHEN THEY ARRIVED AT THE empty shop. Paolo went to a corner diner to fetch two small paper cups of coffee. After finishing his, he folded his arms and leaned back in a chair behind the counter, tilting his head against the wall and closing his eyes.

Mia paced in front of the counter, one arm wrapped around her middle, the other hand clutching the cup near her lips. Her stomach tensed with nerves, which irritated her. She did not like being nervous. She did not want, even for an instant, to give off the impression to anyone watching her that she was nervous. It was the kind of thing Don Catalano told her an enemy would study her for—any sign of weakness in any form was an open invitation to come for her.

She reached the front door, pivoted, and paced toward the back of the room. It was her fourth pass at this point. The weight of the blackjack banging gently against her hip measured every step. She tugged back the sleeve of her coat to check the delicate diamond watch on a silk ribbon around her wrist. A quarter of eleven.

*He said midnight.*

In a little over an hour, this small, fragile building teeming with various feminine delights would be full of gruff, violent, loud, rude men, there to unload dozens of crates of illegal booze. Probably all of them would be carrying guns. There would be coarse language, perhaps threats, and maybe, if someone became insulted enough, actual violence.

Mia's gaze traveled the length of the room. She'd gone to great pains to have the walls repainted in a charming shade of pale yellow with white trim, to have all the glass polished, and to replace the light fixtures with elegant crystal chandeliers. Before leaving for Sicily, she'd spent long days arranging her merchandise to be aesthetically pleasing and inviting, and adding soft, comfortable touches like cushy, pale-green English upholstered armchairs, low coffee tables, and beautiful Tiffany lamps. She even had a coffee and tea service along with sweet pastries from a bakery nearby so that shoppers would feel like treasured guests, and her important repeat customers felt valued and interested in returning again and again.

She didn't particularly care how many deliveries had happened here while she'd been gone, how many times men had trampled through here, perhaps broken things. She had every confidence Trudy would have put to right anything that had been destroyed. But Mia was back, and she'd be damned if anything inside *her* property got damaged by one of these bastards.

A series of three sharp taps on the glass made her jump and whirl around. Paolo was on his feet instantly, his hand on the pistol under his jacket. For a moment, she froze at the sight of the uniformed beat cop standing outside the window. There was something familiar about the tall, paunchy man with graying hair and bushy gray eyebrows.

Then she smiled.

*My old pal.*

"It's all right," she said to Paolo. "He's a friend."

Paolo eyed her doubtfully, but sat back down in his chair.

Mia walked to the door, unlocked it, and pulled it open with a big smile. "Officer Fred. How nice to see you again."

Fred McClarty's bright blue eyes opened wide. "Miss Scalisi! I thought that was you. I haven't seen you in...gosh." His brow furrowed as he tried to do the math.

"About a year," she supplied.

"That's right. Has it been so long? Where've you been, if you don't mind my asking? Your partners just said you were on a vacation. Not real friendly, them two."

"I was visiting family overseas," she said, and the expression on his face told her he understood that was all he was going to get. "And how about you? Did you ever take your wife to Atlantic City?"

Fred flushed slightly and rubbed the back of his neck. "Well, yes, I did. And my Dolores had a lovely time on the boardwalk last spring—I took great pleasure in spoiling her every which way. And you were right—the lobster thermidor at Penny's was just swell."

Mia gave him a sincere smile. "I'm so glad to hear it. How have things been since I've been away?"

"Pretty routine," he said. "Mr. Lazzari and Mr. Schapiro take care of my fee. It's just been me walkin' the beat, just like you told me. Don't get a lot of trouble here."

"And my partners have been paying you fairly?"

"Well, they ain't paying me two grand and a bottle of fancy French perfume every time, but sure. I make out all right."

"Good. I'm expecting a delivery tonight."

Fred's mouth turned down slightly. "That one fella gonna be here?"

"You'll have to be a bit more specific, I'm afraid." Mia lifted a shoulder. "I'm only just making acquaintances again, myself."

"The loudmouth," he said. "Not your two partners, them guys are all right, if a little too serious sometimes. He's a young guy. Always telling everyone what to do. Think he calls himself Gems. Least that's how he introduced himself to me first night we met. He nearly strangled me when he saw me. Took the little Jewish fella pointing a gun at him to get him to let me alone."

Mia shook her head. "I haven't yet been introduced to the infamous Mr. Gems yet." A memory of gold rings with glimmering jewels in them flitted through her mind. Or...perhaps she had.

"He's here all the time now, for the past six months or so," Fred said. "Real wise guy. Thinks he is, anyway. Always trying to ingratiate himself with Mr. Luciano."

"Luciano?" Mia raised her eyebrows. "He comes here?"

"When the shipments are for Mr. Masseria, he comes to oversee the storage, or to take inventory. Seems chummy with your two pals. From what I gather, he introduced Gems to your crew to provide the muscle. Knows him from heroin deals, I hear."

That was a new development, indeed. Before she'd left for Sicily, she hadn't seen Luciano at the shop once. That he'd been coming here now piqued both her interest and suspicion. None of her partners had mentioned this to her earlier that day. *An oversight? An unimportant detail? Or something they're trying to conceal from me?*

She wondered again if there was anyone she could still trust.

"Well," Mia said. "He must think highly of Mr. Gems."

Fred shook his head. "He'll have a field day with you, I'm sure. Just...be careful around him, Miss Scalisi."

The chill of her polite smile settled over her like a powder-soft snow drift. "Or perhaps he ought to be careful around me."

Fred's mouth opened and closed before he could find his voice. "What happened to you?" he said finally. "Meaning no disrespect. You seem very different from the young lady I met here Thanksgiving 1924. When you—when you saved my life. When you *changed* my life. It's like there's..."

"Yes?" When he hesitated, she patted his arm. "It's all right, Fred. You can say anything to me."

"Well, miss, if you'll forgive me for saying so, it's like there's a darkness around you I didn't see before. You were so...kind last time, which was why I was so surprised to see you mixed up in this crowd. You had some…sweetness about you then. You didn't belong. But now… Well, I suppose now you do."

"You don't find me kind and sweet anymore?" she teased.

"Kind, sure. But I think life caught up to you and took that sweetness away, maybe," he said quietly.

Strangely, that stung.

Because it was true.

The sound of engines in the alley behind the shop drew her attention. She turned to call for Paolo, but found him already walking toward her, looking alert and focused. For a brief moment, she wanted to smile, picturing him as he'd been earlier, sitting in the chair with his head tilted back against the wall, mouth wide open as he snored.

Mia looked at Fred. "Please keep watch."

He nodded.

She and Paolo strode past him to the back of the shop. There were boxes of supplies and merchandise scattered about—legitimate wares for the shop. The door at the back of the storage area opened to a staircase, which led down to a much larger, underground storage room where the liquor was kept. She propped open the cellar door, glancing at Paolo.

"Suppose I oughtta myself useful, shouldn't I?"

He smirked.

She went to the back entrance and swung it open. A cluster of men standing next to a half a dozen trucks, smoking, whirled in surprise.

"Gentlemen, good evening," she said, and glanced at her wristwatch. "My, you're early. I wasn't expecting you until midnight."

"Mia?"

She glanced to the right, catching sight of Charlie walking toward her, a wool fedora slicing over his face at an angle. He frowned.

"Hello, Charlie."

"What're you doing here?" he asked in a low voice when he reached her side.

"I said I was going to be here, didn't I?"

"I thought that was just talk for Morelli," he replied.

Mia drew herself up. *Just talk?* He acted as if he didn't remember her. "I never 'just talk,' Charlie. Now where's the booze?"

"Hey, life of the party showed up like she said she would."

Another loud voice came from the other side of the alley. A man walked toward her, smoking a cigarette. His face was concealed by a hat set at a dashing angle on his head, but as he swaggered toward her, ribbons of smoke billowing over his shoulders, she knew him right away.

"Jake Morelli," she said flatly.

"Dollface," he purred, leaning toward her as though to kiss her.

She leaned out of the way at the last second. "If you try to touch me again without my invitation, Mr. Morelli, I will have you pistol-whipped until you lose consciousness."

Instead of appearing offended, his dark eyes gleamed at her, and he grinned wider. "I think I'm in love with you, Miss Scalisi. So you *are* sending out invitations, is that right? I'll come to any party of yours. I like the private ones best."

"Will you just unload, already?" she snapped. "Make it fast. This is my place of business, after all."

"Aw, take it easy, kitten," he replied, flicking away his cigarette. He waved to his men. "Boys. Let's go." Men began pulling crates from the trucks.

Mia stepped back, nodding at the men she knew—Moritz, Bobby, Joey. Charlie remained at her side, barking orders to the others, who eyeballed her with open and frank curiosity. She met their stares, steady and unsmiling, as they passed.

"She acts like she made this shit," one of the men muttered under their breath.

"Since it tastes like shit, maybe she did," another man

replied, and they both chuckled. "Some of that fancy French perfume might improve the taste."

*Improve the taste?* She watched them take a few more steps past her, flipping the words over in her mind. In a matter of seconds, she decided she wouldn't allow that remark to go unaddressed.

"Hey, you," she said to the man who'd made the crack. "Stop. What's in that crate?"

"Huh?"

In response, she blinked slowly.

"Th-the good stuff," he replied, clearly baffled by the question.

"*What* good stuff?"

"The rye," he said, still looking confused. "From Templeton." He glanced at Charlie, his brow knitted.

"I'm talking to you, not him," Mia said sharply, drawing the man's attention again. "Are you sure it's not whatever Mr. Masseria keeps here?"

"Lady, I'm positive," the man said. He jerked his head toward a truck. "Masseria's load is still on those trucks."

Will Wyatt's rye whiskey from Templeton was arguably the finest available on the market. The flavor was distinctive, sharp, and smooth at the same time, and he took enormous pride in it. It was the reason why Nick had worked so hard to set up his operation. It was why Hyman Goldberg had agreed to let her forgo repaying him two million dollars in exchange for selling the product himself and earning his investment back in a matter of a few months. It was why Sal and North Side gang in Chicago had plotted to try to seize control of the operation. It was why Hymie Weiss had whispered promises into the ear of one of Nick's men, getting him to betray her brother. The rye was a product men would literally kill for, and that was worth millions.

So why on earth would the taste need to be improved?

"Put it down," she ordered, and the men who'd had so much to say halted in their tracks, staring at her.

"Mia, what is it?" Charlie demanded.

"Open a crate and pull out a bottle. I want to taste it."

"What for?"

She fixed him with a silent stare.

Charlie studied her for a moment longer, then flicked his head at one of the men. "All right. Do what she says."

"But this is—"

"I said, fuckin' do it."

"Is there a problem, here?" Moritz said, walking back toward them from inside the storage room.

"She wants to taste the rye," Charlie told him, then glanced at the man with the crate. "Hey, you—you got five seconds to get that crate open. Don't make me show you what happens when that time ends."

With a huge sigh, the man set a crate on the ground, then used a knife to pop open the crate lid. He withdrew a plain, dark brown glass bottle, then cracked the sealing and uncorked the neck before handing it to her.

Mia held it up to read the label. It read TEMPLETON RYE, THE GOOD STUFF. She held the bottle up to her nose and sniffed in a deep breath. Immediately, her eyes watered at the sharp stench of alcohol. Anger stirred in her chest like glowing embers from a hearth swept along by the wind as she tilted the bottle opening to her lips.

An unfathomably vile flavor flowed over her tongue, searing a path along the inside of her mouth like gasoline. It was bitter and sharp, sour and putrid, and had a strong chemical undertone that made her eyes water.

All eyes were on her as she coughed, gagged, and spluttered. Her throat closed automatically, as if her body refused to admit the liquid that made her want to retch. *And that's saying,* something she thought as she turned away from the door, *since I've had my share of bathtub gin.* Though it was most unladylike, she spat the mouthful out into the alley, not caring that droplets of it landed on Moritz's pants and shoes.

The men were correct. It tasted like *shit.*

"What the *hell* is this?" she demanded, shaking the bottle.

"I fear you may be hard of hearing. It's the rye whiskey,"

Moritz said, his brow dropping. "And you just spat all over my shoes, Mia."

"To hell with your goddamn shoes," she said, pointing a finger a few inches from his face. "This disgusting swill is *not* Templeton rye whiskey. What is it?"

The glance Charlie and Moritz exchanged filled her with cold fury.

Moritz gave her another condescending smile. "Dear, it's business. That's what your brother planned to do from the start. We manufacture a batch pure for our preferred customers, and then we manufacture a batch that we cut with water to sell to the general public. That's how we make a profit. You do like profits, don't you?"

"I've tasted a cut batch before," Mia said. "And that still tasted pretty damn pure to me. This is not cut with water, and you know it!" She upended the entire bottle, pouring it out in the alleyway. "This is revolting and undrinkable."

Moritz stiffened. "That's twelve dollars you're pouring out there, Mia."

"*That's* not fit for consumption. Why should anyone pay twelve dollars for a bottle of rotgut hooch when they can get it for half that anywhere else in the city?" She shifted her gaze to Charlie. "Did you know about this?"

He looked away.

"How goddamn dare you both," she said through her teeth. She turned to the men still unloading crates. "Listen up. Only Mr. Masseria's crates will be unloaded and stored in my shop. You can take the rest of it back to wherever it came from."

They all stopped, exchanging confused looks.

"Keep unloading, fellas," Moritz said, raising his voice over hers. "*Everything.*"

At a glance from Mia and a flick of her head, Paolo stepped directly into the path of one of the men and drew his pistol. He pointed it at the man's chest. The worker froze.

"Hey, what's the big idea?" he protested. He stared at Moritz with huge eyes. "I didn't sign up for *this!*"

"Mia, call off your bodyguard, all right?" Moritz growled.

"I will, when you get this sorry excuse for liquor out of my shop."

"Hey, listen," Charlie interjected, his voice calm. "We might have gone a little heavy with the water this time around. We'll ease up next time, all right?"

"If we were just talking water here, maybe I'd believe that line of bull," she snapped. "But this tastes like the fermented garbage poor men drink because they can't afford the good stuff. We're *not* selling this. This is *not* the Templeton rye Nick sold."

"I believe that's what it says on the label," Moritz said. "Though I seem to be without my eyeglasses at the moment."

Mia ripped the label from the bottle, then threw the bottle down onto the cobbled street of the alleyway, where it shattered into pieces. Then she tore the label into pieces and threw them at Moritz's chest.

They locked gazes, matching each other glare for glare. If she were a man, she was sure one of them would swing. Her hand itched for the blackjack in her pocket.

"If you speak to me like I'm an idiot again," she said quietly, "I'm afraid our friendship is going to be affected."

"Children. Is there a problem here?"

Mia tore her glare from Moritz and glanced behind her. Hyman Goldberg strolled up to her, a tall man trailing him. His face wore a look of mild concern.

"The problem," she said, "is that the quality liquor my brother manufactured is being reduced to a drop of pure rye, then filled back up with sewage water and chemicals. It's not fit to clean my hotel room. That was *not* part of the operation or the agreement."

"It's also not your booze, Mia," Moritz said tightly. "We've already been paid for those bottles."

"By whom?"

"I believe that's our business."

"You're just all kinds of wrong tonight, aren't you, Morrie?" she snapped. "Anything that concerns this liquor operation *my* brother and Will Wyatt created is, in fact, my business. Let's not forget that you wouldn't even have heard of the product had it not been for Nick. And as I'm your partner, a word *you've* thrown around in the past, and as I am Nick's sister, I say you *won't* sell this garbage."

"You don't get the right to make the ultimate decision simply because you have Scalisi blood," Moritz said. "And let's be clear about something, *dear*—you wouldn't even be considered a partner if Nick were still breathing."

The weight of the blackjack in her pocket again called out to her, begging her to swing its heavy, leather-wrapped steel ball into Morrie's snide face for that comment. But if she gave into the rage churning through her body, she'd do exactly what he wanted her to do—prove she was unfit to be involved.

Charlie drew in a deep breath, his nostrils flaring as he stared at Moritz. At least, he didn't seem to approve of that comment, either.

Mia clenched every muscle in her body, grasping for every ounce of self-control she had ever possessed. A long moment of silence passed before she trusted herself to speak.

"I own this shop," she said, her words clipped. "Not you, not Charlie, not even Mr. Goldberg anymore. And as it's my shop, I won't have this poison stored here."

"Now you are infringing on *our* agreement," Hyman said gently. "The contract you signed explicitly states you agree to hold inventory here relating to my business arrangements. That includes liquor."

"You can store Mr. Masseria's load here," Mia said, "but not that other crap."

"Mia, be reasonable." Hyman put his hand on her shoulder, but it was heavy, and he squeezed. Hard. "You *do* get a cut, remember that."

"Shove your cut," Mia said, and he dropped his hand. "I don't want any money relating to that load. If you leave it in this store, you'll find it running in the streets tomorrow morning."

Hyman's eyes flashed with anger. "That, my darling, would

be most unwise."

"Try me," Mia added softly. A small pocket in her stomach churned with fear, but the call of a challenge made her blood simmer and her pride shoot to the roof of her head. One did *not* speak to Hyman Goldberg this way. And certainly not a woman. But if she didn't show these sons of bitches she meant business and her word carried weight, they would never respect her. She swallowed her fear and lifted her chin, refusing to break her stare.

Her godfather—and before him, her brother—had taught her that.

"Hyman," Moritz said, as though they were squabbling children and he were appealing to the authority.

Mr. Goldberg's tightly clenched jaw twitched several times before he sighed heavily.

Mia looked at Charlie. "Have you nothing to say?"

"We're trying to make money here," he said. "That's the bottom line."

"So quality means nothing? Nick means nothing?"

A look of pain rolled across his face, then disappeared as his eyes narrowed. "The more diluted we make it, the more they need to drink to get drunk, the more they buy. The more bang for our buck we get. It's called commerce, Mia."

She glared at him. He might have tried to gloss over her last question, but she refused to let him. He, Moritz, Hyman—all of them would be called to account here and now.

"Nick was your best friend," she said through her teeth. "You know goddamn well how much it meant to him to have a quality product to sell that he was proud of." She shoved his chest. "You look me in the eye right now and tell me he'd approve of this. That he'd like the taste of that. That he'd be happy to sell it to his customers. Look me in the eye, Charlie, and tell me. If you can do that, I won't say another word. Go ahead."

Charlie looked away, shaking his head. Then he lifted his eyes to hers. And said nothing.

Mia whirled on Moritz. "Get it. Out. Now."

"I think," a deep voice said from behind Hyman, "that you fellas oughtta listen to her."

The tall man who'd trailed Hyman stepped into a pool of light from a sconce on the building. She straightened as she recognized the thick, wavy black hair, heavy-lidded eyes, the leonine features.

Charles Luciano, the man they called "Lucky."

She'd met him a few times over the years—once before Nick had been drafted, once when she'd worked in Atlantic City and Mr. Luciano and several friends had come to Penny's, and once before she'd left for Sicily, when she'd gone to personally deliver a crate of real Templeton rye as a thank-you for the respectful tribute he'd sent to Nick's funeral. Both meetings had been cursory, if polite.

He was only a couple of years older than Nick, but he carried himself with a quiet dignity that made him seem years older than he was. He'd earned nearly half a million dollars for himself by the time he'd been Mia's age. It had been no wonder Nick had looked up to him so much.

Mr. Luciano tossed his cigarette butt away and blew out a stream of smoke. "I been at the bootlegging game for quite a few years now. It's getting to a point where people actually want decent shit, not the bathtub gin like in the early days of Prohibition. I understand wanting to make a profit—why the hell else would any of us be doing this otherwise? But Miss Scalisi has a fine point. They've gotta get what they're paying for, and reducing it to the shit that used to kill drunks in the early days ain't the way to go about it. You'll lose all your clientele that way —especially if they start dying from what you're selling."

She was shocked. Mr. Luciano, one of the biggest and most successful bootleggers in the whole country, *agreed* with her. Agreed with a *woman*.

For an instant, Nick was beside her, a careless, affectionate arm about her neck. *That's my sis*, a phantom voice chuckled in her ear.

"All due respect, Mr. Luciano," Moritz said, his voice

strained, "but this is *our* business."

Mr. Luciano smirked and lifted a hand in mock-surrender. "Yeah, sure, pally. I got no idea what I'm talking about. Go ahead and lose money."

"If you want to sell that," Mia said to Moritz, "you're going to have to find your own place to store it, and you're going to have to change the label. Because that's not Templeton rye."

Jake stepped into the alley then, hands spread wide. "Hey, what gives? I thought I provided men to unload crates, and ain't nothing getting unloaded. Wasting time costs me money."

Mia turned to him. "You can have them unload Mr. Masseria's crates."

"That's it?" He looked from Moritz to Hyman to Charlie.

"That's it," Mia said, the edge in her voice drawing his attention again.

He smirked and gave her an up-and-down look. "Oh, you're in charge?"

"Yes," she said before anyone else could say anything. "You'd better get them started, or else they're going to be here all night. I imagine that'll get pretty expensive for you, right?"

Jake shrugged, then turned to his men. "Fellas, forget about the Templeton for now. Get Masseria's crates tucked in."

She felt a small flash of surprise. At least the loudmouthed Mr. Morelli didn't question her orders.

A tense silence befell the small group as the workers moved into action, except for Mr. Luciano, who looked perfectly at ease as he checked his pocket watch and lit up another cigarette.

"Well," Hyman said tightly, "it's rather late for you, Mia, isn't it? After all, you have a party to prepare for in less than twenty-four hours."

"It will be a very late night for me," she replied, "but luckily, I can sleep late since I don't need much time to rehearse. I'll be staying until you're all done. After all, I have to lock up, don't I?"

"I believe I also have a key," Hyman said. "I'd be happy to lock up for you."

"I'd rather you didn't."

"We're clearly not going to come to an agreement tonight."
Hyman looked between her and Moritz. "Let's just remove the
offending product for now and discuss things later."

"There's nothing to discuss," Mia said.

Moritz gave her a cold smile. "You have a lot to learn about
this business, Mia. A lot to learn. Like remembering who your
friends are."

She stepped toward him until only a few inches separated
them. "I would advise you the same."

OVER THE NEXT TWO HOURS, SHE WATCHED, ARMS FOLDED, AS
the crates of diluted Templeton rye were removed and Mr.
Masseria's stored.

As Charlie and Moritz paid the team, Jake sauntered over to
her. Paolo tensed beside her, but Mia patted his arm.

"So," Jake said. "How 'bout that drink? I've worked up quite
a thirst."

"I appreciate the offer," she replied, "but I need to get my
beauty sleep."

He winked. "You're already plenty beautiful, but I could tuck
you in."

She sighed, exasperated, reluctantly flattered, and a tiny bit
amused. "Don't you ever quit?"

He faced her. "Not when there's something I want real, real
bad."

Mia tilted her head. "Mr. Morelli, you don't even know me to
want me."

"Call me Jake already. And I don't have to *know* you to want
you." He leaned toward her, careful not to touch her. "But I like
what I see. And I'm real curious about what I don't. I can tell
there's more to you than meets the eye. And I want to see it all."

She noted the way his gaze traveled between her eyes and her
chest. "I'm sure you do."

"So, how 'bout it?" he pressed. "Gimme a chance. I think

you'll find I know how to treat a lady."

"You may know how to treat women, Mr. Morelli, but I doubt you know how to treat a *lady*."

"Teach me. I'm a fast learner."

"I wouldn't hold your breath." She waved a hand toward the back entrance, where the crew was filing out. "It appears the men are done for the night. You should be on your way so I can lock the place."

He chuckled. "After I pick my face up off the floor, I'll see myself out."

She couldn't contain a slight smile.

Mia remained by the back entrance as the storage room cleared of the men who'd packed it earlier. At least the inventory for the shop was unharmed.

Hyman strolled over to her. "I'd be lying if I said I wasn't disappointed in some of the conversations had here tonight, but you've only just come home, and there's much about the business you have yet to learn. I hope a good night's rest will help you see things more clearly in the morning." He put on his hat and stepped outside to join Mr. Luciano. Mia wondered when they had become friendly.

Mr. Luciano met her gaze, gripped the brim of his hat, and smiled at her before getting into the same vehicle as Hyman.

Moritz barely glanced at her as he wished her a curt goodnight.

Charlie halted in front of her. "I'm sorry about all this."

She looked away from him, watching as one by one the trucks pulled slowly out of the alley and headed in different directions. "You knew what Morrie was doing. Or you were in on it. Either way…that hurts."

"I knew about it," he said gently. "I didn't tell him not to do it at the time. It was a good business move. The market's getting clogged, and we needed to expand our clientele."

"I'm not an idiot, Charlie," she said. "There's only so much honor among thieves, and this *is* an illegal business, after all. I understand, logically, what you were doing. But this is different.

It's different because of Nick. And I feel Nick was disrespected tonight by two men in particular who should've known better. Who *do* know better."

"I won't insult you further by arguing that point," Charlie said. "Morrie always has the brilliant mind for business, and what he proposed seemed like good business—for us. There's other ventures to get into, you know. Liquor's good, but it's not the best."

Immediately, Mia thought of the heroin epidemic in the old neighborhood. "I want to ask you something. Is Jake the same 'Gems' fella I keep hearing about?"

Charlie shrugged. "People call him that. Why?"

Her stomach clenched at the confirmation, but she wasn't surprised. "He's got a decent operation in one of those other 'good business ventures' you mentioned—heroin. He's poisoning my old neighborhood."

"He makes good money in heroin, and we could too," Charlie said. "We've been telling you that for a year now."

"And I told you how I feel about that," she replied. "My answer is the same. I won't repeat myself. I had a talk with Mr. Masseria about *Gems*. He won't be dealing in the neighborhood anymore."

Charlie lifted a brow. "You sure about that?"

She wasn't convinced she was lining Masseria's pockets for nothing in return, but she refused to admit it to Charlie. "Mr. Masseria, at least, seems to value friendship."

"Mia…"

"You should go," she said. "I need to get back to the hotel and check on Gloria and Emilia. I'll see you tomorrow night."

A look of hurt flashed briefly across his face, but Charlie nodded and walked out the door.

Alone, with Paolo at the front of the store where she'd asked him to pay Fred, Mia shut the door and locked it, then looked at the cellar door.

She'd won the battle she'd fought hard for tonight, but she was fairly certain war was on the horizon—in her own camp.

# CHAPTER FIVE

**M**ia slept until the late afternoon the next day. She hadn't been able to fall asleep until just before dawn, lying awake and staring at the ceiling. Thinking.

She'd managed to sneak into the hotel suite undetected at nearly four in the morning. The soft snores coming from Gloria's room let her know they were safe.

The April day was cool and gray, and gentle patters of rain dropped against her large window beyond the filmy white curtains. She rolled onto her side, staring out the window. She hadn't woken up as much as she'd just become alert. Instantly, her mind fell back to the previous night, and her anger returned.

*What the hell was Morrie thinking?*

She was a challenge to his position, that much was clear. But for that to have even become an issue between them was asinine. She'd never wanted to be part of the business, anyhow—she'd only wanted to make sure her brother hadn't died in vain. That his hard work would come to fruition, that he'd be able to change the lives of his family and friends the way he'd always dreamed. When she'd sailed back to America, she'd considered the words of Don Catalano and Johnny Torrio, cautioning her that things back home had changed. That her brother's operation was

hardly even a Scalisi operation anymore. She hadn't quite understood what they'd meant at the time. After last night, it was
crystal clear.

She had returned home with the intent to focus on her career
at Hyman's nightclub. Perhaps she would check in with the operation, but she'd thought it would be for the best to leave the
heavy lifting to those better equipped—her "trusted" comrades.
They'd have the operation's best interests at heart, she'd thought.
They'd never let Nick's name or hard work be squandered, she'd
been certain.

*I was wrong.*

She sat up and walked to the window, leaning her palms on
the sill.

Things were going to change.

A knock on her door drew her attention. "Yes?"

The door opened, and her niece wheeled in a small cart that
contained a covered dish and a silver pot of coffee.

Mia smiled. "Oh, you must be the new maid the hotel told
me about. Let me see if I have a tip for you…" When Emilia was
within grabbing distance, Mia snatched her up, tickling her, and
they tumbled onto her bed, Emilia shrieking with laughter.

"I brung your breakfast, Auntie," the little girl informed her,
wiggling away from Mia's fingers. "Even though it's afternoon
now."

"Brought," Mia corrected gently, and kissed the top of her
head. "And thank you, dearest."

She glanced up, catching sight of Gloria in the doorway. Her
arms were folded, and she had a slight smile on her face as she
watched her daughter busily arrange the cart beside Mia's bed.

Beneath the plate covering was a generous helping of bacon
and eggs, with a side of buttered toast and jam. Mia bypassed the
food for a moment to pour her first cup of coffee. After adding
cream and sugar and taking a long, fortifying sip, she looked at
Gloria. "What time is it?"

"It's nearly three," she replied. "Mr. Goldberg has rung here
for you three times since ten o'clock."

Mia sighed. "I have to attend his party tonight. And sing a couple of songs."

"Well, he seems rather urgent to talk to you. You should ring him back soon."

"I will." But not before she applied herself to her breakfast.

Gloria reached into her pocket and withdrew a telegram. She set it on Mia's tray. "It came earlier. Raquel is on her way. She arrives in a week's time."

Mia smiled as she read the short message from Carlo's younger sister that echoed Gloria's words. "Good. It'll be wonderful to have her here. Emilia will be so excited, won't you, darling? Your other *zia* is coming."

"Raquel?" the little girl said, hopeful.

"That's right."

"Hooray! Can we go pick shells on the beach?"

"When it grows warmer, we'll go to Atlantic City and you can do just that," Mia promised.

"Emilia, dear, go play with your dolls in the other room, please," Gloria said. "Mama and Auntie need to have a talk."

*Oh brother.* Mia returned her attention to the last bite of her toast, feeling like she was about to be in trouble.

After Emilia obediently trotted from the room, Gloria walked toward the bed. "Where the hell were you all night?" she demanded in a harsh whisper. "It was nearly four in the morning when I heard you come back in."

Apparently, Mia hadn't been as stealth as she'd thought. "I had business to attend to," she said without looking up.

"You just left without saying goodbye or telling me where you were going!"

"Well, our little chat beforehand wasn't exactly conducive to any of that," she said. "Look, Glo. You need to get used to me coming and going at odd hours. For one thing, I'm getting back into show business. You know what that's like. For another, after last night, it's blatantly clear the operation is going to shit. I refuse to let that happen, and that means I gotta be out more to keep an eye on things."

Gloria perched on the edge of the bed. "What do you mean, going to shit?"

Mia set her fork down. Nick probably never would have said what she was about to say. *But I'm not Nick.* "The Templeton is being diluted almost all the way down with water. It's *not* the product Nick was selling."

"Don't all bootleggers do that?"

"To an extent. Not to the level I tasted last night."

"Who's behind that? Goldberg?"

"Moritz. And Charlie."

Gloria's eyes widened. "Why would they do such a thing?"

"They're getting greedy." Mia shook her head. "And, they're getting pressured. You can't just sell booze anywhere. Every part of the city belongs to someone. If you want to do business on someone else's turf, it'll cost you."

Gloria was silent for a long moment. Then she said, "How do you go about getting your *own* turf?"

*You're smart enough to know the answer to that.* Mia studied her, chewing the inside of her cheek, then decided to give it to her straight. "You gotta kill a whole bunch of men."

To her credit, Gloria flinched only slightly. She nodded, very slowly. "And…is that what you're thinking of doing?"

Images of Kiddo Grainger and his bloody mouth, screaming for mercy, of Vinnie Fiore and the hole in his forehead, of Sal Bellomo, oozing blood from his chest flashed through her mind rapidly but one at a time. She lowered the cup of coffee that had been halfway to her mouth back to its saucer, fearing she might vomit if she took the sip.

She had killed before, for her brother. She would kill a thousand men for him. But for business? The thought made her hands tremble.

But she couldn't answer no to Gloria's question.

"I—I need to figure out who I can trust." Mia shook her head. "Things have…changed since I've been away. People have changed."

"Can you still trust Charlie?"

Mia stared down at her half-eaten plate of food, her nausea increasing. She couldn't meet Gloria's eyes as she said, "Part of what I need to figure out."

❀❀

Mr. Goldberg was waiting for her in the foyer when she walked into his opulent penthouse that night. She was early, as he'd ordered. Early for her, that was. The party, though in its early stages, was in full swing. Men in tuxes and women in evening dresses stood about the room, sipping drinks, eating hors d'oeuvres, and chatting pleasantly. An eight-man orchestra—her new band—sat in a corner of the room, filling the place with soft, background jazz.

Hyman was resplendent in a perfectly tailored tuxedo. A fresh, fragrant boutonniere was pinned to his lapel. He gave her a scrutinizing, head-to-toe onceover.

"You are very lovely, Mademoiselle Scalisi," he said, winging his elbow out for her to take. "The Chanel is incredible on you."

She glanced down, running a hand lightly down her side. He'd sent the dress with her after she'd shown up for a brief rehearsal that afternoon at his insistence. It was a filmy, red chiffon number, with beading along the slender straps and in an intricate pattern at the front. Cascades of sheer red chiffon dangled from each side of her hips, where the seam of the drop-waist bodice met the skirt. Jeweled heels, also sent by Hyman, completed the look.

"Thank you for it," she replied.

"Consider it a gift to celebrate the start of our partnership." He smiled down at her and patted her hand as he led her through the foyer to the large receiving room that served as tonight's ballroom. "Do you remember when you visited me around Thanksgiving the year before last, when I gifted you the shop?"

"Yes."

"And do you recall how I suggested you might be able to aid me in my less-than-legal endeavors?"

She glanced up at him. "The bootlegging, you mean? You told me politicians and important businessmen would be more interested in talking to a pretty girl than a crusty, middle-aged man."

"I don't quite recall describing myself *quite* that way," he said drily, "but, yes. That's the conversation I am referencing."

"What of it?"

"Do you see that man right there?" He nodded toward a tall, stoic man with graying hair and a prominent nose.

"Yes."

"Do you know who that is?"

She studied him more closely. "That's the governor of New York, isn't it?" She only knew the man from seeing his picture in the papers. She'd never followed politics particularly closely.

"Al Smith," Hyman confirmed. "He's going to run for president in the next election."

"And...you want me to try to talk him into buying something?"

"No," he said. "I want you to help him change his stance on Prohibition."

"He's a dry," Mia said. "That'll be a challenge."

"The opposite, actually."

She looked at him. "He's...a wet?"

"That's correct."

"Then why..." She trailed off under Hyman's gaze. Then it clicked in her mind. "If Prohibition gets repealed, all of these lucrative business ventures go away. People stop making money hand-over-fist when it's legal."

Hyman's eyes gleamed at her with pride. "I always knew you were a very smart girl, Mia. Yes. You are absolutely correct. Governor Smith is anti-Prohibition because he feels—rightly—that criminality in this country has increased exponentially since it was enacted. And he wants to abolish the cause of that criminality. But in doing so, what he'll abolish is many people's main source of income. And…well, that would be bad."

"How, exactly, do you expect me to change his mind?"

Hyman faced her, halting them in their slow progress across the room. "I want him to hear from one of America's success stories. An immigrant girl, brought to the Promised Land, the land of milk and honey, the place where her poor parents' dreams came true. And how happy you are to see the vile drink abolished from this beautiful country."

"I was born *here*, Mr. Goldberg. I'm not an immigrant."

"He doesn't need to know that, my sweet." He looped her hand through his arm and began walking again. "He only needs to see the sincerity and worry in your pretty brown eyes, and have a good peek down the front of your scandalously low-cut neckline."

*The puppetmaster at work.* She ought to have recalled Hyman never did anything without an agenda. "Some gift," she muttered.

They reached the governor, where he conversed with a man Mia did not recognize. They both turned as she and Hyman approached, and nodded their respect to Hyman, while giving her polite but curious glances.

"Al," Hyman said warmly, releasing Mia to shake his hand. "Joe. How are you gentlemen enjoying my little soiree?"

"Fantastic, as always," Governor Smith responded. "Food is great, drink is better. Music's swell."

"The music will soon get even better, at least for a song or two." Hyman gestured to Mia. "Allow me to present Miss Mia Angela Scalisi, the soon-to-be featured headliner at my new nightclub, and who will be enthralling us with her vocal stylings and charm later this evening. Miss Scalisi, this is Governor Al Smith and his future running mate, Senator Joseph Robinson."

"Miss Scalisi," Governor Smith said, lightly taking her proffered hand and bending over it.

"A pleasure, Miss Scalisi," Senator Robinson said, doing the same.

"Governor, Senator," she said. "What a pleasure and an honor it is to meet you both."

"The pleasure is all ours," Governor Smith replied, "especially if we can count on your vote next election." He winked at her and dug his elbow into Senator Robinson's side. "Now that you women have earned the right, it's time to start using it, eh?"

"Indeed," the senator said. "The future is our young people, and even more, our young women."

"Miss Scalisi here is a good Catholic girl," Hyman added.

"Oh?" Governor Smith said with a smile. "Tell me, to which parish do you belong in our fair city?"

Mia hadn't planned to resume going to church now that she was back in the country. She'd gone as a child, then stopped going altogether when she'd taken the job at the dress factory, since she'd had to work Sundays. In Sicily, she hadn't wanted to scandalize her newfound family by not going to church, so she'd accompanied them every Sunday and gone through the motions like a machine.

But before Nick had died, she'd attended most Sundays with Gloria, though it hadn't been out of interest. Nick would always send her, telling her to say enough Hail Marys to keep him out of hell. She'd assumed he'd been only half-joking.

Mia racked her brain for the name of the church Uncle Joe and Aunt Connie attended—the church most Italians in the Lower East Side attended.

"Most Precious Blood," she replied with a smile. "Though it's been some time since I've been there. I've been out of the country for nearly the past year and a half, visiting family."

The governor looked pleased. "May I inquire as to where?"

"Sicily," Mia replied. "Where I was, er, born."

"An immigrant." Senator Robinson studied her with new interest. "I do love hearing tales of our immigrant friends. Truly, this country would be nothing without our immigrants."

Feeling a bit of a fraud, Mia said, "I immigrated here with my family in—" She faltered; her parents and Nick had arrived in 1901, and she had not been born until 1903. On the off chance the governor and senator decided to investigate her claims and located her family's immigration documents, she'd have to lie about her age. "In 1901," she finished. "When I was just a—a year old."

"Wonderful," Governor Smith said. "And what do your parents do for a living?"

"They're both deceased, but my father was a fisherman and a laborer. And after he passed, my mother worked in factories. She perished in the Triangle Shirtwaist Factory fire."

The governor bowed his head. "I am truly sorry to hear of that, Miss Scalisi. Such a terrible, terrible incident. You know, shortly after that, I dedicated many long months to investigating factory conditions so that families such as yours would never have to endure such horror. We sought to reform labor laws after that tragic occurrence."

Mia drew her head back, genuinely surprised. How ignorant she'd been of all that had taken place in the wake of the disaster that had killed her mother. "I can appreciate your efforts, Governor. Sadly, though, I'm not sure they were appreciated by the men in charge at those factories. You see, after my brother and I became orphans, he was drafted into the war. And I had to take up work in a factory in order to survive. I can tell you firsthand that conditions were nearly as terrible as the ones my mother worked under, and that was several years later."

"We certainly still have our work cut out for us," Governor Smith said gravely. "All the more reason to secure your support in the next election, Miss Scalisi. It's a very important time, indeed. What better candidate for you to support than those you know believe in righting wrongs you and your family have experienced?"

"Well, Governor," Mia said, "I would love to put my support behind you, but I'm afraid we don't agree on one of those very important issues."

"And which issue would that be?"

"Prohibition," Mia said.

The governor and the senator both chuckled. "But my dear,

look around," Governor Smith said, gesturing around the room. "You're surrounded by alcohol. In the hands of very fine men and ladies." He nudged Hyman with his elbow. "And I daresay your benefactor here has made a pretty penny off selling the stuff, as well. Wouldn't you say you're being just a tad hypocritical?"

"Not in the slightest," Mia said sweetly. "You see, Governor, as a good Catholic, I was raised to stay away from liquor. My own father only ever drank wine, and even then, only on special occasions. Growing up in our tenement apartment, and then later, when I became a child vaudeville performer, I saw how drink ruined so many people. Good men and women. I saw the effect it had on our veterans, after my brother came home from the war. And I see what it does now—it turns people into rabid beings. I once worked for a shopkeeper, a very fine woman named Madame du la Boviette, who was also an immigrant Catholic, and a member of the Women's Christian Temperance Union. She influenced me greatly."

The governor and the senator did not need to know that Madame du la Boviette was actually the stage name of a coarse woman named Beverly Marsh from Idaho, whom Mia had met on a dusty vaudeville stage in the Bowery in 1915. It was also the name Mia fell back on when she needed to lie about her dance tutelage, or her own identity.

"But, dear," Governor Smith said, "look at all that has happened since Prohibition went into effect. The rise of the organized crime has men acting like rabid beings, anyway. If we abolished Prohibition, we get a hold of organized crime and the criminals who participate in it. You would be shocked if I shared with you some of the stories I've heard."

Actually, Mia agreed with the governor wholeheartedly. She wasn't so naive that she believed abolishing the 18th Amendment would thereby abolish criminality in its entirety, but she did believe that crime had drastically increased since Prohibition had given birth to those years of blood and whiskey.

"I only know how I feel, Governor," she said, hoping she

sounded grave. "I, and so many other young ladies like me. We've seen what alcohol does to so many of our good men. Meaning no disrespect to you or your endeavors, but I hope Prohibition stands. Or perhaps you might change your mind."

"To change his mind would be to give up the entire goddamn ticket," Senator Robinson objected.

"Miss Scalisi might have a point," Hyman said. "And I believe she and many of her peers will happily exercise their newly granted voting rights in the upcoming election." Then he angled his head, his gaze targeting something or someone across the room. "Ah, Miss Scalisi, there's the lady I mentioned to you earlier that I wanted you to meet. Come, my dear."

*What lady?* Mia bobbed her head at the two gentlemen. "Enjoy your evening. It was lovely to meet you."

They both bowed elegantly.

"It was a pleasure to make your acquaintance, Miss Scalisi," Governor Smith said, "and we look forward to seeing you sing shortly."

As Hyman dragged her away, she frowned up at him. "Who am I meeting now? And what was the point of that conversation? He won't change his mind, and even if he did, you heard him— to do so would defeat the point of his position on the ballot in the first place."

"You're meeting the powder room," Hyman said. "I just wanted to get you out of there. And I didn't expect you to create some kind of epiphany in the good governor. I just wanted you to get in his head, confirm some of the fears and doubts he's been having about running." He smiled. "Mind games, dear."

"We have two long years to see if these little mind tricks of yours work," she said. "So I still don't see the point."

"Seed planting, my child," Hyman said. "Besides, that was an audition of sorts. I wanted to see how you'd fare against men of that class for future…business endeavors. Throwing you in front of a likely presidential candidate seemed like a good way to gauge that."

"More mind games, Mr. Goldberg?"

"I never stop playing, my darling," he said, leading her to the door of the powder room. "You may refresh yourself here. I'd like you to take the stage for the first song in twenty minutes. Are you all set from rehearsal earlier?"

"Rehearsal" had consisted of a thirty-minute, mid-afternoon meeting with the band Hyman had hired to select a couple of songs. The band leader, Gene, was a kindly pianist whom Mia had liked almost instantly. She thought of Billy from Stems Club in Chicago. After the club had closed, the band had gone its separate ways, and she hadn't heard from him since. He'd been a wonderful man. She hoped he was all right.

They'd selected two popular songs from Mia's repertoire, "Somebody Loves Me" and "Nobody Knows You When You're Down and Out."

"Yes," Mia replied. "I'm all set."

"Good. I'll have someone come fetch you when it's time. Break a leg, dear." Hyman shut the door, and she was alone.

The powder room was as big as a walk-in closet, with shining hex tiles, a porcelain sink and toilet, and a vanity with a cushioned stool. Mia slid onto the stool and gave her reflection a hard stare. Her thick, dark hair had grown while she'd been in Sicily, so she'd had it cut back into her old, chin-length bob, so charming with its large waves. Her full, unsmiling crimson lips matched her dress, and her smoky eye shadow made her brown eyes hazy and alluring. She pinched her cheeks a little for color, and then, suddenly, nerves erupted in her stomach.

Her first performance in well over a year, and she was *nervous*. Mia Angela Scalisi, the Saturday Night Special, did not get nervous.

Except she did. She always had, but she had only ever allowed one person to see it.

And Nick wasn't here—would never again be here—to joke her out of her nervousness, to calm the butterflies in her stomach, to say what he always said to her before a show.

*Never let 'em see you sweat.*

Nick had been the one to broker this deal with Hyman—a

deal she'd known nothing about, had had no say in. A deal that felt very much like he'd been selling her in exchange for two million of Hyman's dollars, but one that had been meant to get her away from Sal Bellomo.

If he were here, what would he think? He'd probably be terribly proud of her. He'd tell her to knock 'em dead. He'd tell her not to forget about him when she became a big star. He'd have lots of jokes, but they'd be underscored with his pride in her.

If she stared into the mirror hard enough, she could almost see him behind her, in his own tux, wearing his old, smart-aleck grin, flashing the dimple in his left cheek that completed their shared set. She could almost see his hand on her shoulder, squeezing reassuringly. Then he'd offer his elbow and escort her to the stage himself. And when she was done, he'd be the first on his feet to cheer for her. They'd get late-night steak and eggs somewhere, or have a drink at the crummiest speak in town, and he'd tell her how proud of her he was. How proud Mama and Papa would be if they could see her now.

Tears filled her eyes before she could will them away.

A box of facial tissues rested on the vanity next to a small jar of cold cream. Without a handkerchief available, Mia plucked a tissue from the box and dabbed her eyes.

A knock at the door made her jump. "Mia?"

Charlie.

She considered not answering the door. After last night, it was hard to know if Charlie was still the same Charlie she'd left on the docks last January before boarding the ship to Sicily. And that realization that he might be a very different man…hurt.

"It's Charlie. Open the door."

Mia slid off the stool and opened the door slightly. He peered down at her through the crack. "You gonna let me in?"

She opened the door wider. He stepped inside the small room, pushing the door shut. He looked terribly handsome in his tuxedo. His wavy black hair was tamed, even the stubborn fore-lock that added to his boyish features.

"How you doing?" he asked. "Nervous?"

"Little. First time singing in front of people in a while."

"Ah, you're a pro." He stepped closer, his hands stuffed in his pockets. "It'll be like you never left."

She studied him. "I think we both know that's not true."

His jaw tightened almost imperceptibly.

"I did leave," she went on. "And things are very different. Aren't they?"

"We had to keep going, Mia," he said. "With or without you. We didn't know you'd stay there so long. I didn't know."

"Of course you had to keep going." She stepped closer to him. "But was it in the right direction, Charlie?"

He took a deep breath. "Look, a lot's happened. You know that. We haven't had a chance to talk, me and you. Alone, I mean. Just us. Let me take you to a late supper after this. All right?"

Mia hesitated. An enormous part of her wanted to say yes. A small, but loud, part of her begged her to say no.

"Please," he added softly, and reached for her hand slowly, as though she were a wild animal he was trying not to startle. "I— I've missed you, Mia."

*I've missed you, too.*

She nodded.

He smiled. "Good. Listen, you better get going. Hyman sent me to fetch you. But I know how you always loved to keep 'em waiting."

She laughed softly, but there was no mirth in it. "I'm a very different person from that girl, Charlie." She walked past him, her heels tapping against the tiled floor as she walked back to the small ballroom where everyone was gathered.

"Ah, here she is!" Hyman called when he spotted her. He held a hand out in her direction, and heads turned toward her. Low murmurs began filling the room.

Mia kept her head high as she sauntered past them toward the band and Hyman. She stood next to him, and he lifted one of her hands in his.

"The new star of The Divine, and New York City's It Girl," Hyman said, smiling at her. "Clara Bow has nothing on Miss Mia Angela Scalisi!"

The room erupted into applause.

"Miss Scalisi, will you honor us with a song or two?" Hyman went on.

"Of course," she called in a clear voice. "It'd be my pleasure."

She glanced at Gene, seated at his grand piano, and he nodded to the band. They launched into the opening strains of "Somebody Loves Me."

The song had been Sal's favorite, she remembered. She'd sung it for him at his birthday party a year and a half ago. His *last* birthday party before she'd had him murdered. Because he'd had her brother murdered.

A lump lodged itself in her throat.

Nick had gotten a kick out of teasing her about the song because she'd always hated it. He'd recommended she sing it for her audition at the Chicago Theatre. The same theater outside which he'd been gunned down. Where she'd held his dying body in her arms, felt his blood seep out of him and onto her.

A quick drumroll cued her that it was time to sing.

Mia opened her mouth, but nothing came out. The lump in her throat was too large.

The music behind her seemed to fade. The faces of the partygoers turned blank, featureless. The overhead chandeliers glittered too brightly. She couldn't see.

Her knees wobbled.

*Open your mouth! Sing!*

From the front row, a bloody Sal Bellomo lifted a finger at her and laughed.

The room began to spin.

*Nick*, she thought. *Nick's not here. He has to be here.* Her brother was the only one who could calm her nerves. His mocking grin always put her at ease. He was steadfast and reassuring. One glance at him was all she needed to banish her fear.

But she could not find him in the crowd of faceless people, with a dead, leering Sal Bellomo at the front. Laughing, laughing.

Where was Nick?

*Dead*, the voice in her head said. *He's dead. You're alone. And you're failing.*

She sucked in a sharp breath. Sal's mocking ghost faded, and the room came back into focus.

The crowd was quiet. Partygoers murmured to each other in hushed voices as they cast furtive, confused glances in her direction.

Hyman approached her from where he'd been standing off to the side, a concerned and slightly annoyed look on his face. He leaned close, putting a hand on her back.

"What's the problem, Mia?" he asked in her ear. His voice was nowhere near as gentle as the hand on her back was.

"N-nothing," she replied, smiling. "I just—forgot the words. I remember now."

He narrowed his eyes. "Are you certain?"

"Yes."

He nodded once, still looking doubtful, but stepped back, his highly practiced smile in place as he made his way to the side of the room. Beside him stood Charlie and Moritz. Moritz's face held an unreadable expression. Charlie's brow was furrowed deeply, but he blinked the expression away when her gaze landed on him. One side of his mouth flicked up, and his eyes flashed with encouragement.

She drew in another breath. For a terrible instant, her voice came out hoarse, breaking on the first note. She cleared her throat and skipped to the next word. This time, her voice did not fail her. It rumbled in her throat before smoothing out to an easy vibration. Like breathing, her technique fell over her like a mink coat.

The lyrics, once so despised she'd found them funny, now meant nothing at all. They were gibberish to her own ears. But she sang with convincing emotion, and soon people's faces relaxed from confusion and concern to pleasure and excitement.

She wondered if her old love of singing would ever come back to her.

After the song ended, Hyman led her about the room, introducing her to people whose names she did not even hear. But she smiled and made charming remarks that came to her lips automatically.

"You're doing wonderfully," Hyman muttered out of the corner of his mouth. "Are you feeling better? Something to drink, perhaps? I'm sure there's a glass of champagne somewhere around here with your name on it."

"I don't drink, remember?" Mia kept her smile in place as they passed the governor and the senator. "I'm just a poor, teetotaling immigrant girl. Like you said."

He patted her hand. "You continue to fill me with pride, Mademoiselle Scalisi. That was a test, to see how closely you pay attention to details."

Mia stopped in her tracks. He gazed down at her, brows lifted in mild surprise. "When will you stop testing me, Hyman?"

He gave her a chilly smile. "When things like the beginning of your first number never happen again."

"I told you," she said. "I just forgot the words for a moment, is all. You know, I haven't sung in public in a long time, Hyman. I told you this was too soon—"

He tilted his head. "Are you not the consummate professional you insisted you were, dear?"

She blinked. "Of course I am. But I—"

"Then stop complaining and be a professional." He fixed her with a hard stare before his face relaxed into easy lines. "There are people watching us right now. Smile."

She stretched her lips obediently, though she was sure it looked more like a grimace.

"You can do better than that. You have a charming dimple. You should know how to use it."

Mia took a deep breath through her nose, wishing she could

claw his face. Then she tossed her head and grinned, flexing her cheek. "Better?"

"Much, much better," Hyman said approvingly, taking her arm again. "And so will be your next number. Do I have to question your familiarity with the lyrics to this song?"

"No," she said through her teeth.

"Excellent." He held a hand out toward the band. "Then do what you do best, dearest."

She got through the next song with an ease that surprised even her. Mostly, it was because she refused to let Mr. Goldberg see her fail.

After, she remained with the band as partygoers mobbed her. They wanted to shake her hand, tell her how charmingly she'd sung, how much they looked forward to seeing her at The Divine.

Governor Smith bowed over her hand, pecking her knuckles. "My dear, it was a pleasure to both make your acquaintance this evening and get a sneak peek of what's in store at Goldberg's new place. I look forward to finding myself in the audience some night soon."

"Thank you," Mia said. "I look forward to discussing more factory reform with you on those evenings. And perhaps your stance on Prohibition."

He blinked, then smiled widely. "Beauty and brains. An enviable combination for any young lady in these times of change. I enjoy matching wits with you." He released her hand, then wagged a finger at her. "You've a long career ahead of you, Miss Scalisi. I can sense it."

Mia smiled politely, nodding her goodbye at him. Then she caught Hyman gazing at her from across the room. He lifted his glass of water in a toast to her, a slightly smug smile on his face.

She wondered just how long this career might last.

# CHAPTER SIX

"I hope you're not too sick of Italian food," Charlie said as he guided Mia out of his car, driven by Joey.

She glanced up at the sign. John's of 12ᵗʰ Street. She'd been here before. It was a quiet, little family joint that served the old-world recipes, heavy on the gravy and red sauce, that she'd grown up on. It felt and smelled more like home than anything else. She and Nick had often dined here after he'd started making a little money, when he'd come home from the war. It was one of the few places in the city he felt he could breathe.

"No, it's perfect," she said. "This place has…good memories."

He smiled and held open the door. "I guess this is our version of Sunday dinner, right?"

She gave him a curious look.

"It's Sunday now, and we're having dinner," he clarified. "We should be the only people here."

She'd been dismissed from Hyman's party around midnight, and since it wasn't her scene in terms of having fun anyway, she and Charlie had headed out for a bite to eat. Granted, she couldn't remember the last time she'd had the kind of fun she'd used to, in her past life.

*I guess it was before Sal's birthday*, she mused. Considering she'd nearly been raped that night, it hadn't been what she'd considered a ball.

"Mr. Lazzari," a suited, heavyset man at the door said, wringing Charlie's hand. "So nice to see you again. And this must be Miss Scalisi."

"Yes," she said with a polite smile. "Thank you for having us."

"Ah, for Mr. Lazzari?" the man said. "For all he do for my place? Anything. Come, come."

As Charlie had said, they were the only people in the restaurant. Either the owner had kicked everyone out, or they'd stayed open this late just to accommodate them.

They were led to an intimate table for two near the back of the restaurant—far away from the windows, she noted. Likely also per Charlie's request.

The man pulled out her chair and solicitously dropped her napkin in her lap, then set about filling their glasses with strong, house red wine.

"This reminds me of the wine I had in Sicily," she said after taking a sip.

"You enjoyed your time there?" Charlie asked.

Mia nodded. "I did. Very much. I learned a lot about my parents, about my family. My cousin Raquel is coming here in a week. She should be on the ship now. In time for the club opening."

"That'll be nice to have her close by. I'm sure she'll be overwhelmed here at first."

"Her brother's wife wants her to find a husband here, but I plan to show her she doesn't have to do that if she doesn't want to. I'm sure Isabella will be disappointed."

"Maybe she'll find a nice fella." Charlie shrugged.

Mia made a face. "Are there such things anymore?"

"What am I, chopped liver?"

She ticked an eyebrow at him.

He chuckled. "On second thought, I'm not sure I want an

answer to that. Tell me what else you did over there."

"I learned," she replied. "I spent a lot of time listening to our family stories, things that happened long before Nick and I were born. Meeting people."

"What did you learn?"

"About—well, lots of things."

"Like what?"

"Did you ever know a man called Don Catalano?" she asked.

Charlie's expression changed to one of recognition laced with respect. "Yes. Your and Nick's godfather. Met him a couple times when he'd come to town on business. Good man."

"I spent most of my evenings with him," Mia said. "Sitting in the blood orange groves. Drinking wine. Talking. Listening. He's kept me well abreast of things that were happening here."

"Oh?" Now Charlie's face seemed guarded.

She decided to leave that thread untugged for the moment. "He spoke to me as a father speaks to a son," she went on. "I enjoyed that."

"He knows what you did after…Nick died?"

"Yes."

"Then that's why."

"I picked up on that. He's a good teacher."

Charlie leaned back in his seat. "What else did he teach you?" His dark eyes were focused on her as he toyed with his small wineglass.

"The importance of learning who to trust," she said softly.

Before he could reply, the owner returned to refill their hardly touched wineglasses and take their orders.

Charlie glanced at her. "The clams are some of the best you'll ever have—even having just got back from Sicily."

"Ah!" The owner turned to her, and in Sicilian asked, "You visited the old country?"

She chatted with him briefly in Sicilian, the melodic language flowing rapidly off her tongue as though she were still there. They ordered the clams.

"Tell me," Mia said when the owner had returned to the

kitchen. "What have you been up to since I've been away? *Really* been up to?"

He lowered his gaze, a smile playing around the corners of his mouth. "The don teach you how to stare at a man like you can read the bottom of his soul, too?"

"No," Mia said softly. "Nick taught me that."

Charlie sipped his wine. "It's been...a ride since you went away. Ups and downs. 'Twenty-five was a big year for us. We got Hyman paid back—well, he paid himself back from your sugges-tion. That was brilliant, by the way. We made more money last year than we'd made since the war. It's allowed us to dabble in other business avenues."

"Give it to me straight," she said. "Is Morrie involved in heroin?"

He hesitated. "Look, Mia, I know how you feel about it, but you have to understand. The earning potential with that partic-ular product—"

"Charles," she said sharply.

"Yes," he said with a sigh. "Yes, he's got a nice little heroin business going."

Mia drew her breath in through her nose. She shouldn't be surprised. And she really wasn't. Moritz was a highly intelligent businessman. He went where the money was. And the money, she knew, was in heroin. She thought back to that night at the Hotel Astor when she and Gloria had first landed in New York for Thanksgiving. She'd begged them not to go into the heroin business, and losing that, had begged them not to use any money made from Nick's liquor deal. She couldn't support a product that so thoroughly ruined people's lives. True, there were drunk-ards on every street corner, but heroin was an especially nasty substance, and she'd seen so many young people destroy their lives after getting hooked on it. Moritz had agreed—he'd use his own personal finances, not money from Nick's operation. She'd known at the time she was being placated, but she'd gotten away with it because she'd been Nick's sister.

"Whose idea was it to cut down the Templeton?"

"Both of ours," Charlie said. "I didn't know…I didn't know he'd take it that far."

"What did he put in it?"

He shrugged. "Don't know for sure, but if I had to guess, I'd say it's probably one part pure rye, six or seven parts water. Grain alcohol."

Mia shook her head. "Nick wanted the cut batches to be half and half, with *quality* alcohol being added." She glanced at the table, then lifted her gaze to his. "I don't want that happening again, Charlie."

"I'll talk to Morrie. You have my word."

"And the heroin stays separate."

"Mia," Charlie said gently. "I brought you here so we could catch up. Not talk business. There's more to life than just that, isn't there?"

The owner delivered their plates of linguine and clams. They spent a few moments in silence, eating their meals. The clams were tender, the sauce flavorful and tasting of home.

Charlie glanced up from his plate. "You like your clams?"

She nodded, then offered a small smile. "Some of the best I've ever had."

"I'll bet nothing can beat fresh seafood right from the ocean, though."

"My cousin's wife, Isabella, is a fine cook. She lives for Sundays."

He smirked. "She make you go to Mass?"

"Every Sunday," Mia said. "It…it's hard. Going to church. Knowing everything I've done."

He nodded, eyes on his plate. He took a bite of linguine, then said, "You could always make confession."

She barked out a laugh. "Could I? Is that what you've done?"

Charlie shrugged. "I've made confession before."

The smile left her face. "You have?"

"Nick and I went together once a couple of years ago."

She lowered her fork to her plate. "Nick…made confession?"

"He never told you?"

Mia shook her head slowly. Yet one more thing about her brother she'd never known. He'd rarely attended Mass himself. In fact, the only occasions she remembered him going to church besides his wedding were Christmas and Easter.

"What do you confess?" she asked.

Charlie gave her a look. "That's between me and God, ain't it?"

"And the robed man on the other side of the confessional."

"You blaspheme," he said disapprovingly.

"Don't tell me you're putting stock into priests these days." She chewed her lip. "Do you...think it helps?"

Charlie twirled pasta onto his fork. "Does it make me a changed man, you mean? You know the answer to that."

"Then why bother?"

"Just because I'm in a certain line of work and I've done certain things for that line of work," he said quietly, "doesn't mean I don't have a conscience."

"Does it make you feel better?"

He made a face and shrugged. "Yeah, I guess it does."

She watched him eat for a moment, thoughtfully shuffling clams around her plate with her fork. "But," she started again, and he glanced up at her. "If you confess to...certain things, and then you don't change, what's the point of confessing in the first place?"

"Sometimes the things we carry get a little heavy from time to time," he said. "And confessing helps ease the weight. Maybe you should go."

She scoffed. "Like fun, I should." She didn't even intend to attend church and started to say so, then she remembered the commitment she'd made to Aunt Connie. "Gloria and I promised Joe and Connie we'd go to Mass and then over there for Sunday dinner. I'm pretty sure it'll take being on a death bed to get out of that from here on out."

"You need your family," Charlie said. "Blood or not."

"What about your mother?" Mia spun linguine onto her fork. It was time for a change in subject, because talking of religion and confession made her deeply uncomfortable. "How is she?"

He lifted a shoulder and wiped his mouth. "As well as she can be, I guess. She fell a couple months ago, and it's taking her a while to recover."

"I'm sorry to hear that."

"So my Sundays are booked, too," he said, then smiled.

The sight of it made a sudden rush of emotion fly through her. For the first time since she'd gotten home, the full weight of just how much she'd missed him hit her like blackjack over her head. She'd come to rely on him for so much—support, strength, wisdom. Not knowing who he'd become while she'd been away or if she could still trust him killed her.

"What is it?" he asked softly.

"I just…" Mia's throat tightened suddenly.

He dropped his fork and reached across the table, laying his right hand on top of her left. "Tell me."

The touch of his warm hand, so large it completely eclipsed hers lying on the table, made her heart beat swiftly. He stroked the back of her hand with this thumb.

"Tell me I can still trust you," she whispered. "Tell me that with all of these horrible things we've been through, that—that I've done, all the terrible ways in which I've changed… Tell me you're still the same. The same Charlie you always were." She bit her lip. "My Charlie."

His eyes flared at her last words, and his grip on her hand tightened slightly. "You can trust me," he said. "I swear on my life. I promised your brother I'd always watch out for you. I'd always protect you. And I always will. I just…" He broke off, his jaw flexing. "I wasn't supposed to fall in love with you, Mia. But here we are."

Her heart jumped into her throat.

He leaned forward. "The day you left, I told you I'd wait for you. I meant it. I did. And I still am. You came home with this mile-high brick wall around you. Sicily was supposed to protect you, supposed to show you that you're not alone in this world. But…it changed you.

I don't think it's a bad thing. But I think you feel like you don't know me anymore. I'm still the same guy, Mia. The same guy who'll rip this city, this whole fucking world apart if it means keeping you safe."

He stood up and knelt before her, cupping her face in his hands. "Every day you were gone killed me," he said hoarsely.

"Charlie," she whispered, leaning toward him. She reached up to take one of his hands, the other still on her cheek. She grasped it tightly and shut her eyes as she tilted her head toward his.

His lips captured hers with a careful but ravenous hunger, as though he were straining to hold himself at bay against his true feelings. The first time they'd kissed on the dock the day she'd sailed away from New York, she'd initiated it. She'd given it everything she had, fearing it would be the last time. Treating it as goodbye the kiss it was. But now, he was in control, and this was a welcome home she'd dreamed of every night she'd been in Sicily. Because as much as she loved the country of her blood, being away from him killed a little part of her, too.

Mia lost herself in the movements of his lips, letting him carry her on and on, higher and higher, forgetting they were in a public place, even if they were alone. Emotions she'd never felt before filled her to the brim, each one more intense than the last, and she wondered how she'd lived for almost twenty-three years without this feeling before. Wondered how she could ever live without it again.

She squeezed her eyes closed in case it was all a dream, and gripped his hand tighter to remind herself that it was real. Her fingers slid over his palm.

Then her eyes flew open.

She jerked back, startled, her lips still warm from his kiss. She flipped his hand palm-up and stared in horror at what she knew she'd find.

A long line of raised skin.

Charlie swiftly closed his palm, but it was too late. She'd seen it.

A scar.

The same scar Nick had had. The scar that had tied him to this life forever. The scar that had gotten him killed. And now, Charlie had it.

Her eyes filled with tears.

She looked at him, the tears spilling down her cheeks. "Why?" she demanded in a whisper. "Why? *Why?*"

"Mia," he muttered. "I told you. A lot's happened since you left."

"Who? When?"

He sighed. "Masseria. About nine months ago."

*Masseria.* She touched trembling fingertips to her trembling mouth. "Jesus Christ."

"Mia—"

She stood abruptly. He did too. He reached for her. "Please, Mia—"

"No." She pulled away as though he'd brandished a knife. In a way, he had, since her heart was stung and bleeding. "You know. You *know* what it did to him. What it did to his family."

"Whether I'm made or not, the risks are still the same," he said. He held up his palm. "This? This buys me protection."

"It ties you to him for the rest of your life," she countered, her voice shaking. "To this life. You can't *leave*, Charlie. You can never leave. Until you die. Tell me, how long do made guys live? Nick made it to twenty-five."

"Masseria is the most powerful man in New York right now," Charlie said.

"That's why Luciano was there last night," Mia said. "Everyone knows he's Masseria's right hand. He was there because of you."

"Luciano is a big reason why the business has taken off the way it did," Charlie said. "Nick was friendly with Lucky. He appreciated your show of respect and wanted to repay by helping grow the operation."

"And he brought you into the fold."

"I'm Sicilian," Charlie said, avoiding her gaze. "He couldn't bring Moritz for obvious reasons. This…this is an honor."

She stared at him, horrified. "An *honor.*"

He straightened his shoulders. "Yes. An honor."

"You always gave Nick crap for being a made guy," she said. "You said he sold himself. That he could have been his own boss."

"I didn't understand at the time. Now I do." He encircled her wrist with a gentle hand, but his eyes were hard. "Come on, kid. You know better than anyone than to be naive about all this. Look what you did after Nick died. You can't have one foot in this life and one foot out."

She tugged against his grip, and he released her immediately. "I—"

"You're as much a made man as I am, as Nick was." Charlie held up his hand. "This scar? It's the only difference between me and you. When are you gonna stop lying to yourself?"

She knew he was right, deep down in her soul. Knew it as truly as she knew her own name and that the moon came out at night. But she cringed away from that truth. If she accepted it, it would mean she had become a monster in her own right.

"I'm still the same man, Mia," he said quietly. "You have to know that. This doesn't change anything between us."

She stepped away. Her heart burned from the phantom knife slash. She wished the tears would stop spilling from her eyes. Wished she could accept the truth, about Charlie, about herself.

Behind Charlie, she caught sight of the owner peering out at them from the kitchen, a worried look on his face.

"Thank you," she choked out, "for a very lovely dinner." She turned on her heel and walked to the door.

"Mia," Charlie said. "Don't leave. Please."

At the door, she hesitated, shutting her eyes as she swallowed several times, working to regain her composure.

How she wanted to run back into his arms.

Instead, she pushed the door open and strode out into the cold night.

# CHAPTER SEVEN

E arly Sunday morning, her eyes burning from lack of sleep, Mia followed Gloria, Emilia, Aunt Connie, and Uncle Joe into Most Precious Blood Catholic Church for Mass. She wore a black shift dress with elbow-length billowing sleeves, white lace insets down the front, and plain black T-strap heels. She was so tired from tossing and turning all night since she'd made it home from her disastrous, hurtful date with Charlie that black had been a poor choice. Her olive skin was wan, and the starkness of the color would only make her look more so. Despite this, she'd forgone any makeup. Aunt Connie frowned on that sort of thing. In Sicily, so had Cousin Isabella. Luckily, her snug-fitting black hat was fitted with a lace veil, somewhat allowing her to hide.

It was automatic reflex borne of weekly habit from her child-hood that dunked her fingers into the font. She touched her wet fingertips to her forehead, chest, and shoulders, noting the way Aunt Connie performed the same action, and with such rever-ence, her lips already moving in silent prayer.

Mia prayed for the strength to stay awake.

She strolled behind her family toward their preferred pew, roughly in the middle of the church. The beauty of the building, with its white domed ceiling and bright, tall archways, frescoes painted on the ceilings and in between the huge panes of stained glass, and the stunning altar and tabernacle, did not impress her as they once had, as God had once impressed her. But since He'd robbed her of the things that had mattered most to her—her parents and her brother—she could not bring herself to priori-tize Him as she once had.

And yet, the weight of her guilt as she gazed up at His form on the large crucifix nearly brought her to her knees. She was a murderer, entering the House of God.

But she was not sorry for what she had done.

She genuflected before entering the pew, then knelt on the knee-rest, hands clasped in front of her. She was the perfect picture of piety, though her mind was blank.

"*Psst*," she heard from the aisle.

Everyone in the family turned their heads toward the sound.

A humbly dressed man holding his hat wore a sheepish smile, but stretched out a hand. "I come to pay my respects," he said with a heavy Italian accent. "To Signor and Signora d'Abbruz-zo." He shifted his gaze to Mia and gave her a serious nod. "And to Signorina Scalisi."

Mia drew her head back. Out of the corner of her eye, she saw Gloria turn to stare at her in confusion.

*Me?*

The man maintained his serious expression, his hand still out.

Mia scooted back onto the bench and reached for his hand. "It is my honor to meet you," she said in Sicilian, and his eyes gleamed with pleasure. At her mastery of the language, or that she'd said it was an honor to meet him, she wasn't sure. "You are?"

He bowed, still holding her hand. "Bruno. I am a great friend of Signor d'Abbruzzo."

Mia nodded. "Signor Bruno."

Uncle Joe reached up to pat his back. "We were each other's first friends when we arrived in America. We were on the same boat."

"I come to his shop to buy my family's food, and he come to the dock to buy my fish," Signor Bruno said, smiling.

Mia returned it. "Any friend of my uncle's is a friend of mine."

He fixed her with an eager stare, nodding. He seemed to be waiting for her to say something else.

Then it dawned on her—Signor Bruno was approaching her as he would approach any man of respect. She hoped her shock wasn't written on her face.

"If—if you ever need anything at all, please, come to me," Mia said. "I…would consider it a great favor to assist you."

They were words she'd heard Nick utter hundreds of times to the poorer tenement families before they'd left New York, and even in Chicago.

Signor Bruno beamed, bowed several times, and released her hand. "*Grazie, grazie.*" He waved at Uncle Joe and Aunt Connie, at Gloria and Emilia, before backing away.

"What the hell was that?" Gloria hissed in her ear.

Mia kept her gaze forward. "You're in church, Gloria."

She felt the stares of Uncle Joe and Aunt Connie from her other side, but when she met her uncle's eyes, he only gave her a solemn nod.

As if he understood.

When the Mass began, Mia went through the motions as she used to, the words meaningless on her lips, the hymns echoing hollowly in her ears, the message of Father Alessio's homily flying over her head. When the time for Holy Communion came, she rose and dutifully followed her family out of the pew and into the aisle, her hands folded prayerfully in front of her.

Mia glanced around the cathedral. Every face her gaze landed on was the picture of holiness, of gratitude. These churchgoers were giving and receiving of their spirits and hearts in communion with that of Jesus Christ and all the saints.

She, on the other hand, was numb.

Would she ever stop being angry with Him? Would she ever feel the way these people did, the way her aunt and uncle did?

Would she ever feel gratitude for the Lord, and come to rely on and trust in Him again?

Perhaps her relationship with Him was as dead as the men she'd had killed.

She neared Father Alessio in the Communion line, watching him feed Aunt Connie a wafer. Her throat tightened.

When it was her turn, the wafer between his fingers might as well have been a cockroach. She couldn't eat of His Body. The thought of it was almost repulsive.

*Because I've done murder.*

*Because I'm going to hell.*

The priest's brow creased. Mia placed a finger over her lips and shook her head rapidly. He dropped the wafer back into the ciborium and quickly traced the sign of the cross into her forehead with his thumb.

She dropped her hands and turned away from Father Alessio, the Eucharist, the tabernacle, the crucifix. All of it was simply too much to look at. She could not bear it.

"Looked like you was gonna choke on that little cracker," a voice behind her whispered.

Mia whirled.

Jake Morelli grinned at her. "Didn't know you went here."

"What are *you* doing here?" she demanded in a whisper. "You following me?"

"Attending church like all the good little boys and girls." He rested a hand on her lower back. "Just like you."

She arched away from him. "I told you what would happen if you touched me again without invitation."

He leaned close to her ear. "But I don't see your bulldog anywhere around."

She narrowed her eyes. "That's the point. You're not supposed to see him coming."

Jake smirked. "It's Sunday, Miss Scalisi. This is God's house. That's not very Christian of you, is it?"

"You don't strike me as a holy man, Mr. Morelli," she said. "I know what you're up to in this neighborhood. I've been meaning to talk about that with you."

"Have you?" He cocked his head. "Let's discuss it, then. How about over dinner and drinks?"

"Mia?" Gloria said, coming up on her other side. She looked doubtfully at Jake. "Excuse me. Are you…a friend of Mia's?"

"Oh, yeah," he said, stepping away. "A real good friend. See you later, dollface." With a wink, he disappeared toward the back of the church.

Mia gritted her teeth as she reentered the pew and knelt beside her aunt.

"Do I even want to ask who that was?" Gloria asked under her breath.

"Just some jerk," Mia murmured back.

"Why didn't you take Communion?"

Mia finally lifted her gaze to the huge carved crucifix, to the serious countenance of Jesus Christ. The Son of the God who'd allowed her family to be taken from her.

"I didn't confess," she whispered. But that wasn't the whole truth.

*I don't deserve it.*

"I hope you not too tired of Italian food," Aunt Connie said that afternoon from the stove in her kitchen.

They were the same words Charlie had uttered at the start of what should have been a beautiful night. Mia's heart seared a little, but she forced the pain away to smile at the older woman.

"I could never grow tired of your cooking, Aunt Connie. My cousins in Sicily were wonderful cooks, but you're in a class by yourself."

Aunt Connie beamed with pride as she bustled around the small, tidy kitchen. She and Uncle Joe, currently in the small parlor having a glass of anisette with Paolo, lived above their grocery in a cozy, well-furnished apartment. It always smelled of something baking, either tomatoes and cheese, or the delicious biscotti she sold in the store that never seemed to stay in the display case.

Mia sliced a great, warm Italian loaf, dusty with flour, and stole marinated vegetables from the antipasto dish on the counter. Gloria supervised Emilia setting the table and sipped a glass of Uncle Joe's rich, red wine. Aunt Connie pulled dishes from the oven—chicken cacciatore, meatballs in gravy, spaghetti in simmering Bolognese. Beef braciola sautéed on the stove in the special olive oil Uncle Joe imported.

"Ah," she said, sounding pleased. "Now we just about ready to eat."

Mia dunked a little corner of bread into the meatball gravy and popped it in her mouth, just before Aunt Connie swatted her away.

"Put the bread on the table, girl," she ordered good-naturedly. "Before you eat the whole kitchen."

"She could eat the whole *store* and never gain a pound," Gloria complained, lifting a hand. "You should have seen her in Catania, Aunt Connie. Breakfast, lunch, and dinner, plus a whole jug of wine every night. Look at her. Not one single pound."

"Cheeks look fuller," Aunt Connie argued. "So does the…" She mimed pushing up her breasts with both hands. "Much better than when she left. Too skinny. Good Sicilian girls needa meat."

Mia chuckled. The banter reminded her of her family in Sicily, and of her days growing up on Elizabeth Street. Nothing was off-limits among the women as topics of conversation went. "Well, I can't have *too* much meat. I have to be able to fit into my evening gowns for Mr. Goldberg's nightclub. He'd have quite a few things to say about that."

"You eat more," Aunt Connie insisted. "You fill out the dresses. He got nothing to say about that. Then maybe you get a husband."

"If that Charlie keeps sniffing around, she just might," Gloria teased. "She had a date with him last night, Aunt Connie. One she didn't return from until well into the wee hours of the morning."

Mia shook her head, determined not to let the weight of the discussion she'd had on that date drag her down. "Come on, Glo."

"Ah, well." Aunt Connie reached out and patted Mia's middle. "Then you eat. Soon you might be eating for two." She cackled as she stirred the gravy.

Mia burst out laughing. "You'll have better luck with Raquel, Aunt Connie. Maybe—she's a girl after my own heart."

"Isabella wants her to be married," Gloria pointed out.

"I want her to follow her own mind," Mia said.

"Okay, so between you or her, one of you gettin' married." Aunt Connie lightly banged her fist on the counter.

"Mia with a husband and a child, like a proper woman," Gloria said, and Mia wasn't sure if the wonder in her sister-in-law's voice was real or teasing.

"I would rather die," she said scornfully.

Gloria's face fell, and a hush dropped over the kitchen.

*Damn my mouth!* Shame dropped over her like a net. It had always been her reply whenever Nick frequently suggested the same—mostly, he'd teased, because it'd get her out of his hair and she'd be some other *coglione*'s problem.

But Gloria would never have her husband again.

"Glo, I'm sorry," Mia said quickly. "I meant—I meant nothing by it."

"You think marriage is so terrible," she said softly. "Just wait until you finally fall in love with someone. Start a family. The thought of being without them will be pure agony. And then being without them is pure agony. When you find yourself in that predicament."

Mia didn't know quite what to say. She glanced at Aunt Connie, who gave her a brief, understanding smile before crossing the small room to stand at Gloria's side.

"Go get Uncle Joe and Signor Scarpa," she said softly. "Tell them time to eat."

Gloria nodded and walked from the kitchen without a word.

"I didn't mean—" Mia began, but Aunt Connie reached out to cup her face and pat her cheeks.

"Don't fret," she said. "She still mourn."

"We all do. I do. He was my brother."

"Different when it's a husband," Aunt Connie said. "I want you to get a husband, but I don't want you to know what it's like to lose him."

Mia tilted her head. "Do you—do you know what it's like?"

"I marry a young man long before Uncle Joe, when I was young girl in Sicily." Aunt Connie's eyes took on a wistful look. "He handsome. Treat me good. I was pregnant with our first baby when he get killed over money. He loaned a man, the man never pay him back. When I find out whata happened, I lose the baby, too."

Mia reached up and placed her hand on top of Aunt Connie's. "I'm sorry."

The older woman gave her cheek another gentle pat. "It's a long time ago," she repeated. "Then I meet Joe. He good man, strong, hardworking man. He bring me to America, and we have a happy life. Now, get the bread and put it on the table."

Mia obeyed, setting the basket of sliced loaf on the table. She'd never known Aunt Connie had ever been married before Uncle Joe. Had ever had a *life* before Uncle Joe. Had ever loved and lost before Uncle Joe. The older woman seemed perfectly content with her life, despite the fact that she and Uncle Joe had never had children of their own. That forgotten realization made Mia bite the inside of her cheek. Perhaps she'd also hurt Aunt Connie with her careless remark.

*Perhaps I should just keep my big mouth shut*, she thought.

Would Gloria ever find another love? She deserved it—at twenty-five, she was still young. She wouldn't remain a widow forever. It would be strange seeing Gloria with another man. It would feel like a betrayal to her brother, as unfair as that was. Mia tried to envision the sort of man Gloria might prefer now— someone *not* in the life, that was certain. On the other hand, she was used to a certain way of living. Could she be content to trade in the luxury for a simpler, more modest life?

It was hard for Mia to picture Gloria as anyone but Nick's wife. Her brother's wife. Her sister-in-law. If Gloria married someone else, would she stop being Mia's sister-in-law? Would she even be considered family anymore? She'd have another family instead. So would Aunt Connie and Uncle Joe. Would that kind couple stop belonging to Mia, as well? She didn't share blood with them. They were only in her life because their niece had once been married to her brother. But that commonality was dead. Was the string that tied them to one another unraveling, even now?

Gloria and Uncle Joe came into the room, Paolo behind them. Uncle Joe had an arm around her shoulder, and she leaned into him. She lifted her gaze to Mia and gave her a slight nod before taking her seat at the table. Uncle Joe sat at the head of the table. Aunt Connie had inserted an extra, mismatched chair beside Mia's for Paolo, and he seemed to know without being told that it was his seat. It touched Mia that Aunt Connie and Uncle Joe were so accepting of Paolo. When Mia had explained to her uncle that he was with her for protection, he asked no questions and treated the silent man with all courtesy and respect.

Mia finished helping Aunt Connie carry the rest of the dishes to the table, the delicious aromas making her mouth water. Gloria got Emilia settled nicely in her chair, Uncle Joe rattled off a fast blessing, Aunt Connie served them, and they all tucked into the meal.

After a few minutes of silence punctuated only by the clink of silverware on china, Gloria looked up. "Who was that man at church this morning? The one that came up to you before the Mass began."

"Signor Bruno?" Uncle Joe asked. "He's a good man. Having a hard time right now, trying to care for his family. His wife died last year, and his oldest daughter, who should be helping him run the house..." He met Aunt Connie's disapproving stare across the table.

"It's not good for dinner talk, Joe," she said.

"What is it?" Mia asked. "What's wrong with his daughter?"

Aunt Connie made an impatient gesture with her hand and reached for her wine. "What is wrong with most young people in this neighborhood nowadays. The drug."

"Drugs?" Mia looked across the table at Uncle Joe.

He sighed and nodded. "Heroin. So many good families losing their children to the substance."

She frowned, then stabbed her fork into a meatball. "I spoke to Mr. Masseria at your store the other day. He said he'll make sure the neighborhood gets cleaned up."

"Don'ta hold your breath," Aunt Connie said with displeasure.

"Does he know who the dealers are? Who they're working for?" Gloria asked, placing her hands over Emilia's ears. "Not that this is a suitable topic of conversation in front of a child."

"I doubt she understands what we're talking about," Mia said gently.

"Just the same," Gloria replied, an edge to her voice, "I don't want her repeating anything to the other children she meets. What would their parents think?"

"You mean those rich little brats at the outlandishly expensive hotel we live in?" Mia said, not entirely sure where the surge of irritation she felt came from. "God forbid their parents—who are probably worse than the addicts in this neighborhood—should know we're of an unsavory stripe, is that it?"

Gloria looked at her, shock written all over her face, eyes filling with tears. "Why would you be cruel to me? What have I done to *you*?"

"Mia," Uncle Joe said, his brow furrowed deeply.

Paolo placed a light hand on her forearm, the corners of his eyes tight. He shook his head. Strangely, it was his silent reprimand that stung the most.

"You apologize," Aunt Connie insisted, as though they were children.

"Sorry," Mia muttered.

Gloria sniffed and looked down at her plate.

After a pause, Uncle Joe went on. "Signor Bruno's daughter, she in a bad way. She steals the grocery money for the dr—the powder. She leaves the younger children by themselves. She has nearly died from overdoses several times now." He shook his head. "Poor man."

"I heard from Signora Ricci after Mass there was a fire that took the tailor's shop only last week," Gloria said. "She said the dealers did that to send a message. Can you believe it?"

Mia pushed her pasta around on her plate with her fork, growing angrier with each word. Angry—and helpless. Ten years ago, she'd run the streets of this neighborhood with her brother. There had been bad men around then, but this section of the Lower East Side had been made up largely of hardworking immigrants who simply wanted to claim their tiny piece of the American dream, and nothing more. They came from oppression, violence, and dire poverty, and despite knowing they'd never be filthy rich in this new land, they were safe. They had small but tidy homes, food to eat, friends with whom to fellowship.

The idea that criminal greed could ruin this little, dirt-smudged, peaceful community hurt her. *Is there nothing I can do to change this?*

When the meal was finished, Gloria cleared the table while Aunt Connie put on a pot of strong coffee. Uncle Joe lit up a hand-rolled cigar.

Mia glanced at Paolo, then addressed her family. "I think I'd like to take a little walk before dessert, if that's all right." She patted her stomach. "Ate too much."

"Yes, yes," Aunt Connie said absently from the stove. "Go. Don't be gone long."

Gloria gazed at her, her dark eyes gleaming with suspicion.

Before anyone could make a comment, Mia donned her light coat and cloche and stepped out the door. At the light touch on her elbow, she turned. Paolo frowned at her, his question plain in his eyes.

"Mr. Masseria made me a promise," she said quietly as they strode down the stairs of the apartment. "I want to see how things are coming along."

Paolo held up two fingers. *It's been two days.*

"I know it's been two days since I talked to him," she said, pushing open the door to the grocery and holding it open for Paolo. "But he's a powerful man. He should be able to work fast."

Twilight was passing into the full dark of night when they exited the grocery. The shops were quiet, the street vendors and their carts full of goods and wares gone so they could enjoy Sunday with their own families. She heard the distant strains of Italian folk music being played from apartments, smelled the faint scents of cooking food wafting from several open apartment windows.

They strolled down the sidewalk, Paolo letting her lead the way, but instead of trailing behind her a few paces as he normally did, he walked firmly at her side, not touching her, but well within arm's reach just in case. If he were truly a bulldog, she imagined him padding at her side, hackles up, teeth bared, a low growl of warning rumbling low and quiet in his chest. After a moment, she linked her arm through his.

The deeper into the neighborhood they walked, the seedier things became. They passed the burned ruins of the tailor's shop Gloria had mentioned. Mia paused in front of it. The windows were broken out, the façade blackened with one side collapsed inward. To know drug dealers were responsible for it filled her with an incandescent fury that surprised even her. The tailor and his wife were good people. They had opened this shop shortly after landing in America fifteen years ago. The tailor was a talented man who undercut himself in order to serve the Italian people of the neighborhood to pay forward the kindness other established immigrants had shown him and his wife.

This was a neighborhood where everyone looked after

everyone else. When she had still been a girl and Nick not yet a man, the other families in her building had done what they could to make sure she and Nick never went hungry or cold. They gave what food or scraps of clothing they could. When Nick had been drafted, the tenement families and the other people in the neighborhood redoubled their efforts to make sure she survived. They had all been struggling to make ends meet, but always, always made room for one more.

And the despicable bastards who pushed their white poison had landed like locusts here and sought to destroy the steely backbone that made up the Lower East Side, Mia thought, her fists clenching at her sides. She wondered if Mr. Masseria was aware what had befallen the tailor's shop.

"*Aiuto! Aiuto!*"

A boy's cry for help—a young boy. Mia whirled around to see where it was coming from. Paolo, already scanning the area, pointed to an alleyway half a block down the street. She took off at a trot, Paolo surpassing.

The boy's pleas for help broke off into a single, high-pitched wail of pain.

Mia and Paolo reached the alley. Breathless, Mia shouted, "*Smettila!*"

Four faces turned toward her. Three of them belonged to older boys on the cusp of manhood—old enough to know better. But though they all looked different, their haggard faces and the burning desperation in their eyes could have made them brothers.

The fourth boy was young—perhaps no older than ten years. He lay on the ground, where one boy held him down, a fist cocked back. The young boy had a bloody nose and an already-swelling eye. His clothes were a rumpled mess. One of the other assailants held a fistful of bills in his hand, no doubt what he'd stolen from the child.

The boy closest to her began taking menacing steps toward her, demanding of her in Italian, "Mind your own business, lady!"

"Leave him alone," she snapped. His accent told her he wasn't Sicilian, but Southern Italian, likely from Calabria. "Where are your parents?"

He gave her a rude response that shocked her, then his gaze went over her boldly, impertinently, before he switched to English that carried no trace of Italian accent. "You got any money?"

"She looks rich," one of the other boys chimed in, then kicked the young boy on the ground, who whimpered like a dog in pain. "Of course she's got money."

"Let's take it from her," the third boy said, joining the first, who continued to walk slowly toward her. "This little shit barely had anything, anyway."

"That's my mother's grocery money!" the child cried. The third boy doubled back to strike him in the mouth.

"Leave him alone!" Mia commanded.

Paolo stepped around her. He flicked out a knife.

The first two boys paused in their steps, then glanced at each other.

"You Sicilians are always so small," the Calabrese boy jeered. "He's old enough to be my father, yet I'm twice his size."

It was true; despite the tattered appearances of the boys, their ripped and dirty clothing showcased stocky, well-muscled bodies, vastly different from Paolo's wiry build.

"Take their money and slit their throats," the boy instructed his friends. "I'll show you what a real knife looks like, old man."

"Paolo," she murmured.

Paolo pushed Mia behind him and fell upon the boys. Soon, the alley was filled with shouts that quickly devolved into shrieks of pain. For all their bluster, the only blade in the alley that was being put to use was Paolo's. Mia watched him with a mixture of terror and awe. She'd known he was a brutal man, had witnessed it herself in Sicily, but the ferocity he displayed now mixed with deftness and a blurring speed was unlike anything she had ever witnessed before.

In a matter of minutes, the three older boys lay bloody and beaten against the stone alley floor, moaning. Paolo met her steady stare, and gradually the lines of terrible savagery faded. He nodded at her.

She slid her gloved hands into the deep, slanted pockets of her coat as she walked into the alley. Her heels clacked on the stone as she walked from boy to boy. None of the older boys had life-threatening injuries. They'd been just nicked and scratched with Paolo's knife, and it was clearly intentional. He could have gutted them like a fisherman had he wished.

Mia flicked her head at the little boy, staring wide-eyed at first his beaten attackers, then his saviors.

"Take back your money," she said, pointing at the bills strewn across the ground. To her surprise, the boy took only a few of the bills and left the rest.

"What, are you leaving us a tip?" Mia said.

He swallowed. "They stole from others before me. This is all my mother gave me. To take any more would mean I was stealing, too."

Mia smiled at him, then reached into her pocket and counted off ten dollars. She held it out to him. His eyes went wider.

"Take it," she urged softly. "Give it to your mother. Tell her it's from Mia Scalisi, and that she should come see me at d'Abbruzzo's when she needs more. Got that?"

He nodded, taking the money carefully as though it had teeth. He turned to go.

"Hey, sport."

The boy stopped and whirled around, then froze at the sight of the five-dollar bill Mia held out to him.

"That's for you. Only you."

He reached for the money more hesitantly than before, then gave her a tentative smile. "*Grazie*, Signorina Scalisi."

"No one will bother you again," she told him, glancing at Paolo.

"*Grazie*."

She flicked her head. "Off you go."

With one more astonished, backwards stare, he took off running.

The two other boys scrambled to their feet and followed suit. Mia lifted a hand to Paolo, signaling him to let them go. The third boy, the Calabrese, struggled into a sitting position, hissing with pain.

Mia tilted her head as she studied him. He'd seemed to be the leader of the pack before.

"Why were you stealing some kid's money?" she asked quietly. "Don't you know where you are?"

"I needed it," he ground out, clutching his side. Blood seeped over his fingers, but Mia knew it was just a flesh wound—a warning to these young fools that next time, Paolo would not be so merciful.

"For what? You're nearly a young man. There's work for you in this neighborhood—in this city. Honest work."

"Only chumps work for pennies," he snapped. "And like you're one to talk. I bet you never worked a day in your life, huh, princess?"

She'd had enough of his disrespect. She looked at Paolo and lifted her chin. In the span of a breath, he darted behind the boy and had his arm twisted behind his back, his other hand clapped across his mouth to stifle his shrieks of pain.

Mia went on calmly as though nothing were amiss. "And what does stealing from a little boy make you?"

Behind Paolo's hand, the boy refused to meet her eyes.

"It's just you and me," she said. "Your *friends* have left you. You don't need to act so tough." She flicked her chin at Paolo again, and this time he released the boy. She dug in her pocket for a handkerchief and tossed it on the boy's chest.

He glanced up at her as if confused by the gesture, but warily began mopping the blood from his nose and lip.

"Why," she said again, "were you mugging a little boy?"

"We needed the money," he muttered. "Fast. I know that kid shops for his mother on Sundays. Usually has at least five bucks."

"You and your friends needed it?"

A bob of his head was her answer.

"Why?"

"We owed it to someone."

"Who did you owe?"

"Lady, who are you to be asking me all these questions?" he demanded.

Paolo answered him with a low snarl.

Mia gave him a thin smile. "I can be a pal, or your worst nightmare. Why don't you choose one?" She let the silence linger, her gaze boring into him. He stared back, as though deciding how seriously to take her.

Finally, the boy swallowed with an audible gulp. "We…owed a fella. A—a businessman. He gave us something to sell, but I got jumped by another gang and we lost the stuff. Now I'm into him for twenty bucks, or he'll kill me."

Mia raised an eyebrow. "Over twenty dollars?"

"He's crazy."

"Who is *he*?"

"Some fella, I said. He works for someone else. He said he needed neighborhood boys across the city to sell his product. That we should sell it to other kids our age."

Children. He was pushing the shit to *children*. "And what product is that?"

"You gotta be crazy if you think I'm telling you anything." He shook his head rapidly.

Mia reached into her pocket again. The boy winced, as if expecting the worst. She smirked inwardly—she'd left her black-jack at home today. It *was* Sunday, after all.

This time, she withdrew a twenty-dollar bill. The boy's eyes sauceread at the sight of it.

"It might be worth it to you to tell me what I want to know," she said. "This money could be the thing that keeps you alive, couldn't it?"

The boy licked his lips. "He—he said if I told anyone—"

"Let me guess. He'd kill you."

The boy nodded.

"No one ever need know you told me anything," she said. "In fact, I can keep filling your pocket if you keep bringing me information. That's probably a better deal than you'll get with whoever it is you're working for, isn't it?"

He bit his lip.

"What was the product?"

The boy hesitated still.

"Kid," she murmured, "I don't ask questions I don't already suspect the answers to. I didn't just fall off the turnip truck, all right?"

"Heroin," he admitted, and though that was what Mia expected to hear, a pang went through her just the same.

"Give me a name."

He stared at her in confusion. "Who *are* y—"

"I'm losing my patience," she said softly.

"I…"

"All right." Mia pocketed the money. "Well, good luck to you, kid. If you stay alive long enough, that is. Don't take any wooden nickels." She turned to leave.

"Wait!"

She stopped and sighed.

"Gems," he said quickly. "The guy I work for, works for a guy called Gems."

Another answer she expected, and it further ratcheted up her ire. "And how did you come to find employment with him?"

"Me and the guys, we were just out one night, trying to find some booze at a card hall to buy. His guys snatched us up and brought us inside. Gems asked if we wanted to make some money. We said yes. He said to come back the next night and he'd have something for us."

She shook her head. "You got *any* idea the kind of man you're working for? He's dangerous, kid. The business is dangerous. You could get killed."

"We needed money," he said, and his voice broke a little.

Silence fell over the alley for a long moment as Mia studied him through narrowed eyes.

The boy watched her with huge eyes, not daring to move.

Finally, she said, "Get up."

He rose on unsteady legs, using the wall as support.

She stepped toward him until they were almost nose-to-nose. "This is how it's going to be," she said coldly. "You're not going to sell any more of that shit in this neighborhood again. Not you, or your friends."

"B-but I have to," he said. "He told me to. I have to pay him this money back. Then he's expecting me to show up to his place to get more product."

"Pay back the man you contact directly," Mia said. "And then…you don't show up for your next pickup. You lay low."

"Don't…don't *show up*?"

"Did I stutter?" She waited for an answer, but the boy wisely shut his mouth. "If you obey me, I'll make it worth your while. You seem like a kid in the know—I can use a good source of information in the neighborhood."

"Yeah, sure," he said, nodding so fast she feared his head would fly off his neck. "Yeah, information. I can do that."

"If you lie to me," she continued as though he hadn't said anything, "and keep selling here or try to sell me out to your employers, I will find out, and I promise you, what happened in this alley tonight will seem like kisses from your mother compared to what I'll have my friend here do to you. Tell me you understand."

"I-I understand."

She held up the twenty. "This goes to your contact, and only to your contact. Don't get cute and try to pocket some of it. Pay him."

With bloody, trembling fingers, he reached up and grasped the bill, staring at it like it was gold. "Thank—thank you."

"What's your name?" she said. "I like to know who I'm doing business with."

He hesitated. She waited. She didn't blame him for his uncertainty—it was impossible to know who to trust. Assuming there *was* anyone to trust.

"Nicolo," he said finally. "But everyone calls me Nicky."

It was as though he'd punched her in the chest with those words. All the air rushed out of her body.

She steeled her spine, willing her face to give nothing away. "Nicky. Nice to meet you. I'm Mia. I wouldn't let the fellas you work for know about that. If you have any questions about me, ask around the neighborhood."

"Where can I find you?" he asked.

"Ask for me at the d'Abbruzzo grocery," she replied, "and then I'll find *you*."

She turned her back on him and walked out of the alley, Paolo at her side.

"We should hurry," she said to him. "I'm sure they're probably worried about us, and Gloria will have a million questions for me later."

Paolo nodded, keeping pace with her.

She could make something up—she'd met an old neighbor and had chatted for a while, or had stepped into a shop to look at something. That wouldn't prevent Gloria from asking her about it again, later on, and then she'd probably discern Mia had been dishonest. She could hardly fathom the alternative of telling Gloria the truth. Her sister-in-law would be horrified to learn Mia had ordered Paolo to brutally assault three boys, then turned one of them into her snitch.

It almost made her smile.

Her humor withered away as long-buried grief and the echoes of bone-shaking agony rattled the edges of her mind.

Nicolo, that boy had said his name was.

*But everyone calls him…Nicky.*

# CHAPTER EIGHT

"If you think I'm going to let you go to a man's home and try on *dresses* by yourself, you're out of your goddamn mind," Gloria said on Wednesday afternoon as Mia was on her way out the door.

Mia rolled her eyes. "Listen, I know Paolo's not your favorite person, but he's with me all the time. I won't be alone."

"This is not about Paolo," Gloria said firmly. "This is about what's proper and what's not." She took Emilia by the hand. "Our first stop will be the grocery, where I'll leave Em with my aunt and uncle. And then we'll go to Mr. Goldberg's together."

"But—"

"But good." Gloria walked past her and opened the door. "Come. We don't want to be late."

Defeated, Mia sighed and walked out the door.

After dropping off Emilia, Paolo drove them to Hyman's penthouse in the new vehicle he had acquired for Mia. It was a simple black Ford, sturdily built and reliable. She thought of Nick's bright-yellow Cadillac Phaeton sitting in a storage garage. He had always loved that car, and people recognized it everywhere he went. A chariot fit for a prince. She couldn't bring herself to drive it.

"Really," Gloria griped. "I don't see why this couldn't have taken place in a dress shop, for goodness' sake. What sort of man has a dressmaker come to his place? At the very least, the fitting could have taken place in *our* suite."

"Still his suite," Mia said. "It's just geography. He's a hands-on sort of man, Gloria. You'll see."

"I fully intend to discuss the boundaries of propriety with this Mr. Goldberg."

"You'll do no such thing," Mia said. But to take the sting out of her tone, she patted Gloria's hand. "I'm glad to have you with me, just the same."

"When your cousin gets here, there'll be two of us to nag you," Gloria said. "Although I'm starting to think it'll be me against the two of you, as high-spirited as Raquel is. She's so much like you. You even look alike."

Though her tone was light, she sounded slightly worried. Mia wondered if Gloria was afraid she'd be edged out. Raquel was closer to Mia's age, and they were blood. They'd been more like sisters than cousins.

"She's young," Mia said, looping her arm through Gloria's. "You and I, we'll need to guide her."

Gloria smiled. "Of course. She's family."

When they arrived, Paolo refused to hand the keys to the valet and parked the car himself. Then he escorted Mia and Gloria up to Hyman's residence.

Mia led the way out of the elevators and through the foyer of his penthouse. His usual guards loitered outside his office and glanced over at her as she approached. Their faces turned wary —though if that was due to the introduction of Gloria, or remembering how Paolo had manhandled one of them and pulled a gun on a second, she wasn't sure.

The guard closest to the door knocked on it, then opened it, giving Paolo a wide berth. She noted his bruised neck and smiled at him.

Hyman stood in the middle of the room beside the pool table, engrossed in conversation with a middle-aged, fashionably dressed woman with a tape measure draped around her neck. They both looked up as Mia, Gloria, and Paolo entered the room.

Hyman's eyebrows lifted at the sight of Gloria, but his charming smile spread across his face with practiced speed. "Miss Scalisi," he said with a warmth Mia suspected wasn't entirely genuine. "And Mr. Scarpa. Good to see you again. And who is this lovely young lady? Your sister-in-law, I presume?"

Gloria flushed a little as he turned to her. "How do you do. It's a pleasure to make your acquaintance. I've heard…so much about you."

The pause was not lost on Mr. Goldberg, who flashed Mia a sardonic look. "I can only imagine, Mrs. Scalisi." He held her hand delicately and leaned over it. "It's a pleasure to finally meet you. I trust your accommodations at the Murray Hill Hotel are adequate?"

"More than that," Gloria said, bobbing her head. "Thank you very much."

"You're welcome. A token of my gratitude to your enchanting sister-in-law, who has all but guaranteed the success of our new nightclub." He patted Mia on the shoulder. "I assume you'll be overseeing the dress fittings? A fetching woman such as yourself surely knows much more about what looks good on another woman than I do."

All of the rancor Gloria had possessed earlier regarding the dress fittings taking place in his home seemed to vanish under the cultured man's well-honed charm. Mia fought back a smirk. It was easy for one to let his beautiful manners and polished, friendly demeanor make them forget themselves—if one did not know how to handle Mr. Goldberg, that was.

Although, at this stage in their relationship, Mia wasn't sure who handled whom.

"May I present to you ladies Mrs. Eleanor Astor?" He turned to the elegantly dressed woman waiting silently behind him. "She owns the most popular boutique in the city. She has several lovely options for you to choose from, Mia."

"It's my pleasure to dress a young lady as exquisite as you are," Mrs. Astor said, bowing her head gracefully.

Mia shook her hand. "A pleasure to meet you, Mrs. Astor," she replied. "Astor... As in...the hotel?"

Mrs. Astor smiled. "I married into a talented family, one could say. And an indulgent one, to allow me to pursue my dreams of dressmaking."

"The Mademoiselle Chanel of the United States, she's known," Hyman said with a nod.

"Oh, how you flatter me, Mr. Goldberg." Mrs. Astor gestured to a large dressing screen, beautifully printed with an Oriental floral motif across its half-dozen panels. "If you would, please, Miss Scalisi."

Mia cast a glance at Hyman as he settled himself into one of his deep, plush brown leather easy chairs with a cup of tea. "You hanging around?"

He gave her his best bland smile, lifting his cup from its saucer with a pinky extended. "I have the final approval on the gowns, Miss Scalisi. I imagine that's only fair, considering I'm footing the bill. Wouldn't you agree?" Without waiting for an answer, he waved a hand toward the dressing screen. "Go on."

She glanced at Paolo, who remained standing by the door, his gaze politely averted to the window. He would not leave her alone with Hyman, which simultaneously relieved and embarrassed her further.

Feeling somewhat indignant, Mia stepped behind the dressing screen with Mrs. Astor and Gloria. In a moment, she was out of her plum, printed crêpe de chine dress and standing rather awkwardly in her white lace step-in as Mrs. Astor unfurled the first dress for her to try on.

Mia brightened. It was a sleeveless silk-and-chiffon, cream and gold affair with a handkerchief hem and plenty of beading that would catch beautifully under stage lights. The neckline was daringly low, revealing the top of the sheer, sewn-in bandeau underneath.

The two women slipped the gown over her head, Mrs. Astor

hissing as the beading caught in Mia's hair. "These are handsewn crystals," she fretted.

Mia winced as strands of her hair snagged on the beads tugged her scalp. *Damn the crystals*, she wanted to snap, but held her tongue.

When the dress was in place, Mrs. Astor handed Gloria a pair of golden T-strap heels to slide on Mia's feet as she assessed the drape of the dress on Mia's frame.

"It fits a little tighter in the bust than it's meant to," Mrs. Astor said disapprovingly. "I suppose I'll have to let the top out a bit. My, and you've a pair of hips, haven't you?"

"It's a shame loose silhouettes are in," Gloria said loyally. "You've never a seen a nicer shape than Mia's."

"Most of my clients are *quite* slender," Mrs. Astor said in the same tone.

"I'm an Italian girl, Mrs. Astor," Mia said. "Not some pale, English waif."

Mrs. Astor, every bit a pale, English waif, pressed her lips together and began jabbing pins into the dress. Mia bit back a smirk, then a yelp when one of those pins pricked her skin.

*Perhaps I ought to wait until she's not holding pins to insult her...*

From his seat, Hyman called, "Are you having trouble, dear?" His meaning was clear. He was getting impatient.

Mia rolled her eyes. This had been his brilliant idea, after all.

Mrs. Astor, several pins still caught between her lips, shrugged and gave Mia a little push. Gloria followed her out from behind the screen.

Mia lifted her chin as she strode toward Hyman. He stopped her in her tracks with a hand.

"Perhaps don't approach the crowd as though you intend to kill them," he said. "You're a dancer. Presumably that means you've some grace. That you no doubt learned under the tutelage of—what was the name? Madame du la...Boviette?" He flicked his fingers, dismissing her back to the screen to try again.

She gritted her teeth and walked back to the screen, then pivoted. She pretended she was back on stage at Stems—no. The thought of that had her stomach tightening around a sickening, oily feeling that pooled there. Imagining herself back onstage at the Chicago only intensified that feeling. No, nothing to do with Chicago.

Her mind drifted back to simpler times when she was hardly a woman, but one of the best chorines at Penny's Supper Club on the boardwalk of Atlantic City. It had been an exciting time, her first real gig, and so many interesting people came in and out of the club every single night. She'd lied about her age—or rather, Nick had—to get her the gig, and at sixteen she'd danced in her first chorus line. She'd been at the biggest party on the East Coast when Prohibition had gone into effect. Nick had been a young prince in that city, she a princess, and those had been simpler times. Happier times.

She rarely let herself think of those times these days, but now it was as though she couldn't stop the tidal wave of memories, the feeling of wistful nostalgia so strong she might have wept.

"Mia?"

She looked up. Hyman's brow creased as he studied her. Behind her, Gloria placed a light hand on her back.

"All right?" she murmured.

Not trusting her voice, Mia just nodded.

"How about a turn?" Hyman said, spinning his finger in the air. He stood from his chair and approached her.

Mia extended her arms to either side and spun in a slow circle, then met his eyes with a haughtily raised eyebrow.

His lips twisted sardonically. "Well. Isn't she stunning." He snapped his fingers as he returned to his seat. "That one will do. Next gown, please."

Over the next two hours, she tried on gowns, got jabbed by Mrs. Astor—at this point, Mia was convinced it was on purpose —and spun in circles for Hyman. He systematically rejected and approved a variety of gowns. There was a pile of them Mia had quite liked herself that he'd dismissed for a variety of reasons.

"She'll need a few numbers suitable for dancing," he told Mrs. Astor once Mia was back in her day dress. The dressmaker nodded as he turned to Mia. "Opening night will be one week from this Saturday. Beginning tomorrow morning, you will commence rehearsals. We are still finalizing some last-minute things at the club, so you'll rehearse at the Cotton Club in the meantime."

"The Cotton Club?" Mia repeated. "Aren't they booked full of acts who'd need the rehearsal space?"

"Owney Madden can be very accommodating. For the right price." Hyman smiled thinly. "It'll just be for a few days. I'd like you to be more present at the shop as well. Inform the ladies of the grand opening, encourage them to attend." He glanced at Gloria. "As should the sister of the star. Who ought to have a lovely gown, too. Please, Mrs. Scalisi, choose whichever you like best. On me."

"Oh." Gloria blinked, then glanced at Mia as if for approval, who flicked her head. She was more than capable of purchasing Gloria a bespoke evening gown, but it was best not to refuse Hyman's generosity, though she was suspicious of the probable strings attached. "Why, that would be wonderful. Thank you."

He smiled and extended a hand toward the screen. Gloria stepped behind it, and Mia hid a smirk when she heard Gloria let out a short hiss of pain as Mrs. Astor set upon her with her sewing pins.

"So," Hyman said. "Do you like your gowns?"

Mia cocked her head and smiled. "You don't really care if I did, do you?"

His eyes gleamed with amusement. "No, I don't. Not really. But, it still pleases me to know you're happy."

"Happy?" She considered that. "I guess time will tell, Hyman."

"Indeed. But I do wish you to know that your happiness is important to me, if not necessarily a priority."

She huffed out a short laugh. "You're a real charmer, Mr. Goldberg."

He opened his mouth to reply, but there was a knock on his door.

"Sir," came the muffled voice of one of his guards. "Mr. Yale is here to see you."

*Mr. Yale? As in, Frankie?* Mia glanced at Hyman, who suddenly appeared rather uncomfortable. Apparently, this visit was unplanned.

Johnny Torrio had been a mentor to Frankie, like he'd been to Al. And Frankie was one of the biggest bootleggers in New York. He controlled Brooklyn, and he was in charge of picking up Al's orders of Canadian Club—along with delivering the Templeton, in which there was some interest in Ontario.

*Her* Templeton.

"Tell him I'm busy and he should come back," he called.

*No way in hell.* Mia caught Paolo's eye and nodded to the door. Her bodyguard shrugged, and before Hyman could say another word, opened the door.

The guard, and behind him, a stocky man with thick, dark hair and a handsome face, looked at Paolo, and then at Hyman and Mia, in equal surprise.

"Come on in, fellas," she said.

"Mia," Hyman snapped behind her.

The guard looked questioningly at his boss, but Frankie Yale shrugged and stepped around the guard.

"Seems like this is a bad time," he remarked.

"Yes, it is," Hyman said.

"No, it's not." Mia looked Frankie in the eye and extended her hand. "I'm Mia Scalisi."

At her last name, Frankie raised his eyebrows. "Oh. Well. It's a pleasure, Miss Scalisi." He shook her proffered hand with the gentleness most men used, but she squeezed his hand firmly, forcing him to look at her.

"Johnny tells me you've been running the Templeton up to Canada for us," she said. "I appreciate that. Thank you."

His dark eyes glinted with interest at her use of the word *us.* "I've worked out a nice deal for Charlie and Moritz. And Mr. Goldberg."

"Mr. Yale has been a great asset to *us*," Hyman said, and his emphasis on the word was not lost on her.

"Which version of the product are they buying in Canada, Mr. Yale?" Mia asked. "Pure, or cut?"

"Pure, of course."

"Good. It seems while I was away, my partners took to cutting down the rye to an undrinkable state. I'd never want our friends in the north to be subjected to such trash."

"I believe that's enough," Hyman said, his soft tone full of warning.

She turned to look at him. "Aren't you concerned about the quality of product our clients are receiving?"

Frankie shifted his amused gaze to Hyman, as though also interested in that answer.

Before Mr. Goldberg could reply, Gloria stepped out from behind the screen. "Well?" Then she caught sight of their newest guest and flushed. "Oh—pardon me."

They all turned to look at her.

She was stunning in a shin-length, sleeveless, burgundy chiffon dress with an overlay of netting covered in glimmering beads. The dress's straight lines concealed her slender curves, but the plunging neckline revealed a hint of décolletage.

"Jesus Christ and all the saints," Frankie Yale muttered beside her.

Mia cut her eyes toward him. He held a hand on his chest, and his gaze went over Gloria again and again.

"Gloria," she said loudly. "Come. Meet Mr. Yale." When Gloria reached her side, Mia wrapped a protective arm around her and faced Frankie. "Mr. Yale, this is my sister-in-law, Gloria Scalisi. My brother's *widow*."

He seemed to get the message. "Mrs. Scalisi," he said, bending slightly over her hand. "It's a pleasure to meet you."

"Thank you," Gloria murmured, casting her eyes down. "Mr. Yale." Then her dark eyes flicked up to meet his again.

*Oh brother.*

He smiled widely. "That's some dress."

"Isn't it?" Mia interjected. "It's a gift from Mr. Goldberg for the first night of the club opening."

"Oh, will you be there?" Frankie asked Gloria. "Won't that be nice. Perhaps I can buy you a drink."

"I'd like that," Gloria said with a shy smile.

It was all Mia could do not to gape at her sister-in-law.

"As much as I'd enjoy chatting you up, Mrs. Scalisi," Frankie said, "I do have some business to discuss with Mr. Goldberg." He glanced at Mia. "Well, come to think of it, I suppose it has to do with you, too."

"Mr. Yale," Hyman said. "I'm sure whatever you have to share can wait, can it not?"

"I'm here now," Mia said smoothly, patting Hyman on the arm. "And it concerns me, apparently. So, Mr. Yale, let's talk. You've come all this way from Brooklyn, after all. Isn't that right?"

He nodded slowly, glancing between her and Hyman.

"Let's let Mrs. Scalisi get dressed in peace," she added pointedly, noting the way Frankie's stare followed Gloria back to the dressing screen.

"Yes, we can step out into the lobby," Hyman said, and gave her a penetrating stare.

She'd be in trouble for this later.

Out in the lobby—Paolo standing back several feet behind Mia—Frankie shrugged. "I had some business in the city, anyway. Thought I'd drop in. I just wanted to let you know I made space in my warehouses for the product you're not keeping at her shop."

This was news, that Frankie Yale had become a trusted partner with Hyman Goldberg. Mia glanced at Hyman.

His nostrils flared. "After our friendly little discussion at the unloading last Friday night, I took it upon myself to locate another venue for the cut Templeton that created so much ire. So, Miss Scalisi, your shop should be free of anything that is not up to your standard."

"And how much will that cost?"

"It's a side deal," Hyman replied. "That product, as Moritz informed you, was already lined up for a buyer. The terms are between us and Mr. Yale now."

"As long as those bottles don't still say 'Templeton Rye' on them," Mia said. "Because that's not what it is."

"We had the labels changed," Hyman said tightly. He turned to Frankie. "Is that all? A phone call would have sufficed."

"As I said, I had other business in the city," Frankie replied. "Besides, Johnny always taught me to discuss business face to face and not over the telephone. Figured a businessman such as yourself would appreciate that." His gaze wandered to Gloria as she joined them in the lobby, back in her normal clothes. A slow smirk spread across his face. "I suppose it wasn't a fruitless trip, after all."

"Well, since you've come all this way, I suppose it would be impolite not to offer to take you to dinner," Hyman said tightly. Then he turned to Mia. "Would you and Mrs. Scalisi care to join us?"

Gloria brightened, but before she could say anything, Mia shook her head. "Thank you, Mr. Goldberg, but we'd better be on our way. We have to collect Emilia." She glanced at Frankie. "Her child. My niece."

He didn't seem deterred, keeping his smile fixed on Gloria. "Next time, then."

Mia took Gloria's arm, and the two of them followed Paolo to the elevators.

"Why are you in such a rush now?" Gloria said irritably when the elevator doors shut. "It's barely six thirty. And I *am* hungry."

Mia stared at her in astonishment. "You can't really mean you wanted to go."

Gloria *hmph*ed impatiently. "Well, why not? I'm always at home with Emilia or with my aunt and uncle. You're the one who always gets to have all the fun."

"Fun?" Mia said, her voice raising. "*Fun?* You think having to deal with stubborn men about liquor and money and drugs is *fun*? Or acting like Hyman's little doll? Or constantly having to prove myself to these bastards that I have an operating brain? Which part of that sounds like *fun* to you, Glo?"

In the mirrored door's reflection, she caught a glimpse of Paolo frowning at her. He seemed to have a soft spot for Gloria and especially Emilia, even if the former didn't return his affection. He disapproved of her words, but he could go chase himself. Gloria had no idea what she was talking about.

Gloria pursed her lips. "It sounds better than what I'm stuck doing, which is *nothing* most of the time. I'm still a young woman, after all. Besides, maybe you could benefit from having me around instead of just stuffing me in a room all the time. Did you ever think about that?"

Mia drew in a deep breath to the bottom of her lungs, struggling to hang onto her rapidly disintegrating patience. She tried to put herself in Gloria's shoes.

"I know it must seem…exciting to you," she began. "And sometimes, it is. But, Gloria, you must understand something. I'm trying to keep Nick's business afloat. All of his so-called friends are just… They're driving it into the ground."

The elevator reached the lobby and the doors opened. They stepped out, Paolo striding ahead to open the building's glass doors.

"I thought they could be trusted." Gloria sounded confused.

Mia set her jaw. "So did I. Anyway, I feel like I'm fighting the battle alone. I don't know who to trust. It's not safe right now, and I promise you, it's not any fun. I'd much rather be home with you and Em than doing this, but I won't have it go by the wayside. Nick believed in the rye, so much he died for it. If I let them destroy what he built…his work, his *death*, would be meaningless."

Gloria's eyes glistened. She looked away. As Paolo opened the car doors for them and they climbed inside, she said, "I'm sorry I said it sounded like fun. I just—sometimes I get so lonely, Mia. Even with the baby. She'll start lessons with a governess soon, you know, and what'll I do? You'll be at rehearsals all day for the club, and then you'll be there performing all night."

"Raquel will be here to keep you company."

"Yes," Gloria said, her lips stretching into a polite smile. "She will. But it's not the same as… Well, you've got Charlie, after all. And I— There's no one else…no one."

As Paolo pulled into traffic, Mia put a hand on Gloria's arm. "Filling your…*time* with another gangster isn't going to end in anything but more heartbreak, Gloria."

She flushed and averted her gaze. "I don't know what you mean."

"Come on," Mia said drily. "I haven't seen you look at a man like you looked at Frankie Yale just now since you were sixteen and Nick dragged me to the grocery so he could flirt with you."

"So, what, I'm supposed to be dead, just like my husband?" Gloria snapped, and Mia winced. "I'm not supposed to find a man attractive, or enjoy the attention he gives me? Or like that he obviously seems interested?" She huffed. "I'm sure I'm just an old widow to you, Mia, but I'm only twenty-five years old. I'm not dead. And—and—goddammit, I'm *lonely*." Her luminous brown eyes shone with tears, and Mia slipped an arm around her shoulders. She kept her mouth shut.

There was no sense in warning Gloria about Frankie Yale or what he was—not now. Mia was lonely too, in her own way, but she had never been married. She had never had the companionship, the bond, with a man the way her brother and Gloria had had with each other. She understood Gloria's grief, because she had her own, but she'd never fully empathize with it, because it was different.

Her thoughts crept to Charlie. She had not spoken to him since Saturday night. He had rung their room several times, but Mia had told Gloria to tell him she was unavailable each time. She couldn't stop thinking about the scar on his palm—no better than a cattle brand. The same one Nick had worn.

And she couldn't stop thinking about the truth he'd flung at her feet—about herself.

When Nick had become a made man, it had been a point of pride, of excitement. It had meant a new stage in their life. It had elevated their social position. It had been protection. She hadn't been able to advertise the fact that her brother was a made man, but she walked the walk, silently daring anyone to try her.

She'd been so young and stupid then.

While that scar might still mean honor and loyalty and respect and tradition, it also meant the bearer was property to the men who placed it there. That they could never leave the life once they'd entered it. That the only way out was death. A made man might as well have meant a marked man. And Charlie had signed up for it.

But then, hadn't she?

The scar was the only thing that separated them, he'd said.

*Stop thinking about it.*

She was still thinking about it, she realized miserably a moment later, and sighed and looked out the window.

They arrived at the grocery, and Paolo waited in the car while Mia and Gloria got out to walk inside. Since they lived upstairs, Joe and Connie usually kept the store open later than most other businesses in the neighborhood. There was always someone who needed a bottle of olive oil or a loaf of bread at the last minute, and Joe and Connie were only happy to oblige.

In the room at the back of the store, Gloria's aunt and uncle sat with Emilia at the scarred table, nibbling bread, cheese, and meat. Uncle Joe was teaching Emilia to play checkers.

Aunt Connie made Mia and Gloria sit and eat and drink a little coffee, and they spent a few pleasant moments chatting about the day.

"Where is Paolo?" Aunt Connie demanded. "Tell the old Sicilian brute to come in." But she said it in an affectionate way, and with a smile, Mia went to fetch the grumpy man who'd insisted on waiting in the car. In the back room, Aunt Connie plied him with meat, cheese, and coffee, all the while berating him in Sicilian for not coming in sooner.

This old neighborhood always felt like home. More than the

fancy suite at the Murray Hill Hotel, where every comfort, every luxury, was a snap of her fingers away. She toyed with the idea of what it might be like to move back here, back among her people, back where she felt safe. Could she come home again? And she wasn't just responsible for herself any longer. Would it be in the best interests of her sister-in-law and niece?

Her gaze fell on Emilia, earnestly pushing checkers around the board where Uncle Joe pointed. It was important for her to be among her family, her people, too. It was something that had always been incredibly important to Nick.

Distantly, the sound of the bell ringing over the door reached them. Aunt Connie rose from her chair to go tend to the customer.

"Joe! Joe!" a man shouted.

In an instant, they were all on their feet except Gloria, who remained by Emilia's side, eyes wide.

Mia put a hand on Paolo's shoulder. "Stay here with Glo and Em." She followed Aunt Connie from the room.

Out in the store, Uncle Joe held Signor Bruno in his arms. The man sobbed uncontrollably, crying out in Sicilian.

"*Figghia mia! Figghia mia!*"

*My daughter. My daughter.*

"Lock the door," Aunt Connie said harshly to Mia in Sicilian, pressing her keys into her hand before stepping over to her husband to comfort the hysterical man.

Heart in her throat, Mia did as she was told.

"Come with me," Aunt Connie said, gently but firmly as she led Signor Bruno toward the back room.

Mia trailed the group, lingering in the doorway to stay out of the way as Connie sat the man in a chair and placed coffee and bread before him. Signor Bruno wept into his hands as Connie rubbed his back and murmured soothing, unintelligible noises at him.

"She is dead," he managed to finally utter. "My daughter. Tonight. They found her in an alley."

Mia and Gloria exchanged a startled look.

"How?" Uncle Joe said, his hand on his chest. "It's been a few months since I saw her last, but she looked so strong, so healthy—"

"The drugs," the man said tearfully. "The drugs, she got a hold of them. Started using them. I found out, I told her to stop. She promised she would, but I knew she didn't. Three nights ago, we argued about it. Badly. She left the apartment. I did not see her again until this morning. She said she was sorry, so…I took her in." He lifted the cup of coffee to his lips in hands that trembled. More tears streamed down his cheeks. "What kind of father would I be to turn my back on my child? She was filthy, and for hours she did not say one word. I begged her to stop the drugs, and she agreed. This evening, she said she would go and fetch bread for supper from here. A long time passed, and she did not return. I went looking, and I found some men who told me they were coming for me, to tell me. They took me to see her, and I—I—"

A sickly feeling drained from Mia's heart into her stomach.

She had overdosed, Signor Bruno's daughter. On the drugs she'd been taking.

*Heroin.*

He went on, the Sicilian words tumbling over one another as he struggled to get the story out. "Those who witnessed her final moments said she kept crying out, 'Gems, gems!'"

Mia froze.

Signor Bruno shook his head rapidly. "She must have sold the few jewels she had for the poison. Family heirlooms. But those were her last words." His eyes filled with fresh tears. "Not *Papa*, not *God*. 'Gems, gems.'" He crossed himself. "Let her be at peace now with her mother, while her poor father suffers."

*Gems. Gems.*

Her stomach soured so much, bile rose in her throat.

She lifted her gaze to Paolo, finding him already watching her with a look of comprehension in his eyes. Comprehension, and question.

*What now?*

"I come to you tonight for help," Signor Bruno pleaded.

"Of course we will help," Aunt Connie said. "With preparations. Meals. Anything you need. Don't worry about a thing."

"Anything," Uncle Joe said emphatically.

"No." Signor Bruno shook his head and looked straight at Mia. "I come to *you* for help!"

"Me?" Mia said, startled.

"You are a woman of respect, of power," he insisted. "It is known. The people of the neighborhood, they talk. They know of what befell your brother, how you avenged him so swiftly and mercilessly. They see you talking with Don Masseria. You can help us. Please, will you help me?"

For an instant, Mia had no idea what to say. She had no idea what help she could offer to either Signor Bruno or to the people of the neighborhood. His daughter was only one victim of the horrible poison that had befallen this community. She wasn't the first, and she wouldn't be the last.

Mia looked down at her tightly balled fists.

*But none of that matters to him. He's looking for help—from you.*

The same help she had promised to offer him Sunday at church. *If you ever need anything, I would consider it a great favor to assist you.*

Those words echoed through her mind. He was calling her to account now in his time of need. He was asking her to make good on those words. And she had only a second to decide. If she refused, she would lose any of the small amount of respect she had gained since coming home—just for avenging her brother. She would be looked at as someone who did not keep her word, who did not repay loyalty shown to her, who was not who she appeared to be.

That could never happen.

Don Catalano would never have refused. Nick, certainly, would *never* have refused.

And neither could she.

In the way of her godfather and in the way of her brother, she had to make Signor Bruno's pain her own. She hadn't known his daughter. Hadn't grown up with her, or been girl-chums, or shared confidences.

But the pain in the man's eyes touched her. It reminded her of those horrible days when she'd been a child vaudeville performer, witnessing one starlet full of potential after another getting their bright lights dimmed and then snuffed out altogether from the same killer that had taken his daughter.

Anger lined with sorrow warmed her chest as she lifted her gaze to the hopeful, heartbroken man, and found her entire family staring at her, too.

"Yes, Signor Bruno," Mia said, grateful her voice didn't tremble. "I will help you."

# CHAPTER NINE

The next afternoon, Paolo helped her out of the car after pulling up to the curb in front of the Cotton Club. It was impossible to miss, with its gargantuan sign along the upper façade that would burst into brilliant white lights when nighttime fell.

At this time of day for a Thursday afternoon, 142$^{nd}$ and Lenox was bustling with people skirting past her on the sidewalk. Mia passed beneath the jutting awning boasting a cheap dinner and no cover charge and walked through the double doors, held open by a doting doorman. She nodded to him and strode into the hall, hardly sparing a glance at the tall columns lining each side underneath the huge, arched ceiling covered with hand-painted murals. Her gaze focused on two men who stood at the back, where her band was set up to rehearse.

Hyman Goldberg, and an unassuming man of medium build, wearing a plain, dark suit—the bandy-legged Irishman from Leeds, England everyone on the streets called "The Killer."

"Ah, here she is," Hyman said as she walked over to them, holding a hand in her direction.

Owen "Owney" Madden turned toward her, his boyish face

breaking into a polite smile that carried a trace of warmth. He offered his hand, and she took it.

"Mr. Madden," she said. "How do you do?"

"Owney, please. It's a pleasure to finally meet you, Miss Scalisi," he said. His brogue had perhaps been heavy once, but two decades in America had softened it. "I had some dealings with your brother a time or two. Terribly sorry to hear of him."

She stretched her lips into a polite smile. "Yes. Thank you."

He stuffed his hands into his pockets. "I hear you'll be givin' me old joint a run for our money. Star entertainment over in Midtown at Goldberg's new place. You must be thrilled." His tone was neutral and polite, but a twinkle in his eye told her he understood just how *thrilled* she might truly be.

"I am grateful to Mr. Goldberg for the opportunity, indeed," she replied, feeling Hyman's penetrative stare upon her.

Owney studied her for a beat longer, then swept his arm toward the stage. "Aye. Well, it's all yours. Whenever you're ready."

The pianist, Gene, handed her a sheet of paper with the setlist scrawled down. Mia glanced over it. She'd been given a repertoire of popular songs to familiarize herself with as well as several original songs.

Gene smiled at her. "We'll start with a couple you know to get you warmed up."

"Sure," Mia said. "That'll be swell."

They started with "I'm Just Wild About Harry," then moved onto "I Ain't Got Nobody" and then "My Man." She sang tentatively at first, warming up, then let her voice blossom and open up. By the time she finished "My Man," she was ready for something far more interesting.

"None of Ms. Smith's songs are here," she said to Gene, leaning on the piano.

"Bessie Smith?"

"Yes."

"What do you want?"

"Most of them." Mia tapped her fingers on the paper. "Let's do 'T'ain't Nobody's Business If I Do.'"

Gene considered it, then shrugged. "You got it."

His nimble fingers plunked out the lazy yet jaunty tune. Mia's voice skipped through and around the cheeky lyrics, tasting them with relish. The song was one of her favorites—about a woman who did exactly as she pleased in a man's world and was unapologetic about it. She had always loved the blues, especially Bessie Smith. Something about the empowered way Ms. Smith put herself out there sang directly to Mia. She would never fully understand what black people experienced in this country, but coming from an immigrant family, she understood what it meant to be treated as a second-class citizen, and she felt Bessie's mournful lyrics and melodies deep inside her soul. They gave her an outlet for the pain and frustration she'd experienced after the loss of her brother and trying to find success in the dust he'd left behind.

She shut her eyes and crooned, leaning into the melody and dancing with it and around it, enjoying it. When she finished, she and Gene were both smiling, and Hyman and Owney applauded her.

A third set of hands from somewhere off to the right also applauded. Mia turned in the direction of the sound.

"Almost as good as Miz Bessie herself," the low, velvety voice said, a teasing note laced through it. "*Almost.*"

A beautiful, light-brown-skinned woman with extravagantly coiffed hair and dressed in a chic dark-blue dress stepped out of the shadows of one of the columns off to the side and walked toward Mia, one side of her mouth curled into a smile. The stage lights picked out the diamonds in her earlobes, making them shimmer and dance with rainbows.

Mia felt a matching smile spread across her face. "As I live and breathe," she said. "Annette Maybelle Elliott."

"In the flesh," Annette said.

Mia crossed the stage in a few quick strides and tossed her arms around Annette.

The desire to hug her was an odd one, since they'd never been particularly close, and Annette had come between Nick and Gloria when she'd catted around with him for a while. But Annette had also been brutalized by Kiddo Grainger, the same man who'd pulled the trigger on Nick. Before she'd fled to the South, Annette had been the one to serve up Kiddo to Mia, practically on a silver platter, so she could take her revenge.

And Mia had taken it—for Nick, and for Annette.

For a brief moment, she thought of the young woman she'd been, walking up to that abandoned warehouse the night she'd ordered a man's death for the first time. How far from her she was now.

And as she pulled back to look into Annette's warm brown eyes, keeping her arms around the woman's waist, Mia realized how far they'd both come. Separately, but united in their love for one man and hatred for another.

The last time she'd seen Annette, she'd been nursing a horrific gash across her face, along with lumps and bruises—all courtesy of Kiddo. She'd been convinced her days in showbusiness were over. Looking at her now, all Mia could see was a faint line running across the smooth brown skin and over her full red lips. It was there, but hardly noticeable. Mia had seen it immediately only because she'd been looking for it.

"You look swell," she said softly, touching the end of the scar at Annette's chin.

Annette smirked. "I look like I got my face scarred. But it healed better than I thought it would."

"What're you doing in New York? You didn't want to stay in the South?"

The other woman shook her head. "I spent a good, long time there with my family and my son. But we can't *live* there. White people don't want us to have nothing—no jobs, no rights, not even our lives. My own cousin got lynched last year because a white woman said he looked at her wrong. Folks down there seem like they forget they lost the war."

Mia's spirit drooped. "Jesus Christ. Annie, I'm sorry."

Annette's jaw tightened as she released a sharp breath through her nose. "So I couldn't raise my boy there. I'll be damned if I lose my son that way. So once my face healed, I thought maybe I might still have a chance in a chorus line. I packed up my boy and came up here nigh on six months ago and got real lucky. The Cotton Club is the hottest joint on the East Coast."

"Did you know someone here?" Mia asked.

"Well, yes. I did have an acquaintance up here who helped me get the job. I believe you know him."

Mia tilted her head. "Who?"

Her gaze shifted somewhere over Mia's shoulder, and she flicked her chin. "That man behind you."

Confused, Mia glanced in the direction Annette indicated. Strolling through the back of the club toward Hyman and Owney was a tall, dark-skinned, elegantly dressed man she recognized instantly.

She turned back to Annette, brows lifted. "Wolfy Harold?"

He'd been an ally of hers, had helped her find Vinnie Fiore in exchange for Kiddo Grainger. He'd been Kiddo's boss, and had been planning to off the man himself before Mia had gotten hold of him. He'd considered *that* a favor done him.

Annette lowered her lashes. "Yeah. Wolfy."

"Wolfy…and…you?"

Annette's face remained impassive.

"Are you…happy?" Mia asked softly.

"I'm comfortable," Annette said with soft pointedness. "And so is my son. And *that* makes me happy. Wolfy, he ain't perfect. But he treat me good. Real good. He's real…kind."

That lightened Mia's heart. Annette might not be in love, but she was safe. "And Owney?"

"Mr. Madden, he a good boss, all things considered. He can be sweet. But oh, so vicious."

"Guess they call him 'The Killer' for a reason."

"They do. But he ain't nothin' like Mr. Bellomo." Her serious gaze turned knowing. "Speakin' of. Heard he met with some misfortune the day he got acquitted for murder."

Mia met Annette's eyes.

"I know it was you," Annette whispered, her hands resting on Mia's upper arms and tightening. "And I'm glad."

She'd spent so much of her time trying not to think about Sal. About what he'd done. About what she'd done to him. She ran from the memories and her thoughts and the picture of his face her brain liked to shove in front of her, because she could escape none of it at night when she slept. Hearing his name would make a wave of hot sludge roll through her gut and burble up into her chest.

But now, hearing Annette's whispered words, seeing the intensity in her eyes, feeling the grip of her hands... It was a strange thing to feel proud of ordering a man's death—of committing murder—but Mia's heart bloomed with warmth, anyway.

If anyone understood, Annette did.

"You ladies know each other?"

Mia turned. Owney stood behind them, his head tilted and arms folded.

"Yes, Mr. Madden," Annette said. "Miss Scalisi and I worked together in Chicago, when she headlined the Stems Supper Club."

Owney regarded Mia with a smirk, the twinkle in his eyes returning. "Yeah. Sal Bellomo's old place. Sad thing that happened to him, wasn't it?"

"Downright tragic," Annette said smoothly with practiced sadness. "Working for him was almost good as working for you, Mr. Madden."

Owney smiled and made a humbly dismissive gesture. "Shucks. With talent good as you, 'tis an easy club to run." He checked his pocket watch. "But you'd best prepare yourself for rehearsal, dearie. You two ladies can catch up later."

The words were said with kind deference, but Mia recognized the underlying steel in his voice—there was no room for negotiation. And though she did not work for Owney Madden, Annette did, and Mia wasn't about to cause her strife.

"You sounded real good," Annette said with a smile as she stepped away. "Hope to catch you some night."

"You're welcome anytime," Mia replied. "Whenever you get a night off, let me know."

Annette gave her a little wave, then turned and headed backstage.

Hyman, Owney, and Wolfy stood beside a table, chatting quietly. Mia strolled over to them.

Wolfy caught sight of her and flashed the famous grin that had given him his moniker. "Well, well. The rumors was true. The lady's back in town."

Mia gave him a one-sided smile. "Miss me?"

"Shoot, sure did. Left me dealing with this knucklehead." He gestured toward Hyman, who rolled his eyes good-naturedly. "I been filling my speaks with some of your fine booze. Kids go wild for it. You getting back into the racket?"

"Oh," she said loftily, "where I'm needed, when I'm needed."

"Mia's hands are full with other endeavors these days," Hyman said, then held a hand out toward the stage she'd just vacated. "Such as this."

"Yeah, you sounded real good," Wolfy said. "Y'ain't no Bessie Smith no way, but you ain't bad."

Mia tipped her head back and burst out laughing. "Gee, thanks, Mr. Harold. You're a real charmer."

"Your friend seem to think so," he said, giving her another roguish grin and a wink.

Mia gave him a serious look. "Keep her happy and smiling, all right, Wolfy? She deserves that."

"And a whole lot more," he said, and the sincerity in his voice filled her with relief. Annette might not be in love with him, but it was clear he was head over heels for her.

"So?" she said to Hyman. "What did you think?"

"You sounded swell," Owney said.

"Very good," Hyman said with a crisp nod. "Keep it up."

The praise took her by surprise, but she was pleased. She'd been expecting a thorough critique of how she might have performed better.

A waiter came by with a drink on a tray. He offered it to Wolfy, who nodded his thanks and took a sip. Then he spluttered and coughed, his face screwed up in severe distaste.

"My God, man," Owney exclaimed. "What devils you?"

"The shit in the glass!" Wolfy replied, slamming the glass on the table. Liquor sloshed over the sides. "What the hell I look like, Owney? Some broke motherfucker in off the street who can't afford the booze?"

"Afford it," Owney said, glancing at Hyman and chuckling. "You freeloading son of a bitch never pay a penny in this place."

"Exactly," Wolfy said sternly. "I've invested a lotta money in this joint. I supplied a lot of the talent, including my gal. And *this* what you serve me?"

"What is the problem?" Hyman asked mildly.

"Ain't no problem," Owney protested. "It's liquor, through and through. A fresh shipment I got t'other night."

"From whom, if you don't mind me asking?" Mia asked.

All three men turned toward her.

Owney looked slightly surprised at the question. He shrugged. "I got a deal."

"That's not what I asked you," Mia said.

Wolfy chuckled.

She pointed at the glass he'd abandoned. "May I?"

He drew his head back, then lifted a shoulder and reached for the glass. He handed it to her. "I wouldn't, if I was you, but it's your funeral."

She sniffed the contents. It *looked* like a regular neat whiskey, but the smell was off. And familiar. And when she took a tiny sip, the potent, vile flavor that had the same familiarity in the taste as it did the scent flowed over her tongue as it all burned down her throat.

This time, she managed to not spit it all out like she had the first time she'd tasted it in the alley behind her shop, but let it stream out of her mouth and back into the glass. She might have been horrified at her lack of manners but for the anger she felt.

Nonetheless, her eyes watered as she coughed. Wolfy gave her a handkerchief from his pocket and took the glass from her.

Hyman watched her, his face expressionless.

Owney tilted his head. "Now you, too."

Mia dabbed the corners of her mouth with the hanky. "Have you actually tasted your own product, Mr. Madden?"

"Not this batch," he admitted.

"What exactly did you think you were purchasing?"

"Rye whiskey," he replied, clearly mystified and annoyed.

Mia met Hyman's gaze. He lowered his eyes. "Again, I'll ask, from whom did you buy this crap?"

"Some Italian fella," Owney said. "Gems, he called himself."

Mia heaved a sigh and shook her head. So that was who Moritz had sold the load to after she'd banished it from the shop. And based on Hyman's somewhat sheepish expression, he knew it.

"If I might offer you a bit of advice, Mr. Madden," Mia said, "don't serve this to your customers tonight."

His brow creased. "I'm flush with what I bought from that fella. I haven't enough stock of everything else at the moment."

"Then get ready to lose a whole lot of business when people start walking out of here," Mia said. "This club has a reputation in the city. A high-class place. Some of the best entertainment around. Good food. Great booze. Serve them *that* swill, and that reputation goes into the garbage."

"She know what she talking about," Wolfy said.

"Miss Scalisi," Hyman said, his lips stretched into a tight smile, "I think it's best we let Mr. Madden tend to his own affairs, don't you?"

Mia offered her own insincere smile in return. "Sure. Are we done here for today?"

"Wait." Owney held out his hand for Wolfy's abandoned drink. "Give me that."

He handled his sip with a great deal more control than either

Wolfy or Mia, but the tightening around his eyes told her he noticed the horrible taste.

"There's not enough soda or simple syrup in the world to mix with that and make it drinkable, Mr. Madden," Mia said.

"Goddammit," he cursed, and set the glass down. "That bastard assured me it was the finest rye."

"It *was* the finest rye," Mia said. "Once."

"What do you mean?"

"The details aren't important," Mia said. "How many crates of this stuff did you buy from him?"

"Ten."

"How about this." Mia took a step closer to Owney. He wasn't a tall man, so they stood nearly nose-to-nose. She didn't even have to tilt her head back to meet his gaze. "I happen to have ten crates of the *real* good stuff. Rye straight from Templeton, Iowa. As a thank-you for offering me rehearsal space today, and to help out a *pal* in need, I'd be happy to send those crates to you before you open tonight. And if you like what you taste... maybe there's a deal to be worked out."

Owney's eyes narrowed. "You're a cheeky little bird, aren't you?"

"I'm a businesswoman," she said, allowing a hint of her own steel to creep into her voice.

"Is this the part where we shake?" he said.

"I'm offering a favor," Mia said. "You don't have to shake on a favor."

Behind her, Wolfy said, "You ain't got many choices, Owney. I'd take the lady up on her kind offer. Her shit's the good shit."

"And what am I to do about the Gems man?" Owney asked. "He seems a bit...unpredictable."

Mia shrugged. "That's entirely up to you. I'd never dream of meddling in your affairs."

"Hmph." He looked amused, then sighed. "Well, I haven't much choice, have I? Send the crates, if you wouldn't mind. As long as it's better than this goat piss, it'll do."

"I think you'll find it far superior to anything you've ever tasted," Mia said. "And you're an Irishman. You know your whiskey."

"That I do." He eyed her up and down. "If I like what I taste, you'll be hearing from me again."

Mia smiled. "I would consider it an honor to be the Cotton Club's supplier of rye whiskey. Until then, have a lovely night."

He tapped the side of his forehead. "Yeah. You come back any time as my special guest."

Hyman took her arm and they strolled toward the entrance, where Paolo lounged in a chair beside the door, reading a small, leather-bound book. He glanced up as they approached, then rose and went outside.

The doorman held the door for them as they stepped beneath the awning to wait for Paolo to bring the car. The sky had darkened with the onset of twilight, and though spring had officially come to New York, the evening air clung stubbornly to the chill of winter. Mia wrapped her arms around herself, wishing for a heavier coat.

"Well," Hyman said, facing her. "That was quite a performance."

Mia lifted a shoulder. "Thanks. Overall, I think it went well, though I know I flubbed some of the lines in that new song the boys worked up. Don't worry, though, I'll get them straightened out. Opening night will be perfect."

"What a relief," Hyman said. "I do so appreciate perfection. However, that's not the performance I'm referring to."

She knew that. She cocked her head and braced herself for the scolding. "Oh?"

Instead, to her complete shock, a slow smile tugged across Hyman's face. "The way you handled yourself back there was truly impressive, Mia. Owney Madden is not a man to be trifled with, and though he's still somewhat of a young man, he comes from a less progressive time, where men did not conduct business with women in any capacity—outside the boudoir. And certainly not in delicate matters of illegal operations such as this."

"I…thought you'd be irritated," Mia said. "Since I said I'd send him the crates for free."

"Oh, I certainly am," Hyman said drily. "Do you believe I'm truly happy about seeing two thousand dollars just float away from me? Of course not. On the other hand, I didn't get to where I am by making bad business choices. Nor did I get to where I am by ignoring the simple tenet that it takes money to make money. You're familiar with that expression, Miss Scalisi? Moreover…" His gaze became distant as it traveled somewhere beyond her shoulder. "Moreover, I have been ruminating on that unpleasant scene that took place outside your shop the night we had the unloading. I fear I had begun to rely too heavily on Moritz and Charlie to run the operation. There was too much emphasis on shrewd practicality rather than quality—both are equally important. And I believe you understand that in a way those ambitious young men don't."

"It's what Nick always said."

Hyman nodded slowly. "Yes. I daresay he'd be quite proud of what you just did in there. Not many men would have even attempted that without some lengthy preamble."

"I've never been particularly interested in preamble of any length." Mia flashed a cheeky smile.

He met it with a reluctant one. "That much has always been abundantly clear. Anyway, well done. I believe you've just earned yourself a new customer."

"I've earned *myself* a new customer?"

"Does that require explanation?"

"I just…" She shook her head. "It almost sounds as though you're putting me in charge."

"I'm going to have the boys step back and focus on other things and see how you do in a position of leadership," Hyman said. "After all, I invited you to take a more active role when I transitioned the shop to you. And you've very likely just secured the business of one of the most important men in the city. That's not going to be an easy task. If you can pull this off with grace, then that only excites me for what we may be able to accomplish together at The Divine."

"I don't see Morrie being agreeable to me in a position of leadership."

"Morrie has other endeavors that keep him rather busy," he said in a tone that gave away nothing. "And I'm sure Charlie has his hands full working with Mr. Masseria, as well."

A cloud passed through her mind. Yes, she was sure Charlie was quite busy, too.

"One more thing, and perhaps the most important of all." His voice was low and serious, and he dipped his head to look her in the eye. "In addition to pulling off a risky and brilliant business move in there, you've also just inadvertently made yourself an enemy."

"You said he was a customer."

"I am referring to his previous dealer," Hyman said. "Mr. Morelli. Gems, as he's so colorfully known. He purchased for himself the liquor you so politely refused with the intent of kicking off his own bootlegging business."

"Then he's a moron for ever thinking that garbage was the thing to sell to the Cotton Club," Mia replied, folding her arms.

"I won't argue with you on that point. However, he *did* have an agreement with Mr. Madden, and now you've very likely ended that."

"That's presumptuous, isn't it?" Mia said. "Owney hasn't agreed to anything."

"He would be a foolish man not to capitalize on quality liquor for one of the finest and most popular establishments in town, as would any man in the same business. As I would be. No, he hasn't agreed to anything. You're correct. But I can read people, I daresay better than even you, Miss Scalisi. And I can tell you it's likely a matter of time. And when that time comes, you'd better be prepared for some rather strong feelings from Mr. Morelli."

"So what do you think I should do?"

He tilted his head. "What do you think your brother would have done?"

Mia lowered her eyes as she considered the question. What would Nick have done? A mirthless smile tugged up one side of her mouth.

Nick would have murdered Jake Morelli and eliminated any problems before they could arise.

Don Catalano, on the other hand, had frequently advised her to avoid bloodshed except in the direst of circumstances, when her back was to the wall and she was left with no choice.

*Blood is expensive,* he'd told her time and again. *You are here to make money, not lose it all on a war.*

Would there be a war?

"I know what Nick would have done," she said softly. "But that's not what I'm going to do." She lifted her gaze to Hyman's. "I won't murder a man preemptively."

His eyes gleamed with approval, but he said, "Just understand, whether you intended to or not, you've struck the first blow. Preemptively."

"I'm not trying to strike any blow," she protested. "I'm simply...being a businessman. Woman."

"Come," he said softly. "You're much too intelligent for that sort of naivete. You know what you've just done. And you know you can't undo it."

Damn him for being able to read her so well, he was practically clairvoyant. "Perhaps I can speak with Mr. Morelli. Reason with him."

"Can a matador reason with a bull once he's flashed his red and set the beast to charging him?" Hyman shrugged. "Perhaps it's not impossible, but what would suit the matador the most is to learn to move deftly, anticipate the bull's next move, and...get out of the way."

For a moment, a feeling of deep regret took root in her heart. She hadn't even considered any of this when she'd opened her big mouth to Owney. She'd dismissed Jake as easily as she would a fly, but the impact of her choice carried the promise of consequences she hadn't taken into account.

She'd wanted to play in a man's world, and now, she might be due a man's repercussions.

"Why didn't you intervene, then?" she asked. "And don't tell me you're shy."

"Because I didn't disagree with you." He lifted a shoulder. "Moritz purchased a quantity of our booze from me. He did with it what he did. You rejected that batch. So, he did what any enterprising person would have done—he marked it up and sold it all off to someone who was desperate for it. I just never thought it would wind up in the hands of a man like Owney Madden. *He* must have been desperate for it if he didn't bother to sample it first. That, or Mr. Morelli is quite the silver-tongued, snake oil salesman." Hyman slid his hands into his pockets, a casual stance Mia rarely saw him take. "I got paid for the rejected batch either way. And I'll make my very handsome cut from any future sales with Mr. Madden. It benefits me no matter what."

"And leave me out to dry?"

He withdrew his hands and placed them on her shoulders. "Not at all. Should you need my help, you'll have it."

She wasn't sure what the full breadth of his "help" would look like, but she took some comfort in knowing she wouldn't have to fight alone. *Perhaps Mr. Madden will keep our arrangement quiet, if there is one.*

"Ah," Hyman said, gesturing to something behind her. "Your chariot has arrived." Graciously, he opened the back passenger door for her.

"Can I offer you a ride somewhere?" Mia said.

Hyman checked his pocket watch. "No, but thank you. One of my men will be along shortly. I have some business to take care of at The Divine." He tucked the watch back into his waistcoat. "I'll expect to see you back here tomorrow at three. The choreographer will be here to work with you through the numbers, and the chorines will be here as well. Consider today a rehearsal for your rehearsals. I'll also expect you to know all your lyrics, yes?"

"Yes. Of course."

He gave her as kind a smile as he was capable of. "Go on, then. You'll have a busy evening preparing that little favor to Owney, so make sure you get a good meal and some rest."

"Yes, of course, Papa," she said sarcastically.

"I would never presume, Miss Scalisi," he replied, then shut the door once she was seated inside.

Paolo turned to her from the front seat and mimed eating.

She shook her head. "Later. Take me to the shop, please. We got some work to do."

# CHAPTER TEN

Late Tuesday morning, Mia walked into Most Precious Blood with her family to pay her last respects to the daughter of Signor Bruno.

It was the third time she'd been to the cathedral since returning home. Aunt Connie had accepted her first visit to Sunday Mass with them as acknowledgment that she should expect Mia every single Sunday now. Mia understood Aunt Connie didn't give two slaps how late her Saturday nights kept her out. She was expected with Gloria and Emilia in her Sunday black.

The past Saturday night, she'd spent several long, frustrating hours in a meeting with Hyman, Charlie, Moritz, and later, Frankie Yale at Hyman's penthouse. He'd made it clear Mia was to be placed in charge of the Scalisi operation, given her successful new deal with Owney Madden, who had thanked her for the crates she'd sent over and wanted to discuss the details of their new partnership very soon. Mia's triumph was short-lived when Moritz had, predictably, protested Hyman's suggestion, but Hyman had gently reminded him of his other business ventures.

It had been his exquisitely polite way of telling Moritz to go chase himself, she had noted with amusement.

"Give Mia a chance," he'd added. "You didn't see her tête-à-
tête with Mr. Madden, but suffice it to say, it would appear the
*mademoiselle* knows what she's doing. Besides, she brokered this
deal, not you, Moritz."

The doubt that had clouded her mind outside the Cotton
Club had crept back in that moment, but she would rather have
died than let anyone—certainly Moritz—see it.

Charlie had advised her to hold a meeting with Jake. The
man was a loose cannon, Charlie had told her, and she needed to
prepare for the fallout of her impetuousness. It would be held at
the grocery, and Masseria would act as mediator.

"Be patient," Charlie had said. "Make him an attractive offer.
Cut him in at a good percentage. Just remember you can't take
back what you did. So you better push forward."

It was risky, but with Jake's obvious interest in her, combined
with the pretty numbers she'd put before him, she was confident
she could work something out to her advantage and avoid
making an enemy.

Besides, there was something else she wanted from him.
Something she would demand of him tonight at their meeting.
Something she was reminded of now as she followed her family
into the somber atmosphere of the cathedral.

She wanted him to stop his heroin business in the neighborhood. Immediately.

She had paid for the funeral—every last dime. The service,
the reception at a local hall, supplies for the meal to be served,
the burial itself, and money for Signor Bruno.

Word seemed to travel fast over the weekend, because by the
time she and the family arrived at Most Precious Blood, heads
turned in their direction—in *her* direction.

Signor Bruno met them at the back of the church. "I wish to
offer you a place behind my family, up front," he said, shaking
Uncle Joe's hand and accepting Aunt Connie's embrace. He
seemed to have aged twenty years since Mia last saw him. His
face was drawn and pale, and he had lost some weight. "Come.
Let me lead you."

"No," Uncle Joe said, slipping an arm around his shoulders. "We will walk with you."

Aunt Connie and Uncle Joe flanked the grief-ridden man, and Mia, Gloria, and Emilia trailed behind.

As they walked toward the front, every so often, a hand would shoot out from a pew to take Mia's wrist, to pull her down for a kiss on each cheek, to thank her for the tremendous kindness she had done the Bruno family. Mia stopped each time to accept the murmured words, responding with her own, shaking hands, patting cheeks, and always, always saying, "Should you ever need anything, come and see me."

She hardly heard Father Alessio's words. Her gaze was fixed on the still face rising just above the casket—the profile of a young woman, hardly eighteen, gone much too soon. When Mia had paid Signor Bruno and his family a visit last Sunday, he'd shown her a sepia-tinted photo of his daughter taken only the year before. The girl had been beautiful in her healthier days, all huge eyes and wide smile and flowing black hair. A sweet girl, her father had said, a dutiful daughter and a doting big sister who had put her grief at losing her mother aside to care for her siblings and look after her father.

Perhaps that grief had not been totally forgotten, Mia thought, studying the girl's waxy, pale-yellow skin drawn tight over the bones of the face. Perhaps that grief had driven her to try to dull the pain with the chemical. Plenty of people did it with booze.

She knew she was a hypocrite. She was part of an operation that sold alcohol to anyone who wanted it, regardless of whether they had a problem with the substance or not, but she was staunchly against drugs. Moritz had once called her on that, and she'd leaned on her stories of witnessing firsthand what the drugs did to those who fell to their evil siren song. And she still believed in what she'd told him—a snort of heroin was by far worse than a shot of liquor, but that didn't change the fact that plenty of men and women abused it the same way. Plenty of men consumed so much they lost themselves and beat their wives, their children. Poor women sold themselves for a few dollars to buy a bottle of the rotgut product that would see them dead in half a year. Children took to the stuff at a young age, become prolific and heavy drinkers long before adulthood.

Knowing all of this, she still pressed Nick's operation forward. She still drew her cut from the quantities that were sold and stored.

And yet, there was something inherently vile about drugs she could not look past. Perhaps Moritz was right and she could become a millionaire inside a few months if she would only put her beliefs to the side and view it as a business, a commodity, a product people wanted they couldn't easily get, and that she could furnish for them. She could operate out of her own shop, out of Hyman's nightclub. Even if she limited her clientele to those two areas, the addictiveness of the drug would keep her earning potential high. And the things she could do with that money...

*No.*

Another look at Signor Bruno's dead daughter's face, the memories of the starlets she'd seen overdose, and the echoes in her ears of the weeping and wailing and cries to be mercy-killed and for someone, anyone, to just bring them one hit ran through her mind in a blurred instant.

She might be a murderer, a criminal, and a hypocrite, and for the things she'd done in the name of vengeance for Nick, she was already likely going to hell, but she would not do this. She would not be a poisoner of her own people. Of anyone. Not for all the money in the world.

After the service, Mia and her family joined Signor Bruno and everyone from the neighborhood at the reception hall. She had told Hyman over the weekend she would not be at rehearsal today, explaining a family friend had a death in the family. To her surprise, though he did not sound pleased whatsoever, he asked no questions as he granted her the day off, but warned her the following day he would expect twice the effort from her.

At the reception, she tried to stay in the background, even

when Signor Bruno publicly thanked her for handling all of the preparations.

Mia shook her head. "It was the strength of the family values of the neighborhood that made this day possible." Her short words drew a round of applause, which embarrassed her.

She'd just taken her seat at the end of a long table, a plate of chicken cacciatore in front of her, when a young woman only a few years older than her approached. A child was half-hidden behind her.

"Signorina Scalisi?"

Mia set her fork down and stood to meet the woman. "Yes. What is your name?"

"I am Signora Cancio," she said in a shy voice, taking both of Mia's hands in her rough ones. "I have come to thank you."

"Thank me for what?" Mia said, not unkindly.

"You rescued my boy from bullies, thieves," Signora Cancio said, and pulled the small boy from behind her.

His large, dark eyes set in his sweet face immediately tugged on her heart. "Of course. How are you?"

"He is well, and so am I," the signora said. "We thank you from the bottom of our hearts. For helping him, and me. The… money you gave him. For us."

"Yes. I only did what anyone else would."

Signora Cancio shook her head. "What you gave him—we had our electricity turned off for a month because I was unable…" She lowered her eyes in shame. "I had been sick, not able to work at the factory. They fired me anyway, even when I came back before I was strong. My husband died last year. I had to choose between food and lights. I picked food for my boy. But thanks to you, we could put our lights on this month."

Mia's mouth tightened. She knew all too well the harsh conditions found in factory work.

"My boy, he is not in school because he must sell newspapers to make us a little money," Signora Cancio went on, laying a hand on his shoulder. "I am trying to find work so that he can go back to school. But—"

Mia held up a hand. "Come and see me tomorrow morning at my uncle's grocery. We'll discuss your bills and your monthly expenses. We'll talk about your skills for work. I'll help find you a job—a good one, no more factory work. I own a shop, and I have a girl there now who needs help. I can offer you a good wage and good hours. Your boy can return to school. He can keep the paper job if he likes, but only on the weekend." She smiled at the boy. "Would you like that?"

He nodded. "*Grazie*," he murmured.

Signora Cancio had begun to weep softly. She used the sleeve of her worn black dress—likely her Sunday best—to dab her eyes. "You are so good," she said, her voice breaking. "I only meant to thank you. I do not want you to think—"

"Nonsense," Mia said. "I want to help you. Come to the store in the morning. All right?"

Signora Cancio nodded rapidly and kissed Mia's hands. Mia knelt in front of the boy and patted his arms.

"Take care of your mother," she said. "After all, you're the man of the house. Aren't you?"

He nodded, his face serious. "Yes. I am."

She had only taken a few bites of her meal after they left before she had a new visitor—this time, a middle-aged couple, neighbors of Signor Bruno. They'd heard all about what she'd done for the man, and wished to pay their respects. After a few more minutes of chatting, Mia discovered the husband had been out of work for a few weeks due to some back trouble, for which he was unable to afford treatment. Mia promised to speak with her doctor friend—that was, Hyman's doctor friend—and get him an appointment and some relief.

More and more people, emboldened by the visitors to her side they watched come and go, came up to her. Many simply wanted to formally introduce themselves and pay their respects. Some had requests—money, assistance of some sort, trouble with a job. She offered her pocketbook and aid whenever and wherever she could.

Her uneaten meal had long since turned cold when she finally returned to it.

After the burial, Paolo drove Aunt Connie and Uncle Joe back to the store, where they planned to reopen for a few hours in the evening—before the meeting. Aunt Connie seemed a little bewildered as she kissed Mia goodbye.

"Perhaps I should start calling you Godmother now, eh?" she teased in Sicilian, a bit uncertainly.

Mia only smiled and clasped the older woman's hand, the fingers still gently and teasingly pinching her cheek. "No, Aunt Connie. I just—I want people to know they can come to me for help. That I *can* help them."

"I hope you do," Aunt Connie said softly, then patted her cheek. "We'll see you later for the meeting."

"Don't go overboard, Aunt Connie," Mia said, knowing the woman would have cooked a three-course meal for Mia's guests if she didn't say something. "I don't want them feeling *too* comfortable."

She hadn't realized something in her voice had changed, gone colder, but Connie's brow knitted slightly as she nodded and backed away before turning to walk into the store.

Uncle Joe slipped an arm around her shoulders. "You did well today," he murmured. "I had people coming in here asking about you since you got home. Word travels fast about things you do, Mia. People here know more than you think. You made a lot of allies today, but you made a lot of promises, too."

"Promises I fully intend to keep."

He patted her shoulder. "About tonight. You want me to get some boys from the neighborhood to stand outside?"

On the one hand, she could always use the extra security. On the other hand, if things went sideways—and that was a fair assumption with how volatile Jake was, and what she had to tell him tonight—she wouldn't be able to look their mothers in their faces if any of the boys got hurt. Or worse.

Mia shook her head. Perhaps unwise, but she had Paolo, and Charlie had arranged for a couple of his men to join them. She had her own plans to beef up extra security that might be more effective than neighborhood boys. "No. Just..." She paused, then looked up at him. "Don't set the table by the window, all right?"

It was meant to be a joke, but the coldness seeped back into her voice before she heard it.

Uncle Joe's bushy gray brows lifted a fraction of an inch. He bobbed his head. "Of course not. You know, I've held meetings like this before here."

"You have?"

"Many times. In fact, back in 'twenty-three, I hosted Don Masseria and Signor Luciano. He was in big trouble." He laughed. "That is why the *padroni* pay me respect. I respect them. I provide neutral place to conduct business. I pay my tributes, my protection money."

"You help keep the peace," Mia said, still amused over the idea of the fearsome Lucky Luciano getting an earful from Mr. Masseria right here in Uncle Joe's store.

"I do my best." He bowed his head. Then he studied her, head tilted, and clasped her hand in his. "I never thought my niece would be the one to have a meeting with the *padroni*."

*Niece.* She patted his hand. "I'm honored you think of me as blood."

"Aunt Connie and I, we never had children. That we had Gloria sent to us from her parents was a blessing. In a way, we think of her as our daughter. And we've come to think of you as our daughter, too."

She smiled teasingly. "Or maybe a son?"

Uncle Joe pecked her forehead. "Better than a son, though I worry more. Go and rest. Everything will be ready for tonight."

Paolo drove them back to the hotel. Gloria carried a sleeping Emilia toward the elevators, but Mia caught sight of the two people she'd asked to meet her at the hotel restaurant.

"Go on ahead," she said to Gloria. "I'll be up shortly."

Gloria had been uncharacteristically silent on the ride home. Mia had expected a barrage of questions, more than usual, but her sister-in-law stayed silent. It was more unnerving than the questions.

"All right," she said, and walked toward the elevator attendant.

"Go with them," Mia said to Paolo quietly. "Make sure they get settled, then come back here."

He gave her a sharp nod.

Mia turned and walked into the restaurant, offering hellos to the host staff who recognized her, and headed straight for the round table in the back of the room, where two hulking, suited, dark-haired men sat.

When they noticed her, they both stood.

"Bobby, Joey," she said, holding out her hand.

"Miss Scalisi," Bobby said, taking her hand.

"Miss Scalisi," Joey said, doing the same.

"Let's sit." Before she could touch her chair, the men shuffled around the table as if in a choreographed movement, and Bobby pulled out the chair whose back faced the wall. He gestured for her to sit.

When they were settled, she looked each man in the eye. "Thank you for coming to meet me on short notice. I should've called you yesterday, not this morning on my way out the door."

"It was no trouble," Joey said.

"What did you want to meet with us about, Miss Scalisi?" Bobby asked.

"Where we stand, the three of us," Mia said. "I've been gone a year. A lot's changed, hasn't it?"

Both men nodded gravely.

"I've been feeling rather…alone," she went on. "It's hard to know who I can rely on these days. Men who I once called 'friend' because of their friendship with my brother seem to have gone their own ways. And there seem to be some new faces hanging around that I'm not sure I like too much."

The two men exchanged a look.

She leaned forward, bracing her elbows on the table. "I need to know where you stand. Who you're loyal to. It's all right if it's not me. I get it. I've been away. I haven't done much for you. But my brother trusted you both. With his life. I want to be able to do the same."

The two men looked at each other again for a beat.

"Miss Scalisi, do you remember when we brought you to the train station in Chicago for your first trip here after Mr. Scalisi was killed?" Bobby asked.

"Of course."

"We pledged our loyalty to you then," he said. "And we pledge it to you now."

"We've known you'd come back," Joey added. "Sure, we've had to do what we needed to do to make ends meet. We drive the trucks. We provide security at drop-offs and pickups. We do whatever Mr. Schapiro and Mr. Lazzari ask of us."

"Are you contracted to them in any way?" Mia said. Behind Bobby, Paolo walked toward them, a silent shadow in the mostly empty dining room. He took a seat just away from the table at her right side. Not part of the conversation, but near her.

Bobby shook his head, glancing at Paolo. "We work for them. But we've pledged no oaths of loyalty to anyone…but you."

"I need to know why," she said. "Why me?"

"Your brother saved my life," Joey said earnestly. "I don't know if he ever told you how I came to work for him."

She shook her head.

"Just after the war, I was home and looking for work. I'd discovered my wife had left me while I'd been off fighting. I found odd jobs here and there. Dock work, deliveries. I used to work for a butcher on Mulberry. He had a bad gambling habit. One night, he wasn't feeling well, he said, and he asked me if I could stay late to handle the customers. I'd done some of that the more I proved myself to him. Of course, I said yes. Three fellas came by, looking for the money my boss owed them from a card game. They told him he'd pay them, or they'd kill him. They decided to try to use me as a message. I fought back as hard as I could, but three against one, what're you gonna do? They beat me, sliced me open, left me for dead in the alley. Your brother was out on the streets that night coming from a different card game. He found me, took me to the hospital. Saved my life. Came to visit me too, asked me about what happened. He said for all they sliced me open and I didn't die, I must be a tough son of a bitch. When he found out I fought in the war too, he gave me a job on the spot. Said he could use a reliable bodyguard. And he never turned his back on me. Ever."

Mia thought back to that terrible night when her world had changed forever, when Nick had been murdered. Joey had been crouched over his body on the sidewalk. He'd looked up at her with tears in his eyes, agony on his face. *There's nothing I can do*, he'd said in a broken voice. *I couldn't get to him in time.*

"I used to work as bouncer at this Irish joint in the Bowery," Bobby spoke up quietly. "All the work I could find, and I had a sick mother to take care of. Nick come in one night, he sees me takin' all kinds of shit from the owner, some of the patrons. He walked up to me and said, 'Hey, *paesano*, how about a real job?' He had me start driving for him for a while. We'd talk, I'd tell him about my mother. The cancer eating away at her. He fixed her up with a good doctor to get her medicine to make her final months as painless as possible. Paid for everything. He always used to come visit her too, bring her flowers and books and little things like that. When she passed, he paid for her funeral. Stood right by my side the whole time, cried with me like a brother." Bobby swallowed and looked down at his hands for a moment.

Mia's eyes stung. She should not display this much emotion in front of men if she wanted them to take her seriously, but hearing of the kindnesses her brother had shown these men, the second chances they'd gotten because of him, the loyalty he'd shown them and had earned in kind, moved her beyond measure.

"The one thing he always asked of us," Bobby went on, "was that if anything should ever happen to him, we look out for you. He only asked that of us and Mr. Lazzari. He never would have trusted anybody else to watch out for you, but he trusted us. I made him a promise I would do that. And I intend to keep it."

"Me, too," Joey said. "And even if you'd never done the things you did to avenge him, we'd still keep that promise. But... you did."

"We respect you," Bobby added. "And we respect what you're trying to do now—save his business. It ain't my place to say so, but...it ain't the same as it was before you left. It's like the rules changed."

"It's like they forgot whose business it was in the first place," Joey said, a sharp edge in his low voice.

"I'm hoping you'll help me make them remember," Mia said.

Bobby stood, then Joey. Bobby clasped her hand. "I pledge my loyalty and service to you, Miss Scalisi, until the day I die." He kissed the back of her hand.

Before she could lower it, Joey took her hand next, kissed it, and said, "My loyalty is yours, Miss Scalisi. Now, until I die."

For a moment, brief panic set in, though Mia struggled not to show it. What exactly did this mean? What had she gotten herself into?

From the depths of her mind, a frightened girl's voice cried out. *I just want to sing. I just want to dance. That's all. I don't know what to do with this. I don't know I don't know I don't—*

She drew a deep breath, and the frightened girl's voice lowered into the voice of Nick, speaking now to a grown woman —one resigned to her destiny, loyalty to her blood. Loyalty to her dead brother, who had been a prince in this world still so foreign to her.

*It's your world now,* surrùzza.

There in the empty dining room of the Murray Hill Hotel, with only three trusted men as witnesses, a young queen was crowned.

# CHAPTER ELEVEN

When Charlie walked into d'Abbruzzo Grocery with Joe "The Boss" Masseria and Jake Morelli ten minutes early, Mia was waiting.

She'd already been sitting at the scarred, round table for thirty minutes to ensure she was the first one there, anticipating they might try to catch her unawares by arriving early. They hadn't disappointed her, but she sincerely hoped she'd disappointed them.

The table was laden with four glasses and a bottle of strong red wine from Uncle Joe's personal collection, which she would be sure to mention so Mr. Masseria understood the respect her uncle had shown tonight. Along with the wine was an antipasto spread of a big dish of marinated vegetables, a loaf of fresh bread baked personally by Aunt Connie, still warm from the oven, a bottle of Uncle Joe's finest olive oil straight from Sicily, several kinds of cheese, and thick slices of salami. Her "guests" would not receive a full meal, but they would not leave hungry or disrespected.

After she'd gone up to her room at the hotel, she'd changed out of her funeral black and debated on the proper attire for the meeting. Nothing too low-cut; it would never do for them to accuse her of using her "feminine wiles" to get her way. Nothing too boring or simple, either.

In the end, she'd selected a dress of a deep purple-brown with a high neckline cut straight across her collarbone, a filmy, knee-length, handkerchief hem, and long, sheer sleeves gathered at the wrist into a jeweled cuff, its only decoration. She'd kept her makeup light, with only a touch of rouge on her lips. The only other ornaments she wore were the dangling diamond earrings her brother had given her the Christmas before he'd been killed.

Uncle Joe met them at the door, greeting Mr. Masseria first, then Charlie, then Jake, and took their coats. He held a hand out toward the back of the room, toward her.

Mia did not smile as they approached, remaining seated with her forearms draped along the chair's armrests, ankles crossed, back straight, and chin lifted. Paolo, Bobby, and Joey were lined up like sentries directly behind her.

When they reached the table, Paolo pulled her chair out for her, and Mia stood beside it. She greeted first Mr. Masseria with a kiss on each cheek and a shake of the hand—the most respectful greeting for a man of his station. Then she greeted Charlie with a cold handshake—all that was proper for the meeting facilitator. He held onto her hand for a beat longer than necessary, forcing her eyes up to meet his.

"Good evening, Miss Scalisi," he said in a low, meaningful tone.

Her heart ached at the thought of the chill she'd forced between them, but as his hand slid away from hers, the raised line of flesh on his palm reminded her why it was there.

And for Mr. Jake "Gems" Morelli, who would either be her partner or her enemy when he left tonight, she offered her hand.

His dark brows shot up. "Is this an invitation to touch you, Miss Scalisi?" He eyed her up and down with a roguish admiration.

"It's a gesture of courtesy."

He slid his larger hand around hers with confidence. It was warm and firm. He tugged her closer, and she went willingly.

"I'm eager to hear this business proposal of yours, honey. I hope it involves lots of time for us to get close and put our heads together."

She couldn't think of a single polite thing to say in response to that, so she offered a tight smile instead and gently extracted her hand. She gestured to the chairs. "Gentlemen, please sit."

When they were all seated and settled, Mia nodded to Paolo, who uncorked the bottle of wine and poured some into each of their glasses.

"Ah," Mr. Masseria said, taking a deep, appreciative sniff. "Your uncle's special wine, no?"

"Yes," Mia said, pleased. "How did you guess?"

He waved a finger in the air as he took a sip. "He sends me big case every year for Christmas. No other wine has aroma like this." He fired off a trail of flowery praise in Sicilian.

She nodded to the spread in the middle of the table. "Please, help yourselves. The best of the best of my uncle's store."

Shrugging, Jake helped himself to bread, olives, salami, and cheese. He popped an olive into his mouth and chewed lazily, leaning back in his chair and crossing his legs as if this were a social call.

"So," he said between chomps, "where's your Jew daddy? Goldstein, right?"

"Goldberg," she corrected softly, though she was aware, as was everyone in the room, it had been an intentional slight. "Is this how you'd like to begin, Mr. Morelli? With disrespect?"

He grinned. "Just teasing you, toots."

"Jake," Mr. Masseria said disapprovingly, shaking his head. "Don't be insulting to our host."

It was time for her to establish control, as Don Catalano had instructed her. In matters of business, he'd told her time and again, control over the situation, big or small, was paramount. Should anyone suspect her control was slipping, she was done for.

She hadn't asked him to elaborate on what "done for" meant, precisely.

"Mr. Morelli," she began.

He reached out to pat her hand. "Jake. You call me Jake."

To withdraw her hand would be a sign of disrespect, so Mia clenched her jaw and gave him a patient smile. "Thank you. Jake. I appreciate you coming out here this evening, as I'm sure you have more pressing matters to attend to on a Tuesday night."

"I'd like *you* to be a pressing matter," he said with a grin.

"Morelli," Charlie snapped. "Let her fucking finish, already."

Still grinning, Jake lifted his hands in surrender and leaned back in his chair, his body angled toward her, and crossed one long leg over the other. "You got the floor, dollface."

Lengthy preamble, as Hyman had called it, was not going to work with a man like Jake Morelli. Neither would common courtesy, apparently. She folded her lips together and faced him head on.

"I have a business proposition for you," she said briskly. "I'll cut you into my liquor operation as a partner. You'll receive twenty percent—out of my share."

He blinked slowly and regarded her for several long seconds. Then he said, "*Your* operation?"

"I got a new buyer," she said. "It's a hot deal."

"Mm-hmm." He rubbed his forefinger beneath his bottom lip, his eyes narrowing slightly. "What kinda hot deal? Who's the buyer?"

*Here we go.* She wanted to look over her shoulder at Paolo, Bobby, and Joey, to make sure they were still there, but she kept her gaze on Jake.

"Owney Madden."

Charlie shifted slightly in his chair. Mr. Masseria looked up sharply from his glass of wine. Only Jake remained completely immobile. He didn't even blink.

She waited.

"Owney Madden," he finally said, drawing out the name. "You don't say. Fella owns the Cotton Club, right?"

Mia sighed softly. He was toying with her now, like a cat with his prey. "There's only one Owney Madden who matters in this city."

"Mmm." He tapped his chin, then unfolded his legs and leaned toward her. "I find that to be a funny coincidence. Because, see, *I* had a booze deal with Owney Madden."

"Not anymore," she said.

Finally, anger flared in his dark eyes. "Oh, no? Want to tell me how the fuck that came to be?"

"Jacopo," Mr. Masseria said in a soft, warning tone.

"Very simple," Mia replied. "You sold him the crap Moritz tried to pass off as Templeton. Mr. Madden made the mistake of not tasting it first. I just so happened to be rehearsing there, and Owney and I, we got to talking. He expressed interest in my product once he had assurances it was of the utmost quality."

"You had no right," Jake said, his voice low and dangerous. "You had no fucking right to steal my business out from under me like a no-good thief."

"It wasn't intentional," Mia said. "Hence the reason why we're sitting here right now. I figured you'd be put out—"

"Put out," Jake interrupted. "Put out? Yeah, you could say I'm a little fucking *put out*."

This time, Mr. Masseria laid a hand on his forearm and gave him a disapproving frown. "Settle yourself."

"As a gesture of goodwill and friendship," Mia said between her teeth, "I'm offering to make you my partner in this deal exclusively. Twenty percent in it for you."

Jake tilted his head back and laughed. "Twenty percent. He was *my* customer first."

Mia's patience cracked. "You can't possibly have thought one of the most prestigious and famous clubs in the city would've wanted that rubbing alcohol you sold them," she said sharply. "Once his patrons started dropping dead from whatever's in that garbage, it would have only been a matter of time before Mr. Madden came knocking on my door. And let's not forget, Mr. Morelli, you would have had no product had it not been for *mine* in the first place."

"Yours." He chuckled, the sound low and ugly. "Yours. That's rich, sweetie."

"Twenty percent," she repeated. "I suggest you take it before it expires, Mr. Morelli."

He fished a cigarette from his pocket and lit it. "Make it fifty, then we can negotiate."

Mia tilted her head. "I'm genuinely curious as to why you think I would *ever* offer you fifty percent."

He blew a stream of smoke just over her head. "Because I'm better off being your friend than not. And after the slight you just dealt me, my wounded feelings are worth at least fifty percent. And a blowjob, which I'm sure Madden had thrown into his deal, am I right?"

Instinct made Mia shoot her hand out to land on top of Charlie's the moment he lunged out of his seat. She lifted her other hand into the air without turning to stop the three men behind her as well, hearing the sharp rustle of suit material as they moved toward Jake.

"It's all right," she said softly to all of them.

Mr. Masseria shook his head. "Apologize, Jacopo."

"No, to hell with that," he replied, violently flicking ash off his cigarette. "She steals my customer and then insults me with a twenty-percent deal?"

"It's hardly an insult," she replied. "I call that being awfully generous."

He leaned toward her. "You got any idea what you're doing, little girl? Going up against a man like me? You need to stay on stages and prance around for the fellas like the little dick tease you are."

His voice was too low for the others to clearly make out, which was just as well—for him. Mia gave him a cold smile.

"I thought you wanted to be friends," she said. "It's not my fault you made a poor business decision, and it's also not my fault Mr. Madden happens to want quality liquor for his establishment. Less is it my fault that he wants *my* quality liquor. This is called business, Mr. Morelli. I'm sure there's plenty of poor folks and average joes who want your swill, but Mr. Madden isn't one of them. In light of the fact that he was your customer before he was mine, I decided to do the friendly thing and offer to cut you in. But you've made your feelings on that entirely clear. So I'll take your words to mean your 'no' is final."

Jake hesitated.

She'd boxed him into a corner, as she'd intended. He hadn't actually said no—he'd simply pissed and moaned about the way her deal had been orchestrated. Now, he'd have to either humiliate himself in front of the rest of the men by accepting her deal, or he'd be forced by pride into giving up twenty percent of a very handsome deal.

She gave him another second to weigh out the obvious dilemma, then placed her hand over his. It was time to place her bet.

"I'd be willing to make it fifty," she said, allowing just a touch of honey to creep into her voice, "but you'd have to do something for me in return."

Charlie gave her a sharp glance.

Jake glanced down at their hands. "That's a tall goddamn order, all things considered."

She used her thumb to stroke the back of his hand, once. "Once you hear my request, I doubt you'll think so."

"Then lay it on me, sister. I do so want us to get back to being the best of friends."

She didn't miss the slight note of interest in his voice as she leaned back in her seat, pulling her hand from his. "Today I attended a funeral. A young woman died last week. She was the daughter of a good friend of my uncle's. Do you know how she died?"

Jake lifted a shoulder. "Can't imagine."

"She overdosed," Mia replied. "On heroin. That she purchased in this neighborhood."

Mr. Masseria slowly turned his head toward Jake.

"She died calling out the word 'gems,'" Mia said, her voice growing softer with each word.

Jake said nothing, his eyes steady on hers.

"I tell you not to sell in this neighborhood," Mr. Masseria said. "Didn't I?"

Jake shrugged. "I don't recall. Did you?"

"You work for me," Masseria said coolly. "I hire you for protection for my deliveries. I make you a rich fellow, no? I got other interests in this neighborhood besides booze—and I got a valuable friendship with d'Abbruzzo and his family. You make me look bad, Jake." His voice turned cold. "I don't like to be made to look bad."

"Listen," Jake said in as reasonable a tone as Mia had ever heard. "I got a lot of business ventures. Deliveries. Protection. Booze. And, yeah, heroin. All due respect, Joe, but my business with you extends to delivery protection. You don't control where I do my other business. And neither does she."

"*She* is sitting right here," Mia said. "You can address me."

"Oh, sorry, sweetheart," he said. "See, broads ain't usually present in these kinds of situations unless they're pouring my drink." He patted his knee. "Maybe if you sit on my lap and feed me some olives, I'll stop forgetting you're here."

Behind her, Paolo grunted angrily.

"You wouldn't want me putting anything in your mouth, Mr. Morelli," she said. *Because I'd make sure you choked on it.* "We can sit here and squabble all night about who does what and where. What I'm offering you is simple: fifty percent of my deal with Owney Madden, and you'll stop selling drugs in this neighborhood."

"I should get fifty percent anyway," Jake said. "Since it was my deal to start with."

"Enough," Mr. Masseria said irritably. "She made you a fair deal. More than I would offer. Take the deal and be done with it."

"That's for me to decide," Jake said and pulled another cigarette from his silver monogrammed case. "'Cause I don't report to neither of you."

Mr. Masseria's face went a deep shade of red. Jake was toeing a very thin line.

Mia didn't know whether to be impressed or shocked by his impertinence. Then she recalled again what Hyman had told her at the showcase—Jake was rumored to be in Maranzano's pocket, where his real loyalty lay. And Masseria and Maranzano disliked each other.

"There are plenty of other places in this great, big city that have people who want heroin," she said flatly. "This is not one of them. This is a community of families. Of elderly, of hardworking people, of young children just trying to get by. Go find the socialites in Manhattan to sell to. You could sell at the Cotton Club."

"You want a little?" Jake leered at her. "'Cause it would sure mellow you out, hon. You ever felt ecstasy before?" He glanced at Charlie, then shrugged. "No, probably not. I'll cut you a real swell deal."

"Why are you so insistent on this neighborhood?" she asked. "Business has to be much better elsewhere."

"Maybe I just like getting under your skin," he said with a smirk.

"You're giving yourself too much credit."

"I don't think I am."

"Now you're just wasting my time," she said. "I made you a deal. I'm waiting on an answer."

"It ain't a deal when you're putting even more limitations on my business," Jake said. "And I ain't decided yet."

"Then you should know this deal will expire the moment you walk out the door."

"What if I wanna sleep on it?"

"I'm afraid that's not an option."

He tilted his head. "What happens if I accept your first offer and refuse the second?"

She stared at him in disbelief. "Selling heroin in this neighborhood means more to you than fifty percent of a lucrative liquor deal?"

The corners of his mouth turned down as he shrugged. "I just wanna know what happens, is all."

"It's fifty percent and no drugs in this neighborhood, period," she said flatly. "That's the deal."

"Or...?" He smiled patronizingly at her.

Her patience reached its breaking point, and she spoke the first words that bubbled up her throat. "Or you're asking for a war."

The entire room went silent. She felt the heat from the stares of Mr. Masseria and Charlie, but did not spare them a glance, keeping her gaze steadily on Jake.

Internally, she was kicking herself. *Goddamn Scalisi temper.*

"Yeah?" he said. "You and what army?"

She gave him a wintery smile, all the while asking herself the same question.

He shook his head. "I'll forgive you for those words. Because I know you're in over your head, threatening me like that, and you got a bad temper," he said. "But the next man might not be so nice to you. So you'd do well to watch your mouth."

"Would I?"

"You need to remember something. You're a woman, doll-face. A gorgeous one I'd love to ride like a Kentucky Oaks filly, but a woman nonetheless. You ain't your brother, whatever he used to be. And he's dead now."

*You ain't your brother, whatever he used to be.*

The familiar words rushed back to her, spoken by a different man, in a different time, when she had been a different girl. And that night, the night she'd first heard those words, she'd set herself on an irrevocable path.

"A man once said those exact words about my brother to me," she said. "Do you know what became of him, Mr. Morelli?"

Jake said nothing, just lifted an eyebrow.

"I had him killed."

His eyes gleamed at her, recognizing the threat even as the expression in them turned mocking. He cocked his head with false concern. "Was he your first?"

"Yes," she said. "But not my last."

"Baby, I killed my first man when I was half your age. I've lost count since. It's cute, you trying to scare me."

"You're speaking awfully loudly, Mr. Morelli," Mia said. "Are you feeling all right?"

He sucked down then blew out an angry stream of smoke, stubbed his cigarette out right on the table, and stood up. Behind her, Mia felt the air move again.

"Look, I came here out of respect for you, Joe," Jake snapped. "This broad's threatened me twice in the same breath, and I'm the asshole, right? You just gonna sit there and let her say this shit?"

He seemed rather excited, Mia noted, pleased. She had gotten to him after all.

"Jake, sit." Charlie, annoyed, pointed at the chair Jake had just vacated. "Now you're just being a jerkoff. *Sit.*"

Jake hesitated a moment before taking his seat.

"You both say rude things, you both make insult, now you both make truce," Mr. Masseria said firmly.

"Sure," Mia said. "The truce is, I never see him or hear about his product in this neighborhood again."

"That ain't no truce," Jake said. "What happened to fifty percent?"

"Off the table."

"Since when?"

"Since you decided to bring my brother into this," she replied.

"That ain't how you do business, sweetie," he said menacingly. "Besides, you can't enforce where I sell my product. You need men for that. Just like you need men for your little war." He waved a dismissive hand to the three behind her. "More than them yahoos."

"You don't know what I've got," Mia said, but she was bluffing. He knew it, too, and that meant she needed to work on her poker face. *Nick would be disappointed.*

"Just face it—you're gonna see me around here whether you

want to or not. I got protection business around here. I need to make my collections. Make sure everything's *safe*."

She decided right then and there that protection business would come to an end as soon as she could make it so.

"This is getting out of hand." Charlie shook his head and looked at Mia. "I know he insulted Nick, but think business for a second. Put the deal back on the table. Fifty percent of the Madden deal, and he don't sell heroin here. Right, Morelli?"

Jake folded his arms. "I want her to offer it to me."

Charlie nudged her foot with his under the table.

Mia swallowed hard. "Fifty percent of my deal with Madden," she ground out. "Absolutely no heroin in this neighborhood anymore."

He glanced down at the table, where it smoldered from his cigarette. Then he looked up, and smiled. "I accept, partner."

Mia looked him in the eye. "I'm willing to forget about all your insults toward me this evening, but if you renege on this deal in any way, I promise you I'll make you answer for each and every one."

"It gets me hot when you talk to me like that," he murmured under his breath so only she could hear.

She glared at him.

He grinned and bit his lower lip. "Fine. By the way—speaking of protection." He made a big show of looking around. "Your uncle's shop here need protecting? 'Cause the neighborhood's been a little dangerous lately, you know."

"This store already under *my* protection," Mr. Masseria cut in, his tone deep and threatening. "Why you think I'm here? It is in your best interest not to overstep what I've allowed you to do. Because I *do* have an army, Jacopo."

Jake shrugged and glanced away under Mr. Masseria's penetrating stare. "I didn't mean nothing by it. Lookit, in the interest of new partnerships, I got a booze deal now. My own thing. Don't worry, I ain't selling in your territories," he added, glancing at Charlie. "But I could use some warehouse space." He flicked his head at Mia. "What do you say to selling me some space, partner? I'd pay you a good rate. I just secured fifty percent in a great deal."

She fixed him with a stony stare. "You must be joking."

He lifted his hands. "Right hand to God Himself, I'm being serious. C'mon, don't be so selfish with all that space. I'll pay you. In fact, take six months in advance outta my cut. How do you like that?"

"I don't," she said flatly. "I don't care if you pay me six *years* in advance. The answer is no."

A storm passed over his face. "Why?"

"I think it's fairly obvious why."

"What the hell's a guy supposed to do?" he demanded.

*Go jump off the Empire State Building.* "That's entirely your problem, Mr. Morelli. We have one business transaction, and it doesn't include warehouse space."

"Thought we're all *paesan* here."

"You thought wrong," Mia said. Then she shrugged. "I'm told Frankie Yale's got warehouse space in Brooklyn. Maybe you should try talking to him."

He glowered at her. "I conduct my business in Manhattan. I need space *here*."

"Then perhaps you should conduct your business in Brooklyn."

"I *can't* conduct business in Brooklyn—that's Frankie's territory," he growled.

Mia smiled. "That's right. Darn it all."

"Mia," Mr. Masseria said. "Don't be unreasonable."

"I'm not being unreasonable," she said. "The fact of the matter is simply that it's my shop. I don't have the room to accommodate any more product. My brother's operation comes first. Then, Mr. Masseria, as you have a standing agreement with Mr. Goldberg, and that agreement was written into my contract when I took over the shop. And that's all."

"That's a load of shit," Jake said. "You got room. Kindly remember *I* was the one who unloaded all those crates for Mr. Masseria. I'm intimately acquainted with your storage space, and you got it, especially with how fast rye moves in and out of that place. You can make room for mine." He hesitated. "Cut my share back to twenty percent, and let me have a corner." After another long pause, he added, "*Please*."

That word hung over the table in the silence that stretched out, as though it had caught everyone else off guard, as well as Mia.

She studied him. He was a handsome young man, as handsome as Charlie, with an irreverence she might have once found immensely appealing. He was the kind of man who would stand up to her stubbornness and her smart mouth, and under different circumstances, she might rather have liked that.

But he was also a man who didn't care about poisoning people, who didn't care about loyalty or honor, and who would, she was certain, put a knife in her back the moment she took her eyes off him.

His dark eyes bored into hers as her gaze went over every inch of his face, the humility in the last word he'd spoke still thick and heavy in the air. She knew what that *please* must have cost him, especially in front of men like Mr. Masseria and Charlie—a good chunk out of his pride. It would have been a hard word to say to another man in front of other men, but he'd said it to her—a woman, in front of one of the most powerful men in New York, if not *the* most powerful man in New York.

And now, everyone waited for her answer.

She thought about what Don Catalano would have done in this situation. She thought about what Nick might have done.

Both men would likely have weighed the cost of doing business with a man like Jake Morelli against what he was offering— agreeing to her first offer of twenty percent of the Madden deal, *and* she'd still get her way of him not selling drugs in Little Italy. All she had to do was cough up a corner of her warehouse.

Her godfather, her brother, and probably every man in this room right now would have made the deal, and then they would have hired extra men they trusted to keep a very close eye on

Jake. But they *would* have made the deal, and profited handsomely from it.

That was what she should do.

She lowered her eyes to the still-burning mark in her uncle's table made by Jake's cigarette. Made by *him*, as a sign of disrespect. The same disrespect he'd shown her from the moment he'd sat down at her table.

Then she looked him in the eye.

"Thank you for the generous offer. My answer is no. And that no is final."

Every pair of eyes swung toward her.

Jake stared at her, his mouth setting into a tight line. "That's it, then? That's how you're gonna be?"

"I don't understand which part of the word 'no' you struggle with, Mr. Morelli." Mia stood up from the table, and Charlie and Mr. Masseria followed suit.

Jake remained in his chair, glaring up at her.

She tilted her head. "Mr. Madden will receive his first shipment in a few days. Once I receive payment, I'll have your fifty percent couriered over to you. In return, you'll no longer deal heroin here." She paused, giving him a quick onceover. "Good luck in all your endeavors, as they no longer conflict with mine." She stuck out her hand.

Jake looked at her hand, draining his glass of wine.

"I know I'm just a woman and new to business," she said softly, "but I believe it's customary to shake someone's hand when you make a deal."

"Shake her hand, Jacopo."

Jake slammed his empty glass on the table and stood to his full height, several inches over her. He slowly grasped her hand in his and held it tight, giving it a couple of hard shakes. Then he jerked her against his chest.

"I sure hope you're as smart as you think you are," he whispered.

One side of Mia's mouth curled up into a sneer as she yanked her hand from his. "I do so hope that we can go back to being the best of friends now. Isn't that what you said you wanted?"

He backed away, nodding slowly. He glanced at Mr. Masseria and Charlie. "Thanks for a pleasant evening, gents. I'll see myself out."

He strode to the coatrack by the door and put on his hat. With a long, backward look at Mia, he strolled out the door, whistling.

"Charlie," Mr. Masseria said, snapping his fingers. "Come. We got other business tonight." He took Mia's hand and kissed it. "I hope the arrangements tonight are satisfactory. It seems the best we can do with a fellow like that." He shrugged. "Thank your aunt and uncle for us, please."

"I will," she said.

She watched with disappointment as Charlie started to follow Mr. Masseria to the door. Was that part of the scar on his palm? Being at Mr. Masseria's beck and call, answering his every order as though he were still in the military?

Charlie put on his hat, said a few soft words to Mr. Masseria, who nodded and slipped outside, then doubled back to Mia.

"I'm sorry," he said, and she wasn't sure exactly what he was apologizing for. "You're going to need to watch out for Morelli."

"I guess so."

"Very closely, now." He leaned toward her, and her heart ached too much to let her pride push him away. She let him kiss her cheek gently, squeezing her eyes shut and wishing they were alone.

When he pulled back, he swallowed several times, taking one of her hands in his. "Can we—can we talk? Soon?"

"I don't know, Charlie." His face fell, and her heart tumbled down after. "It's a busy week. Rehearsals. The load on Friday. Saturday's opening night, you know."

"I'll be there with bells on," he promised, then gave her a crooked smile. "Unless you told the bouncer to kick me out if he sees me."

"No," she replied. "Of course not."

He sighed and nodded, toyed with her fingers for another moment, then dropped her hand. When he raised his eyes to hers, there was a look of worry in them. "Maybe you should've given him warehouse space, Mia. He's unpredictable. Dangerous."

She just gave him what she hoped was a reassuring smile. "It'll be all right. When he gets his money, he'll forget all about that."

*I hope.*

# PART II

# CHAPTER TWELVE

"Over there," Mia said on Friday night, pointing to a corner of the warehouse beneath her shop. "Stack them. We got nearly a hundred crates coming in tonight, so make some space."

The two young men Charlie had sent over nodded and began pushing crates around and stacking them in the area she'd ordered, grunting from the effort of it. She wrapped her arms around herself from the chill floating in from outside, where a light rain fell.

The days since her failed meeting with Jake Morelli had seemed to stretch on forever. Between rehearsals, she had upheld her promises to Signora Cancio and the other families who had reached out for help at the funeral reception. She'd spent a great deal of money, giving to them what she could to help lessen the burden of simply trying to *live*. But helping them made her happy. The money she doled out would, she hoped, improve the quality of their lives, even if that meant they didn't have to worry about rent or electricity for six months.

The alley behind the shop was going to be rather crowded shortly. Trucks were arriving from Iowa with crates of pure rye whiskey, and even more trucks belonging to Frankie Yale would arrive to load up a number of them to take over the border.

More trucks bearing newly cut batches of Templeton from a still outside Atlantic City would be dropping off a load as well.

She'd made sure she was early so she could review her ledger and ensure everyone was paid accordingly. Hyman would not be present tonight, as he was seeing to final preparations for the club's grand opening the following night.

"Must you be there?" he'd asked her at rehearsals this afternoon, with a wide smile that relayed his severe annoyance. "I can't stress to you enough how important tomorrow night is. You should be home resting. If you are anything less than bright-eyed and bushy-tailed tomorrow night, I shall be very put out with you. *Very* put out."

"Hyman," she'd replied, patting his shoulder. "You got nothing to worry about."

"If only that were true, Miss Scalisi."

She liked to imagine he knew better than to try to tell her to do otherwise.

The previous night, she'd sent her first official delivery to Owney Madden as his supplier. He was nearly out of the rye from the ten crates she'd gifted him last week, to her surprise, and he'd come back to order eighty more from her. Eighty crates at three hundred dollars apiece—twenty-four grand, just like that.

The money had been brought back to her by a young driver handpicked by Charlie. Mia had discreetly checked afterward and found not a cent missing. Had there been any money missing, she would have been surprised at his audacity but not at the thievery. Then what would she have to do? It wasn't a situation she wanted to deal with, though she knew, at some point, theft was to be expected.

She'd divvied up the money accordingly, paying first her team of fifteen drivers—a handsome one hundred dollars apiece. They were arguably the most important cogs in the wheel, since they delivered and protected the shipments, and if they were hijacked, how much money she paid them determined whether or not they would fight to keep the load and her loyalty.

Next, she subtracted Will's percentage, which included padding for his supply expenditure. She would have put Bobby or Joey on a train to Templeton to make the delivery, since she trusted the mail service not at all, but Will was on his way to New York now for Mia's debut the following night. He'd insisted on coming to see her, stating in his never-loquacious manner that it had been too long and he wanted to support her. It pleased her that he'd go to all the trouble, and she took pride in being able to hand him his cut in person.

That left almost eighteen thousand dollars to split four ways between her, Hyman, Charlie, and Moritz. From her share, she'd paid Bobby and Joey each five hundred dollars, then grudgingly divvied her remaining portion in half, which she'd had Joey deliver to Gems this morning.

All that work, and she had not even two thousand dollars to show for it. Twenty-four grand went fast. At least new orders were coming in from different directions each day, and Owney had promised her he'd buy from her each week. Moreover, she was buying the safety of her neighborhood, and she hoped it would be money well spent.

She'd met with Signora Cancio on Tuesday, and as promised, had offered her help the best way she knew how. Dollars. Signora Cancio had been so moved by the money Mia had given her to cover her expenses for the next several months, she'd dropped to her knees, pledged her undying loyalty, and kissed Mia's hands over and over, until Mia, thoroughly embarrassed, begged her to stand. She'd started her new role as Trudy's assistant at the shop that morning.

"Mia, look alive."

The sharp voice brought her out of her reverie, and she glanced up as Moritz strode toward her from the front of the shop just as the rumble of truck engines met her ears.

"Mind on other things?" he asked as he passed her to open the back door.

"Money," she replied.

He smirked. "Soon, that'll be all you think of."

Curious, how he made that sound like a good thing.

"Did your cousin get settled in all right?" Moritz went on as she fell into step beside him.

"Yes." Raquel had arrived early that afternoon, brimming with excitement. As they'd led her from the dock, Mia had been amused at the way her head swiveled this way and that as she soaked in all the sights of New York. So vastly different from Catania. "She had a big afternoon, sightseeing, lunch. I took her to some fine shops to get some new clothes. And now she's resting." She'd moved out of the suite she and Gloria had shared to her own room on the other side of them. It was adjoined, so she still felt close by. Emilia had wanted to be close to her "*zia*," and the arrangement suited Mia's need for privacy.

"That's fine," Moritz said with a nod and smile. "I hope she enjoys life here. Will she be at your debut tomorrow night?"

He was being suspiciously friendly. "Yes, and she couldn't be more excited. We want to take her out for a real night on the town."

"I'm sure she'll find it thrilling."

At the door, Mia peeked out into the alley. Charlie shouted directions to the drivers and unloaders. "Who're these men?"

"From the still outside Atlantic City," Moritz replied. "With the cut batches."

She glanced at Moritz. "Do I need to be concerned?"

He sighed. "Look, Mia, I think we got off on the wrong foot ever since you came home. For my part in that, I apologize. I know how important this operation is to you, and it's more than just money. I've never lacked in ambition, and it became easier and easier to cut corners. The tension between us lately has been unpleasant, and I do hope we can start over. What do you say?"

His boyishly handsome face, round with youth, was open, and his large brown eyes were sincere behind his eyeglasses. He offered a small smile as well as his hand.

Moritz Schapiro did not offer apologies easily, so Mia reached for his hand. "Let's bury the hatchet, then, Morrie."

His smile grew. "That's swell. And just to prove it to you, I want you to pick any crate at random, and select any bottle inside. You'll see I'm a man of my word."

Mia lifted her eyebrows, but pointed at a young man carrying a crate into the shop. "You."

He stopped and looked at Moritz, who nodded. "Go ahead. Open it for Miss Scalisi."

Shrugging, the young man lowered the crate and flicked open a pocket knife. He jimmied the lid open, then looked up at Mia. "What's your fancy?"

She selected a random bottle from a lower corner of the crate, and the young man pulled it out, sliced open the seal, pulled the cork out, then offered it to her.

Mia took the bottle and sniffed it. The sharp, familiar aroma of the rye whiskey she remembered wafted up her nose. Then she took a sip, carefully swishing the liquor around her mouth to examine the taste.

It could kick a person's teeth in, but the flavor was distinctive and...*good*.

She looked at Moritz and smiled.

He looked pleased with himself as he directed the young man to continue his task. "I wanted to thank you also for the timely delivery of my cut from the Madden deal this morning. I take it everything went smoothly?"

Mia set the bottle on a nearby table. "Owney's a seasoned businessman, so that certainly helps."

"Certainly." Moritz adjusted his eyeglasses. "I understand Mr. Morelli received his money as well."

Instantly, her hackles rose. She put her hands on her hips and fixed him with a steady stare.

Moritz lifted his hands. "I mean no offense, Mia. But you're new to running deals yourself."

"So you feel the need to father me and breathe down my neck?"

He smiled politely, but she felt their old tension simmer and bubble beneath the surface. "I'm still a partner and an investor in this operation, and all related business deals and transactions," he said stiffly. "As such, I believe I'm entitled to ask questions."

"I believe Hyman told you to mind your potatoes," Mia replied. "And let me handle this. Besides, you got your money, didn't you?"

"Mr. Goldberg has a fatherly fondness for you I believe affects his critical thinking at times," Moritz said. "You're not ready to lead a deal on your own—as evidenced simply by the fact that you interfered in another man's deal and stole it for your own."

Mia stared at him in disbelief. "You gotta be kidding me."

"I've never been accused of having much of a sense of humor."

Her temper shot to the top of her head, fiery hot, as though a switch had flipped. For the first time, she understood why her brother had always had a rep for being a hothead. She'd prided herself on being the cooler of them, but matters of business could be *so* very aggravating.

Mia forced herself to draw in a deep breath before she opened her mouth again. "I'd like to invite you down off your high horse. You act as though this sort of business has any rules of polite engagement, Morrie. We aren't some blue-collar, working stiffs. This is a cutthroat business and anyone—any *man* —would have done what I did in an instant, and they likely wouldn't have tried to negotiate peace by cutting in the man they *stole* from. You've got a lot of nerve acting this self-righteous when I know you've done the same or worse."

"You're missing the point," he said impatiently. "I don't make a habit of crossing men like *Morelli*. He's half-crazy, and that's the good half. You have no idea what you did, Mia. You can't do something like that to a man like him and expect there to be no repercussions."

Mia folded her arms. "Aren't you supposed to be on my side?"

He shook his head in frustration. "This isn't about sides, Mia!" His raised voice drew the curious stares of the men still toting in crates. Moritz lowered his voice. "This is about common business sense, which you're still developing. You should have consulted with me and Charlie first."

"And why's that?"

"So we could prevent you from making irresponsible, impetuous decisions and potentially putting us all at risk."

"How do you know Jake got his money?"

The question seemed to catch Moritz off guard. He regarded her uncertainly. "Beg pardon?"

"How," she said, knowing full well he'd heard her the first time, "did you know Jake got his money from me?"

Moritz straightened his bowtie. "He…informed me. When he stopped by my poker room this afternoon."

"Oh?"

"He likes cards, Mia. Like most men in this city."

"A frequent patron of yours, is he?"

"Just what are you driving at?"

"I had no idea you and he were so very close."

He frowned. "I don't like your tone."

At that moment, a young crewmember stuck his head in the doorway. "Sorry to interrupt, Mr. Schapiro, Miss Scalisi, but the trucks with the load for Mr. Yale are here. If it's all the same to you, can we just stack the crates in the alley? It seems an awful lot of work to tote them in here then back out again. Mr. Yale's due any moment, and we gotta move their trucks to make room for his."

"Yes," Mia said before Moritz could. "That's fine, but don't let the crates get too wet."

"Oh, they won't get wet at all," he replied confidently. "We got tarps to cover 'em with."

"Swell," she said. "What was your name again?"

The young man, hardly more than a boy, flushed pink, his freckles standing out alarmingly on his skin. "Paul, ma'am. Paulie. Whatever you like."

"Paulie it is. You get Mr. Yale loaded up and on the road

inside thirty minutes, you can come see me about a bonus. All of you."

Paulie grinned. "Yes, ma'am!" He ducked back out into the alley, and Mia could hear his shouting voice echoing off the brick walls.

"Wasting money again, Mia?" Moritz sighed. "Those boys could get Frankie Yale loaded inside twenty minutes without breaking a sweat."

Mia recorked the bottle of rye. Perhaps Fred, patrolling out front, would like to take it home. "Yeah, thanks, I figured that."

"Then why do you insist on throwing your money around so carelessly?"

She was getting awfully tired of his constant criticizing. It wasn't that she couldn't take advice—she found advice, solicited or otherwise, tremendously helpful. But Moritz delivered his with a nasty air, a lilt in his voice that suggested everything she did was of the utmost stupidity.

"Because I want those boys to look at me and see something to be loyal to." The sharp edge in her tone was plain. "Because I want them to know I serve a job well done properly. Because I want them to work *harder* for me. You call it buying loyalty. I call it buying insurance."

"Everything all right in here?" a voice from the doorway asked.

Mia and Moritz turned to see Charlie lingering in the doorway, drops of water from the rain sliding off the tilted brim of his hat. His dark eyes flicked between them.

"Fine," Moritz said, beating her to the punch this time. "Just swell. I was trying to find out why Mia pulled the move with Morelli that she did. And trying to impress upon her how stupid it was."

Her temper burst through its carefully lashed restraints. She slammed the bottle back onto the table. "You got something to say to me or what, Morrie?"

He smiled. "I think I've just said it."

"No." Mia shook her head as she stepped closer to him.

"You've been talking around it. Ever since this whole thing started, ever since Nick died. So spill it. I'm letting you have your say, free and open, right here, right now. Go ahead." She lifted her chin, meeting his piercing gaze head on.

He tilted his head, eyes tightening at their corners. "Fine. You asked for it, sweetheart. I think you're in well over your head. I think you have no idea what you're doing. I think you should just worry about your business arrangement with Hyman, and tend to the shop, and relinquish all control of the bootlegging to those of us who actually know what we're doing. Do you have *any* idea how much money we made while you were away? Have you checked your bank account lately? I personally made sure to hand-deliver your cut of the profit to Hyman every single week to deposit into your account. You can still get paid for doing none of this work. And as far as your stance on heroin—I find it unimaginably foolish."

"Yeah, I'm sure you do," she shot back. "That's because you got no sense of loyalty to the community. You grew up in the Lower East Side, too, Morrie. You grew up poor like we all did. Don't you care about the people you left behind?"

"That's what leaving something behind means. You don't look back."

"I feel sorry for you," she said.

He grunted. "Please don't. You'd rather stand on a hypocritical pedestal and preach about how terrible the big, bad drug is, all the while peddling another version of it to anyone with money to buy it—you've seen the drunks around this city, haven't you? Do you think any of them benefit from yet another sip? But when it comes to a product that has unfathomable earning potential, you'd rather let your emotions do the deciding instead of your rational brain. Then, you go and do a thing like what you did with Morelli. You have no idea what sort of man he really is, or what can happen to us now. You made a very poor choice where he's concerned. And *that* is why you're ill-equipped to be a real part of this, let alone lead anything."

His words hovered in the air for a long, timeless moment. A

queer numbness befell her as she heard them, over and over, in her mind. Was she hurt, or enraged? She had no idea, so she felt nothing at all.

*And besides,* a voice in her head whispered, *is he wrong?*

Deeper than the surface cuts his words made was the sinister realization that accompanied them. She no longer had Moritz's support. He'd made that clear. He was a partner in Nick's business, but he did not support her or believe in her.

He might as well have been an enemy.

Charlie was the first to speak. "Morrie, that ain't fair."

Moritz flashed him a scathing look. "Says the man who's in love with her. Listen, Charlie, I've been meaning to ask you where *your* common sense has gone lately, too."

"I'd be real careful, I was you."

"Would you?" Moritz shook his head and reached for his hat. Then he looked at Mia. "I've had my say, Miss Scalisi, as you invited me to do. I'm going to go see if the boys need a hand." He put on his hat and brushed past Charlie into the alley.

"He's right, you know," she said in the silence that followed his departure.

Charlie frowned and walked toward her. "You off your nut? He's just being a jerk."

She gave him an exasperated look. "Come on, Charlie."

He released a long breath. "Look. I think you're a lot like Nick in that you know good business when you hear it, and you act fast. Sometimes that ain't the best way to go about things. But that doesn't mean it won't work out."

She flung her arms out to the side. "What am I *doing* here, Charlie? I'm a showgirl, for Christ's sake. I'm not a gangster or a bootlegger or even a decent businesswoman. I'm just Nick Scalisi's sister."

"Bullshit. You're just as smart as Nick ever was—smarter. What you did with Owney Madden would have made him *proud.*"

"But the fallout," Mia said. "He would've thought about that first. I didn't think about it until Hyman pointed it out."

Charlie shook his head. "That's because he's been at this game for a long time. He'd know what to anticipate because he had years and years of experience with this. You've had, what? A few months altogether, considering you were in Sicily for a long time. Yeah, Morelli's fucking crazy and unpredictable, but he's not a strategist. He wants money more than anything. The deal you worked out with him at the store the other night? That *was* good business. Nick would never have been so fair."

"You said I should've let him have storage space, too."

"I think it would have been a show of good faith, and he would've seen he was getting more than he was giving up," Charlie conceded, "but I doubt he cares too much about that since he's seen that you'll deliver his money in a timely manner. Again—he wants money, Mia, not a war."

"Would Nick have sold him warehouse space?"

Charlie sighed impatiently. "Listen, do you know how many times Nick ever fucked up in business? Plenty. You never heard about those times, but there were plenty of meetings we left where he regretted something he did or didn't say, did or didn't offer. Sometimes, those things came back to bite him in the ass, sometimes they didn't. He learned from them all."

Before she could respond, Fred called to her from the front of the store.

"Miss Scalisi, some fella out here's asking for ya. It's all right, Mr. Scarpa and I'll be right there."

"I'm coming," she called back, then looked at Charlie. "I did hear about one of those times." She watched understanding and realization dawn in his eyes. "And he didn't learn from all of them. 'Cause he's dead now."

She turned away and walked to the front of the store. Now her words hovered in the air, dreadful and heavy.

Fred was outside on the sidewalk and Paolo waited for her near the door he held open. A deep crease formed between his eyebrows as he looked at her, and he gave her a slight shake of his head.

He was not pleased.

He followed her outside, close on her heels, his head and eyes swerving side to side. At the curb, a black car idled, the driver chatting with Fred. She couldn't make him out.

Fred turned to her. "He, er, wants to buy a bottle of the good stuff."

Mia directed her stare and her reply to the driver, concealed in the shadows of his car. "I don't sell *perfume* to people I don't know. That's the only good stuff we sell here."

"Aw, come on, toots," came the deep voice from the car. "I know what's really going on here. Hell, I see them trucks in the alley."

"I sell a lot of perfume." Mia folded her arms. "You want some, you'll have to come back another time. Shop's closed, mac."

"Even for a hundred clams?" A hand snaked out of the window. A folded C-note was pinched between his index and middle finger. "Come on. I know you got the real good stuff in here. Best in the city. The pure stuff."

She snorted. "You think I'm a rube or something? Even prohis aren't as bad as this. Or are you a rookie on the Bureau? Either way, get lost."

A low peal of laughter drifted over the curb to her. "Nah. I ain't no prohi. Fine. If a hundred bucks ain't good enough, maybe this will be."

Her body sensed it before her mind could understand, and she was already throwing herself to the side even as Paolo's arms snaked around her waist to jerk her backward into the store.

"Fred!" she screamed. "*Move*! Move, Fred!"

But it was too late.

Bullets ripped through the air. Air whooshed out of her as she hit the floor hard, Paolo atop her. He was surprisingly strong, and even as she tried and failed to pull air into her shocked lungs, he was already dragging her backward, farther into the store and under cover. At the same time, he drew his pistol with the speed of lightning and emptied it into the car. But he hadn't quite been fast enough, as the car pulled off with a scream of tires.

An odd, muted grunt came from his throat as he dropped his pistol and held her head in his hands, looking her over with alarm in his eyes.

Finally, her lungs unlocked and she sucked in a whistling, gasping breath. "I'm fine," she choked, sitting up. "Fred?"

Paolo looked over his shoulder. He wouldn't meet her eyes as he shook his head.

Charlie and a handful of men burst through the door that separated the front of the store from the back. "What the fuck was that?" he bellowed, his gun drawn. All of them had guns, Mia realized.

His dark eyes pinned on her where she remained on the floor. "Mia—Jesus Christ—"

"Help me up," she said to Paolo, and he pulled her to her feet. Immediately she stepped around him and hurried to the door.

"No, Mia!"

Outside, she swiveled her head in both directions. Whoever that had been was long gone. There weren't any other cars on the street, not even parked, empty ones.

Behind her, Charlie tugged her elbow. "You can't just go running around like that," he said harshly. "What the fuck happened?"

But she couldn't answer him as her gaze drifted down to the man sprawled on the sidewalk on his back, his eyes still wide and open. Unseeing.

*Fred.*

He was dead.

She knelt beside him, resting a hand on his forehead as she surveyed the damage. His chest was riddled with bullet holes, and all of them oozed. It reminded her so much of—of—

*She knelt next to her brother's body, then sat down. She pulled his upper body up into her arms and, with a shaking hand, turned his face toward hers. It was still, pale, his eyes half open and glazed over, staring unseeing at something beyond her shoulder. Blood soaked his entire front and most of the lower half of his face. She felt warmth and wetness against her legs where his back was pressed and knew it was his blood, too.*

*He was gone.*

With a hand that shook, Mia gently closed Fred's eyes as an invisible iron vise closed around her throat. He'd been a good man. A crooked cop on the take, but he hadn't always been that way. *She* had corrupted him. He'd been a hardworking man who'd just wanted to provide for himself and his wife the best he could.

And now, another widow had been made.

"I'm sorry," she whispered to him, settling her hand on his pale, waxy forehead. "I'm so very sorry."

Charlie knelt beside her. "Mia," he said in a gentle voice. "We have to move his body."

"His wife deserves to bury her husband."

"We'll work all that out," he said, touching her shoulder. "But we gotta move him before we get our people on the police force involved. It's real bad for business if it gets out he was killed here, in front of your shop."

She wanted to argue, though she had no idea why or what she'd accomplish. Instead, she just nodded mutely and rose on legs that trembled slightly.

Charlie snapped his fingers and four men came forward. In a matter of minutes, Fred's body had been carried off and loaded into one of the empty trucks, and one of the men used a tarp and a few bottles of liquor to wash away the blood.

She stared at the spot where Fred had been lying. Where he'd fallen. Where he'd died.

It was as though nothing had happened at all.

"Damage to the storefront's not so bad, actually," Moritz said from behind her.

She turned to look at him. She hadn't even realized he'd come outside. He stood with his hands in his pockets, studying the places where stray bullets had peppered the glass.

"I know someone who can fix this. I'll send him over first

thing in the morning. It'll be good as new before the shop opens."

"Thank you," she said in a dull voice.

"Of course." He opened the door and gestured her inside. As she passed, he gently caught her wrist. "*This…*is what you've signed up for." His voice was almost kind, understanding.

And once again, he was right.

She stepped inside the shop. All the warmth had gone out of it. "I want weekly payments set up to be delivered to Fred's widow. All of their expenses covered plus a little extra."

"And just where is that money—"

Mia whirled around. "I don't give a shit where it comes from, Morrie, just *make it goddamn happen!*"

Without waiting for his reply, she turned on her heel and stalked into the back room. There, she found Charlie talking to Frankie Yale. They turned as she approached, and she hoped she didn't look nearly as rattled as she felt.

Frankie flicked his chin at her. "You all right?"

"Fine." She hoped she sounded convincing.

"You oughtta go home," Charlie said quietly but firmly. "We're about done here, anyway."

"Your boys got me loaded up in no time at all," Frankie added. "Good boys. I just hung around in case things got hot. And Charlie's right—you need to go home and tend to yourself."

"Make sure the boys get paid a little extra," Mia said to Charlie. "I promised them."

He nodded. "Don't sweat it. I'll make sure they know it was you took care of them."

She hesitated, glancing over her shoulder. "Fred— The shop—"

Charlie took her hand. "I got it under control, Mia. I promise. Let Paolo take you home."

Feeling a little bewildered and heartsick, Mia bid them goodnight and followed Paolo out the back door, down the alley, and across the street to where her black Ford was parked. He helped her inside, then slid behind the wheel.

It occurred to her as they drove toward the Murray Hill Hotel that no one had even questioned who had done the shooting tonight. Perhaps they'd been distracted with more immediate matters. Perhaps, like her, they'd been in shock. Or perhaps, she thought as her shock faded, it was obvious who had done it.

"Apparently, I've underestimated Mr. Morelli," she said to Paolo.

That wouldn't happen again.

# CHAPTER THIRTEEN

S he didn't sleep that night.

But when dawn came and she still lay on her side, staring out the window, her mind wasn't on her debut at The Divine that night. It wasn't on how tired she felt. She wasn't worried about finding the energy to make it through the night, nor did she feel even a little trepidation at Hyman seeing her with the bags under her eyes.

She wasn't dwelling on the fear that someone had very well tried to end her life last night. When she closed her eyes, she saw the snub nose of the revolver pointing at her, over and over. She heard the crack of the shot, and she felt the phantom searing burn of the bullet tearing through the flesh of her body.

Which would have happened, had it not been for Paolo pulling her out of the way.

Yet, she was numb to the realization that she could have been killed. Someone had tried to kill her before. She was well acquainted with that fear, but she could not give herself over to it now.

Her mind was on Fred's widow.

In the short time she'd known him, he'd referenced his wife, Dolores, many times. Dolores, to whom he'd been married nearly twenty years by now. Dolores, who had surely already been alerted of her husband's fate. No children to take care of her. Dolores, by herself. Alone.

Mia knew the feeling.

How had Dolores spent her sleepless night? Had she screamed her anguish, or had she mourned silently? Had she known what her husband was up to or what had led him to his death? Had she been prepared for this?

*No. This is never something you can prepare for.*

Eyes burning with exhaustion, she walked out of her bedroom. Now that she'd moved into a smaller suite by herself, she didn't have to worry about waking Gloria or Raquel. Gloria's door was still closed. She picked up the telephone where it rested on a sleek side table and rang Charlie.

"You know what time it is?" he said by way of greeting, his voice harsh and sleepy.

"I don't care," she replied.

"Oh, Mia." His tone changed. "Sorry. Why aren't you sleeping still?"

"Couldn't sleep at all," she said. "Listen, I need you to do something for me. I'd ask Morrie, but…"

"Yeah, I got it. What do you need?"

After she told him and hung up, she shuffled back to her bed. The delivery would not come for another couple of hours yet. And she really should try to sleep.

But each time she closed her eyes, his face was added to the lineup of dead men she saw. Men who had died by her hand or order. She hadn't killed Fred, but…hadn't she?

And the thought that loomed over all the others, the one that kept her mind chugging along like the faithful engine on an old train.

Jake Morelli.

She felt it, a hard pang in her chest, that he was responsible somehow. It had his stink all over it. But she couldn't prove it. The shooter had left nothing behind, had given no indication for whom he worked, and his car had been a generic black Ford with no license plates. She had no concrete evidence or reason to believe he'd had anything to do with it, yet she believed it, deep in the pit of her stomach.

He'd tried to have her killed.

Perhaps she was naive for thinking he *wouldn't* try something like this. Perhaps she was the worst fool to ever exist to think her sex protected her from such things. Men tried to kill one another in this business—they did not try to kill women.

*But they do. And they will keep trying.*

By the time Charlie arrived and Paolo led him into the suite's sitting room, Mia was waiting on the sofa with a cup of coffee, dressed and only slightly more refreshed from the one fitful hour of sleep she'd managed to claim.

Charlie sat in an easy chair beside the sofa, holding up a hand to refuse the coffee she offered. He studied her face. "How are you?"

She sipped her coffee. "Didn't really sleep."

"That's gonna hurt later. You got a long night ahead of you."

Mia lifted her shoulders.

Charlie reached inside his suit coat and withdrew an envelope. "Here."

She took the unsealed envelope and peered inside. It was stuffed with money. "It's all here?"

"Every last cent you asked for, all given with extreme prejudice from our pal Morrie," Charlie said drily. "He asked me to kindly remind you Fred was a member of the police union and they'll take care of his widow."

"You can kindly remind him to go jump in a lake," she said tiredly.

He gave her a quick smile. "We found his place, on the west side. Are you ready?"

She nodded and stood up. Paolo approached her, holding her light spring coat open. She allowed him to slide it over her shoulders. "I need to say goodbye to Gloria and Raquel."

When Charlie opened the door to the suite, she was surprised to see Bobby and Joey waiting outside. Both men nodded respectfully to her.

She bid them good morning as she walked to Gloria's door and knocked on it. It opened a moment later, and Gloria looked at her in confusion.

"I thought you were going to have breakfast with us. Where are you going?"

She stepped aside so Mia could walk in. Raquel sat at the small table by the window, laughing with Emilia. She caught sight of Mia and leaped to her feet, then hurried to her and took her hands.

"Cousin Mia," she said. She spoke splendid English, with only a trace of an accent. She had been studying the language since she'd been a young girl, and when Mia and Gloria were in Sicily, had insisted in conversing exclusively in English.

This morning, she wore one of the fashionable dresses Mia had bought her the previous day, a lovely lavender frock with insets of lace and chiffon. She greeted her cousin with a kiss on each cheek. "Good morning, Raquel. You look beautiful."

Raquel spun in a circle, the flowy skirt swishing around her legs. "Thank you for the dresses, Cousin Mia. Today we are going to meet Gloria's aunt and uncle. Then, do some more exploring. I see you're ready to go."

Mia put her hand on Raquel's shoulder. "I have some business to attend to this morning, Raquel." She pointed out into the hallway, where Charlie, Bobby, and Joey waited politely. Paolo, she was already well acquainted with.

Raquel's eyes widened. "You have business with...those men?"

"Most of them work for me."

"They work...for *you*?"

"I'll explain it to you soon." Mia led Raquel a few steps closer to the door. "Boys, this is my cousin. She just arrived from Sicily yesterday. Miss Raquel Scalisi."

"Miss Scalisi," Bobby and Joey said with respect.

"Nice to meet you," Charlie said.

Paolo nodded a greeting to her.

Mia turned back to Raquel. "I came to say good morning to you. I'm sorry I haven't been able to see much of you since you got here. I'm quite busy."

"It's all right," Raquel said, then added carefully in a quieter voice, "I know some things from Carlo. Why Paolo came with you."

Mia only nodded. There wasn't time to pull at that thread. "We'll have fun tonight. I'll see you later." She turned to Gloria, who'd been silent during their chat, watching Mia. The question was obvious in her dark eyes.

It was on the tip of Mia's tongue to default to her old response that told Gloria absolutely nothing. But then she hesitated.

If anyone could understand Dolores's pain, it would be Gloria.

She stepped around Raquel and paused in front of her sister-in-law. After a beat, Mia said into her ear in a soft voice just above a whisper, "The cop who walked the beat around my shop got killed last night. I'm going to see his widow. Pay my respects."

Gloria's brows rushed together.

"You need to be careful," Mia added, placing a hand on her forearm. "You and Raquel both."

"Why?" Gloria whispered. "Was it you they were after?"

"I...don't know. I don't think so." The whole truth wouldn't do for now, so Mia patted her arm and turned away. In the hall-way, she turned to Joey and Bobby. "Would you two stay here, please? Just outside the suite. Until we return."

"Of course, Miss Scalisi."

She glanced back as Paolo pulled the door shut, catching one last glimpse of Gloria's face and the despair written on it, and the confusion on Raquel's.

"Was that smart?" Charlie murmured to her as they walked toward the elevator bank, Paolo following. He dismissed the attendant when the young man tried to enter the car with them and pushed the buttons himself. "Especially in front of your cousin?"

Mia shrugged. "Maybe not, but I can't keep leaving Gloria in the dark. Besides, you and I both know what was really meant to happen last night, and if I'm in danger, she and Raquel and Emilia are, too. I can't have that."

"Gems," Charlie spat.

"We don't know that."

"It don't take a genius to figure it, Mia," he said as the elevator descended.

"It doesn't," she agreed, "but I won't make a move until I know for sure."

"And give him the chance for another try at you?"

"Why else you think I got all yous around?" she cracked, affecting a real wise-guy accent.

Charlie didn't smile. "This is serious, Mia."

Paolo turned from where he stood in front of them and made a soft grunt of agreement.

The little smile dropped off her face. "I know it is. And I'm taking it seriously. But I need to know who was responsible for the order before I do anything." She fixed her stare straight ahead at her reflection in the mirrored doors. "Or I'm no better than he is."

"You can't have anyone looking at you, at *us*, as weak."

"I also won't solve my problems with murder," Mia replied. "Unless I have no other option."

"One foot in," he said softly, "one foot out."

In the mirrored doors, they locked gazes until she couldn't take the weight of it any longer and glanced away.

Charlie led her to his waiting car. A man she didn't recognize sat behind the wheel. "He's one of mine," he told her before she could ask. "He's solid."

They drove to the modest, six-story apartment building in Hell's Kitchen, where Fred McClarty had lived with Dolores for years. Charlie's driver kept the car running.

Charlie led her up to the fourth floor and pointed out which door was Dolores's. She placed a hand on his chest. "You and Paolo wait out here. I'm going in alone."

Without waiting for a reply, she turned and walked the few feet down the hall and stopped in front of the door. She drew a quick, deep breath, then knocked on the door.

After a long pause, a woman's voice called out, low, unsure. "Who is it?"

"My name is Mia. I knew your husband," Mia replied. "I've come to pay my respects."

There was another long pause, then she heard the click of a lock unlatching. The door opened a few inches, the chain still in place. A middle-aged woman peered out at her, her bloodshot eyes narrow and suspicious. She eyed Mia up and down.

"You...knew my husband," she repeated.

"He worked for me." Mia cursed her choice of words and hoped she hadn't caused the woman any additional heartache. There were only so many places a woman's mind could go when another woman showed up at her door claiming to be acquainted with her husband.

Dolores's brow creased. "He worked for *you*? My husband was a police officer."

"He provided security at my shop." In a kind voice, she added, "May I come in, please, Mrs. McClarty?"

Dolores studied her again. "I s'pose that'd be all right." She shut the door, and Mia heard the slide of the chain before it opened again, wider. Dolores gestured her inside.

She was a small woman, shorter even than Mia, and her blonde hair was shot through with gray. It was gathered in a messy knot at her nape, as though she hadn't wanted to bother much with it. She wore a severe, high-collared black dress and she looked like she hadn't had much sleep, either.

"I just put some coffee on. May I offer you some, Miss, uh...?"

"Scalisi. And that would be wonderful, thank you." Mia could use another cup herself, and something told her it would be rude to refuse the woman.

"Please have a seat. It'll just be a moment."

While she bustled around the small kitchen, Mia took a seat on a faded sofa that had seen better days at least two generations ago and glanced around as she tugged her gloves off. It was the sort of place Mia envisioned Fred had lived—cramped but cozy, with furniture that was functional only and well-worn. The mantel was crowded with pictures and knick-knacks, and there was a bookshelf in one corner with great, dusty tomes.

Dolores joined her in the tiny living room, carrying a tarnished silver tray with a coffee pot, cream, sugar, cups, and a dish of shortbread cookies. She poured Mia coffee and offered the cream and sugar, then the plate of cookies.

"Shortbreads were his favorite." Her eyes filled and she pressed her handkerchief to her lips.

Mia hastily took one and bit into it. "It's delicious. I can see why he enjoyed them."

Dolores nodded, dabbing her eyes. "You said you've a shop?"

"Yes. A ladies' shop in Midtown."

"You need security in a place like that?" The older woman's forehead knotted and her gaze took on a suspicious look again.

She was a sharp one, Mia thought, and understood Fred hadn't shared his side job with her. "Burglary, you see. Since it's such a nice area, and, well, the city's been full of criminals these past few years, hasn't it?"

"He certainly had his hands full. But his hard work paid off, you know."

"Did it?" Mia sipped her coffee.

"Why, yes. He was so courageous and brave, he got awarded with a big bonus. Bigger than I could have ever imagined. And he took me to Atlantic City with it."

Mia smiled into her cup. "Did he? And did you have a lovely time?"

"It was a bit risqué for my tastes," Dolores admitted, her cheeks reddening, "but, yes. We saw a wonderful revue and enjoyed a delicious meal at a place on the boardwalk."

"Penny's, was it?"

Dolores's eyebrows lifted. "How did you know?"

"Mr. McClarty mentioned it," Mia said. "He said the lobster thermidor was quite nice."

"It was." Dolores nodded vigorously. "If you ever go, Miss Scalisi, I highly recommend it."

"I'll keep that in the front of my mind," she replied with a private smile.

As quickly as it had lit up, Dolores's face fell, as if recalling the entire reason for Mia's visit. As if the knowledge that her husband was gone came and went, came and went. Mia understood that, too.

"We'll never go again, Fred and I. Never." Her voice quivered off into a fresh wave of grief.

"I'm so sorry," Mia said. "I came here today because I…was worried about you. Mr. McClarty spoke of you often, and mentioned you don't have any living family or children."

Dolores flushed. "I—was unable, you see. Barren, the doctor—"

Mia held up a hand. "It's none of my business. I bring it up only because I don't want you to feel you're alone."

"But I am," Dolores cried. "I *am* alone now. He was my everything, and now he's gone."

An invisible needle stabbed Mia through the heart. "Mr. McClarty was a valuable employee of mine," she said. "And what happened to him was unfair. But you're not alone. You're not." She reached into her pocketbook and withdrew the envelope of money Charlie had brought her.

Dolores's eyes went wide. She made no move to take it, so Mia set it on the coffee table.

"Wh-what is that?"

"Money to cover his funeral expenses, to live on, whatever you need," Mia said. "I assume he has a pension, from his work with the police force. But anything else you need—anything else you *want*—that money doesn't cover, this money will. And when you need more, you come and see me. There's a slip of paper in that envelope that has the address to my store as well as the telephone number to my suite. Should you need anything, you call me."

Dolores finally picked up the envelope, her hands shaking. She stared at Mia. "Who *are* you?"

A nice girl, Fred had called her once. "Just a friend."

Dolores leaned across the small coffee table and grabbed her wrist. "It was gangsters who killed him, wasn't it?"

Mia looked at her, startled. "Ah, beg pardon?"

"He said he'd been dealing with a lot of gangsters on the street lately, bootleggers. Was it them?"

"Why…are you asking me?"

Dolores gripped her hand almost fervently. "You do know, don't you? Look at you." Her wide eyes rolled over her like a hysterical horse's. "Fine clothes. Jewels. I can smell the expensive perfume on you—in fact, one night Fred came home laden with gifts. Lip rouge…perfume. Just like yours. He said it cost fifteen dollars. Fifteen whole dollars, and it smells just like yours. You're not just some shopkeeper, are you? What were you really paying him to do?"

Mia withdrew her hand from Dolores's crushing grip, leaned back against the sofa, and crossed her legs. She sipped her coffee again. "It's Shalimar, actually."

"What?"

"My perfume. I only wear Shalimar. I sent him home with the Chanel for you."

Dolores's mouth fell open.

"How much do you really want to know?" Mia asked.

The question caught the other woman off guard. "What have you to tell me?"

"If I tell you the truth, how much can you really handle? Wouldn't you be content to know your husband died in the line of duty, and that you're going to be a wealthy widow? Because the truth isn't far from that, but it's much darker. And risky —for me."

Dolores opened and closed her mouth as she stared at Mia as though she were a mirage.

"If we're going to have a real chat, then you'll need to pull yourself together," Mia added in a gentle voice.

Dolores drew in a breath, and then in an abrupt movement that took Mia by surprise, she launched herself out of the easy chair and went to the cupboard that seemed to hold her china. She opened a door on the bottom left and pulled out a bottle.

Mia's brows lifted slightly.

Dolores made her way back to her seat, uncapped the bottle, and took a healthy pull. She let it settle, then offered the bottle to Mia.

With half a smile, she grasped it and took a small, conspiratorial sip.

The older woman took the bottle back and tipped it into her mouth again, then added a splash to her coffee and set it aside. "Consider me pulled together."

Mia regarded her for a long, silent moment. Then she said, "I'm an entertainer in town. A singer. At a nightclub called The Divine. I also own the shop your husband provided security at. A perfume and cosmetics shop, and yes, it was me who sent him home with those gifts for you. And I gave him the two thousand dollars he used to treat you to a lavish vacation in Atlantic City and, I imagine, many other things."

"He—he put most of it in the bank," Dolores whispered. "All that—that was you? Why?"

"To buy him," Mia replied. "To buy his silence, his cooperation, his loyalty. The night we met, he was walking his beat, doing his job. He wandered into my store at the wrong time, and frankly, he didn't have a choice. I wanted to keep things friendly with the gifts and money."

"Friendly?" Dolores shook her head. "I...don't understand. Did he...did he try to proposition you?"

"Absolutely not," Mia said. "I know how it must seem, to have some strange, young woman knocking on your door, telling you she knew your husband. But he was devoted to you."

"Then what do you mean?"

Mia released a light breath. "He was being held at gunpoint

by my partners. Who fully intended to kill him. I didn't want that to happen, so I used the moment and the gifts to bribe him into my service. I wanted to save his life, yes, but I needed a beat cop on my payroll, too."

"Why?"

Mia gazed down into her coffee cup, then at Dolores. The truth she was about to admit would be the first time she admitted it to herself. The first time she said it out loud.

"Because I'm a bootlegger, Mrs. McClarty. I run an operation from my shop, which is a front. The night Mr. McClarty—mind if I call him Fred?—walked in, my partners were overseeing a whole lot of booze being unloaded in the alley."

Dolores went very still.

"And ever since that night, he worked for me. I told him when shipments were coming in, and he made sure he was the only cop in our area on his beat during those times. He was our lookout. And in return, I paid him. When you go to the bank to have his assets rolled to you, you'll see just how handsomely."

The older woman picked up her handkerchief and wadded it in her hands. "He just never said anything," she said. "He just never said a word. He told me everything."

"This is a dangerous business," Mia said. "I'm sure he wanted to protect you from it."

Dolores snapped her head up. "That's why he died?"

She'd come this far. There was no point in stopping now. "Yes. A car came by while I was outside talking to Fred. The driver pulled a gun. My bodyguard pulled me out of the way. But Fred…"

She stopped as fresh tears gathered in Dolores's eyes and slowly oozed down her cheeks. "That's why it was important for me to come see you today, Mrs. McClarty. Because of what your husband meant. Because…because…"

"Because it's your fault," Dolores whispered, but the accusation was as loud as if she'd screamed it.

It stung. Mia swallowed hard and lifted her chin. "Yes. It was my fault. Had I not hired him, he would never have been in a position to get shot while working for me. However, had I not hired him, my partners would almost certainly have killed him. Or, Fred would have gotten away and brought the New York City police to my doorstep. And then...I would have been on yours."

Dolores stared at her with wide eyes, the veiled threat clear.

"So you see, Mrs. McClarty, the likelihood of us meeting, one way or another, was always high. To be frank, I'd much rather us meet this way than the other. Because this way, I get to tell you your husband died a hero, and reassure you you'll never want for anything again."

"How do you know I won't go to the police and tell them what you've just told me?" Dolores asked, her voice trembling.

A tiny part of her felt horribly guilty for threatening this poor woman when she was up to her ears in grief. She'd just lost her *husband*, after all. But she'd wanted the truth, and Mia had given it to her. And her truth was costly—so Dolores needed to know the exact price.

"Because if you did, I would know it was you, and whatever happened next, you would know it was me," Mia said.

Dolores went as white as the cream in the little, tarnished silver pitcher on the tray between them.

"But I believe a woman in my position needs friends she can rely on. And a woman in your position needs the same. Wouldn't you agree, Mrs. McClarty? Can I call you Dolores?"

"You...know my name?"

"He spoke of 'his Dolores' often."

Dolores looked down at her lap. "What about the man who shot him?"

"I will find him," Mia said, ice creeping into her voice, "and I will make him pay for that."

"You're...going to kill him?"

Another truth forced out of her, that she wasn't even ready to admit to herself yet. "There aren't many other ways of dealing with someone who does what he chose to do. Not in this life."

"You could go to the police," Dolores said. "Then they'd catch Fred's killer, and he'd be out of your life."

"Your husband was one of the few decent, honest men on the force," Mia said.

"He was on the take," the older woman said bitterly.

"That doesn't mean he wasn't a good man," Mia said. "But don't be fooled, Dolores. The police department is as corrupt as any criminal in the city these days. They could do nothing to whoever shot Fred, whoever tried to kill me, that would keep them from getting out of jail and doing it all over again."

"So you mean to say you *are* going to kill that man?"

Sometimes silence was as much of an answer as words, Don Catalano had told her, so she said nothing.

After a moment, Mia reached for her purse and gloves. "I should be on my way. It was nice to chat with you, Dolores."

Dolores rose a bit uncertainly to her feet and walked her to the door. "I do appreciate the visit," she whispered. "And—and the money. That was very kind of you. Unnecessary."

"I hope you'll consider me a reliable friend in the future," Mia said.

Dolores hesitated, her throat bobbing. "I've...I've nothing to offer you in return. I'm not my husband."

"I would consider you not going to the police to share what I've told you a great favor," Mia said. "One I won't soon forget."

"Is that what that money's for?" Dolores said. "To buy my silence?"

"What I told you, I did of my own accord. Because I felt you deserved to know," Mia replied. "I didn't have to tell you anything in order to give you the money. I simply wanted to help you, because your husband helped me."

"You seem like a nice girl," Dolores said, her eyes wide and sad. "What're you doing, mixed up in all of this?"

It was another question that would go unanswered. Mia put her hand on the older woman's arm. "Please accept my condolences, Mrs. McClarty. And don't hesitate to contact me if you need anything at all." She opened the door and stepped out into the hall.

"I won't say anything."

Mia turned around.

Dolores stood with her head high, eyes streaming. "You have my word. Mia."

Mia gave her a small smile, and a bob of her head. "Good day to you, Dolores."

She walked down the hall until she found Charlie and Paolo. The former leaned against the staircase wall, arms folded, and the latter sat on the top step, leaning against the railing, snoring softly. He woke instantly as though a switch had been flipped when the sound of her heels on the wooden floor reached them.

"In there making friends?" Charlie said.

"Yeah, actually," Mia replied, glancing over her shoulder at Dolores's door. "Can't have too many."

# CHAPTER FOURTEEN

"Well," Hyman said, leaning against the doorway of Mia's new dressing room, "I daresay we've quite the turnout tonight. Quite the turnout, indeed."

He looked quite pleased, and Mia smiled. "Congratulations seem to be in order then, Mr. Goldberg."

"I've merely packed the house with the promise of entertainment," he said. "It's up to you to make good on that promise."

"Don't you believe in me?"

He walked over to where she sat at her vanity, putting the finishing touches on her makeup. She'd had to apply extra powder underneath her eyes tonight to cover the dark circles. Despite taking a three-hour nap that afternoon, filling up on coffee, and Gloria doing her best to reduce the puffiness around her eyes with cold spoons and cucumber slices, the darkness remained. The powder and heavy, dark eye makeup helped conceal the worst of it.

Hyman stood behind her, bending to place his hands on her shoulders as he met her gaze in the mirror. "I have every confidence in you." He straightened and reached into the interior pocket of his suit coat. He handed her a wide, flat jeweler's box.

"A gift for you, to celebrate a night that's been a long time coming."

Mia looked at him in surprise. "Hyman. You shouldn't have."

He smiled at her. "Yes, I should have. Please, open it."

Mia popped the spring lid and blinked down at a delicate diamond and ruby necklace. It sparkled up at her in the low lighting of the dressing room. She fingered the drop-shaped ruby. "It's stunning."

"I thought it would complement your ensemble this evening well." He took the box from her and removed the necklace, then draped it around her neck.

The ruby settled in the center of her collarbone. It *was* the perfect complement to the sleeveless, ruby-red silk shift she wore, draped with a mesh overlay of silver thread, giving her the appearance of glimmering all over. The matching headpiece, made of the same silver mesh, rested right over her dark, waved bob like a close-fitting cap.

She reached up to adjust the necklace so the ruby hung perfectly in the middle. "Thank you, Hyman."

"I, er, know our partnership came about in a way that must have seemed rather…sneaky to you," he said. "Considering the conversation happened between me and Nick, apart from you. But, I do hope you know he only wanted the best for you, and I haven't forgotten how he very nearly threatened my life if I didn't care of you properly."

She smiled a little. "Sounds like Nick."

"He would be very proud of you if he could see you," Hyman said gently. He checked his pocket watch. "I must go and ensure everything is running smoothly. Break a leg, Miss Scalisi." He snapped his heels together with all the elegance of an English lord and made her a formal bow, then slid out of her dressing room door, shutting it silently behind him.

Mia turned back to the mirror, studying the necklace. It was beautiful, but she was under no illusions about it. It wasn't just a thoughtful gift from employer to employee. It was yet another reminder of how Hyman owned her. If she were to tell him tomorrow she quit, he couldn't stop her. But she knew he would stop being her ally and join the ranks of her enemies...whoever they were, and however many of them there were.

*Besides,* a small, slightly taunting voice asked, *isn't this what you always wanted? Better stages and opportunities?*

The Divine was what Sal Bellomo had always wanted the Stems Club to be, but could never achieve. Hyman's joint lived up to its name, and the first time Mia had set foot inside the place, she'd seen with her own eyes how he had spared no expense to create a truly lavish, extravagant experience for New York's upwardly mobile.

A knock on the door drew her from her reverie. "Who's there?"

"Annette."

Mia blinked in surprise and smiled. "Come on in."

The door opened and Annette stepped instead, breathtaking in a dazzling, all-white dress. She glanced around, taking in the dark-brown marbled floors, the dark cherrywood vanity and coffee table, the plush, upholstered loveseat and chair, the wallpapered wall.

"Well," Annette drawled, "I suppose this is a little better than that old broom closet you used to have."

They glanced at each other, then burst out laughing.

"Go on," Mia said, waving a hand at the loveseat. "Sit down. I'll fix you a drink."

She poured a couple fingers of bourbon into two short tumblers and joined Annette on the loveseat. "So you got the night off."

Annette smirked. "Helps that Wolfy and Owney have a good working relationship." She sipped her drink. "So, you nervous?"

Mia swallowed all her bourbon in one go. "Not really." She set the empty glass down.

Annette lifted a brow. "Suppose that helps, don't it?"

"My first one for the night," Mia replied with a shrug.

"Hmm. Well, it's good you ain't nervous. It's a full house out there, and let me tell you, they ain't the kinda crowd we had at Stems."

"No?"

Annette shook her head. "A highfalutin group, that's for sure. Even the waiters are wearing tuxes. I saw a few fellas Wolfy told me were political types. And it seems you can't be a lady here if you ain't dripping diamonds." Her gaze drifted down to Mia's neck. "Though I see you got that part covered already."

Her fingers flew to the necklace. "It was a gift."

"From who?"

"Mr. Goldberg."

"Oh," Annette said with a knowing lilt. "I see."

Mia gave her a look. "It's not like that."

"I ain't no judge."

"Just...yet another reminder he's the boss." Mia shrugged.

"Well, it is gorgeous." Annette leaned close to examine it. "Looks like that cost a pretty penny."

"I'm sure it was hardly a drop in the bucket for him. He has the means to hand out jewelry like it's candy." She smiled at Annette. "Want a new job?"

The other woman chuckled, finishing off her drink. "Nah. I'm happy where I'm at. The Cotton Club's bigger than this place, honey."

She hadn't meant it as a jab, but Mia couldn't ignore the words' barbs. "Can't argue that."

"Give this place time, though," Annette said quickly. "Plus with you on the marquee, why, we'll lose business left and right."

"If Owney doesn't treat you right...I'll get it straightened out."

Annette smirked. "Oh, will you?"

"One way or another," Mia said, her tone wiping the smile off Annette's face.

"Well, I guess I better find my man. We have supper coming." She got to her feet, and Mia stood with her. "Break a leg, girl. I'll see you after."

"Thanks, Annie."

When she was alone, Mia sighed deeply and contemplated another drink. The bourbon she'd downed a few minutes ago warmed her, and she wanted to stay warm. Without it, she feared her performance would be cold and lifeless. Mechanical.

Because that was how she felt—like a machine.

Another knock sounded on her door.

"It ain't ten yet," she called. "Go away."

"It's Charlie."

She turned away from the decanter on a side table and opened the door. Charlie loomed in the doorway, handsome in his tux. "What're you doing here? I thought you were rubbing elbows."

"Schmoozing gets old for some of us," he said, stepping inside. "Morrie's still at it."

"What a shock. Did Will make it?"

Charlie nodded and smiled. "Said the trip was long, but he seems to be having a good time. You know, for him."

Mia chuckled. Will Wyatt, manufacturer of their rye, was straitlaced and sarcastic, and if he'd ever kicked his heels up, she'd eat her hat. But she hadn't seen him since Nick's funeral, and was looking forward to catching up with him.

"He's been getting chummy with Raquel," Charlie added.

Mia frowned, protectiveness surging through her. "Tell him she's not that kinda girl."

"He knows. He's just trying to figure out how to get the words 'Can I buy you a drink?' out." His dark eyes fell on the necklace. "That's a pretty bauble."

"A gift from Hyman."

"Generous."

"Calculated," Mia corrected.

"Well, it looks beautiful on you." His lips curved up on one side. "And you look gorgeous."

"Thanks." Her cheeks heated as she turned away. Yes, time for another drink. "You know me. Just the pretty little show pony."

"You're a lot more than that," he objected.

"No. I'm not." She poured out two more bourbons and handed him one.

"That's a pretty bleak way of looking at things." He took a sip.

Mia tossed back her drink in one gulp again. What was the point of sipping it? She uttered a dark laugh. "I'm a bleak gal these days."

He looked like he wanted to protest, then relented. "I guess I can't blame you. A lot's happened since you've been home."

"Including watching a man die from the bullet meant for me." A third drink? No. It wouldn't do to wobble through her steps or slur song lyrics.

Charlie sighed and set his glass down. He reached into his suit coat and withdrew a small jewelry box. "It ain't expensive diamonds, but maybe this'll cheer you up."

He handed her the box and she took it, her head tilting with curiosity. It was smaller than the box Hyman had given her, and it was larger than a ring box. She opened the lid and froze.

A small, round pendant attached to a delicate silver chain gleamed up at her. One side of the pendant was engraved with the image of a bearded man with a staff, a small child on his back.

"It's..." Her throat tightened, squeezing off the words.

"Nick's St. Christopher medal."

It had once belonged to their father. She'd given it to Charlie from the personal effects recovered from Nick's body after his death. She'd insisted he have it.

Mia stared up at him, speechless.

"I knew you'd want it back one day," Charlie said. "It's yours. Nick was your brother, and it was your pop's before that."

She swallowed. "But I gave it to you."

"Let it stay in your family. Give it to Emilia one day." His lips twisted into a small, teasing smile. "What do I need a medal for? I got you to protect me now, tough girl." He reached into the box and pulled it out. "I had it made into a bracelet for you. I don't think it complements your ensemble for tonight, but—"

Fighting through the tightness in her throat, Mia held out her arm. She wanted her brother with her tonight, in whatever way that could be managed. "Please."

He gently fastened the bracelet around her wrist, then lifted her hand to his lips.

"Thank you, Charlie," she whispered.

"You're welcome."

They held each other's gazes, and Mia couldn't stop herself from falling into his arms. In many ways, he was the same Charlie she'd always known him to be. He was, perhaps, one of the very few people in her life who had stayed consistent, scar on his palm or not.

Her door swung open, and she and Charlie both started. Gloria stood in the doorway, her eyes going wide at the sight of them. "Oh. I—sorry." But she didn't leave. She folded her arms and stared at Charlie.

He cleared his throat, his arms dropping away from Mia. "I'll clear off. Break a leg, Mia." He stepped around Gloria and disappeared.

Gloria shifted her attention to Mia. She looked beautiful in the burgundy dress she'd tried on at Hyman's. A matching head-band wrapped around her forehead, and Mia had applied dark, smoky eye makeup to enhance Gloria's big brown eyes. She'd insisted she was only coming tonight for moral support and to assist Mia and look after Raquel, but she wasn't fooling anyone. She was thrilled to be out at a real nightclub in the city. Emilia was spending the night with Aunt Connie and Uncle Joe, and had been none too pleased to hear her mother was leaving her behind for the night. Earlier that evening, she'd pitched a tremendous fit in front of the store, and only Paolo, who scooped her into his arms and hummed some nameless tune deep in his throat, could pacify her.

"Who'd have thought he could be so gentle," Gloria had mused when they'd left the store and were on the way to the club. "Perhaps I ought to have him look after her permanently."

Though Paolo was clearly fond of the little girl, and she him,

Mia had blanched at the thought. "But then, who would look after me?" She'd been only half kidding.

"Hope I wasn't interrupting anything," Gloria said with a pointed smirk, shutting the door.

Mia flushed. She was still warm from Charlie's embrace. "Where's Raquel?"

"Will's keeping her company until I get back. She seems quite taken with him. He's polite enough, for all he's a bootlegger. She even made him smile once or twice."

"Smile? Will?"

Gloria chuckled and nodded. "So what was Charlie doing here?"

Mia cleared her throat and glanced at his abandoned glass. He'd only had a sip of his drink, and one sip remained. She snatched the glass and polished it off. "He came to give me a gift and wish me luck."

Gloria tilted her head with real interest. "What'd he give you?" She gasped softly, a hand going to her chest. "That necklace? Jesus Christ, Mia. That had to have cost a fortune. What'd he do, propose?"

"What? *No.*" Mia held up her wrist. "He gave me this bracelet. It was—it was Nick's St. Christopher medal, the one our father used to wear. Nick wore it after Papa died. Went to war wearing it."

Gloria grazed the medallion with her fingertips. "How lovely."

"One day, it'll be Emilia's," Mia said softly.

Her sister-in-law gave her a watery smile. "She'll love it. But her aunt needs to wear it for a long time, first." Then she cleared her throat. "So, where'd that necklace come from, then? Are those real diamonds? A real ruby?"

"Yes, it's all real," Mia said. "It was a gift from Mr. Goldberg. That's all—just a gift."

"Oh, really, now? Some *boss* you got there."

"Don't you start, too," Mia groaned. "Annette already—"
She snapped her mouth shut as fire erupted in Gloria's eyes.

*Shit, Mia!*

Annette had been a sore spot between Nick and Gloria, as he'd been catting with the leggy dancer before he died and Gloria had found out about it, despite Nick and Mia's combined efforts to lie to her and tell her otherwise. Their affair had swayed Kiddo Grainger to accepting the job to murder Nick.

Things were far from forgiven as far as her sister-in-law went.

"She's *here?*" Gloria hissed.

Mia hesitated, helpless.

Gloria stalked toward her until they were nose-to-nose. "Don't even think about lying to me, Mia Angela Scalisi. That goddamn tramp is here?"

"She's not a tramp, Gloria."

"You're defending her?" Her eyes went huge, full of betrayal and hurt. "After what she did? After she stole Nick from me?"

"Hold your horses," Mia said quickly. "Listen—what she and Nick did was wrong. And it will always be wrong. But it was never about you, Glo. And she's moved on now. She's with—"

"She's moved on because my husband is dead," Gloria snapped. "If he were still alive, she'd still be trying to take him."

"You can't take a man who doesn't want to be taken," Mia said, then immediately regretted it. She sucked in a sharp breath that hurt her throat. "I didn't mean it like that."

"Your meaning is plain," Gloria said, stepping back from her.

"Gloria, don't leave," Mia begged, stepping toward her. "Please—just sit down for a moment and hear me out."

"That's quite all right, dear," Gloria said with an angry sneer. "Because, you see, I've got a handsome gentleman waiting on me with a bottle of champagne that I intend to drink. In fact, I intend to get very drunk tonight. And perhaps, I'll let him do with me as he pleases."

"What?" Mia exclaimed. "Who? *Frankie Yale?*"

"Perhaps it's best not to wait up for me tonight. *Good luck,* Mia." Gloria whirled around and slammed the door shut behind her.

❀

*NEVER LET 'EM SEE YOU SWEAT.*

The bourbon, however, had other ideas. She'd wanted to be warm—well, she was absolutely glowing now. Two and a half drinks were child's play on most nights, but her heightened nerves—*ah, there they are*—and the unpleasant scene with Gloria had given the alcohol a boost she hadn't counted on.

Nonetheless, she was a professional. Had been since age eleven, and one of the old vaudeville starlets told her that a bee could fly into her bloomers and sting her where the sun didn't shine, and not a single person in that audience should ever know something was amiss.

The first three songs of her set went smoothly enough. They opened with the mid-tempo "I'm Goin' South," then slid right into "I'm Nobody's Baby," which rolled into "I Ain't Got Nobody."

Mia's voice carried nicely through the large room, as though it had been built with that in mind. The ceiling had a dome shape to it, allowing her voice to slide along the curves and shower down over the crowd.

The club had been designed with meticulous care. The floor was the same dark marble as in her dressing room, the tables made of glossy cherrywood as dark as could be found, and draped with crisp, white linens. Roman columns lined either side of the room, and she knew from closely examining them that they were made of pure ivory.

The walls had been painted with murals to resemble those found on the ceiling of the Sistine Chapel, but instead of featuring God, they showed scenes involving each of the Greek gods and goddesses in their most divine moments.

And Annette had not lied—the club was absolutely packed.

A cursory glance from side to side as she'd sung the first few numbers had shown her quite a few famous and familiar faces— Lucky Luciano and his business partner, Meyer Lansky, were in the crowd, sitting with Frankie Yale at a large table. Charlie and

Moritz had joined them, with Will Wyatt in tow. Gloria and
Raquel sat with them, Gloria beside Frankie and Raquel seated
beside Will.

Mia also spotted Governor Smith and his crony Senator
Robinson in the crowd with very young women on their arms
that could not possibly have been their wives.

Now it was time to change into her dance number and bring
out The Divine Angels. The chorus line was made up of
seasoned dancers, some of whom had danced with Ziegfeld,
though why they'd left his troupe for Hyman's was a mystery.
They were polite with Mia, but not friendly.

Mia's dance costume was certainly beautiful—a short, snug
silver dress with crystal fringe, with a bodice of netting and more
crystals coating the straps and down the front to catch the light—
but it scratched her terribly all over where it touched her skin.
The dancers' costumes were similar but much scantier, though
elegant. None of them seemed to be struggling against the urge
to scratch violently at themselves.

Hyman had hired a choreographer from Broadway to work
up some special routines. He was an arrogant, impatient man,
and since Mia did not have the technical skill of the other
dancers—despite her oft-repeated lie about the lengthy ballet
tutelage she'd received at the hands of good, old "Madame du la
Boviette"—she'd had to spend long hours alone with him,
marking out the steps and listening to him berate her until she
longed to beat his teeth out with Nick's blackjack.

After the first dance number, they launched into the second,
"Everybody Loves My Baby." The tune would forever tug a taut
string of pain in her heart, since it had always been one of Nick's
favorites. Focusing on her steps kept her from wallowing in the
grief that threatened to rise to the surface. She'd once loved the
song, too, but she could not bear it now.

Movement near the middle of the room caught her eye. A
dark-haired woman in a burgundy-colored dress lurched to her
feet from where she sat at the same table as the gangsters Mia
had spotted earlier, flinging out her arm. The drink she was

holding sloshed onto the couple at the table in front of her. Her mouth opened and she sang loudly along with Mia.

Her Charleston faltered slightly.

*Gloria.*

A stocky man shot up beside her, wrapping his arms around her and speaking rapidly into her ear as he pulled her down into her seat.

Though Mia was grateful for the intervention, her hackles still rose at the possessive way Frankie Yale clung to Gloria, as if she were little more than a drunken flapper he'd conned into a date.

They finished the song to raucous applause. Mia pasted on her brightest smile as she curtsied gracefully, then led the dancers off the raised stage. The band remained to continue playing through the intermission.

She'd hardly disappeared behind the curtains that fell on either side of the stage when she practically stumbled right into Hyman's arms.

His face was taut with irritation. "Your sister-in-law appears to be in her cups," he said sharply. "This isn't that kind of establishment, Mia. I must say, I'm rather surprised by her behavior."

"She's just...having a hard night," Mia said. "She doesn't normally act this way. I'll speak with her later."

"See that you do," he said, then grabbed her elbow. "Come. The governor and the senator wish to congratulate you."

She really just wanted a few moments of peace in her dressing room to catch her breath and scratch herself. "Can't it wait?"

Hyman gazed down at her. His bland face fell into its normal, polite smile, but his eyes gleamed with menace at her. "No. It cannot."

He practically dragged her out into the side hallway the talent used to get from their dressing rooms to the stage and led her down to a door at the end, which opened to the main room. As soon as they stepped out of the hallway, his grip on her arm relaxed and he looped her arm through his, as though they were the dearest of friends, and his gait slowed to a leisurely stroll.

As he led her to the center of the room where the senator and the governor were seated, people reached out to compliment her on her performance. She responded in kind, staying in character of the Saturday Night Special, flashing her dazzling smile, making sure her dimple popped in her cheek, offering saucy compliments to the women to make them laugh and blush, and almost-but-not-quite flirting with their male companions. She winked so many times, she was sure her eyelid had permanently acquired a tic.

"Well done," Hyman said under his breath. "Keep it up, Mademoiselle Scalisi."

"Yes, boss," she replied.

He led her to Governor Smith and Senator Robinson, who rose to greet her with smiles on their faces. The liquor they'd drunk seemed to embolden them as their gazes went over her, still in her dancing costume, and Mia realized it had not been a coincidence that Hyman insisted she greet them dressed this way.

"You are ever charming, Miss Scalisi," the senator said, pecking the back of her proffered hand.

"Yes, indeed," the governor added. "A vigorous dance number, that was. You must have quite a set of powerful lungs to sing and dance so at the same time." And his eyes drifted down, as though trying to see her "lungs" through her costume.

Mia glanced at Hyman, who smiled blithely at her. "Thank you so much, gentlemen. That's just the first half of the show. I do hope you're ready for the rest."

"After this fine food and this even finer booze, I'm ready for anything," the senator said, and pinched the rosy cheek of his young companion. "Isn't that right, dolly?"

She smiled, playing her role as much as Mia was. They exchanged a brief glance of camaraderie. "That's right, Joey."

"So, Miss Scalisi," Governor Smith said, "have you reconsidered lending me your support in the next election?"

"That depends," she replied. "Have you reconsidered your stance on Prohibition?"

He tipped his head back and laughed. "Still on that? Look around, Miss Scalisi. Nearly every person here is imbibing. Do you see any crimes being committed? Do you see any terrible things taking place? No. We are all adults who can handle our cups. To assume otherwise is preposterous. All this ridiculous law does is provide a breeding ground for criminals."

"Well, our booze had to come from somewhere," Mia said sweetly. She caught Hyman's sharp look out of the corner of her eye. "Doesn't us procuring it make us criminals, as well?"

"Merely victims of circumstance," he replied. "Mr. Goldberg is a solid businessman. You're just a poor, immigrant showgirl trying to get by the best way she knows how."

*You're a fool*, she thought, biting down hard on her cheek to fight off the sneer that threatened to twist her lips.

"If this law didn't exist to punish honest businessmen merely trying to provide an in-demand service," the governor continued, "you could never even have asked that question, my dear. Of course, you're no criminal."

"I'm sure the country's brave Prohibition agents would beg to differ," she said.

"All the more reason to abolish it."

Before Mia could open her mouth to argue, a woman's voice rose above the crowd.

"You're nothing but a goddamn, lousy, man-stealing *whore!*"

Eyes wide, Mia whirled toward the voice, already knowing who it belonged to.

Gloria stood unsteadily in front of Annette, where she was seated at a table with Wolfy, Owney, and a few other men and their companions. Annette kept her gaze steadily on Gloria, a look of stoic understanding written on her features as she slipped out of her chair and rose to her feet.

"Oh, dear," Governor Smith commented in a mild tone.

"Catfight," the senator said with a laugh.

"Mia," Hyman said in a low, warning, commanding voice meant only for her ears.

Raquel held one of Gloria's wrists, looking terrified as she tried to tug her away. Gloria, too hellbent on screaming at Annette, kept jerking away from Raquel. She jabbed a shaking finger in Annette's face, and Mia wouldn't have blamed her friend if she decked her sister-in-law.

*Just the same—no one touches her.*

"Pardon me," Mia muttered, shoving between the governor and the senator and hurrying toward the two women. A small crowd gathered around them—not to break them up, but to spur them on.

It seemed Charlie had the same idea as her, as she caught sight of him across the room, throwing his napkin on the table and striding toward the crowd. Moritz remained coolly in his seat, smoking a cigarette as he nodded at something Mr. Luciano was saying to him. He glanced up almost casually as Mia passed his table.

"Why don't you do something!" she snapped at him.

"She's not *my* sister," he replied.

Mia clenched her fists as rage flashed through her, but there was no time to deal with him. She none-too-gently elbowed her way through the crowd, ignoring the little cries of pain she elicited along the way. *Serves these lousy bastards right.*

Raquel turned toward her and practically fell into her arms. Her face was a mixture of beauty and terror. "I don't know what to do," she stammered. "I—I—"

"It's all right," Mia reassured her cousin, patting her cheeks with a calmness she was far from feeling. She felt horrible that Raquel's first night out in New York City, when she looked so charming in a brand-new, glitzy, dark-blue dress, was turning out this way. "Please go find Mr. Wyatt and stay by his side."

With wide eyes, Raquel nodded and slipped through the crowd. Mia turned toward the two women, facing off.

"...couldn't find your own man?" Gloria was shouting at Annette. "You had to take mine? You knew he was married!"

Annette slowly brought her hands up, and Mia jolted forward. But Annette just rested her hands on Gloria's shoulders.

"You're makin' a scene just now, Miz Scalisi," she said in a gentle voice. "Perhaps no one should see you like this."

"I'll make as many fucking scenes as I want," Gloria snarled, shoving at her hands. "And I want answers. I've been waiting to talk to you for a long time, you floozy."

"Gloria," Mia said harshly, and yanked on her elbow.

Gloria lost her footing, stumbling into Mia, her bloodshot eyes wide with surprise. "Mia? Get off me!"

"*No.*" Mia wrapped both her arms around Gloria's from behind, using all her might to keep Gloria's arms pinned. She caught Charlie's eye as he pushed his way to the front. He reached for Gloria.

"C'mon, Glo," Charlie said. "Don't do this here."

"You can go to hell!" she shouted, kicking a foot out at him. "All of you. I hope you fucking burn there! You knew! You knew what he was doing all the time!"

Charlie scooped her off her feet and headed for the nearest door. Gloria beat him with her fists, thrashing this way and that, her cries fading beneath the band the farther away he carried her.

Mia faced Annette, who stood still, her face the same, impassive mask it had been since the ugly scene started.

"I'm—sorry," Mia said. "She's drunk. And we had a row earlier. She's real sore at me for something I said. I don't know—I don't know what's gotten into her."

"Seeing me didn't help," Annette said gently.

"Still. I'm sorry for those terrible things she called you."

"I been called worse. And I *did* sleep with her husband." Annette shrugged. "I wanted to apologize to her, but I don't think she'll forgive me."

"No, she won't," Mia said. "But I did, a long time ago, if it means anything. And…thanks for not decking her."

"Never." Annette gave her a one-sided, sad smile. "Take care of her."

Mia nodded and strode for the door Charlie had gone out of. She ripped it nearly off its hinges and slammed it shut behind her, as hard as she could manage.

In the service hallway, Gloria was on the floor, sobbing in Charlie's arms. Raquel hovered nearby, wringing her hands, and Will stood beside her. He shot her a look of sympathy.

Mia's nostrils flared. She wanted to be furious with Gloria, but her heart broke at the same time.

"I'm sorry," Gloria wept. "I'm sorry."

"Glo, you're drunk," Mia said. "You need to go home and go to bed."

"You stay with her," Charlie said. "I'll go find Bobby or Joey."

Just then, the door opened again, and Paolo stepped into the service hallway, looking distressed. On his heels was Frankie Yale.

Paolo caught Mia's eye. He flicked his gaze briefly over his shoulder toward Frankie, then back to Mia and frowned.

He did not care for Mr. Yale.

"Paolo, would you please go find Bobby or Joey? Mrs. Scalisi needs to go home."

Paolo glanced once more at Frankie, then nodded and went back into the main room.

"I'm happy to take her," Frankie said, leaning against the wall. "I had her under control earlier, 'til she got away from me."

"My sister-in-law is not and will *never* be under any man's control," Mia bit off.

Frankie just chuckled. "Suit yourself."

"C'mon, hon," Charlie said to Gloria, helping her stand. "You're gonna go home and sleep it off."

Paolo reemerged with Joey in tow. "Bobby's been waiting outside, keeping an eye on things," Joey said. "I'll have him take Mrs. Scalisi home."

"I—I'll go, too," Raquel said, looking at Mia. "She needs someone to take care of her."

"I'll help." Will lifted his brows at Mia. "All right?"

"Thank you." Mia glanced at Frankie, still eyeing her drunk

sister-in-law. "Please tell Bobby to stay out in the hallway after the girls get settled." She put her hand on Paolo's arm. "Can you help Raquel and Will?"

He gave her a reproachful look, as if offended she would even ask.

The door opened again, and Hyman stepped out. The carefree smile he'd been wearing dropped away the instant the door shut behind him.

"I'm normally not given over to using coarse language," he said through his teeth, "but what the goddamn *hell* was that?"

"Sorry, I'm sorry," Gloria mumbled, tears still coursing down her cheeks.

Hyman looked at Mia. "Get. Her. Out of here."

Raquel stared at him in shock.

Mia said quietly, "Joey."

Joey whipped off his suit coat and draped it around Gloria. "Time to go, Mrs. S." He wrapped an arm around her waist to steady her, then walked her toward the exit door at the end of the hall, Paolo trailing. More than once, Gloria's legs wobbled and her ankles gave out. Joey caught her each time before finally scooping her into his arms.

Mia grabbed Raquel's hand. "I'm sorry, Cousin," she said, looking into her dark, kohl-rimmed eyes that brimmed with tears. They were nearly the same height, and did favor each other more as sisters than cousins. "I promised you a fun night out."

"I did have fun," Raquel said with a tremulous smile. "For a while. You were splendid, Mia. Such a wonderful performance. Thank you for inviting me."

"I'll make it up to you."

Raquel nodded and glanced at Will. Mia couldn't help noticing the respectful, solicitous way he offered his arm, and the awe in his eyes each time he looked at her. Something to address, but now was not the time.

Hyman watched them all go, breathing deeply in and out through his nose as his jaw muscles twitched. He fixed Mia with a long stare, the look on his face terrifying and unlike anything she'd ever seen before.

Finally, he said, "*That* does not happen here. This is not *that* kind of place."

Mia bristled immediately, her slight fear of him vanishing. She was angry with Gloria for acting out, too, but Hyman was toeing a delicate line with his words. "What's that supposed to mean?"

"You know very well what it means," Hyman said, his voice sharp as a knife. "The Divine is not some sleazy speakeasy with brawls and drunkards."

"She is *not* a drunkard. She made a mistake."

"A mistake that's costing me my reputation," he snapped. "This place was built for people with *money*. Real money. Old money. You saw the governor and the senator here. This is not the place for grieving widows to act like drunken floozies arguing over who's a better piece of ass!"

Mia hadn't realized she'd lunged at Hyman until she felt arms locking around hers and heard her own snarl of killing rage echoing in her ears. Charlie was pressed to her back.

"Stop it," he ordered.

Hyman blinked at her in shock.

Her heart pounded almost painfully. She wrestled her arms out of Charlie's. "Let go of me."

After a tense moment of silence, Hyman took another deep breath and straightened his tuxedo bowtie. "Tensions are high," he said finally, his words clipped. "As they usually are after a disagreeable scene like what we just witnessed. The best course of action is to proceed with the evening as normal. Miss Scalisi, you will go back inside and be your charming little self. You will continue with your set and make everyone forget the unpleasantness they witnessed. And *I* will overlook what just happened here. This. Once." He pointed the opposite direction down the hallway. "I believe you know the way to your dressing room. You have five minutes to change."

If she remained in the hallway a moment longer, she was

going to say something that would get her in deep, irrevocable trouble.

Mia spun on her heel and stalked down the hallway. When she reached her dressing room, she slammed the door with enough force to shake the building.

# CHAPTER FIFTEEN

S omehow, Mia made it through the rest of the night. She did exactly as Hyman had told her—she sang more songs, talked and joked with the crowd, mingled during the next short intermission, and charmed away their lingering memories of the scene Gloria had caused. She made sure to avoid Hyman directly, though during the remainder of her set, she tossed teasing, flattering remarks his way, inviting the crowd to applaud him for a successful opening night of New York City's hottest new nightclub.

"Perhaps one day we'll be as big as the Cotton Club, eh, Mr. Madden?" she called. "How kind of you to help us celebrate our grand opening! Isn't he swell, everybody?"

He smiled modestly, waving to the crowd as it applauded him. "Anything for my friend, Mr. Hyman Goldberg."

"I can think of no better friends to celebrate with," Hyman said, bowing graciously to the crowd. "And, to close out our spectacular first night—champagne for everyone, on the house!"

Mia slipped out as the crowd went wild and the sounds of corks being popped peppered the air. She walked down the service hall to her dressing room, unlocked the door, and slipped inside. She packed her small suitcase that had followed her from vaudeville to Penny's to Stems to the Chicago, and now here. She could change her clothes later.

Mia stepped out of the room and stuck her key in to lock it.

"Not gonna spend time with your adoring fans?"

The voice brought her up short. Her heart sped up again, clanging against her ribs.

"Mr. Morelli," she said to the door with a calmness she didn't feel. "Fancy that."

She was trapped. There was nothing else in this part of the hall besides her dressing room. No other exit. She might be able to duck inside and slam and lock the door before he caught up, but wood didn't stop bullets.

So she summoned her courage and spun around slowly, and looked him in the eye.

He was handsome in a neatly tailored tux, if the bowtie was a little crooked. His hands were in his pockets. He prowled closer, his dark eyes raking her head to toe.

For the last part of her set, she'd changed into the beautiful cream and gold dress with the handkerchief hem, the first one she'd tried on at Hyman's. Mrs. Astor had let out the appropriate inches in the bust and hips, and now, it draped on her in a fashionable way, and the top was even low enough to reveal a bit more of her décolletage than it had before. Mrs. Astor had, however, forgotten a pin on one side of the dress at her waist, and it had been poking and scratching her since she'd first noticed onstage during "Saint Louis Blues." It scratched her now, but she remained motionless, watching Jake's every move as he neared.

"Ain't you a sight for sore eyes," he said admiringly.

"Yeah," Mia replied. "A few less bullet holes than you'd prefer, I'm sure."

He raised one thick, dark eyebrow. "Whatsit?"

"Don't play coy, Mr. Morelli. That's my role."

"Someone shot at you?" He tilted his head.

"As if you didn't know."

"I didn't. Who was it?" His eyes narrowed as he gave her a roguish smile. "Guess I oughtta thank 'em for trying, at least."

"What. Do you want."

He held up his hands. "It was a joke, dollface. A bad one. I didn't try to have you shot, I swear to God. We're partners after all, ain't we?"

"Do I look a fool to you?"

Jake shook his head. "Listen, you sent me a whole pile of dough the other day. I'd be stupid to try to get rid of you. Besides, I like lookin' at you too much."

She glared at him.

"When did it happen?" His voice was quiet, almost gentle.

"Last night." Suspicion pinged through her body. She was reluctant to tell him anything. Was he truly innocent, or was he just playing her? "You had nothing to do with it?"

He huffed impatiently. "Hell no. I was at a card game in the Bowery, anyway."

"You don't have to be present for a hit."

"I like to do my own work." He stepped closer to her until he was less than an inch away. His body heat practically radiated through her. He smirked. "See, I ain't touching you. Though I don't see no pistol on you to do any whipping, unless you got one in that suitcase or…under that dress."

"You have no idea what's under this dress."

"Is that my invitation?" His gaze dropped to her lips.

She backed up until she hit the door. "Only if you enjoy risking your life."

"Ah, come on," he drawled, bracing an arm on the door beside her head and leaning in close. He pulled the suitcase from her hand before she could react and set it down out of reach. "You ain't gotta be so mean all the time. I ain't so bad. Gimme a chance. Besides, a woman like you needs a man like me. Not some little prick like that Lazzari. The way he just pussyfoots around you. You need a man who's not afraid to take what he wants."

"And what is it that you want, Mr. Morelli?"

"You to call me Jake, for starters." His breath brushed her lips. "And I think I've made it pretty clear what I want."

"To kill me?"

He put his mouth beside her ear and chuckled. The sound made her shiver. "You're the most beautiful dame I ever seen. Why would I want to kill you?"

She turned her head and their lips nearly touched. "Because I made you look like an ass."

His jaw tensed. "You got a smart mouth for a broad."

"And what are you gonna do with it?"

He held her gaze for a long, heated moment, then deliberately tilted his head. An instant later, his mouth was on hers. His lips were soft and rough at the same time, and tasted of tobacco laced with whiskey. He reached up to cup her jaws in his hands in a grip that was as rough as his lips, but it wasn't unpleasant. In fact, if she hadn't despised him, she might have felt herself getting swept away on a thrilling rush of passion.

His mouth left hers abruptly when he stumbled back several feet, roaring in pain and clutching his neck just beneath his jaw where she'd stabbed him with the little sewing pin from the side of her dress.

"What the fuck?" he bellowed, his chest heaving with rage. He pulled his hand away, and she was mildly fascinated by the thin stream of blood rolling down his neck. The wound was far from fatal, but it produced more blood than she'd expected. "You fucking stabbed me!"

"Oh, it was just a little pin," she said, flicking it away. "Anyway, I warned you not to touch me."

"You crazy bitch," he spat, his tone a mixture of wonder and fury. He clenched his fists, blood still trailing down his neck, as he stepped toward her. He backed her into the door again, the front of his body pressed to hers. "I *was* gonna take it easy on you, but now I see you're a bitch who needs the man in charge to put you in your place."

She gazed up at him impassively. "Oh? Tell me. Who's in charge, then? And what's my place?"

He opened his mouth to answer, but a metallic click stopped him. He froze as a revolver's snub nose suddenly pressed to his temple.

Behind him, Paolo bared his teeth as he shoved the gun against Jake's head so hard, the other man's neck bent from the force of it.

"Yeah, all right, now," Jake said in a very different tone than what he'd just used with Mia, lifting his hands into the air. "Take it easy."

Paolo grunted.

"Mr. Scarpa would like you to back up," Mia said. "You're making him nervous. And when he gets nervous, his hands get real shaky."

Jake backed up slowly. "Mia, baby, come on."

"Baby? What happened to 'crazy bitch'?" she said, cocking her head.

"I was just—"

"Kidding around?" She stepped toward him. "Me, too. So why aren't you laughing?"

"You got a fucking loaded gun to my head!"

"And you had someone point one at me last night," she said in a deadly quiet voice. "And instead of hitting me, you hit one of my employees. And he's dead now."

"How many times I gotta tell you, it wasn't me?"

"About as many times as I gotta tell you to keep your filthy hands off me," she replied. "And I don't think you've quite got the message yet."

"I got the message," he muttered.

"Do you? Maybe I should have Paolo blow your brains all over this hallway to be sure."

With a little answering growl, Paolo shoved the gun even harder against Jake's skull.

"Jesus Christ, Mia—"

She touched Paolo's arm, and he immediately stepped away from Jake. He did not lower the gun. She had no intention of actually killing him. But it was a tactic she'd seen Nick resort to on occasion to drive home the point that he was capable of it, and it almost always did the trick.

*One foot in, one foot out.*

The truth Charlie had pointed out to her, the one she was so desperately trying to run from, seemed to reach out and grab her by the soul.

Jake straightened with the speed of a snail, his cautious stare locked on Paolo, who glowered at him from Mia's side. He shifted his gaze to Mia, his nostrils flaring as he sucked in deep lungfuls of air like he'd run a mile.

"You look a bit unwell. Perhaps you should go home and get some rest." Mia picked up her suitcase and started past him, patting him on the chest as she went. "Partner."

"Yeah," she heard behind her. "Thank you."

Outside, Joey waited by the car. "Miss S. Your sister-in-law's all tucked in. I left Bobby outside her door. I believe she's resting comfortably."

Mia sighed inwardly. Something else, and more immediate, she didn't feel like facing. "Good. I'll be home to look after her."

Joey nodded and opened the back door for her.

"Mia," a voice called as she was climbing inside.

She looked over her shoulder as Charlie strode toward her and stepped back onto the sidewalk. "Hi."

"I was lookin' for you," he said. "Hard to get through that mob in there. Surprised you didn't hang around."

She shrugged. "I'm ready to call it a night. Besides, I should go pick up Emilia."

"I was going to ask if you'd let me make up our date to you." He gave her a wry smirk and held up his hands, palms facing her. "No more surprises. I promise."

It was on the tip of her tongue to refuse, but she looked up at him. His handsome face was open and earnest. His bowtie hung undone around his neck, and his insistent, errant curly forelock hung in the middle of his forehead, giving him the boyish quality she'd always found endearing.

He and Jake were both, she admitted, exciting men in their

own ways. And in an odd way, she appreciated Jake's gusto for going after what he wanted, but there was no denying she could never trust him, and despite his pleas to the opposite, she was sure he'd had something to do with Fred's murder—that had her as the intended target.

On the other hand, Charlie kept the dangerous edge he used when dealing with everyone else well away from her. He was a man she could rely on, and she knew instinctively she could trust him. He didn't want anything from her...except her.

"I guess Em will be okay with Joe and Connie until tomorrow," Mia said. "They were expecting to keep her overnight, anyway."

One side of Charlie's lush mouth curled up. He said nothing, waiting for her.

"We could have a late supper in my room," she said. "We'd have to be quiet so we don't wake Gloria."

"As a mouse." His dark gaze leveled on her, and Mia suddenly had the urge to shiver deeply. He flicked his head down the street, where his car waited. "Want to ride with me?"

"I just need to let Paolo know." She turned and leaned into the car, grateful for the darkness in the cab to hide her hot face. "Mr. Lazzari is going to see me home. We're going to have dinner."

Joey didn't even flinch. "Sure thing, Miss S."

Paolo narrowed his eyes at her, but nodded once. She knew he would respect her privacy.

She shut the door and smiled at Charlie. "Ready when you are."

He took her arm and looped it through his as they strolled down to where his car waited. He opened the door for her, then climbed in after. A comfortable silence settled between them during the drive to her hotel. The driver didn't even bother with small talk. Meanwhile, Charlie's hand rested atop hers in the middle of the back seat, his thumb stroking lazy circles on the back of her hand and up her forearm. Tingles burst over her skin with every swipe and shot through her body.

When they arrived at the Murray Hill Hotel, he helped her out of the car and pulled her close as they walked through the lobby. The arm he snugged around her waist felt as if it had always been meant to be there. She said a few quiet words to the elevator attendant when they reached her floor, to have him pass along that she wanted two steaks and wine sent up to her room.

Inside her room, she stepped out of her shoes with a soft groan of appreciation. She padded over the plush carpeting to enter Gloria and Raquel's suite through their adjoining door, then checked on both women, who were fast asleep in their bedrooms. Her sister-in-law's breathing was deep and even, and she didn't stir when Mia placed a hand on her forehead.

She shut the door behind her as noiselessly as possible and reentered her suite. "I'm going to freshen up before the food gets here," she said to Charlie. "When the steaks arrive, just put them on the table there."

"Yes, ma'am." He pulled off his tuxedo jacket, his eyes locked on her in a way that heated her down to the bottom of her belly.

She scurried into the bathroom and drew a hot bath. She wouldn't indulge in a long soak, but one long enough to get the grime of the night and the memory of Jake's rough, burning mouth out of her mind.

*I suppose I ought to tell Charlie about that*, she thought, stripping naked and sliding into the tub with a sigh.

After a too-quick bath, she reluctantly toweled off. A clean nightie and her robe hung on the hook on the door and nothing else. The nightie's silky material slid over her skin like a lover's kiss.

She swiped her hand across the fogged mirror over the sink. She'd washed her face in the tub, and the smoky eye makeup, rouged cheeks, and stained red lips were gone. The Saturday Night Special had retired for the night, and now she was just…Mia.

A soft knock from the door made her turn. "Food's here."

She slid on her robe and stepped out into the living room.

Charlie set dishes on the small table by the window. He glanced at her as she walked over, his gaze lingering on her attire. She couldn't remember having worn so little around him before, but it felt perfectly natural now. At any rate, he didn't comment on it, though a little appreciation flicked through his eyes.

They cut into their steaks, but after a few bites, Mia pushed her plate away and settled back in her chair with her wine.

Charlie set down his fork and knife and wiped his mouth on a linen napkin. "Still thinking about Glo?"

"The whole evening. It was going so well…for a while. I feel terrible about Raquel."

"She'll understand. She seems like a sweet girl." His gaze dropped to her throat. "What'd you do with that necklace?"

"It's in my jewelry box." She held up her wrist, where the bracelet he'd given her dangled. "This stays on."

He smiled into his wineglass.

"After the show, I ran into Jake."

The smile vanished. "The fuck did he want?"

She smirked. "To steal a few moments alone, I guess. I accused him of trying to kill me. He denied it. Then he kissed me."

Charlie's jaw clenched. "I see."

"Then," Mia went on, "I stabbed him in the neck with a pin from my dress."

One of his dark brows lifted. "You…*stabbed* him? With a pin?"

"Well, Paolo showed up in time. He put a gun to his head."

"Good. Arrogant prick deserved it."

She swirled the dark red liquid in her glass. "Maybe he really didn't try to have me killed."

"If not him, then who?"

"That's what I can't figure." She set her glass down and rose from her chair, then went to the big window that overlooked the city. "I can't seem to figure much these days."

"What do you mean?"

"I came back here and thought I'd just be Hyman's little

porcelain doll. I'd let him make me a star here in New York, I'd make good money, take care of Glo and Em, and maybe one day bring Nick's remains back here, so he can lay beside our parents. But it seems like at every turn, something throws me off course."

Charlie joined her at the window. "Some of us ain't helping with that, I'm sure. I suppose in a way, we forced you to get back into the liquor business."

"You didn't force me," she said. "It—it was the nudge I needed. To step up. I never wanted to be a bootlegger, but…it's a good business. And it's my family business. And I don't trust everyone around me. I can't."

"You can trust me." Their gazes locked in the reflection of the window. "I've done some things that hurt you, but I had my reasons. Joining with Masseria."

"I know."

He raised his eyebrows. "You do?"

"I've been thinking a lot about what you said at John's," she said. "You know. One foot in, one foot out."

"And?"

She lifted a shoulder. "It's something I'm still struggling with, but I understand it. And I know why you did what you did. I guess…to be made always meant a death sentence to me. Look at Nick."

"It doesn't have to be the same way for me." Charlie paused. "Or for you."

"Me?"

It was his turn to shrug. "Your brother was a made man. You're not so different from other Mafia chiefs, you know. You've made your bones. If you were a man, you'd have a scar, too. You're head of the Scalisi family, Mia."

"There *isn't* a Scalisi family."

"Bullshit." Charlie pulled her into his arms, her back to his chest. "You got Paolo. Bobby and Joey. I know they pledged their loyalty to you."

"They're good men. They did it for Nick."

Charlie sighed. "They did, but give them some credit.

They're not just blindly loyal machines. If you weren't up to snuff or worth fighting for, trust me, there ain't enough money in the world to buy their loyalty. Just own up to the fact that you're stepping into your brother's shoes. The sooner you do that, the better off you'll be."

She tilted her head back against his shoulder. "How do you figure?"

"Two feet in."

"I remember a time when you wanted me nowhere near all this."

Charlie was quiet for a long time. "A big part of me still doesn't. But you changed that when you killed three men for Nick. I thought after Kiddo you'd get scared and stop. But you just kept charging ahead. And that day when you came home, and I looked up and saw you standing in Hyman's doorway... I saw you, the changes in you."

"I did gain a little weight, I suppose."

"You look even more beautiful than before you left. But that's not what I mean." He tipped her face up with a finger beneath her chin. His eyes were serious and a little troubled. "It was like I could see inside you. The way you carry yourself now. It's hard to describe, but I took one look at you and I knew."

"What did you know?"

"That everything you did after Nick died was just the beginning."

She turned her head away from him. "You make me sound like some kind of crazy, rampage killer."

"No. I mean, if you're the kind of person who believes in *destiny*, it became clear to me in that moment that you'd stepped up and claimed yours."

Mia tightened her jaw. "I'm just trying to protect my family."

"It's okay to want money and power, too. Why the hell do you think any of us do the things we do?"

"It's not what I want."

"Bullshit."

Infuriated, she whirled in his arms, but he held up a finger before she could unleash.

"The night we unloaded. When you and Morrie were getting into it. You told him—told us all—what we could do with those cut batches. I saw what you did."

She wrinkled her brow. "What did I do?"

Charlie tilted his head, lifting one eyebrow slightly. "One look at Paolo. One tiny little flick of your head, and he had a gun pulled on Morrie's men. That's power. And you ordered it like you were signaling a waiter to bring you another cocktail."

"Don't be so dramatic," she muttered, looking away from his gaze. The intensity in it was making her uncomfortable.

"Or how about when we all met with Morelli at Uncle Joe's grocery? He was flinging insults that probably would've gotten him killed in any other situation. But you kept control of the situation."

"I'm not sure who was in control that night."

"Morelli can be an idiot sometimes, but he ain't stupid. If he didn't understand the power you have, he would've brushed you aside like a fly."

"He *did* likely try to have me killed."

Charlie ran a finger down her cheek. "He'll never succeed."

"You sound pretty sure of yourself."

"I am."

"I don't need more bodyguards," Mia said.

"What do you need?"

She lifted her gaze to his. "Maybe I don't need anyone at all."

"I don't believe that for a second."

"Maybe you don't know me the way you thought you did." She made to step around him, but he caught her by the shoulders to stop her, then cupped her face in his hands.

"I know you," he murmured. "I see you, right down to your core. I see your light. I feel your heat. I felt it the very first time I ever saw you. Like my heart just stopped in my chest."

She thought back to that night, at Penny's on the boardwalk in Atlantic City, when she'd begged Nick to bring her to the party he was going to that night. When he'd relented and brought her, she'd strolled in like she owned the place and turned every head she passed. Then, the crowd had parted, and she'd spotted a young, dark-haired man, danger radiating off him like an aura. He'd puffed a cigar, laughing with some pals, dark eyes scanning every single face. And then they'd landed on her, and it had felt like her heart just stopped, too.

"I'm so very different from that girl."

"In some ways. In others, you're the same you've always been." A furrow formed between his eyebrows. "Either way—I love you, Mia. All of you."

And he kissed her.

Her body went liquid at the first touch of his lips. It was so different than Jake's burning, forceful kiss. Charlie was gentle but sure, assertive but yielding, and oh, so very skilled.

Her brain went dizzy immediately. She slipped her arms around his neck to pull her body as close to his as possible as his hands went their separate ways, one sliding into her hair, the other wrapping tightly around her waist.

When he pulled away from her mouth to graze her neck with his lips, she swallowed against the curious urge to burst into tears. "Please don't be another thing that changes," she said, a tremor in her voice. "I couldn't bear it."

"Never," he promised. "I'll always be here for you. With you."

She pulled him to her for another kiss, her mouth blooming beneath his to allow their tongues to meet. She unbuttoned his shirt and pushed it off his shoulders while he pulled off his collar. His hands settled at her waist, slowly tugging the sash of her robe.

"No pins under here?" he teased against her lips, turning her insides to liquid. "You gonna stab me, too?"

She tried to catch her breath. "I supposed you'll have to see for yourself."

He scooped her into his arms and carried her into the bedroom, where he unwrapped her like a gift, taking his time, layer by layer. The belt loosened, then he opened first one side of her robe, then the other, then slid it slowly over her shoulders to pool at her feet. Then he ran his hands down her silk-covered sides, the cool material sliding against her hot skin. His fingers toyed with the straps of the nightgown as he caressed her skin before nudging one strap over the slope of her shoulder, and then, as though she were fragile, the other.

The nightgown dropped straight down to join the robe. Bare before him, Mia held his gaze and waited.

His eyes went over her languidly, as though she were a work of art he wanted to drink in. "You're exquisite."

She bit her lip as she reached for him. She helped him pull off his undershirt, then lower his trousers. His body was lithe and firm, his muscles sculpted as though hewn from stone. "So are you."

He gathered her in his arms and laid her down on her bed. Beneath her bare skin, the down in her pillows and blankets were soft and cushy, like clouds keeping them afloat near the heavens. It was as though she were feeling every sensation for the first time.

Charlie worshipped her with his mouth and hands, leaving no inch of her skin untouched as she arched up to meet him, soft cries falling from her mouth like wishes. When his lips returned to hers, warm and moist and hungry, she made one last wish.

"Charlie...please..."

The ache of his entry was all sweetness. He interlocked the fingers of one hand with hers, sliding it up over her head as he took her on a leisurely journey to ecstasy. His lips broke from hers only to whisper her name in a reverent voice other men might have used to say *Amen. Amen.*

When she fell, shattering, over the cliff, it was his name she uttered like the ending of a prayer, the echo of it pulling him down with her.

Mia slipped under warm waves of a relaxing stream, letting the current carry her along, buoyed by bliss.

Charlie kissed her throat. "Are you all right?" he said into her skin.

"More than all right."

He shifted to one side and maneuvered her so that her back pressed to his front. His warm skin heated her all the way through. He dropped another kiss on her shoulder and draped his arm protectively over her. "Sleep."

She didn't need much encouragement, considering she hadn't gotten much for some time, and it had been...well, never, since she'd felt so safe and warm and comfortable. Because she'd never had Charlie there to make sure she could relax so deeply, knowing he would destroy anything that threatened to disrupt her peace.

So, for the first time possibly since her parents were alive, Mia rested.

THE SOUND OF A FIST BANGING ON THE DOOR MADE THEM BOTH shoot up in bed.

"What time is it?" Mia asked groggily. *What* day *is it?*

But Charlie, alert, was already halfway into his trousers. "Stay here." His voice was gruff and left no room for discussion. He tossed on his dress shirt and left it unbuttoned, but grabbed his pistol and slipped out of the bedroom, leaving the door ajar.

A deep breath helped awaken her mind more, as did three more thumps on the door. She slid out of bed and slipped on the nightgown, then tied the robe tightly around her. She peeked out to the main area, where she heard several low male voices, and a slightly higher, youthful voice. It was a voice that belonged to a boy, not a man.

It was a familiar voice.

She threw open the door and walked out of the bedroom. Joey had a boy by the scruff of his neck. Paolo held him by the arm, and Charlie was in his face, demanding to know who he was.

"Nicky?"

All four faces turned her way. The men looked confused, as if she'd lost her mind. The boy looked hopeful. "Mia!"

"Let him go," she said softly to the other men.

"Yeah, get off me," Nicky said crossly, shaking Joey off and rubbing the back of his neck.

"What are you doing here, kid?" Mia asked in a low, threatening voice as she walked toward him. She wasn't exactly the picture of malice in her bathrobe, but his eyes widened anyway. Probably because he likely hadn't seen too many women in this state of undress before.

"Found him wandering in the hallway, asking for you," Joey said.

"How'd you know where to find me?" Mia demanded.

"You said to ask for you at the grocery," he said meekly.

She glanced at the clock on the wall. "It's a quarter after three in the morning."

"I know, and I'm sorry. But your uncle came to the door and he said I could find you at this hotel. He said I should be careful of your dog." He glanced around. "But I don't see no dog."

Mia glanced at Paolo. He smirked. "It's a long way from the store. How'd you get here?"

"I told your uncle I had something real important to tell you. So he gave me cab fare."

"Well?" Charlie said testily. "It's three in the goddamn morning, kid."

"Come and sit down," Mia said with a sigh.

The door that joined the two suites opened, and Gloria poked her head out. "What's going on?" Her eyes were still bloodshot, but she wasn't slurring. Her gaze landed on Charlie. "What are you doing here?" Then Nicky. "Who's that?"

"Pal of mine," Mia said. She looked at Nicky. "You hungry?"

His brow scrunched up. "It's three in the morning."

"I don't think that means a whole lot to you, does it?"

"Well...yeah, I could eat," he admitted.

Mia turned to Gloria. "Would you call down to the front and have them send up some steak and eggs?"

Gloria glanced at Nicky, then shrugged, a little bewildered. "Sure." She disappeared back inside her room and shut the door.

Mia pointed at the sofa as she took a seat in the chair. "Start talking."

Nicky plopped down on the sofa. "The Murray Hill, huh? Fancy digs. I knew you were an important lady."

"I'm also a tired lady who had a very late night and hardly any sleep," Mia said.

"Right," Nicky said. "Well, uh, you said to come and see you if I had information for you."

"This better be life or death, kid."

"I was hanging around a card hall, and heard some fellas talking. Some bootleggers. They said a few trucks Frankie Yale outta Brooklyn sent up north to Canada got hijacked before they even reached the border."

Mia froze. "What?"

"Yeah, they said the drivers all got shot and the product was all stolen, along with a whole bunch of money. Nobody knows what happened to it now, but they heard that some of the product on those trucks was rye whiskey from Templeton. The good stuff." He cleared his throat. "*Your* stuff. Right?"

"What makes you say that?"

"You told me to…ask around the neighborhood about you," he said hesitantly.

There was a knock on the door—a hotel butler with the steak and eggs Gloria ordered. Joey tipped the man and Mia pushed the cart in front of Nicky and removed the plate covering.

"Dig in," she said. "You did a good job."

As the boy complied, Mia joined Charlie and Joey a few feet away, close to the door.

"Well, what the hell do we do now?" she demanded. "There's customers over the border expecting that whiskey. Customers who paid very good money for that."

Charlie looked at Joey. "Get some men and see what you can

find out about who's behind the hijacking. Whoever it was has balls—that was Capone's money they stole, meant for his Canadian Club."

Joey bobbed his head. "We'll look into it right away."

"What about our buyers?" Mia said. "Morrie said we got paid in advance."

"We did." Charlie sighed and rubbed the back of his neck. "He's got the business contact up there. We'll tell him in the morning, and maybe he can use that slick tongue of his to buy us some time. Then we can get on the horn with Will and see how much product he has on hand right now, get their replacement order ready."

"I don't want it coming through New York." Mia folded her arms. "Whoever this was is familiar with our routes. I want Will to send it straight from Iowa."

Joey shook his head. "That's risky, too. New York ain't the only place with hijackers."

"It's a risk I'd rather take than do this again," she argued. "Especially if we're being targeted."

"We'll call him in the morning. First thing," Charlie promised.

"I wonder if Frankie's in the wind yet," Mia said. "He didn't seem too bothered by anything tonight."

"He might know by now, but not earlier. He'd have blown his fucking top, trust me."

Mia returned to her seat. Nicky was just about done with his meal, using his fork and a crust of bread to coax an enormous bite of eggs piled on a piece of steak into his mouth. It was as though he hadn't eaten in days.

"You don't know the fellas who were talking about this?"

He shook his head, chewing rapidly. After he swallowed, he said, "I never saw 'em before."

"Did it sound like they were in on it?"

Another shake of his head. "Nah. They seemed real surprised anyone would cross Frankie Yale like that."

"Whose card hall were you at?"

"Mr. Luciano's."

Charles Luciano wasn't above thievery, she was sure, but he seemed to be doing well enough in his own affairs that he didn't need to resort to stealing anyone else's shipments. Besides, as far as she knew, he and Yale were friendly. At least, they didn't seem to want to kill each other. *Same thing.*

When Nicky was finished with his meal, she gave him a twenty-dollar bill. His eyes grew large as he reached for it.

She held tight to the money and looked Nicky in the eye. "I keep my word, don't I?"

He nodded vigorously.

"When you get back home, you never came here. You never talked to me. You don't know where I live. We never had this conversation. Understand?"

Another nod.

She released the bill. "Joey'll give you a ride home."

"Come on, kid," Joey said, opening the door.

"Thanks," Nicky said to Mia.

She flicked her head at the door. "Go home to your mother."

After he and Joey left, and Paolo retired to his room, Mia and Charlie crawled back into bed. Gloria's door remained closed.

"Is this as bad as it seems?" Mia murmured into his chest.

Charlie sighed. "Could be pretty bad. But I'm not worried about the Canadians too much. I think Morrie can work something out. But it's the not knowing. First the shooting the other night, now this."

"What'll happen next?" Mia mused.

Charlie didn't answer, but his arms tightened around her, and that confirmed her own thoughts. The possibilities of what might happen next were narrowing, and none of them were pretty.

Most of them ended with her dead.

# CHAPTER SIXTEEN

Early the next morning, Mia went into the other suite and
knocked gently on Gloria's bedroom door before opening it
a few inches. Gloria roused herself, glancing at the glasses of
water and orange juice Mia carried on a tray.

"Good morning," she offered in a meek voice.

Mia set the tray on Gloria's nightstand and handed her two
aspirin. "How are you feeling?"

"Humiliated." Gloria popped the aspirin in her mouth and
tilted back the glass of water. She drained it in a moment and
wiped her mouth on the back of her hand. She reached for Mia's
hand. "I'm sorry."

Mia sighed, looking down at their hands. "Why?"

"I was...enraged when I found out she was there. I haven't
gotten over any of that. I never had time, you know." Gloria
drew her hand back. "Nick and I were trying to work through
things, and he died before we could really get started. I was
thrown into mourning him. And seeing her brought everything
back. And to learn that you *knew* she was there... Why wouldn't
you tell me that?"

"I didn't know she was going to be there," Mia said. "She

showed up at my dressing room. I didn't even think to mention it to you. I...had a lot on my mind."

"What you said in your dressing room," Gloria murmured. "It was a betrayal, Mia."

Mia drew her head back. "What?"

"That she didn't steal Nick from me."

"Gloria, you and I both loved Nick, in very different ways. But let's cut the bullshit—he was a cad," Mia said sharply. "Annette wasn't the first, and despite his best efforts, she probably wouldn't have been the last. She didn't have to do much more than crook her finger. Nick wasn't cut out to be faithful."

Gloria reeled back against her pillows, her face draining of its color. "You...you *begged* me to give him another chance. You begged me not to leave him!"

"And I meant what I said then. I didn't want you to leave him. For all he was a cad, he loved you. To death. But you know as well as I do it was a matter of time before he reverted to how he's always been. So a man like that can't be stolen when he's begging to be taken by any broad with legs and a pretty smile. And at the end of it all, you made a scene at my place of employment, and you nearly ruined everything."

The conversation had veered violently off the rails. How had it gone this way? Why couldn't she just have accepted Gloria's apology and made up with her?

*Why are you shoving her away? Why are you hurting her like this?*

Gloria stared down at her hands, silent tears rolling down her cheeks.

Mia's heart seared. What had she done? "Glo... I'm sorry. I—I didn't mean that. Any of it. I'm just—"

"You're just being honest," Gloria said in a cold voice. "Thank you for the medicine, Mia. I need to get up and get ready for Mass. My family's waiting on me and your cousin."

*My. Me. Your.* No longer *our, we.*

"I'm going, too," Mia said. "Obviously."

"Is it obvious?" Gloria slid out of bed and disappeared into her bathroom, shutting the door.

Mia stared after her. Goddamn her mouth. Gloria was the closest thing she had to an actual sister. And she'd kicked her—hard—when she was already down. Like Mia, Gloria was stubborn with her feelings and her forgiveness. The fissure that had been growing between them had just cracked wide open, and Mia didn't know how to fill the chasm.

She heard the sound of running water, and beneath it, the sound of weeping.

Mia slid off the bed and lingered by the bathroom door, hand poised above the knob. Then, after a moment, she turned and went back to her suite.

The early morning light cast its golden beam on Will Wyatt, who sat on the sofa, drinking a cup of black coffee and wearily rubbing his forehead. Charlie stood by the large window, curtains opened, talking on the candlestick telephone.

Mia sat beside Will and sighed.

"Seems like it went real well," he said, nodding toward the adjoining door.

A humorless smirk twisted at her lips, and she wondered if it looked as ugly as it felt. "It always does, these days."

"That was quite the scene last night."

"Sure was," Mia said, a note of bitterness in her voice. "Half of New York saw it, and the other half probably heard it."

"It's all a part of the grievin' process." He set his cup down. He was a handsome man, if the features of his face appeared to be carved from stone. He so rarely emoted or spoke, it was easy to privately think he was all cogs and motors beneath his tanned, freckled skin. A war vet, he and Nick had fought together in France. Nick had saved him from meeting his end at the wrong side of a Jerry's rifle, and their friendship and later, business partnership, had been born and cemented.

"What's a part of the process?" Mia asked. "Making drunken scenes, humiliating yourself and the people trying to take care of you, and pushing away the ones you love? That's all a part of the process?"

Will refreshed his coffee, then poured her a cup. "Sure, to

some. As much as killing men in the name of revenge is to others."

Her mouth opened, but she couldn't think of anything to say.

"I ain't judgin', mind you." He held out the cup to her. "Here, woman, take it and stop looking at me like I'm next. I'm just saying, there ain't no rules when it comes to mourning some-one's loss. No time limit. No right or wrong way. Lots of people do things they never woulda otherwise done in the name of pain. Mrs. Scalisi ain't no different, and neither are you."

Mia sipped her coffee and made a face. It was black.

Will ticked an amused eyebrow at her. "Cream and sugar, miss?"

"No, thank you," she murmured.

"Anyway, I don't mean to jabber at you about your own family affairs," Will went on, "but my advice you didn't ask for is to cut her some slack and give her some grace. She's finding her way."

"Grace?" Mia repeated.

"I know. Rich, coming from me."

"No, I…" She trailed off and swirled her coffee. "That's very wise. Thank you."

He nodded. After a moment, he added, "I thought you did a real nice job last night."

"Thanks." She gave him a sidelong glance. "So how *does* the Iowa hick like the big city?"

Something that was as close to a smile as she would ever get from him crossed his face. "The Iowa hick liked the big city very well, though it's a trifle smelly here."

"I saw you being a gentleman with my cousin," Mia added. "That was kind of you."

He cleared his throat and scratched his neck. "She seemed a little out of place, like me. Thought she could use the company." He sipped his coffee and adopted a casual tone. "Nice girl."

"Pretty, too," Mia said, narrowing her eyes slightly, but smiling.

"That's a fact," he agreed. "Might I inquire as to how long she'll be in town?"

"Quite a while. Her brother wants her to find a husband while she's here."

Will spluttered into his coffee.

Mia grinned, then set her hand on his shoulder. "She's twenty, Will. A woman grown. But she's a country girl. She's innocent. She needs someone to take care of her, not look at her like a good time."

"I don't look at her like a good time," he said quietly. "She's...sweet." His mouth curled up in a slight, sardonic smile. "I'll forgive her on account of the fact she looks an awful lot like you."

Mia returned the smile with a snort and an elbow to his ribs. Then the sound of Charlie's raised voice drew their attention toward the window. He paced, his shoulders tense.

"...we still don't know," he was saying. "All that matters is we buy a little time to get them a replacement. I don't fucking know, Morrie. That's up to you. You made the contact." He paused, staring out the window and shaking his head. "Look, just call them, all right? Run that slick mouth of yours and ask them for more time. It's your ass, too." He slammed the receiver onto the base's hook. "Goddammit."

"Sounds like he was very willing to help us out," Mia said.

"Yeah," Charlie muttered. "Willing. For him."

"So can he do it?" Will said, spreading his hands.

"Says he'll probably be able to, but he can't guarantee nothin' without talking to Canada."

"Will," Mia said. "How soon can you get trucks on the road? From Iowa, straight to Canada."

"Today," he replied. "But oughtn't we wait for Morrie to confirm?"

"You can always turn a truck around, or stop it in a place we distribute," Mia said. "I want trucks on the road immediately. If Canada says they'll give us a bit more time, I want them to have that booze no more than a day after they were supposed to. The rest of it, we'll deal with."

"Fine." Will gave a laconic shrug. "I'll place a call. But who stole the first shipment?"

"That's what we're working on," Charlie said.

A single, sharp knock sounded on the adjoining door, then Gloria said, "If you're coming, we're leaving."

Mia had been up and dressed since dawn. She glanced between the two men. "I have to go. You two are welcome to stay."

"We won't stay long," Charlie said. "Will and I got some work to do today, anyway."

"And you best not keep Gloria waiting when she sounds that het up," Will added.

Mia gave him a half smile. "You're not leaving right away, are you?"

"Bought a one-way ticket here," he replied. "Didn't know how long I should stay."

"Well, don't hurry off." Mia reached for her cloche and handbag. "I'll see you later."

Paolo drove them to Most Precious Blood. Gloria was silent, and Raquel was uneasy at the tension between her and Mia, so Mia did what she could to put the girl at ease and rattled off nonsense stories from her childhood about Sundays. Soon, Raquel seemed to relax.

Mia walked inside behind Gloria and Raquel and dunked her fingers in the small font of holy water mounted on the wall just inside the door, scanning the packed church for Joe, Connie, and Emilia.

Gloria spotted them first, her face breaking into a wide smile. "Up there. I see them."

"Lead the way," Mia said.

They'd made it halfway up the aisle when Jake Morelli stepped into their path. "Ladies, Mia. Good morning. Happy Sunday."

He smiled innocently at them, giving Mia a long look before

settling his gaze on Raquel. He put a hand over his heart. "Holy Christ, who's this?"

"My name is Raquel," she said shyly.

Her accent seemed to give her away. Jake bent over her hand and a stream of flowery compliments poured out of his mouth in Sicilian as he kissed her knuckles, his lips lingering a beat too long. His dark eyes cut to Mia, and she felt her face turning red with rage.

Finally, she reached out and snatched Raquel's hand away. "That's enough."

"What, I can't say good morning to…who is this? Your little sister?"

"Cousin," Raquel said with a smile. "I just arrived. From Sicily."

"Cousin," Jake repeated. Before she could move, he grabbed Mia's hand and tugged her close, then kissed her cheek in the same lingering manner he'd kissed Raquel's hand. "Me and your ol' cuz Mia here, we're dear friends. Aren't we, dollface?"

"I wish that pin had been a knife," she hissed in his ear.

"Oh, come now," he said loudly. "That ain't real Christian of you."

She shook him off. "What're you doing here?"

"I told you last time. I go to church here. What, you think you own this place, too, dear?"

She glared at him.

"Maybe I'll see you in the Communion line later, huh?" He flashed a charming smile at Gloria and Raquel, then gave Mia's arm a friendly squeeze. "Mm," he said in her ear. "You should have finished what you started last night, 'cause I ain't letting up now."

If she could have, she would have shot him right there, church or no. Instead, to the shock and horror of her sister-in-law and cousin, and the awe of her niece, Mia spat at his feet.

He chuckled in her ear. "Be seeing you, toots."

She couldn't contain a low growl as he returned to the pew, adopting an earnest expression as he chatted with a couple of middle-aged people Mia recognized from the neighborhood but couldn't identify. He caught her eye and winked.

She turned on her heel and stalked up the aisle to catch up with her family, acutely aware of his stare on the back of her head the entire Mass.

At the end of Mass, Aunt Connie went to chat with some of the women while the rest of them waited near the aisle. Mia checked the back of the church where Jake had been, but he seemed to have left. *Good.*

An anguished cry came from the front of the church near the altar. Mia whipped her head in the direction of the sound. Aunt Connie had her arms around a younger-looking woman, who was supported on her other side by Father Alessio. A third woman stood off to the side, silently clutching her rosary, eyes shut as tears rolled down her cheeks.

"What on earth?" Gloria murmured, sliding an arm around Emilia's shoulder.

"Who's that lady?" Raquel asked.

"That's Signora Cancio," Mia said as she got a better view. She blinked. She hadn't been as present at the shop since Friday as she would have liked, but Trudy had not called to give her any indication there had been a problem.

"And that other woman is Signora Franco," Gloria added.

"Excuse me," Mia said to her family before striding across the pews toward the front.

Aunt Connie caught her eye as she approached, and hers were filled with aggrieved tears.

Mia touched Signora Cancio's shoulder. "What is it?"

The woman turned and blinked, then collapsed into Mia's arms. She stumbled back a few steps from the woman's weight, but held her steadfast. "Signora Cancio, what's wrong?"

"My boy," she said in a voice choked with grief and devastation. It was practically guttural. "My boy. *Figghio mio!*"

A knot of dread tightened in Mia's stomach. The small boy from the alley, whom she'd rescued from bullies and given money to. She pictured his big, gentle, dark eyes that had been filled with terror and then with awe. He'd had such a sweet face. A tender face that had seen too much for his youth and been hurt by it. He'd been a child she'd instinctively wanted to protect. He reminded her of herself when she was a child.

And something had happened to him. Something terrible.

The idea of what that might be was too horrendous to utter aloud. Mia drew back and cupped the signora's face in her hands, silently pleading with her to say it all and say nothing, at the same time.

"They killed him," the boy's mother whimpered, clutching Mia's wrists. "They killed my sweet boy. They cut him down in the streets like a dog. My little boy…"

A tremor rattled Mia's heart.

"This is God's will," Father Alessio murmured helplessly. "You must seek strength through Him."

*God's will.*

Mia jerked her hands back as her grip tightened on Signora Cancio's face.

"What is becoming of our home?" Aunt Connie said, weeping with the signora. "Who would murder a child? Rape a young girl?"

"Rape?" Mia whispered.

Connie nodded to Signora Franco, on her knees clutching her rosary. "Two nights ago. Her daughter is eight. Brutalized in an alley. And now early this morning, Signora Cancio's boy."

Mia's hands shook at her sides. A strange sense of guilt made her head go light. Was this her fault? What could she have done to prevent this?

They looked helpless, these mothers who'd had their precious children ripped from them and defiled. And they were helpless to do anything against the men who destroyed their lives. It wasn't fair. They needed someone to stand up for them, to strike back at those who had struck them and send the message that it wouldn't be tolerated.

"Who will give me vengeance?" Signora Cancio cried in a broken voice.

*Vengeance…*

"I will."

The words were out of Mia's mouth before she was aware she had spoken.

The three women and Father Alessio slowly turned their gazes on her.

"T-to seek vengeance is to sin," the priest stuttered.

She stared at him. Through him, past him. The church faded. She was in a dark room, staring down at Kiddo Grainger where he sat tied to a chair. She saw his bloody mouth, the look in his eyes that had gone from hope at being released to a horrifying realization when she'd given his death order and turned her back. She saw Vincenzo Fiore, his smug, self-satisfied expression, thinking he'd gotten over on her, thinking he'd won his life back. She saw the terror bloom in his dark eyes in the instant before she'd leveled Charlie's pistol at his face and pulled the trigger, twice.

And she saw Salvatore Bellomo as she confessed to him she'd planned his hit so he would spend his last few moments on earth understanding it was she who had killed him.

All men she had killed, one way or another. All men she had sought vengeance against in the name of the brother they'd taken from her. They'd stolen her blood, so she'd claimed theirs in response. The weight of that blood was so heavy upon her shoulders, upon her conscience, that she hardly noticed it now.

She had sinned. She would likely go to hell when her time was up. And for avenging her brother, she would go, her chin held high.

And now these women, the simple, goodhearted people of the neighborhood she cared so much about, had suffered horrible losses. She felt their pain, down to the last atom of her being. She understood the devastation, the anguish, the agony.

They could not avenge their losses. But she could do it for them, for the people she thought of as hers.

Mia walked toward Father Alessio in slow, measured strides.

His eyes widened. If her face even remotely reflected how she felt inside, she understood his alarm.

"Then I will sin," she said. "I will accept their blood on my hands, Father. And I will not seek forgiveness, because I am not sorry for what I will do."

Her voice carried through the church, which had gone silent when the sounds of Signora Cancio's aggrieved cries caught the attention of those left inside.

Mia turned, catching the remnants of the congregation watching her closely, as though she were a wild animal outside its natural habitat. Only a few dozen people remained, but she scanned each of their faces. In them was a kinship that went deeper than sharing the same small neighborhood in the Lower East Side. It was ancient, a bond born in blood from the dawn of time, shared with men gone for centuries, awakened with the death of her brother.

"I will take vengeance on those who have wronged these women," she said to them in Sicilian, her voice rising to the rafters, maybe to heaven itself. "I will take vengeance on anyone who wrongs any of you. Anyone who helps me find the people responsible for these crimes will become my trusted friends. I offer my protection, my loyalty, my friendship to all of you today, as I have offered it to Signora Cancio, as I offer it to Signora Franco." She paused, making eye contact with each person who remained inside the church. "But this offer goes both ways. Anyone who protects the men responsible will become my enemies. I swear that to you."

She let her words linger in the air as she glanced from face to face again. She wondered if anyone would laugh at her, but no one dared utter a word, not even Father Alessio.

The silence stretched on before it became unbearable. Without another word to anyone or a backwards glance, Mia walked down the aisle toward the double doors, shoved them open, and went outside.

She just needed to *walk*. She didn't know where she was going, but she picked a direction and went that way.

Her heart was sick and sore at what she'd just learned. She felt lost. On the unlikely chance she hadn't already, she was sure she had become God's enemy today by declaring vengeance by bloodshed, by murder, in His house. What had come over her to say such things?

Mia clenched her hands into fists to keep them from shaking. The force of her emotions was so strong that if she stopped moving, she feared she would collapse on the sidewalk. Fury. Sadness. Hopelessness. Helplessness.

Someone wanted to make her look foolish. Someone wanted to cut her off at the knees. Someone wanted to torment her by tormenting the people she cared about.

What had Jake said to her that morning?

*You should have finished what you started last night, 'cause I ain't letting up now.*

Her instincts told her he was behind what had been happening—the shooting, the hijacking, and somehow the murder of Signora Cancio's son and the rape of Signora Franco's girl. But she had no proof. She had staunchly refused to move on him without proof, because no matter what she had done in the past, no matter how much she loved her brother, she did not want to be a coldblooded murderer as he had become.

But when would enough be enough?

Spring was warming up in New York, tinging the air with a touch of humidity to temper the chill that stubbornly clung to the breeze. Ahead was a small café owned by Signor and Signora Bagnoli, whom she'd met at the reception following Signor Bruno's daughter's funeral. The baker had told her of his troubles, how he'd recently fallen on hard times and had been unable to repair the front windows broken out by a vandal. Mia had given him the money to repair the glass and the damage to the hand-painted sign the following day when he'd visited her at the grocery. Seeing the new, shining windows and the fresh, gleaming paint brought a faint smile to her face. She ducked inside.

Almost instantly, Signor Bagnoli spotted her. "Signorina Scalisi!" he said warmly. "I was hoping to see you today. Ah, my wife and I could not make it to Mass this morning."

"The window looks very nice," she said.

He bowed, shaking her hand vigorously. "If it weren't for you, we would still be struggling."

"I am always here to help you, Signor Bagnoli."

"Have you come for a cup of coffee?" He gestured to a small table near the back of the café. It was mostly empty, since most of the neighborhood had been at Mass. "Please, rest your feet. I will bring you refreshment."

She knew better than to argue, and let him lead her to the small table. Besides, it would be nice to hide out here for a moment. She was sure Paolo was furious with her for walking away like this, and he was likely prowling the streets looking for her right now. It was interesting how a man who could not speak could still scold her like a child with just one reproachful glare.

Signor Bagnoli brought her a cup of strong coffee and a plate of freshly baked biscotti.

"It looks wonderful. How much do I owe you?"

He shook his head. "You have already given me so much. Please, accept this with my gratitude. Is there anything else you desire? A cake to share with your family, perhaps, or some cookies for your niece?"

"I won't let you give anything else away." She placed a hand over his. "You've shown me so much kindness as it is."

A twinkle came into his eyes. "Well, perhaps I can ask one more favor."

"Anything, Signor Bagnoli."

"My daughter's wedding is next weekend. On Saturday. We would be honored if you attended."

Mia smiled, genuine, warm pleasure blooming inside her heart. "The honor would be mine."

"Please bring your family. We will have more food than people to eat it, with the way the women have been carrying on, and I'm baking her wedding cake myself. So many honored guests," he added proudly. "Including Don Masseria. We'd love to have you among us, too."

"Yes, of course we'll be there," Mia said. "Thank you. The groom, is he from New York?"

"He's a fine lad," the baker said with a nod. "His family hails from Palermo, but he was born here. A real American boy."

"That's wonderful."

He left her in peace with the day's newspaper and retired to the back, where the smell of baking bread wafted out in thick, pleasant waves. It made her hungry, as she never ate before Mass. Not because she wasn't supposed to—she hadn't been taking Communion, so it didn't matter—but because Aunt Connie always cooked a small feast on Sundays. She'd learned after her first Sunday home not to eat all day in preparation.

Mia sighed, turning the page of the newspaper. She would finish her coffee, biscotti, and paper, then return to Aunt Connie's. Hopefully Paolo would be there and not still looking for her. It wasn't as though she could get very far on foot, anyway.

She was just dunking her second piece of biscotti into her coffee and reading a story about factory workers' conditions when the bell over the door jangled. She glanced up, expecting to see Paolo and his disapproving frown.

But it was a different man entirely.

He was tall, with pale skin and freckles that gave his weathered face a youthful appearance. Strawberry-blond hair poked from beneath a fedora before he swept the hat off his head. He walked straight toward her.

Mia straightened in her seat, never taking her eyes off him.

There was no preamble when he took the seat across from her. "You're Mia Scalisi."

"That depends on who wants to know," she replied.

"I've been looking for you for a long time," he said. He had looked quite young at a first glance, but now that he was closer, she noted the deep lines etched on either side of his mouth and the crow's feet at the corners of his eyes. There were tiny red marks on the sides of his neck where he'd nicked himself shaving. She also noted his accent. He was from Chicago.

"Have you." She leaned back in her seat and folded her arms.

At that moment, Signor Bagnoli came out, a cheerful smile of welcome on his face. It faltered when he spotted the man.

"Ah," he began, his brow knitting.

"Coffee for the gentleman, please, Signor Bagnoli." Mia kept her stare on her newfound and unwelcome guest. "My friend...?"

He reached into his coat pocket, and she stiffened, waiting to see the snub nose of a revolver pointed at her. But instead of a pistol, he withdrew a leather wallet. When he flipped it open, she saw it was a badge announcing him as a detective.

"Detective Abner Wallace," he replied. "Of the Chicago police department."

Signor Bagnoli was back in practically no time with a cup and saucer and a pot of coffee. His hand shook slightly as he poured a cup for Detective Wallace and refilled Mia's. He gave her a fleeting, questioning look, then disappeared into the back again.

"Well, Detective Wallace," Mia said, sipping her coffee in a relaxed manner she was far from truly feeling. "You're a long way from home, aren't you?"

"I could say the same of you." He stirred his coffee with the little silver spoon that rested on the saucer.

She allowed herself a small, polite stretching of the lips. "Chicago is not my home."

"No? But I had it on good authority you lived at the Lexington Hotel for the past few years."

"Then your authority is mistaken." She set her cup down. "I haven't lived in Chicago for nearly a year and a half now."

"No, I s'pose not." He pulled a notebook from his pocket and made a show of reading what she assumed were notes. "No, I s'pose it does say here the last time you was in Chicago was for the trial of one Salvatore Bellomo."

"What of it?"

"Well, you see," he said, leaning forward and putting his elbows on the table, "after that trial—and I do mean immediately after—Sal Bellomo was found dead. Shot to death."

"Yes. I heard about that."

He picked up his cup around the rim for a sip. "You seem real broken up about it, considering he was your boss and all. Family-like, let you Eye-talians tell it."

"I've had time to make peace with it," Mia said, unable to keep an icy note out of her voice. "He ran with a rough crowd. I suppose that sort of thing catches up with a man after a while."

"Yeah, you're right about that one." Detective Wallace nodded. "'Cept, it sure was odd the way you up and disappeared shortly after his death. We've been wanting to talk to you for quite some time. But it sounds like you left the country altogether for quite a long while."

She raised an eyebrow. "I didn't know I needed anyone's permission to travel."

"Just odd, is all," he said. "See, if you were suspected of something, we'd call that fleeing."

"Am I suspected of something?"

"Not officially," he replied smoothly. "I just wanted to ask you about some interesting coincidences."

"Then ask," she said, her voice carrying an edge. "I got somewhere to be."

"Oh, sure." He consulted his notebook again. Mia was willing to bet if she snatched it away, she'd find his attempts at circles and stars. "So, I have it on good authority your brother was a *capo* in Chicago before he died."

"I don't know what you mean," she said.

He peered at her through narrowed eyes. "Oh, I'm sure you do. See, I know you was well-known in the city when you were there. One of the premier showgirls in Chicago, certainly on the South Side. The Saturday Night Special, ain't that what you was called?"

She did not reply.

"Yeah. So anyways, we know all kinds of gangster types was in and out that joint all the time. Johnny Torrio, Al Capone and his boneheaded brothers—until the one got killed. The Genna brothers, those apes." He flipped his notebook closed with a sharp snap. "And Dean O'Banion."

"If you're asking if I know those men, the answer is yes. As you said, they were regulars, and Sal was a welcoming host."

"You never noticed nothing strange? No booze being passed around? No beef between the two camps?"

"I thought you were a detective, not a prohi," she said. "And beef? I don't know what you mean."

He smiled. "I know you want everybody to think you're just some dumb chorine, Miss Scalisi, but you and I both know that ain't true. Everybody in Chicago knows about the beef between the North and South Sides."

She shrugged one shoulder in as nonchalant a way as possible.

"See, I might be inclined to believe you if you didn't have the brother you had," Detective Wallace went on. "We been set up on Nick Scalisi for a long, long time. Watching his every move."

"You couldn't watch his *every* move," Mia said snottily. She couldn't help it.

"We saw more than you think. No, we never caught him murdering nobody. He was a little too smart for that. But that night of Sal's birthday party? The night them three prohis turned up dead? Guess what? The Bureau knows they went there. They were only playing at being dirty."

Mia stared at him. "What?"

"They had orders to make it seem like they wanted to buy booze and hookers and the like," Detective Wallace said. "To buy from *your* brother and boss. One of 'em called after they got there, said they'd had a meet with Sal already. The Bureau and the department knew where they was. And they never came back." He leaned across the table, fixing her with a hard stare. "Turned up in a river couple days later. Funny coinkydink, huh?"

Mia thought back to that night of Sal's party. Those three

prohis had shown up at her door—as directed by Sal—and tried to rape her. Nick had shown up just in time and beaten one of them to death. The other two had been shot to death, and all three had been dropped in the river. Nick had leaked that story to the press to deflect the crimes away from Stems, away from Sal —at first. It hadn't been breaking news when the bodies had been discovered.

*He's trying to trip you up.*

He was trying to bait her into admitting more than she should know by tossing random facts at her—facts that might not be true. Nick had friends in the department and in the Bureau, and not one of them had said anything about some undercover mission the three in question had been on.

"That is a funny coinkydink, indeed," she said calmly. "But I recall learning about those three dead prohis in the papers. And then the next thing I knew, Sal was being arrested for murder. It was a dreadful time."

The detective's face fell. "Tell me about the day you testified."

Mia folded her hands demurely on the table. "Why?"

"I'm curious, is all."

"I'm afraid that's not a good enough reason."

"You're not in any trouble," he said.

She smiled thinly. "Yet."

"Have you done something to get into trouble, Miss Scalisi?"

*Murder, bribing an officer, bootlegging.* Where should she start? "Not at all."

He shrugged. "Then you shouldn't mind talking to me. So. The day testified, you were spotted leaving the courtroom out the back way. Sal Bellomo told everyone he was going outside for a smoke and didn't want to be bothered. A few minutes later, he was found dead of three gunshot wounds by the back door. His cigarette was still burning."

*It was a cigar.* The words burbled to her lips, but then she hesitated. That was another detail the good detective should know.

An oversight, or was he trying to trip her up again? She pressed her lips together.

"And you was nowhere to be found," he went on.

"We said our goodbyes," she said. "I left. What did I need to hang around the courtroom for?"

"And you saw no one? No one at all? No one suspicious?"

"No," she said flatly, then rose from the table. "I got somewhere to be, Detective Wallace. Good day to you."

It was rude to leave without saying goodbye to Signor Bagnoli, but she wouldn't stay in the café with that detective for one more moment.

She walked outside without a backward look, then turned left to cut through an alley. It led to Elizabeth Street, where she could quickly make her way to the grocery on Mulberry.

A hand dropped over her mouth, cutting off the scream that instantly bubbled up her throat.

Her brain went dizzy as the brick wall of the alley slammed into her back. Her head knocked against the hard wall, and for a moment she saw stars before she blinked them away.

Detective Wallace leered into her face. "You're good, aren't you?" he hissed. "You think you're very, very good. But here's the problem. You're jamming up a lot of business, being all high and mighty like you are. The fellas I work for don't appreciate it. And I got orders to make sure you end up just like your brother—six feet under. Almost had you the other night, but you was too smart to get close to me, weren't you?"

So it had been him who'd tried to shoot her outside her shop. "You bastard," she gasped.

He gripped her face in one hand and flicked a switchblade open with the other. He placed the tip of the blade right beside her eye. "My boss says he'll sell dope wherever he wants. Oh, and Chicago sends its regards."

She fought against him. The tip of the knife scratched her face. She shoved against his hand hard, knocking him off-balance a tiny bit, but it was enough for her to get her knee up where it would do the most damage between his legs. He doubled over, grunting in agony.

Mia fumbled her blackjack out of her pocket, slipped her finger through the leather loop at one end of the tether, then swung her arm up. The small, heavy, leather-wrapped ball connected with the underside of the detective's chin. His head snapped back and he stumbled backward several feet, then dropped to a knee.

"You're dead, bitch!"

Mia had no doubt he would make good on that threat if she lingered. She turned and sprinted down the alley as fast as her legs would carry her.

# CHAPTER SEVENTEEN

"Y ou're not leaving until we nail their asses to the wall,"
Charlie said furiously later that afternoon, back in her
hotel room. His fists clenched tightly at his sides.

"I can't stay here. I got a job," she pointed out.

Her family hadn't seemed to know how to deal with her after
her impassioned speech at the church, so they'd almost seemed
relieved when she told them she had a terrible stomachache and
wouldn't be able to attend the family dinner. Poor Raquel had
offered to keep her company, but Mia had insisted she spend the
time with Joe and Connie, getting to know them as they were
eager to get to know her.

As she'd suspected, Paolo had been at the store, pacing like a
caged animal as Uncle Joe tried to reason with him. His face had
lit up with both relief and utter rage at the sight of her, and for
the first time, she was grateful he couldn't speak, because she'd
never hear the end of it. The rage on his face had quickly faded
to concern when she'd confessed to feeling ill, and he'd escorted
her home. As soon as they were alone, she'd told him everything
that had happened with Detective Wallace.

Now, she sat huddled on the couch in the living room of her
suite, clutching a glass of bourbon. As soon as they'd made it

back to her room, she'd telephoned Charlie to come at once. He'd arrived with Moritz and Will, and Joey and Bobby arrived soon after.

"That's it, then," Bobby said decisively. "Me and Joey, we don't leave your side. Not after this."

"Good idea," Charlie said.

"But my family needs protection now more than ever," Mia argued. "I have Paolo."

"No offense to Mr. Scarpa, but I doubt that'll be enough," Moritz said from where he sat across from her in the easy chair. "Make no bones about it, Mia. You've got a target on your back now. We all do."

"To hell with Hyman and that club," Charlie added. "That detective prick can easily find you there. And you perform on a raised stage—you can't get an easier shot."

"That's easy for you to say," she said. "You haven't got Hyman Goldberg breathing down your neck."

"I think he might understand this time," Will drawled. He sprawled in the other easy chair as though he owned it. "At the very least, he'll understand you're no good to him dead. Can't make him no money if he ain't got no singer."

Mia drained her bourbon and shot to her feet. Sitting down made her feel restless, though her knees still shook as she paced. She was rattled, and it angered her.

*My boss will sell dope wherever he wants*, the detective had said. *Chicago sends its regards.*

She repeated the words aloud.

"His boss. Morelli," Charlie spat. "Who else could he mean?"

"You think he's workin' for Weiss and the North Side?" Will asked.

"Unless he explicitly stated a name, we don't know that for certain," Moritz said. "Have we called Chicago yet? The Capones. Surely they'd be able to find something out about this detective."

Mia hadn't called the Capones, but she *had* placed a call to Chicago shortly before the men arrived to her old pal Maurine

Watkins of the *Chicago Tribune*. She'd covered a number of gangland stories in Chicago over the past couple of years, and had been there the day Sal had been acquitted of murder and then murdered himself. Maurine had sounded both shocked and pleased to hear from her.

"Calling to have that interview with me finally, Miss Scalisi?" she'd asked in her cheeky manner.

"Not this time, Miss Watkins," Mia had said, and the urgency in her voice seemed to have caught Maurine's attention.

"Something...I can do for you?"

Mia had asked her to tell her everything she knew about one Detective Abner Wallace and hadn't given any reasons why. The reporter hadn't asked. Maurine was excellent at her job—nosy, pushy, experienced, and smart as a whip. She'd do a better job uncovering facts than the Capones would.

"When was Al planning to go ahead and take care of that pesky Weiss problem, anyway?" Will said, resting one ankle over the other knee. "What the hell's he waitin' on, an engraved telegram?"

"Hymie Weiss is sneaky." Moritz rubbed his bottom lip with a finger. "He's not an easy man to get to. The Capones know that. Besides, they've got to watch their backs, too. They're in an active war with the North Side."

And now that war had been brought all the way to New York to her door.

Mia wrapped her arms around herself. A glance at the clock on the wall told her she was in danger of being late to rehearsal, and subsequently one of Hyman's lengthy lectures on the importance of promptness.

"I gotta go to rehearsal," she said dully.

"Is that really wise?" Moritz asked. "That detective could be watching the hotel, waiting. He might not be working alone either."

"Then whoever's with him can die, too," Charlie said

A silence fell over the room. The men exchanged glances.

"I thought you wanted to avoid a war," Moritz said. "This is not how you go about that."

Charlie glared at him. "So she should allow *two* attempts on her life to go unanswered? Is that what you would do? You just said so yourself—we're *all* at risk here."

"I'm saying, be smart about this," Moritz insisted. "We don't know how much support he has. You were a soldier, Charlie. I'm sure they taught you all about the lessons learned from Pickett's Charge, no?"

"Killing those bastards is the first priority," Charlie snarled. "Morelli. The detective. Weiss. Maybe when you stop acting like a coward, you'll realize that."

Mia sucked in a breath.

Moritz's face went pale with anger, and he rose slowly from the easy chair to step toward him. "It's not cowardice, Charles. It's strategy."

Both men were close friends. Both men had been her brother's most trusted allies, after her. That they were now practically at each other's throats made her heart burn. No matter how at odds with Moritz she'd been, or how complicated things between her and Charlie were, she could not let their bond fray. Nick would never have allowed that, and it would have broken his heart had he seen it.

"Hey." Mia stepped between them, placing a hand on each of their chests and pushing gently. "I think we're all smart enough here to figure Morelli's got that detective on his payroll, but maybe we should wait until that's confirmed. I'm with Morrie on this one. I don't want unnecessary bloodshed."

"It's *not* unnecessary," Charlie said shortly. "He tried to kill you, Mia. You don't let something like that go. Because he's gonna keep coming at you until he gets lucky."

"Don't you think I know that?" She shook her head. "I learned today a young boy I helped, whose mother I helped, was murdered last night. I learned another woman's girl was raped. By the men who work for Jacopo Morelli. These are *children*. If they'd do that to kids, of course I know I'm fair game."

"All the more reason to take him out."

"Maybe not," Moritz said. "His men, sure. But Jake is motivated by one thing—money. Maybe there's a deal to be struck with him."

Charlie scoffed in disbelief. "You gotta be kidding me."

"I'm not." He straightened his glasses and looked at Mia. "Your last meeting with him went poorly. Maybe it's time to really reason with him."

She sighed, folding her arms. "Do you *truly* believe he's someone who can be reasoned with?"

"To avoid unnecessary bloodshed, I'd say it's worth a try." Moritz held up his hands. "Listen. Morelli's a regular guest at a card game I operate. Why not have a meeting with him and try to hash things out? On neutral territory. We'll all be there to help mediate things. Come to an agreement. You're not Nick, Mia. You don't have to resort to murder."

She glanced at Charlie, whose mouth was pressed in a tight line. He didn't like the idea much more than she did.

"One last try," Moritz added. "No one could say you didn't make the effort."

Her jaw clenched. The thought of sharing a table with Jake Morelli now was abhorrent. But Don Catalano had warned her against the price of bloodshed.

*And you never wanted to become a murderer. Remember?*

"Fine," she muttered. "Tonight, after the club." She stared hard at Moritz. "But this is the final time I'm willing to sit down and try to *reason* with Mr. Morelli."

It was easy to stay out of Hyman's way that night at The Divine, as he was obviously still angry with her. He spoke to her with cold politeness during her rehearsal, and after ensuring she had what she needed to prepare herself for the show in her dressing room, made himself scarce. She spoke to him only once more when her performance concluded shortly after one in the morning. The band was contracted until the club closed at three.

At the end of her set, Mia changed out of her cream and gold gown into a black number with a plunging neckline, elaborate silver beading, and plenty of sheer, diaphanous chiffon that floated about her shins and wisped along behind her. She touched up her lips with her favorite bloodred shade and blotted them together, then tossed the lip rouge into her clutch. Then she locked her dressing room door behind her and walked through the service hallway to the back door.

It was time for her sit-down—her last sit-down—with Mr. Morelli.

"Mia."

She froze at the sound of Hyman's voice. *What does he want?* Slowly, she turned to face him. "Yes, Mr. Goldberg?"

He frowned as he walked toward her. "Are you all right?"

She stiffened. "Was there a problem with my performance tonight?"

"Not at all." He spread his hands. "You are, as I always say, a consummate professional. Not a missed lyric, not a forgotten dance step, and your smile was as bright and charming as ever."

She shifted her weight, uncomfortable that he'd been watching her so closely. "Then why would you ask if I was all right?"

He tilted his head. "You didn't really think news of your attack after church this morning wouldn't reach me, did you?"

"I—"

"I was deeply concerned when I received a call from Moritz this afternoon. So much so, I was surprised to see you walk through the doors this afternoon. Why did you not tell me of your troubles?"

She briefly shut her eyes. *Morrie. Bastard.* "I'm a consummate professional, as you said. I didn't want to worry you or allow you to think what happened this morning would somehow affect my work here."

"Still, it's not like you to not share such things with me. We are partners, in more ways than one."

"After last night, I believed it best we give each other a wide berth," she said.

He sighed heavily through his nose. "Yes. We said some unpleasant things last night, didn't we? I insulted your sister-in-law, and you tried to attack me." He lifted an eyebrow. "Cooler heads prevailed, though, did they not?"

"For the time being."

To her surprise, he grinned a little, but it faded quickly. "Moritz also informed me of the other issue that arose last night, which you also failed to mention to me. And this one is an issue that leaves no option of informing me or not. The hijacked truck."

*Morrie's a goddamn snitch,* she thought. "We're working on that."

"Just the same," he said, his voice sharpening, "these are things I need to know. I remain an investor, Mia, and you don't get to choose what you decide to tell me when my money is involved."

She swallowed her own sigh. "I'm sorry. I didn't want you to worry."

"I think you did not want to be lectured. And yet, here we are. I am very worried. Because you see, our friends in the north were expecting quite a lot of fine alcohol. Alcohol they paid handsomely for. Ninety thousand dollars, in fact. And that alcohol they paid so much money for never reached them, because someone who has it out for you all decided it would be fortuitous to steal your trucks. Why in the world, Mia, would anyone feel that acceptable?"

"One of the answers I'm seeking."

"And when you find that answer," he said, angling his head slightly to look her in the eye, "what do you intend to do about it?"

She hesitated. "Nick—"

"No." Hyman reached out and placed his hands on her

shoulders. "I'm not asking Nick Scalisi. I'm asking *you* what to do about the people responsible for attacking you this morning, for hijacking your trucks, for shooting your police officer friend—by the way, I assume that bullet was meant for you. What does Mia Scalisi intend to do?"

She studied him. He was not mocking her. He was not goading her, or jeering at her, or teasing her. He was asking a real question.

"I intend to make it very clear to that person they made the last mistake they'll ever make," she said.

Hyman's eyes gleamed. His hands dropped away from her shoulders. "When you come to a satisfactory arrangement with our Canadian pals, do let me know. I won't keep you. We seem to understand each other, and you appear to have a pressing social engagement just now."

She nodded, then stepped around him for the door.

"Mia."

She paused without turning around. "Yes?"

"Do try not to get killed anymore," he said wryly. "You are a very expensive employee, and I'd hate to have to start from scratch."

He had a unique way of showing concern. She smirked and opened the door. "I'll do my best, Mr. Goldberg."

Paolo was waiting outside the Lincoln idling in the alleyway, leaning against the door. When he saw her, he opened the back door for her, then immediately slid behind the wheel. She did not have to tell him where to go.

Half an hour later, they arrived at a nondescript brick building in the Lower East Side. Paolo parked the car in another alley as Moritz had instructed. After helping Mia out of the back seat, he knocked on the heavy steel door. A moment later it opened, and a tall, burly man with a cloud of light-brown curls peered out at them.

"Mia Scalisi," she offered.

He nodded and waved her in. He and Paolo exchanged wary looks. "They're in a room at the back. I'll show you the way."

"Thank you." She glanced around as she followed him down a dim hallway. The walls were brick, and the wooden floor had seen better days—a century ago. As she passed various rooms, full of smoke and men, she heard raucous cries—some exuberant, some agonized. Men were winning fortunes or losing them here tonight, and more than likely, there'd be at least a handful of shootings.

"Poker is a passionate game," her host said with a slick smile over the din. "Hope the noise don't frighten you too much."

She arched an eyebrow. "I know my way around a card hall."

It was possible she and Nick had haunted this very same place once upon a time, a dozen years ago. They'd been in and out of so many places like these, hustling poker games, they blurred in her memory.

"You play?" the man asked with keen interest. "Don't see too many broads."

Paolo grunted.

"Er, pardon me. *Ladies*."

Mia gave him an innocent smile. "I've played once or twice. I always get the suits mixed up, though."

"Hands, you mean," he corrected with a chuckle. "A suit is like diamonds, spades. Hearts."

"That's my favorite," she said, pitching her voice just a tiny bit higher. "The hearts."

"They'll eat you alive," the man mumbled under his breath. He stopped at a pocked red door with chipped paint. "All right. In here."

He knocked sharply three times, then pushed the door open. The small room was full of people. At a large, round table, she spotted Charlie, Moritz, and Will clustered on one side, with Jake, Wolfy Harold, and Annette Elliott around the other. Bobby, Joey, and a few other men she didn't recognize stood close to the walls, watching the game in progress. The sconces fitted on the walls cast the room in a dim, yellow glow, and the air smelled of a mixture of cigarette and the richer cigar smoke, fine whiskey, and masculine ego.

She studied Jake, loudly guffawing as he slapped his hand of cards down onto the table. It was clear from the grin on his face he'd been having quite the grand evening. His suit coat hung on the back of his chair, his waistcoat was unbuttoned, and his collar was off. The top few buttons of his shirt were undone and his thick, dark hair was mussed.

His face froze mid-laugh as he caught sight of her in the doorway.

She tilted her head. "Boo."

A hush fell over the room, but Annette smirked at her as she rose out of her chair and sauntered over to where a small bar had been set up.

Jake snapped his mouth shut with a pop. "What're you doing here?" He glanced around the table. "What's she doing here?"

Mia pouted as she stepped into the room. She shrugged off her light jacket and handed it to Paolo, who folded it over his arm. "What, I can't come play some cards, Mr. Morelli?"

Moritz patted the air. "I invited her here. I know there's been some…tension between the two of you lately. I thought it best for you to meet on neutral ground, in a relaxed environment, and try to come to an understanding."

"And knock off the bullshit," Charlie added.

"You couldn't have told me she was coming?" Jake demanded. "You fucking planned it, and couldn't give me advanced warning?"

Mia approached the table. Wolfy flicked his head at one of the players, who immediately relinquished his chair and offered it to her. She nodded her thanks and sat down, then peeled off her gloves. "Aren't you happy to see me?"

"I—"

"Considering the fact that you're responsible for two attempts on my life now, I'd say you at least owe me a conversation." Her words sliced through the air between them like a knife.

"I told you, I didn't have nothin' to do with that," he said.

"No? Then how about siccing your detective friend on me. Abner Wallace?"

Jake wrinkled his nose as he slugged some whiskey. "Don't know the guy. So I guess our chat's gonna be a short one. I told you the other night, we're partners. I don't make money unless you make money."

"Let's not be naive," Mia said. "I'm probably worth more to you dead."

Annette tapped her on the shoulder and handed her a short tumbler with just a finger of whiskey. "Drink, honey?"

"Thanks." Mia took a sip. It was a coin toss as to whether or not it would stoke the angry fire already crackling in her veins, or calm her, like tossing cool water on embers.

Jake cleared his throat loudly. "Look, I came here to play cards. Apparently, so did you. There's a lot of money on the table. We playing, or what?"

"I'm out." Charlie got up from the table.

"I'm in," Wolfy said. "Love to take some of your money, Sonny Jim."

"You're not getting a dollar, you bastard," Jake said. "Who else? Morrie?"

"I think I'll sit this one out."

One of Wolfy's men agreed to sit in as well, but Jake wasn't satisfied.

"We need one more," he said, looking from Charlie to Moritz to Will. "Come on."

"What am I, chopped liver?" Mia spread her palms. "I'll play."

The men at the table regarded her with doubt.

Jake laughed aloud. "You? Come on, sweetie. You don't have to keep bluffing for me. This ain't Old Maid, after all."

"I'm aware of that."

"Come on," he said again. "You can really play?"

"A little. My brother taught me. A long time ago."

Jake's smile grew. "Fine. But, Mia, baby, you know I ain't gonna go easy on you."

"I don't like it when fellas go easy on me." Jake's eyes, she noted with satisfaction, flashed with heat. "But I'll let you make an exception just this once, if you want."

Jake chuckled. "Fine. Deal the lady in. Minimum bet's fifty bucks. Pot's at about..." He trailed off, eyeing the stack of cash in the middle of the table. "Eight grand, thanks to Morrie's losing streak."

"Yummy." Mia glanced sharply at the dealer. "New deck, please."

Jake frowned. "What gives?"

Wolfy let out a quiet chuckle. "She thinks you got greasy fingers."

"Fresh start." She batted her lashes just a little. "What do you say? Humor me."

Jake sighed, then flicked his head at the dealer, who retrieved from under the table a brand-new deck of cards. He opened the box and passed them to Mia for her inspection. She quickly flipped through them, then nodded and handed them back. He dealt the cards with quick flicks of his wrist.

Mia gathered her cards, arranging her face into a neutral expression as she shuffled through them with dismay. It was the saddest hand of cards she'd ever been dealt. *Terrific. Not even a pair.*

Jake lit a fresh cigar. "So your brother was a good player, huh?"

"He was the best," Mia said. "Even when he was barely out of boyhood. Won almost every game. Played with the Gallucci boys before the big gang war of 'fifteen. Took their money, but they didn't get mad—they respected him."

"Ain't that something," Jake said. "And he taught you?"

"A little. He said I oughtta know something useful in case I ever needed cash in a jiff."

Wolfy's man, sitting to Mia's left, discarded his hand with a shrug and followed it up with a bolt of whiskey. "Out."

Jake got rid of two cards and picked up two new ones. His expression, she noted as she studied him closely beneath her lashes, was smug.

She resisted the urge to smile. Mr. Morelli, it seemed, did *not* have a good poker face. Apparently, he had quite the hand—and she didn't.

That was okay, she thought. Nick had taught her how to win a card game even with the crummiest of hands. She hoped she could still pull it off.

*Showtime.*

"You know," Mia began, shuffling her cards around again for effect, "Nick had a secret to that winning streak of his."

Jake puffed his cigar as he leaned back in his chair. "Oh yeah? What was that? Clairvoyance?"

"Nope." She flashed him her dimple. "Me."

He tilted his head. "How's that?"

Mia glanced at Wolfy as he rifled through his hand. "What none of the men he played against knew was that every single night, Nick would make me stay up and learn everything there was to know about poker. I'd go with him to the games and peek at everyone's cards. I'd use hand signals to tell him what they were."

The men at the table turned to stare at her.

"You mean to tell me," Wolfy said slowly, "your brother was *cheating* the whole time?"

"Not the *whole* time." Mia smirked at him over her cards. "Just until he got good on his own."

Jake gaped at her, then tipped his head back and roared with laughter. "Nick took Gallucci's men for everything they had— because of a little girl?"

Mia shrugged. "I just helped."

He shook his head. "Well. You say your brother was so good? He never got to go up against me. I've been playing cards since I was old enough to count."

*You lousy, arrogant shit.* "So, just for the past year or so, then?"

A chorus of low chuckles rose up around the room. Annette coughed to cover up her giggle.

Jake's eyes narrowed. "Ain't you a scream. At least I didn't have to resort to cheating to win. But I'm sure I oughtta be nervous right now sitting here with you, huh, doll?"

"Oh, no. Those days were so long ago." Mia discarded three cards one at a time with leisurely snaps of her wrist before picking up three new cards. They were as lousy as the ones she'd discarded. She refrained from wincing as she made a show of rearranging them in order, card by card. "Now I'm lucky if I remember anything above a straight."

Jake gave her a predatory smile.

He'd taken her bait, the same way a shark would if she dangled a thick, fat, raw steak in front of him.

"Truly, I can barely remember what comes after that," she went on. She trailed her fingers over the edge of her cards, staring down at them. "There's…flush. Full house. Four of a kind?"

"You're doing fine, honey," Jake said with a mocking, encouraging wink. "Keep going. What else? Straight…"

"Straight flush, sure," Mia exclaimed, as if it had just come to her with his help. "And then a… A royal flush, right?"

Across the table, Wolfy watched her with steady, intense dark eyes.

Jake exchanged a contemptuous glance with the dealer and nodded indulgently at her. "That's right."

"I always loved that last one." Mia glanced at Jake over her cards, slowly fanning them out. "Royal flush. *Scala reale*. The sound of it in Italian. It's like music. And you just knew if you were playing against someone who had a royal flush…it was all over for you."

Jake snorted. "Nobody ever gets a royal flush." He held up a hundred-dollar bill and tossed it into the pot.

"No one? *Ever?*" She let her words hang in the air for a moment. Deliberately, she laid her hand facedown, opened her purse, and withdrew a wad of cash that totaled a thousand dollars. She held it up, noting the way Jake's eyes arrowed to them. "A grand. All in."

Jake's eyes narrowed as she tossed the stack on top of the pile of cash in the middle.

She lifted her brows at Wolfy in silent challenge. *You're out.*

Annette didn't miss the look, and Mia caught the subtle nudge of her elbow into his side. He glanced at her, then at Mia, then at his cards, then at Jake, before tossing his hand down. "I rather keep the rest of my money where it is—safe in my lady's pocketbook. I fold."

Mia gave him an almost imperceptible nod of appreciation and shifted her gaze to Jake. *Never let 'em see you sweat.*

"Have you ever in your poker career had a *scala reale*? Were you one of the rare ones?" She tilted her head, making a show of scrutinizing him. It struck her how no one else in the room was talking, and she felt the heat of every gaze pinned to the table in that moment. "No, I doubt you were. You don't strike me as a believer, Mr. Morelli."

He sucked a tooth, returning her gaze with dark eyes that grew increasingly tight at the corners.

"Well, I'm a believer," she went on. "I don't play often, but when I do, I just seem to get…real lucky."

Jake stared at her for what felt like a year, his eyes so piercing Mia was sure he could see to the back of her brain. But she lifted her chin, keeping her confident smirk in place. The dead silence in the room made no space for even the sound of breathing.

"Well? Are you ready, Jake?"

He clenched his jaw, then snatched his glass off the table and gulped a mouthful of whiskey. He stared down at his hand, then slammed them down on the table.

"Fuck it," he spat. "I'm out."

"You sure?"

His lip curled. "Well, let's see your *scala reale*, then. You've been taunting me with it. G'head, show it off."

Mia glanced at his discarded hand. A deliciously mean thrill went through her. He'd folded with three of a kind—queen of spades, queen of clubs, queen of diamonds, eight of spades, ace of hearts.

Her smirk widened into a chilly smile as she looked down at her cards. "You know what the most important thing was my brother taught me about the game, Mr. Morelli?"

He puffed impatiently on his cigar. "Can't imagine."

She lifted her eyes to his. "The best poker face isn't one of impassivity, like most people think. It's the one that makes your opponent believe…whatever you want them to." With that, she laid her sad little cards down, one by one.

Three of diamonds. Seven of clubs. Seven of hearts. Ten of spades. Queen of hearts—the card that would have given him four of a kind, had he pulled it.

*How was that, Nick?*

She wished her brother could see it, see how she'd won a poker game with only a pair and the bluffing skills he'd relentlessly taught her to refine.

"I'll be goddamned," Wolfy said, sounding both admiring and irritated. "She made you fold with a three of a kind."

"Bullshit," Jake muttered, leaning over to snatch her cards. "Bull. *Shit.*"

Mia stood up. "You can keep the money, Mr. Morelli. I didn't come here for that, anyway."

In a movement so fast she almost missed it, he jerked a switchblade from his pocket and flicked it open, then drove it through the center of the nearest card—the ace of hearts from his hand.

"My," she remarked. "Aren't you in a temper?"

Slowly, he rose and stepped so close to her she could smell the whiskey on his breath. "What'd you come here for? Just to try to show me up?"

"I came to reason with you," she replied. "Or try to, anyway."

"Yeah? What about?"

"We had a deal, and you reneged. Not only that, you stole my trucks, and your men murdered and raped two innocent children from my neighborhood. And as if that weren't bad enough, you sent your detective pal after me, and he tried to kill me." She clenched her jaws tight for a moment, her nostrils flaring as she met his gaze that grew more smug by the second. "That wasn't very nice. Thought you wanted to be friends."

"Well, I did, see," he purred. "But I got to thinking about how I didn't appreciate you strong-arming me at your uncle's store the other night. And, I guess you could say my feelings are still hurt about you stealing my deal with Owney Madden."

"Are we back to that? Was fifty percent not good enough for you?"

"Not when it was a hundred to start with."

"He would've wised up and kicked you to the curb soon as he tasted that cat piss you call whiskey," Wolfy said with a lazy chuckle. "Win some, lose some, Jakie."

Jake shot him a murderous look before turning back to Mia. "I guess I ain't feeling too reasonable."

"Surely," she said, "there's something we can work out before we resort to uglier means. I want the neighborhood people left alone. You want more money. Perhaps there's a gesture of goodwill I can make." Moritz had coached her to say that, and to offer to raise his percentage in the Madden deal to seventy-five. She braced herself.

Jake made a face, his mouth pulling down at the corners, as he glanced around the room. "Yeah, well. I guess I've considered it and decided your goodwill can go fuck itself."

In that moment, she understood things between them had just taken an irreparable turn, and unless she was very careful, she was as good as dead.

"You piece of shit," Charlie snarled behind her, shoving forward toward Jake.

"Not here, Charlie," Moritz hissed, grabbing his arm.

Mia ignored them both, her attention focused on Jake. "I'm truly sorry you feel that way. I suppose our friendship is over, then."

"Mia." Moritz's tone was sharp. He had *not* recommended she say that.

Jake's eyes flashed bright, then black. He yanked his knife from the table. The ace of hearts flew up from the momentum, then settled by the edge of the table.

Mia reached for the card. The jagged tear from his knife was almost perfectly centered. "Think I'll keep this as a reminder of the night I took you for everything you had just because it was something fun to do. Maybe it's good luck."

His face darkened with fury, and there was no doubt in her mind that if he could have gotten away with slitting her throat in that instant, he would have.

"That's enough," Moritz interjected, waving his hands. "This is not the purpose of this evening. You're supposed to be reasoning with each other."

"You're outnumbered here, anyway, Morelli," Charlie said.

"Oh, so this is how you planned to play it along?" Jake demanded. "You fucking pricks."

"This is what *you've* made it," Charlie replied. "I suggest you take your losses like a man and leave."

"Or what?" Jake turned slowly to face Charlie.

"Or I'll give you exactly what you've been asking for ever since you landed here," he growled, his hand hovering near his waist where he carried his pistol.

Wolfy stood up and casually flashed his own pistol tucked at his side under his suit jacket. "You gon' have a whole room of pissed-off motherfuckers to deal with, Sonny Jim. A whole mess of us against one of little ol' you."

"Jake," Moritz said quietly. "I think it's best you leave."

Jake's jaw twitched as he clenched it. He stubbed his cigar out violently, then snatched his suit coat from where it was draped over the back of his chair. "You've all spit in my face tonight— that's clear."

He paused in front of Mia and spoke in a voice only she could hear. "Things could have been so good between us. But now you've ruined it."

"Oh, have I?"

He eyed her up and down, then tapped the side of his nose. "See you around, dollface. I got a bad habit of popping up at the damnedest times, in the damnedest places." He stepped close to her, his breath tickling her cheek as he leaned in to murmur into her ear. "I hope that ace of hearts card is as lucky as you think it is."

The threat lingered in the air as he cast one last sweeping look around the table, then walked out of the room.

After a long silence, Moritz looked across the table at her.

"I tried," he said quietly, "to tell you."

As much as the man irked her, Mia had to admit he was correct. He had warned her that a man like Jacopo Morelli had to be handled delicately, and there was nothing delicate about the way she'd treated him.

What happened after tonight might be as much her fault as his. She gazed at the door Jake had stormed out of, flipping the card between her fingers.

"Yeah, well. I learn things the hard way."

# CHAPTER EIGHTEEN

E arly the next morning, Charlie pressed a kiss to her bare shoulder blade.

"I'll clear off in a minute," he murmured into her skin. "You should spend some time with your family today."

Mia stretched, enjoying the cool slide of sheets beneath her belly and his warm body at her back. "I won't have much time today, either. Now that Signora Cancio's gone, Trudy's short-staffed at the store. She needs help. Besides, I've hardly been there since I've been back, and Raquel expressed an interest in working there."

"Thought she was going to nanny for Gloria?"

"I'd like her to decide what she would rather do," Mia replied. "She might able to do both. But not having daily chores to do is new for her, and I don't want her to get bored."

He trailed a finger down her spine. "We need to talk about how to handle Morelli. He made it pretty clear he's coming after you now."

Mia rolled onto her back and gazed up at him. "What would you do?"

He lifted a shoulder. "Get rid of him," he said bluntly. "Then

I'd claim his men as mine and put them to work. For the right price, loyalty can be bought."

She sat up suddenly, holding the sheet to her bare breasts. "His men murdered a child and raped a young girl. You would have men like that working for you?"

"What they did was terrible, but you gotta think in terms of business, Mia. You can't recruit everyone off loyalty. You need people who can be bought, to be frank. The more men you have working for you, the more layers there are between you and the law. You and other families." He tucked a lock of her hair behind her ear. "I know this shit eats you alive, but at some point, if you want to stay in this game, you're going to have to make hard choices you don't like."

"I've done that," she said quietly.

"You have. But it doesn't stop there."

"Maybe I don't want to stay in this game…whatever that means."

He sat up next to her, the sheets sliding down his naked chest to pool around his waist. He cupped her chin. "It's very, very hard to get out once you're in. Sometimes, impossible. And deny it all you like, but Mia—you're in. You were in ever since that night you decided you wanted Kiddo Grainger dead." He pressed his lips tenderly to hers, then slid off the bed to dress.

She watched him. Perhaps he had a point. Perhaps she ought to suspend some of her loftier values for the sake of success and security. Besides, what values could she stand on with the things she'd done? She'd done murder, too. What separated her from the men who'd destroyed those children? Killing for revenge was still killing.

"Penny for your thoughts." Charlie slung his tie around his neck and shrugged into his suit coat.

"I—it's nothing."

He rested his knuckles on the bed. "You don't go anywhere alone from now on. I mean it. None of you. Promise me."

There was no time for any feminine outrage at being told

what to do. The threat Jake had made last night still hung over her—and her friends were as much at risk as she was.

*I got a bad habit of popping up at the damnedest times, in the damnedest places*, he'd said.

She slid her hands over Charlie's shoulders and gripped his lapel, tugging him close. "I promise," she replied against his lips. "Bobby, Joey, and Paolo will take good care of us."

"It's Monday. At least you don't have to work at the club tonight," Charlie murmured.

"I'll have to go back Wednesday," she reminded him. She stroked his cheek. "You need a shave."

He turned his head to kiss her palm. "I'll shave when I get back to my place. I'll be around as much as I can. As much as you can stand." His dark eyes twinkled at her. "Gotta check on some things for Masseria today. I'll be in touch." He kissed her again, this one carrying a burst of heat, then walked out the door.

It was nearly half past seven. Likely, the girls were awake by now. She called down to the front desk to order a lavish breakfast. It was the very least she could do after neglecting them so much, especially since Raquel had arrived.

She bathed and dressed, and by the time she knocked on Paolo's door, the breakfast cart arrived. She gave the butler a tip and pushed the cart toward Gloria's door, smiling over her shoulder at Paolo. "Hungry?"

He shrugged as though unimpressed, but the gleam in his eye as he surveyed the spread—the entire breakfast menu the hotel offered—told her the food wouldn't last long.

Raquel opened the door to answer Mia's knock, and her face lit up at the sight. "Cousin Mia!" she exclaimed. "What's all this?"

"I thought we could have breakfast together." Mia wheeled the cart in and arranged it by the table at the back of the living room as Raquel hurried over to help her with plates and silverware.

"It looks wonderful," she said. The slender young woman

had taken to American cuisine with gusto, and despite her small frame, could never seem to get enough of it.

"What's all this?"

Gloria stepped out of her bedroom. She and Emilia were both dressed for the day, but she carried a brush in one hand and a handful of Emilia's unruly dark curls in the other. Emilia squirmed; getting her hair brushed ranked as high as bedtime and vegetables on her list of hated things.

"Hungry?" Mia gestured to the spread.

"Not for a week if we eat all that," she replied, but she was smiling. "Hold still, Emmy."

"Mama," Emilia whined.

"Can't she get her hair brushed after she eats?" Mia wheedled.

Gloria rolled her eyes. "Fine. Em, go see if Auntie Raquel will fix you a plate. Mia, could I speak to you for a moment?"

*Damn.* She'd been trying to avoid the conversation she knew was coming. She followed Gloria into the bedroom.

Gloria set the brush down on her vanity and glanced at Mia in the mirror. "Are you feeling better? Your...stomachache?"

"Yes." Mia felt the flush of guilt at her lie heat her cheeks. "Thank you. I'm sorry to have missed supper."

"It's all right." Her sister-in-law reached for a small, mirrored silver tray of creams and perfumes and idly began rearranging them. "We're all concerned about you."

*If you only knew how much you had to be concerned about.* "I'm feeling much better today. Hence the enormous breakfast."

Gloria smiled briefly. "Yes. But that's not quite what I meant."

Mia waited, watching her.

"The things you said at church yesterday. About...vengeance. Did you mean it?"

It would be easy and probably for the best if Mia brushed off her remarks, but something prompted her to entertain Gloria with all seriousness. "If I had, what would you think?"

Finally, Gloria faced her. "I would be glad."

Mia drew her head back. "You…would?"

"It was jarring to hear," Gloria said. "In a church. With Aunt Connie and Uncle Joe there. And Raquel. And my daughter…" She bit her lip and shook her head. "Signora Franco's daughter. She was only a few years older than Emilia. And Signora Cancio's boy. He wasn't much older, either. It occurred to me they were doing what we all did when we were children. We all ran errands for our families. Ran the streets. You and Nick were orphans. You had no parents to look after you. Those children did nothing that we did not do. I began thinking about what I would do if…if that had happened to Emilia."

"I would *never* let—" Mia started, her voice suddenly thick with emotion.

Gloria reached for her hand. "I know you would never. But if it had, I would want those bastards dead. The same way those two women want the bastards who ruined their children dead. I…understand. As a mother. I understand."

"What are you saying, exactly?" Mia asked.

Gloria drew in a breath through her nose and stepped closer, still holding Mia's hand. "I'm saying I think you should do… what you think is right. No one with the means to do anything to change this neighborhood cares about it as much as you do. Because you understand what it's meant to us all. For the people who left Sicily and came here, Little Italy is all they know. The community here they've worked for a generation to build, to make a safe place. It's being destroyed, and our children are getting hurt. Raped. *Killed.* People are afraid to walk the streets by themselves. None of the *padroni* are doing anything about it."

She shook her head and dropped Mia's hand, pacing toward the vanity and back again. "Uncle Joe told me Don Masseria hasn't been to the store since that meeting you held. He used to stop by a couple times a week, just to make his presence known on the pretense he was checking on the people of this neighborhood. No more. People have gone to him for help, for justice, and he does nothing. Nothing is *changing*. And it's time things changed."

"What I said," Mia began, "the things I'm involved in… It means the rest of you are in danger, too. And if I make a move, I'm afraid of what it could mean for you. All of you."

Gloria put her hands on Mia's shoulders, her tone lightening. "That's why we've three bodyguards now, isn't it?"

"Glo…"

"I want my daughter to be safe," Gloria said. "And I want other mothers' children to be safe. We all want the same thing." She folded her lips inward for a moment. "I won't ask any more questions. If you want to talk to me about it, you know you always can."

"Thanks," Mia whispered.

Gloria cupped her face. "Now, let's see if they left us anything to eat."

They were halfway through breakfast when a fist suddenly pounded on the door.

"Mia, open up!"

"Is that Bobby?" Gloria asked.

Mia was already out of her chair. She hurried to the door, then slid out into the hallway. Bobby's face was lined with urgency.

"I just got a call from one of my guys in Midtown," he said, keeping his voice quiet. "The shop's burning."

For a second, her mind went completely blank. The words he'd said made no literal sense to her whatsoever. All she could manage was, "What?"

"Someone hit your shop early this morning. It's burning. My guy said the firefighters are trying to put it out now."

"Trudy?" she said with a gasp.

Bobby shook his head. "Don't know if she was there or not."

"Jesus Christ," she breathed, holding onto the wall for support.

*I got a bad habit of popping up at the damnedest times, in the damnedest places.*

She looked up at Bobby. "Take me there now."

❀

BY THE TIME THEY ARRIVED, THE SHOP WAS JUST A CHARRED, smoking pile of rubble.

Hyman was already there, standing beside a firefighter and speaking earnestly. The police were there as well.

"Holy Mother," Gloria said, pressing a hand to her mouth.

"I'm so sorry, Cousin Mia." Raquel squeezed her hand.

It had been a battle not worth fighting when Gloria insisted on coming along, which meant Raquel and Emilia came, too. But none of them followed her when she pushed open the car door and jumped out.

*Trudy*, she thought, her leaden feet stumbling a little as she hurried forward. *What about—*

"Mia," Hyman called.

She turned to see him striding toward her, his face taut with stress.

"Where's Trudy?" she demanded, her voice ragged.

He cupped her elbow to steady her. "Calm yourself. She's fine." He pointed over his shoulder where the small Irish woman stood shivering beside the firefighters. "She was walking here when the shop exploded."

"Thank God." Then, the next horrible thought popped into her brain. "The liquor?"

Hyman sighed. "Fortunately and unfortunately, it's all gone. It appears that's what went first. These officers are on my payroll, so no need to worry about the public discovering that their darling Italian songbird moonlights as a bootlegger. There's no evidence it was ever here. I'll talk to a couple of reporter friends about putting a spin on things."

Mia shook her head, watching smoke curl up into the sky. "All of it. Gone."

"That's what insurance is for," he said briskly. "I'm far more concerned about who was behind this, and the most important inventory that we've lost. We not only had our product destroyed, but also some of Mr. Masseria's. This could get ugly."

She turned to stare at the remains of the store, her pretty little shop that she'd had so briefly. She hadn't cared so much about it when Hyman had first offered it to her. Indeed, she'd been a little bewildered at the transaction when it had first taken place. But then she'd made it her own. A place of serenity and beauty—at least, at the front of the store. A place where she'd been able to give an Irish immigrant a good job with managerial tasks. A place where she'd been in charge.

She'd been proud of it, she realized too late. And now it was gone.

"I'm guessing things didn't go well with Mr. Morelli?" Hyman asked.

Mia thought back to their card game and the dark promise he'd made her. "We did not have a productive conversation, no."

"Our options for dealing with him are growing more and more narrow." Hyman glanced at the police officers as they continued their investigation. "He's made two attempts on your life, hijacked your trucks, and now he's burned down your shop. He's infringed on a business arrangement *I* had with Masseria, and now he's put *me* in a bad position." The muscle in his jaw twitched as he peered down at her. "In this business, Miss Scalisi, there are a limited number of ways unreasonable and unpredictable men like him can be handled, particularly when they take certain action that suggests a supreme lack of respect for a healthy business relationship."

She watched the fire's dark smoke roll up into the sky. "I doubt he'll be easily found after this. And if he is, he won't be alone. He does foolish things, but he's not stupid."

"Then we'll need to draw him out, won't we?"

Mia's chest heaved with quiet fury as she examined what was left of her shop. Yes, as Hyman had unnecessarily reminded her, Mr. Morelli had very likely burned it down. That was a move that called for retaliation. To do nothing would send the message that they were weak—that *she* was weak. The next move had to be well thought-out. Deliberate. The message had to be clear.

Mia ran down the list of men in her life and considered what they would do next. Don Catalano and Moritz would have pressed to talk it out, to reason, because both men hated bloodshed and its inevitable expenses. Charlie and certainly Nick would have moved against Jake himself. And, at this point, so would Hyman.

She had already attempted to talk things out with Jake and come to a reasonable agreement. That had failed.

The problem, she realized, was that Jake did not think she was a worthy adversary.

The problem, she realized, was that she did not trust herself to make her own decisions. To listen to her own inner voice of reason. And that voice was very smart—much smarter than she gave it credit for being.

She turned to look up at Hyman. "I'll give that some thought."

His eyes narrowed at whatever expression he found on her face. "Very well."

"What happens now?"

Hyman nodded toward the police officers sifting through the wreckage of the shop. "They've asked to speak with you, as you are the store owner. I recommend telling them as little as possible. You know nothing of arson, nothing of booze. You're just a—"

"A simple showgirl, distraught over the loss of her pretty shop," Mia finished. "Yes. Of course."

"Unless you have any pressing objections, allow me to handle the paperwork for the insurance adjustors for you. If you wish, you and I can go over things in the morning." He studied her with that same narrow gaze. "You should be with your family. I'm sure this is all very shocking and upsetting for all of you. And Trudy."

"Yes." Mia turned away to head for the terrified, redheaded Irish girl. "I am *quite* upset."

SHE SPENT THE REST OF THE MORNING WITH TRUDY, ASSURING her she would always be taken care of. She'd vowed to find a suitable position for Trudy, perhaps in an office as a secretary.

"With respect, miss," Trudy had said, "I wish to work for *you*. In whatever capacity you can find. If you need a governess for your little niece, I do hope you'll consider me."

"Absolutely," Mia had replied. "My sister-in-law has been looking for a good governess. I'll speak to her about it."

From there, Mia had taken Gloria, Emilia, and Raquel to the grocery to spend the afternoon and part of the evening with Uncle Joe and Aunt Connie, both of whom had been horrified to hear about her shop, but Mia assured them it was just faulty wiring that had caused the blaze, and no one had been hurt. Raquel had watched Emilia up in the small apartment while Mia and Gloria had gone to visit Signora Cancio and Signora Franco, together at Signora Cancio's apartment with a few other women of the neighborhood. They'd chatted with the women for long hours. Signora Cancio planned to bury her son in three days' time, on Thursday. It would cost her the last pennies of her meager savings to bury him and have a small reception, but she would do it, she said, her chin lifting with pride. She would do it because he had been a very good boy and had done his best to take care of his mother throughout his short years.

It was that pride that made Mia refrain from offering her money, but after she and Gloria left the flat, Mia had Paolo drive her to Most Precious Blood, where she gave Father Alessio enough money to cover the service, a nice casket, and a good meal following the service.

"Don't tell her where the money came from," she'd added. "She's a proud woman."

Finally, they all returned to the hotel in the evening. Gloria wanted to go down to the restaurant for supper instead of ordering up.

"No," Mia said firmly. "We've been out all day. We should stick close to our rooms now."

"Oh, come," Gloria said. "It's not as though we're leaving the building, just our rooms. We'll bring Bobby and Joey with us. And Paolo."

"It'll be nice to sit downstairs," Raquel added hopefully.

Mia hesitated, then glanced at Paolo, silently asking for his opinion. He was frowning, as usual, but he flicked his head up slightly, glanced at Gloria, and gave a nod.

"Fine," Mia relented. "We'll eat downstairs."

For the excitement that caused, it was as though she'd suggested eating at the Ritz.

Just as they stepped into the hallway, the telephone rang from Mia's room. "You go on ahead," she said, waving them on. "I'll meet you downstairs."

Paolo hesitated at her door.

"Go with them," she insisted. "I'll catch up."

She hurried back into the room and scooped up the phone, hoping she hadn't missed the call. A nasally operator's voice came on the line.

"Connecting you to Chicago," the woman said. "Please hold."

A moment later, there was a faint click. Then another woman's voice. "Hello? Miss Scalisi?"

"Miss Watkins," Mia said. "What a surprise. I didn't think I'd hear back from you so soon."

"Well, I've heard you've been having a hell of a time up there," Maurine said. "And that you lost your shop to a fire this morning."

Mia blinked. "How could you possibly know that already?"

Maurine laughed. "Fella I used to date in college is a reporter in New York. Told me everything. Including the hush money he got paid to *not* mention that arson is suspected."

"Damn, you're fast."

"And I'm good, too," Maurine added smoothly. "Lookit, I really am concerned for you. You're just a kid, after all. And you're running with some real unpleasant fellas."

"Speaking of that," Mia said, "have you got anything for me on the unpleasant fella I asked you about the other day?"

"Why I'm calling. Looks like that Detective Abner Wallace really is a Chicago detective, but he's as dirty as they come. My source tells me he's been on the payroll of the North Side Gang for years now. Even back when you still lived here."

"What a shock," Mia said drily. It was good dope to know, even if she'd suspected as much.

"Even more than that, he's directly in Hymie Weiss's pocket. By that I mean, there's no buffer between them. From what I hear, Weiss gives his orders straight to Wallace. So that means, Weiss likely told Wallace directly to punch your ticket."

She figured Weiss would have it out for her because she was Nick's sister, and she'd killed a number of Weiss's buddies, but she'd never had any direct dealings with the man. It surprised her, perhaps naively, that he would want her dead before they'd even exchanged two words.

"Any idea when this order was given?"

"Wallace has a track record of moving fast. You say jump, he doesn't even waste time asking how high. My source tells me he bought a train ticket to New York on Thursday, April twenty-second. That means he landed in New York Saturday the twenty-fourth, and he made your acquaintance the very next day."

"So Weiss told him within the last, what, month to come after me?"

"It's possible. I'd say it could have been anywhere from the evening of Wednesday the twenty-first back to the first of the month. Likely not earlier than that—as I said, my source tells me Wallace moves fast, especially where it concerns Weiss."

*Then how does Morelli factor in?* Mia wound the telephone cord about her fingers. Wallace had mentioned "his friend." Had they known each other before?

"Wallace was to meet a contact in New York," Maurine continued. "Being new to the city and not knowing where to find you, he'd need someone familiar with your whereabouts for guidance."

It was as though Maurine had read her mind. "Any idea who this contact might've been?"

"Another business contact of Weiss's," she said. "Let me see... I wrote all of this down to tell you."

"Make sure you burn those notes."

"Fire's already crackling, darling. Ah, yes—I doubt this is a real first name, but his contact was some fellow called Gems. That ring a bell to you?"

Mia closed her eyes. "Yes."

There was a beat of silence as though Maurine were waiting for her to continue. When it became apparent she wasn't going to, the reporter cleared her throat. "Well, that's all I've got for you. My source is a dirty prohi. He knows a whole lot of things about a whole lot of people, but rarely does he know any hard and fast details because these people are good—they don't keep record of hard, fast details. I hope that's enough for you to go on. What'll you do with that information, by the way?"

*You don't want to know.* "Sleep better at night. Eventually."

"Good luck with that. I take it that pesky little dragon isn't slain yet, huh?"

A little smile crossed her face as she recalled the words she'd said to Maurine on the occasion of their first meeting, at Sal's trial, the day she'd had him murdered. Maurine, with her astute intelligence, had been sure there was more to Mia's false testimony than what she was letting on, and had pressed her for an exclusive.

*Perhaps one day, Miss Watkins, when the dragon is slain, I'll take you up on that.*

"Not quite yet," Mia said. "But this dope helps."

"My goodness," Maurine drawled. "This is going to be *quite* an exclusive, isn't it? Even though I'm working on screenplays these days more than news articles, I'll drop everything for you whenever you say the word."

Mia chuckled. "And don't think I've forgotten about that. It's just not a good time."

"Shucks. Anyhow, I do have a little play in the works. You ought to come see it if you ever come back for a visit. Then we can kick up our heels and have some drinks out on the town."

"I'd love to. What's it about?"

"I based it on these murder trials I covered a couple years ago. Two broads killed their old men and got off scot-free. Isn't that a gas?"

"Sounds riveting," Mia said with a private grin. "What's it called?"

"*Chicago.* Do ring me up next time you're around—I'll make sure you get the best seats in the house."

"When does it premiere?"

"December, but there's a special limited engagement in October."

"I'll be there," Mia promised. "You got a deal."

Her levity dissipated as she hung the receiver up on the candlestick base. Now, it seemed, she had the confirmation she'd been looking for, the little push she needed to ensure what she wanted to do was the right thing to do.

That her conscience would be eased when blood ran in the streets again.

# CHAPTER NINETEEN

J oe "The Boss" Masseria pursed his lips, drumming his
fingers slowly on the white tablecloth that covered a round
table at the back of John's of 12$^{th}$. A small dish of tiramisu
sat in front of him, from which he took small, almost dainty, bites
in a sporadic pattern that made sense only to him. A tiny cup of
espresso sat beside the dish, which he stirred occasionally.

The location had been his suggestion, as it was a favorite
restaurant of his in town, and, as he'd said, according to Charlie,
he wished to hear bad news in the presence of a comfortable
atmosphere with a sweet in front of him, to counteract the bitter
information.

Beside him, Lucky Luciano sat smoking, a small smile on his
lips. He'd studied Mia intently as she'd spoken, but waited for
Mr. Masseria to speak first.

After Mia had told him of the demise of the shop, Mr.
Masseria had taken four bites of the dessert and three sips of
espresso. Finally, he broke the silence.

"I do not like it when other people's problems become my
problems," he said. "I have enough of my own. And now, you tell
me I have a new problem. Is that right?"

Mia sighed.

Charlie spoke up. "Look, Joe, it's *her* problem, too. It's everybody's problem. Your stock wasn't the only one that got burned up. We lost all the booze, and she lost her shop. You're on the same side here."

"Only one side," Mr. Masseria said sharply, waving his index finger in the air, cutting a look at Charlie. "My side. That's it." He shifted his gaze back to Mia and shrugged. "So what you want me to do?"

"I didn't come here looking for your help or favors," Mia said coolly. "I came out of respect, as a business associate. To allow you to hear from me what occurred before you read it in the papers and put two and two together."

"He burned your stock, too, Joe," Mr. Luciano said, tapping ash off his cigarette butt. "That's a move against you."

"So what you saying?" Mr. Masseria said. "I should take him out? He works for Maranzano. I kill him, Maranzano retaliates on me."

"Leave Mr. Morelli to me," Mia said.

Three pairs of eyes shifted toward her. Charlie wore no expression, but Mr. Masseria and Mr. Luciano both looked mildly surprised.

"What you gonna do with him?" Mr. Masseria asked.

Mia glanced down at the dish of blood orange sorbet in front of her. It was starting to melt. She spooned up a little and tasted it—it reminded her exactly of the ripe blood oranges that grew in the grove behind Cousin Carlo's villa.

"Whatever I do," she said, "is it safe to assume you'll have no hard feelings if some misfortune befalls him...permanently?"

Luciano chuckled, the sound low and dangerous. "Not from me."

Masseria tilted his head. "You gonna kill him?" he asked bluntly. Fortunately, the owner had quickly cleared the place of any lingering customers once they'd arrived.

Mia met his gaze. "If he makes me."

Mr. Masseria lifted one bushy eyebrow.

"I still have one more offer I'd like to make him," she said, ignoring Charlie's inquisitive glance. "I think it might allow him to see things my way before it comes to what you've suggested."

"You been pretty generous with him so far," Luciano said, his eyes narrowing slightly. "What else could you possibly have to offer him at this point? He's destroyed everything you got."

"That's my business," she replied. "Mr. Luciano."

He drew his head back ever so slightly, and she got the impression he was deciding whether or not to be angry. She doubted many people spoke to Charles Luciano like that, but she didn't care.

Finally, his hesitation gave way to a smirk. "Good luck with that business, then."

"Don't hesitate too long," Mr. Masseria advised. "He's a bomb, waiting to explode."

"I've set him off once or twice," Mia said.

He finished the last bite of his tiramisu with painful slowness, then set down the sterling silver spoon and pushed the china plate away. "Look, you want my help, you got it. You come to Lucky, you come to me, whatever. I just want this mess resolved. No messing around."

"Absolutely none," Mia said. She stood when he did and kissed both his cheeks. "And thank you. If I need your help, I will certainly come to you."

Mr. Masseria lightly pinched her cheek, then patted it. "You need a ride home?"

Mia nodded over her shoulder. "Mr. Scarpa will see me home."

He nodded at Luciano and Charlie. "*Amunninni.*"

"I'll catch up," Charlie told them, hanging back. When they were out of earshot, he looked at her, his brow creased. "What offer?"

"Something I've been thinking of for a few days," she replied, keeping her face in neutral lines. "I've decided Moritz is right. I ought to try reasoning with him instead of siccing our men on him. So, I've come up with something I think will show him how serious I am about mending fences. And if he refuses even after this offer, well, then I'll know where we stand."

Charlie cupped her face in his hands, looking deeply into her eyes. "What're you not telling me, Mia?"

It was no use to be this deliberately obtuse with Charlie, since he knew her well enough to know she was concealing something. But the plan she had been formulating in her mind since the shop burned was too delicate to discuss with him. He would try to talk her out of it, and she wouldn't be talked out of it. Moreover, if things went sideways, she didn't want him involved for his own protection.

She reached up and placed her hands on his wrists and gently removed his hands from her face. "I'm telling you not to worry, Charlie. And I'm asking you to trust me." She nodded toward the door, where Mr. Masseria and Mr. Luciano impatiently waited. "Now, you should go. They're waiting for you."

He hesitated. "Mia…"

She sat back down in the seat Mr. Masseria had vacated, her back to the wall and looking out over the whole restaurant. She dragged her dish of melted blood orange sorbet toward her and stirred it with her spoon.

"It's all right, Charlie," she said to the dish. "Things will be different. Soon."

He took a deep breath and shook his head, then joined Mr. Masseria and Mr. Luciano at the door.

Finally by herself in the restaurant, she finished her sorbet and leaned back in the chair, steepling her fingers and losing herself in her thoughts.

The owner approached her, his hands behind his back as two waiters quickly cleared the table. "May I bring you anything else, Signorina Scalisi?"

She caught sight of Paolo walking up the sidewalk to the restaurant door, Bobby and Joey in tow, and smiled at the owner.

"A bottle of your best wine, please," she said. "And four glasses."

The owner dipped his head. "At once."

She reached out and touched his elbow before he turned away. "Would you mind keeping the restaurant closed for us? I'll compensate you for the inconvenience."

"Of course," he said with another bob of his head. "No compensation needed. It is an honor to serve you, Signorina Scalisi."

"Thank you, but I insist," she said as the three men approached the table. "We'll be here a while, you see. We have much to discuss."

❦

ON FRIDAY AFTERNOON, MIA LEANED ON THE PIANO AT THE Divine, chatting quietly with Gene about the setlist. The musicians were also taking a short break, though there was the occasional trumpet riff and low laugh.

All week she had left the hotel only to go to rehearsal and, beginning Wednesday evening, performances at the club. In addition to Charlie's driver from Brooklyn, Mia, Gloria, Emilia, and Raquel never went anywhere without Paolo, Bobby, and Joey. At the hotel, the latter two shared Paolo's room and they took turns standing guard in the hallway through the night. At the club, Hyman furnished his own security detail as well. One of her team was always stationed outside her dressing room whether she was in it or not, and between their two camps, no door or window into the club remained unguarded.

Detective Wallace hadn't shown his face again, though Mia knew better than to relax. She hadn't seen Morelli, either—now that the shop was gone, it would be much more difficult for him to reach her. Her gut told her he was far from done trying, and was likely plotting something else against her.

In the meantime, though he seemed to be lying in wait, his men were busy. They had performed a series of coordinated attacks throughout the city, attacking bookies, card halls, and other warehouses operated by Charlie, including those he controlled at the behest of Mr. Masseria. It was a bold declaration of war against anyone associated with Mia.

And despite it all...she still had a job to do.

Hyman stepped on stage from where he'd been lingering at a table where Gloria and Raquel were sitting. Mia had forced Hyman and Gloria to make amends since she refused to go anywhere without them unless absolutely necessary. Coming to rehearsal was something they enjoyed, Raquel especially. Due to the circumstances he'd been gracious enough, but had told Mia privately Gloria would not be served alcohol in the club.

"Mia," he called. "New song. Just for you from a musician friend of mine. Here." He handed sheets of music and lyrics to her and Gene.

Gene glanced over it and shrugged. "I can cook up an arrangement with the boys easy enough. Simple melody."

"Think it could be ready by tomorrow night?" Hyman asked. "Sunday?"

"Shouldn't be a problem."

Hyman looked at Mia. "And you?"

She scanned the lyrics, shaking her head. "I'm not singing this."

"I beg your pardon?"

"Have you read these lyrics?" she said, holding up the sheet.

"Of course I have. I had to make sure it was up to Divine standards, friend or no."

She shrugged and set the sheet on top of the piano. "Then you know how stupid it is. I'll sound like some simpering fool, singing that."

"Men love simpering fools, especially ones who fill out very expensive, bespoke evening gowns." Hyman folded his arms and fixed her with his famous bland smile, the one that predicated severe annoyance.

"I can't sing Bessie Smith, then turn around and sing *this*." She picked up the paper and cleared her throat. "'Every fella I kiss is just good practice for when I'm loving you'," she sang along the bubbly-sweet melody Gene plinked out on the piano.

"'For there's no fella around I'd love to love more when I'm loving you.'" She fixed Hyman with a pointed glance and tossed the paper aside.

"It's just a song, Mia," Hyman said, throwing a hand out to the side. "The crowd will eat it up."

She frowned at him. "Then *you* sing it."

He glowered at her. "My dear girl, I'd advise against testing me."

"As the headlining talent, I think I should have a say in what I sing," she insisted.

"You can have a say," he snapped, "but I make all final decisions. Now stop being difficult and sing the song, Mia!" He stormed off the stage.

"You know, he can be a real ass sometimes," Mia grumbled, and snatched the paper up.

Gene chuckled. "You two could have your own act, you know?" He patted her hand. "Come on, let's just run through it a few times."

During a break where Gene consulted with the band about the music, Paolo walked toward the stage from the back entrance. She met him at the edge of the stage, kneeling down to speak in a low voice to him.

"Is everything ready for tonight?" she asked.

He gave her a firm nod.

"Bobby and Joey know where they need to be and when? And they have all the men they need? Men they can trust?"

Another firm nod.

Mia returned it, biting her lip as she stared off into space, her thoughts whirling like a tornado. "You must be very careful. I don't want anything traced back to us, to me—by the authorities. And if these men can fold—"

Paolo pointed at her, then tapped the stage. *You'll be here.*

She tightened her jaw. "I keep wondering if we've overlooked anything."

He waved a hand, shaking his head as decisively as he'd nodded. He pointed at her again, then at the stage, then slashed his hand through the air in a sideways motion. *You sing. That's all.*

His confidence helped ease her mind. Yes, she would sing. She would resume her role tonight of the simple showgirl, as far from a strategist as possible. But as she'd promised Charlie the other day, things would be very different after tonight.

❦

"Look, Cousin Mia!"

That evening, Mia turned from her vanity to look at her cousin. Her mouth fell open as she took in the young woman's appearance. She wore a stunning, pale-yellow dress that sparkled with beadwork and stood out beautifully against her olive skin, but it was her newly shorn hair that took Mia by surprise.

"Your hair!" she exclaimed, sliding off the stool and walking toward her.

"It's like yours," Raquel said, patting her new bob with a little self-conscious smile. "I just had it done at the beauty parlor down the street."

"It's beautiful," Mia said admiringly, lightly touching a lock that brushed Raquel's cheek. "You look like a real American flapper." A flash of mischief went through her. "I'm sure Mr. Wyatt will like it."

"Will?" Raquel said, then blushed. "You think so?"

"I think so."

"He said he has to leave to go back home in a few days," Raquel said. "He asked if he could take me to dinner."

"Oh, did he?" Mia lifted a brow. This was news to her.

"Should I go?"

"Only if you want to," Mia said. "But Will is a very nice man. Not particularly chatty, but nice."

"And handsome," Raquel added, her blush deepening.

Gloria and Raquel were accompanying her to the club tonight, to make up for Raquel's disastrous first night out. That was what Mia had told them, but the truth was, she didn't want them out of her sight tonight. It pained her that Gloria had delivered Emilia to her aunt and uncle earlier that afternoon, but there was nothing else to be done. A nightclub was not an appropriate place for a little girl, and Mia had guards stationed around the grocery for safekeeping.

"Well, I am your assistant tonight," Raquel said, straightening. "What shall I do?"

"You can be in charge of my garment bag," Mia said, nodding to the large zippered bag that contained all of her costumes. "When we get to the club, just make sure everything's out of the bag and hanging on the rack in my dressing room. And when I do costume changes, you can help me in and out of them. It's much easier and faster when I have some help."

"What happened to your last garment girl?"

Mia tipped her head back and laughed. "You're looking at her, doll."

Raquel smiled. "Well, leave it to me. I'll be the best garment girl you never had."

As they giggled, Mia was struck by how young and carefree she felt. It seemed it had been a long time since she'd giggled with a girlfriend.

Gloria poked her head in through the adjoining door. "Time to go, girls."

She hadn't had so much as a sip of booze that night, and Mia appreciated her for it. She knew Gloria was still embarrassed by what had happened last time, but Mia was determined to make her forget about it. And if she wanted so much as a glass of champagne tonight, she would have it, Hyman be damned.

At the club, Paolo escorted the three women back to Mia's dressing room. Before she closed the door, they exchanged glances. She nodded slightly at him, and a chill went through her at the slight smile she got in return.

Her plan was in motion, and there was no stopping it now, even if she wanted to.

Friday night at The Divine brought a considerable crowd. The kitchen staff was busy fixing the gourmet meal orders that flowed in from the guests. A member of the waitstaff delivered three covered dishes to Mia's dressing room, but she was too on edge to eat. She made a big show of pushing her food around and taking miniscule bites while keeping up a steady flow of chitchat to hide the fact that she was hardly eating, something Gloria would surely pick up on.

She went over the setlist with Raquel so she would know which songs were her cues to meet Mia back in her dressing room, then she sent her cousin and Gloria out to the main room to enjoy themselves.

She left the dressing room herself to get a drink, peeking into the main room to make sure Charlie and Moritz were there, and they were, with Will and a few other men. Good. If they were here, then they were not *out there*, where her plan, of which they had no knowledge, was unfolding.

Mia returned to her dressing room, a New York Sour in hand. Finally alone, she took a deep breath as she sat on the cushioned bench at her vanity. After a moment, she dragged her eyes up to her reflection. Somehow, it got harder and harder to look at herself in the mirror.

Her plan had been in motion for days now, but as the night crept into the wee hours of the following morning, the true bottom line would be put into action. The days of discussions with the few men she trusted, the hours of careful planning, her specific, clear, and direct orders, would all be carried out tonight. Tomorrow would be a new day, indeed. And she would be a different woman.

Her plan would, perhaps, not resolve everything. But for her intended recipient, it would send a message, loud and clear.

How that recipient decided to respond was what made her grip her glass so tight it nearly cracked.

She bolted the contents of the glass to fortify herself. She had one job tonight—to do her job. To sing, to dance, to give everyone out there a night they'd remember until the next one. None of them should know the tumult she was in right now. None of them should know that she was in any way connected to her plan, which would almost certainly make headlines tomorrow.

The St. Christopher medallion on the bracelet around her wrist clanked gently against her glass as she set it down. She fingered it.

*What would you think, dear brother? What would you think of this plan? What would you think of me?*

Nick might have been indescribably proud, if he'd been alive to see it all unfold.

He might also be indescribably horrified.

There was a gentle knock on her door. "Mia?"

She froze. It was Charlie. She'd managed to avoid him since the meeting with Mr. Masseria the other day, but he knew she was in here, and there was no running.

With a soft sigh, she stood up carefully so as not to upset the delicate netting or beading on her dress, and opened the door.

"Hi," he said. "You look beautiful."

"Thanks," she said, offering half a smile.

He leaned down to graze her cheek with his lips. She turned her head at the last moment so that his mouth landed on hers.

"Came to check on you," he murmured, brushing a lock of her hair behind her ear. "I don't see your Sicilian pit bull anywhere."

*Damn.* Mia stepped back, waiting to close the door until he entered the room. "I asked him make the rounds outside. There's enough people in here that would make an attack on me pretty hard."

"Not that hard," Charlie said, spinning to face her. "No guard outside your room, either."

Mia shrugged, feigning innocence. "I decided I didn't want some joe breathing outside my dressing room. Makes a girl uneasy, you know."

He frowned. "You know better than that. This is not the time to be lax. He wants you *dead*, Mia. He's been coming at us from all sides the past week. I've lost four men so far because of him."

"I'm sorry about them," she said, reaching for his hand. "Really."

He nodded, the muscles in his jaw twitching. "You need to make a move with him. He's forcing my hand. I've been sitting idle for you."

"Just give me a little more time." She rested her hand on his chest. "I'll be approaching him soon. I promise. Your men won't have died in vain."

"So what about that offer?" Charlie asked. "You gonna tell me yet?"

Mia sighed and dropped her hand. "I haven't worked out all the details." She walked to her vanity and busied herself with spritzing on some perfume.

"Bullshit."

She whirled to face him.

His eyes were hard. "I know you're up to something. With Paolo, with Bobby, Joey. Nobody can look me in the eye or give me a straight answer. What're you hiding?"

Mia stared at him for a long moment. Finally, she said, "I kept you out of it for your own safety."

He strode toward her and grasped her shoulders. "Kept me out of *what*? What are you planning?"

"Charlie," she warned. "I will tell you when the time is right. That time isn't now. Just *trust* me."

His hands tightened slightly on her arms. "I won't stand by and watch you get yourself killed."

She glared up at him and shook off his grasp. "You have no faith in me at all, do you? You think I'm still just some dumb little girl, don't you?"

"Mia—"

"Pay close attention to the papers tomorrow," she said coldly, sidestepping him and opening the door. "Then you'll see what happens when men underestimate me."

PAOLO REAPPEARED AT THE CLUB AROUND TWO A.M., WHEN guests began to drift out of The Divine, fed, drunk, entertained, and with their selected bed partner. Hyman was pleased with another fortuitous night.

Raquel accompanied Mia to her dressing room, where Joey now stood guard. He glanced at Mia and nodded slightly before shifting his eyes away, focusing on the hallway.

It was more than a simple acknowledgment. Mia's belly turned a backward flip, but she kept a firm grip on her control as she and Raquel stepped inside the dressing room.

While Mia packed up her small case of cosmetics and other toiletries, Raquel carefully packed all of her costumes except the one she was wearing into the garment bag.

"Are you sure you wouldn't like to put your street dress back on and pack that in here?" Raquel asked, gesturing to Mia's sheer, billowing, bloodred dress.

"It would certainly be more comfortable, but that's all right, Cousin," Mia said, patting her shoulder. "We'll be home soon enough, and I'll hang this up right away."

"All right." Raquel buttoned the garment bag and cradled it in her arms as Mia latched her small suitcase.

"Well, did you have fun, garment girl?" she asked with a smile, looping her arm in Raquel's as they strolled out of her dressing room and down the hall.

"I did." Raquel beamed. "It's so much more exciting with a job to do. I don't know how you managed before I came along."

Mia chuckled. "Me either. Don't ever leave, all right?"

Raquel turned sparkling brown eyes on her. "Not for anything. But, can we go home and visit sometimes?"

Mia hugged her arm. "How about every Christmas and a couple long months in the summertime? Would you like that?"

"Yes, but will Mr. Goldberg let you leave for that long?"

He would never allow that, but Mia didn't want to dash the girl's hopes. She was practically buoyant after an exciting evening.

*If only she knew about the real excitement.*

"I think we can work something out," Mia said finally. "He knows how important you are to me. How important family is."

"I must admit," Raquel said, "while I do like it here, I miss my brother and his wife and their children very much. And, well, home."

"I completely understand." Mia thought of long, cool nights in the blood orange grove talking with Don Catalano, listening to the stories of the days long before her birth, sipping homemade wine and eating the succulent fruits from the trees that hung overhead. She thought of late nights leaning against the balcony outside her room, feeling the salty air on her skin, listening to the crash of the ocean, the cry of gulls.

She missed home, too.

"We'll always make time to sail home," she promised her young cousin.

At the club's back entrance, Paolo waited with Gloria. He met Mia's gaze briefly. His dark eyes were bright and piercing, lit by some inner fire, and she felt the burn of them before he turned away to open the car doors for them. Raquel sat up front beside Paolo, and Mia and Gloria sat in the back.

Mia kept up the quiet chitchat Raquel started, wondering if they had seen so-and-so's dress and did they think so-and-so's jewels were real, and did they find Will as handsome and resplendent in his tailored suit as she did.

"Charlie seemed troubled," Gloria said to Mia. "Moody. More than normal. I noticed when he came back from your dressing room. Did you two have a spat?"

Mia shrugged. "I guess it was a minor disagreement. Business. We don't quite see eye-to-eye."

"Don't let that come between you," Gloria said softly, surprising Mia. "I can see how much he cares for you, and you for him, you stubborn thing. He wants to love you, Mia. If you care, you must let him."

The words touched her heart with a strange pang. She covered Gloria's hand with her own. "I will, *soru*."

Gloria smiled. After a moment, she said, "I prepared the gifts for Signor Bagnoli's daughter's wedding."

"Thank you," Mia said, relieved. She had nearly forgotten about the gifts she'd intended to bring.

"I love weddings," Raquel piped up. "It's been so long since I attended one. And a real American wedding."

"It'll probably be a little of home, too," Gloria said. "The Bagnolis are a good Sicilian family. His daughter is quite the American girl, though. It should be a nice time. Many people are coming to pay him respect."

"He's a good man," Mia said. She'd put a guard detail around his bakery. Since the detective had tracked her there, she feared he would return and the bakery would suffer the same fate as her shop. Worse, that Signor Bagnoli or his wife would be hurt.

"How are things with the shop?" Gloria asked. "You've been spending a lot of time away from the hotel. Is there trouble with the insurance?"

"No," Mia replied. "It appears the insurance will cover everything. Hyman said it's up to me to decide if I want to rebuild or not."

"And?" Raquel twisted around. "Do you?"

Mia nodded. "Yes, but bigger and better. With my design choices. Of course, that'll mean something I'll have to do that I really don't want to."

"What's that?" Gloria said.

"Take a loan from Hyman," she said wryly. "He loves being owed money."

Gloria chuckled. "It might be worth it."

"Perhaps." Mia flashed a smile at Raquel. "It would give Raquel something to do."

"Unless Trudy wants her job back," Gloria said, "though I do hope she'll remain Emilia's governess."

"She's quite fond of Em," Mia said. "She'd be hard-pressed to quit."

"I suppose it makes me selfish to say so," Gloria said, "but that makes me happy. Emilia is fond of her, too."

As they lapsed into comfortable silence, Mia caught Paolo's gaze in the rearview mirror. They gleamed with approval of her performance, how she'd given nothing away that anything was amiss.

At the hotel, Paolo dutifully carried her garment bag and suitcase to Mia's room while she kissed her family goodnight. The guards outside their room, furnished by Charlie, shuffled off a few feet out of respect.

"We'll get Emilia first thing in the morning," she promised Gloria.

"She's so excited for her new dress," Gloria said with a tired smile. "She's never been to a wedding before, you know."

"It'll be a wonderful day to celebrate something so lovely," Mia said softly. "Goodnight, Glo. Goodnight, Raquel."

They bid her the same, and she walked down the hallway the short, few steps to her room, then opened the door. She cocked an ear, waiting to hear their door shut. A moment later, she heard the latch. Then she looked at Paolo, leaning against the wall beside her door. He had dropped off her things and stepped back outside.

"Let's go," she said.

He nodded, and lifted a hand. Mia glanced over her shoulder down the hall. The two guards nodded at them, their faces solemn.

Mia and Paolo walked down the hallway back to the elevators, rode them down, and went back to the car. It was still warm from having just been running. She slid into the back seat and Paolo behind the wheel, and in the next moment, they sped toward the Lower East Side.

It was nearly four in the morning. The sky was still black, heavy clouds puffing up high and concealing the stars, threatening another April storm. The ground was wet and shiny from a rainstorm that had passed over the city a few hours ago. The air smelled clean, fresh, promising new beginnings with the rising sun.

The old neighborhood was oddly silent. It had nothing to offer young whoopee-seekers. No speakeasies, no jazz clubs. No brothels or card halls. There might be the occasional get-together hosted in a home, but most people knew where to find the liveliest places to have fun. A family-based community was not it. Therefore, silence at this hour was common.

And yet, there was an ominous quality to the silence, one that reeked of death. An echo of stillness that seemed to bounce off the corners of her mind, over and over.

Paolo turned a corner onto Mulberry Street, where so many hardworking, family-operated businesses lined the street on either side. It was one of the hearts of the neighborhood, where people came to do their shopping, to socialize, to fix things, to make a life. The tailor's shop had been burned here, because of the degradation that had poisoned the community. Other shops suffered from theft, vandalism. Others still paid exorbitant protection fees to a man who cared nothing for them, a man who employed other men to peddle that poison, to commit atrocities that would destroy mothers and families for generations.

Paolo rolled to a stop.

Mia opened the car door and stepped out. Her heeled evening shoes slid a little on the slippery ground. The edges of her gauzy dress trailed in a pool of water before she stood up. The only sounds in her ears were the click of her heels with each step forward, the jingle of her long, bejeweled earrings as they swayed, brushing the tops of her shoulders.

She paused, her soft breaths in and out now the only sounds in the still, still night. She surveyed the fruit of her plan.

A small, cold smile pulled at one side of her mouth.

Lying side-by-side along the block, in the middle of the street, were bodies. Eighteen of them.

They were the corpses of the men who worked for Jacopo "Gems" Morelli. Bodies of the men who, in life, had murdered children. Raped young girls. Peddled drugs to young people with bright futures. Vandalized property that belonged to hard-working immigrants who had nothing else to their names. Ruined lives. They'd also organized hits on her friends' businesses, murdering more than half a dozen of those men. They'd encroached on the business dealings of the powerful Mr. Masseria. They'd destroyed her shop and hundreds of thousands of dollars' worth of liquor.

At the meeting she'd had at Johns of 12th with Paolo, Bobby, and Joey, they'd identified these men, gone over who they were, where they lived, and what their habits were. After ensuring they were peddlers for Jake and that the murderer of Signora Cancio's son and Signora Franco's daughter's rapist were among them, Mia systematically ordered them all executed, as punishment, as a favor to the people of her community, as a warning to Mr. Morelli that he should be very, very careful. That his attempts on her life, the destruction of her shop and business, the attacks on her people would not be taken lightly.

Mia walked down the long row of dead men, gazing down at them without feeling. The man who had murdered Signora Cancio's young son appeared to be covered in a thin layer of melting ice. Even the blood that coated what had once been his face glistened with tiny icicles under the street lamps. That had been Joey's handiwork. He'd told her he had an in with the owner of the restaurant the child-killer liked to eat at, and the restaurant owner had a large ice box he was willing to let Joey use for a day or two in exchange for fifty dollars and Joey's gratitude.

Next, she stopped in the middle of the row and looked down at the man who had raped the daughter of Signora Franco. Mia studied his face—the slack jaw, the heavy-lidded eyes that no longer saw anything, the yawning U-shaped gash across his throat, courtesy of a deftly wielded garrote. Paolo had wanted him for himself.

All of these men might have had lives that could have stretched on for many more years. But they had chosen to cast their lots in with a man like Jake Morelli. And even if these dead young men were not all guilty of heinous crimes like the ones Mia was aware of, that didn't matter. They still worked for Jake, still peddled his poison, and had to be lines in her message that he had made a grave mistake in underestimating her. Their blood belonged on Jake's hands, not her own.

She reached into the pocket of her evening jacket and withdrew the ace of hearts card she'd taken from the poker game with Jake and kissed the center of it, over the hole made by his knife. Her lipstick left a red stain. She knelt and placed the card on the young man's chest, face up.

Mia stepped back, taking in the long stretch of dead men for another beat before turning to walk back to the car. No, this blood was not on her hands. She would sleep soundly tonight.

Paolo waited beside the back door and opened it for her as she neared. Before climbing in, she lifted a hand to his cheek.

"*Grazie*," she said softly.

He bowed his head, then scooped up her hand and kissed the back of it. A simple, ancient sign of respect and loyalty.

She climbed back into the car, and did not look back.

# CHAPTER TWENTY

The wedding of Signor Bagnoli's daughter to her groom was scheduled to take place at eleven o'clock the first morning of May, with a lavish reception to follow at a neighborhood social hall that afternoon.

After dressing for the day in a prim, jade satin dress with sheer bishop sleeves, flowing chiffon side panels for movement, and a matching satin ribbon tied in a small bow at the shoulder, Mia joined Gloria and Raquel in their suite for breakfast. Both women seemed to be in high spirits, and Gloria was particularly excited about picking up Emilia soon, though she was certain the girl would fuss terribly over having her hair brushed and plaited for the wedding.

Mia smiled and laughed with them, chatted, resuming the same innocent role she'd played last night. They would find out soon enough what had happened. Part of her preparations had included paying a few reliable homicide detectives that one of Bobby's men knew to clean up the scene that morning, after the people of the neighborhood saw it and understood she was striking back for them. That she had taken vengeance for them, as she'd promised she would.

The guard outside Gloria's suite knocked on the door. "Paper, Mrs. Scalisi," he called.

"Bring it in," she replied. "Thank you."

The door opened, and the young man entered the suite, a different guard than the one from last night. He handed Gloria the paper. Then he walked back into the hall and pulled the door shut behind him.

Mia poured herself another cup of coffee. Though she was altogether pleased with how seamlessly things seemed to have gone last night, she was tired. She felt she could sleep for an entire day. Hyman had allowed her to miss rehearsal with the promise she would show up earlier in the evening to at least run through her setlist quickly with the band once before her scheduled performance, so she likely had no time for a nap. Late tonight, after the club, she would meet with Paolo, Bobby, and Joey to learn about how things had gone, if there had been any trouble, and to give them the money to pay the loyal men they'd hired whom she would likely never meet. Then again, she mused as she took a sip, perhaps she should meet them. Reliable, trustworthy, loyal men were hard to come by these days, and she needed every one she could get.

She'd asked Joey and Bobby to lay low today. She trusted them to cover their tracks properly, but after the events of last night, she thought it would be best for them to stay close to their homes, in case someone had inadvertently spotted them last night and recognized them today.

It had been useless to try to convince Paolo of the same. As soon as she'd broached it when they'd returned to the hotel in the wee hours of the morning, he grunted and dismissed her words with an annoyed wave of his hand.

"Oh, sweet Mother," Gloria breathed, staring down at the newspaper.

Mia glanced up, pausing with her coffee cup halfway to her lips.

"What is it?" Raquel asked, setting down the small plate over which she nibbled a pastry.

Eyes downcast, Gloria slowly turned the paper around so they could read the headline:

## EIGHTEEN DEAD IN GANGLAND MASSACRE, BODIES DISPLAYED ON MULBERRY STREET

Beneath the headline was a grainy photo of the bodies laid out on the street, taken from a nearby rooftop.

Unbidden, Mia felt that iciness that had swept over her last night as she'd surveyed the scene in person. She resumed drinking her coffee. "How unfortunate."

A heavy silence sank down among them. She felt the stares of both women as she reached for a piece of biscotti and dipped it demurely into her coffee.

"Not as good as Signor Bagnoli's," Mia told them, "but really, the hotel makes quite a nice biscotti. Don't you think, Raquel?"

"A-ah," her cousin stammered, glancing at Gloria, who maintained her silent, level stare at Mia. "Yes. They're very tasty."

"Not as good as Isabella's, either, I'm afraid," Mia said, setting down the cookie and brushing off her fingers. "I loved the ones she made with the blood orange juice and the dark chocolate. Delicious."

"Yes," Raquel said faintly, her gaze dropping back to the newspaper.

Mia leaned across the table and plucked the newspaper from Gloria's hands, then folded it to conceal the grisly photo and set it on the side table beside the sofa. "No use in having such unpleasantness lying around at breakfast. It's supposed to be a happy day." She glanced at the clock on the wall. "We should leave to get Emilia. Are you girls ready?"

Without waiting for an answer, Mia scooped up her hat and went to the gilt-framed mirror on the wall. The light wool, picture-style hat was a creamy beige color with an asymmetrical brim that swooped low on one side of her face in a most dashing way. A wide, jade silk ribbon wrapped around the crown beneath a cluster of pale pink silk flowers positioned at the side of the hat, the ends of the ribbon trailing over the brim and brushing her shoulder. She settled it on her head and arranged the dark waves that peeped beneath the brim around her chin. It had certainly cost a pretty penny at the milliner's, but it made her look so charming, it had been worth the indulgence.

When she turned around, both women remained on the couch, watching her. Raquel's eyes were wide, but Gloria's were slightly narrowed.

"Well?" Mia said, allowing a bit of her old impatience to creep into her voice as she tugged on a pair of white, wrist-length silk gloves, making sure her bracelet and watch were visible.

"Go on, dear," Gloria said softly to Raquel, patting her knee. "Fetch your things."

Raquel swallowed and nodded, then hurried to her bedroom.

Gloria rose and retrieved her own hat and gloves from where they rested on a small table and walked toward Mia. She steeled herself for an inquisition, but was wholly surprised when Gloria lightly placed her hands on Mia's shoulders and brushed her thumb over her cheek.

"What a lovely hat," she said. She touched the bow on the shoulder of Mia's dress, then tightened it. "You were coming undone, darling."

Mia blinked.

"Raquel," Gloria called. "Please don't forget Emilia's dress."

"I won't," came the faint reply.

She turned to Mia. "We discovered late last night that some of the lace had come loose, so she stayed up even later to sew it back on." She reached for the door, cocking her head. "Are you all right, dear?"

"Yes," Mia said, clearing her throat. "Thank you. That was very sweet of Raquel."

"That's one of the things I love about her most," Gloria said. "Her willingness to do anything at all for her family and the people she cares about, even if it's to her own detriment."

They locked eyes, and Gloria gave her the slightest of nods.

She understood.

❀

Most Precious Blood was nearly as full as it was for a Sunday Mass. Most of the neighborhood had turned up for the wedding, unsurprisingly. Signor Bagnoli and his family were well liked, and weddings were always an excellent excuse for an enormous party.

Emilia danced along at her side, thrilled with her lovely new dress made of pale pink and white lace, fluffy layers of organza and a big ribbon sash around her waist. She loved less the process of plaiting her hair, but she'd been surprisingly well behaved that morning, putting up only a minor complaint when her mother approached her with the hairbrush.

From the moment they'd arrived at the grocery to get Emilia ready, the air had felt different. Uncle Joe and Aunt Connie seemed to fuss over her more, finding every excuse to call her "niece" and pat her shoulder or cheek. When they'd arrived at the church, crowds of wedding-goers standing outside enjoying the fresh spring air had parted for them, their eyes on Mia. All she could hear as she bid polite good mornings were hushed whispers behind hands. Others rushed to greet them. They grappled for her hand and showered her with well-wishes as if she were the bride.

Inside the church, a Bagnoli family member spotted them and rushed over, insisting they sit with the family near the front despite Mia's polite refusal. The young man would have none of it.

Acutely aware of the congregation's collective stare, she led her family to the proffered pew and sat. She'd expected word to travel quickly and assumptions to be made, but she hadn't expected quite so much scrutiny so soon. She shifted in her seat, trying to focus on the lovely sprays of flowers that had been set up at the front and listen to the cheerful organ music that filled the entire building.

"Stop squirming," Gloria whispered. "You're as bad as Em."

"I feel like everyone's staring at me," Mia whispered back.

"When did that ever bother you before, Saturday Night Special?" Gloria gave her a teasing nudge with her elbow. "Besides, everyone *is* staring at you."

"Great."

"It's fine." Gloria squeezed her hand.

For the duration of the ceremony, Mia managed to ignore the heat of dozens of stares. Signor Bagnoli's daughter was so lovely and radiant in her wedding costume, her pretty face lit up with joy, that the attention immediately pinned to her. Her groom, a handsome young fellow, looked joyous as he watched his veiled bride make the trip down the aisle to him on her doting father's arm.

Mia studied the young couple once they were joined at the altar in front of Father Alessio. She'd never seen such a look of love between two people before—not even Nick and Gloria. She tried to recall Nick's face at his and Gloria's wedding ceremony, but failed. Had he looked so positively blissful to be wedding Gloria as this young man did?

She sent up a prayer that they would never forget this moment or that bond of love between them. Though God was likely disgusted with her, she hoped the unselfishness of her prayer for happiness for the young couple would allow Him to overlook from whom the prayer was coming.

After the ceremony, Paolo drove them to the reception hall a few blocks away. Uncle Joe, Aunt Connie, Raquel, and Emilia went inside while Paolo took Mia and Gloria to a specialty shop, where she purchased fine Italian cigars for the groom and Signor Bagnoli to accompany the array of gifts she'd brought for the couple, the bride, and her bridesmaids, which included an envelope stuffed with a generous amount of cash for the newlywed couple, bottles of expensive French perfume for the bride, her bridesmaids, and Signora Bagnoli, and some of Uncle Joe's finest wine and imported olive oil for the parents.

It took several long moments before the gifts were arranged and packed to her satisfaction. There was so much, in fact, they'd had to make a quick stop by the grocery to swipe an empty wooden crate in which to carry everything.

By the time they returned to the reception hall, it was an hour later and the smell of baked cheese and tomato sauce rolled out the doors and into their noses. Mia's stomach rumbled as she slid out of the car behind Gloria.

"Let's hurry," she said to Gloria, trying to keep the whine out of her voice. "I'm so hungry."

"You're *always* hungry," Gloria said good-naturedly.

"Signorina?" a woman behind her said.

Mia turned to where two middle-aged women approached the reception hall. Both women seemed to hesitate for a moment, then they stepped closer to her. One of them took her hand and kissed the back of it, followed by the second woman. They simply murmured, *"Grazie, grazie"* as they dipped their heads.

The fervency in their voices took Mia by surprise, though she was hardly naive to what exactly she was being thanked for. Before she could recover her wit, the two women disappeared inside the reception hall.

A little terrified thrill shot through her at the realization that many people knew, or strongly suspected, what she had done. There was no proof, of course, but between her declaration after Mass last week and the scene on Mulberry this morning, it left little doubt in the minds of the shrewd people of Little Italy.

On the heels of the fear was a burst of pride. She had heard their pleas and delivered her promise. She'd taken up for them when no one—no man—had.

Gloria stepped up beside her. Mia glanced over, then drew her head back as she noticed Gloria's piercing stare. "I got something on my face?"

Gloria's dark eyes swept over her face as if seeing her for the first time. A small, fond smile stretched her lips. "Yes. You do." She put her palm to Mia's cheek. "Pride."

Mia's cheeks heated as she reached up to squeeze Gloria's hand. She turned toward the car, reaching out for the crate of gifts. "We should head in."

Gloria's hand shot out and closed around her wrist. "You can't carry that in."

"Why not? It's not that heavy."

Her sister-in-law gently pushed her aside. "You're a woman of respect now," she said evenly. "Paolo, would you please carry the box?"

As Paolo came forward to retrieve the create, Mia couldn't help a little incredulous chuckle. Gloria, who would have before been horrified by even thinking about the possibility of what Mia had done, what she'd become, was now scolding her for not acting according to her newly acquired station. It was absurd and touching and a little painful.

Gloria caught her expression and lifted her brows. "What? What's funny?"

*Everything, and nothing at all.*

"Nothing," Mia said as Paolo stepped around her and headed for the building.

People waited for her inside, to see her, to speak to her, to ask her for help. And other respected men attending the wedding—like Mr. Masseria—had certainly heard the rumors by now. What would they think of her? What might they say? Would they take her seriously and treat her as a peer, or would she be dismissed?

*What* they *think doesn't matter.*

She swallowed her nervousness and straightened her shoulders. "How do I look?" she asked Gloria, teasing just a bit.

Gloria's smile, still proud, turned a little sad. "Beautiful. And terrifying." She put her hand on Mia's shoulder and squeezed. "Now be serious."

Mia nodded.

"Because," Gloria added, "they must respect you. And they must fear you."

She turned and walked to the building, opened the door, and held it, looking back at Mia.

Mia glanced down at her shoes and drew in a deep breath. Releasing it, she looked up.

*Never let 'em see you sweat.*

With her head high, she walked past Paolo and Gloria without looking at them and stepped inside the hall as if it were her own reception.

A long set of stairs led up to the large, open room, where the sound of loud, cheerful voices floated down to her on the music of a quartet of Italian folk musicians. As soon as Mia stepped into the room, several women flocked her to welcome her, including the mother of the bride. Mia received their greetings with quiet enthusiasm, shaking hands, accepting pats and kisses to her cheek.

"I've brought gifts," she said, gesturing over her shoulder as Paolo carried the crate over.

Signora Bagnoli called for her daughter, who playfully tossed Jordan almonds into the mouths of her bridal party. The young women hurried over and exclaimed with delight over the gifts Mia had brought. Several of them, the daughters of hard-working and simple immigrants, had never worn perfume, much less owned her own bottle. Mia showed them how to apply it, dabbing behind the ears, on the wrists, brushing her fingers across her collarbone.

Signor Bagnoli joined them, heartily wringing her hand. He leaned close to speak in Sicilian into her ear. "The neighborhood thanks you."

She gave him a small smile. "These gifts are to honor you and your family on your daughter's wedding day." It was the closest she was willing to come to outright acknowledging her actions. His meaning was clear.

He nodded solemnly. "We are honored to receive them. All of us."

Mia swept her hand toward the crate. "There are still more. Wine and olive oil, from Uncle Joe."

"Ah, Joe!" Signor Bagnoli called laughingly over his shoulder.

Mia craned her neck, catching sight of her uncle vigorously performing a traditional Southern Italian folk dance as the band played a lively *tarantella*. She caught Gloria's eye and grinned, and her sister-in-law burst into peals of laughter.

Finally, Mia took the bridal envelope full of cash and reached for the bride's hand. She wore a white satin wedding purse over one shoulder stuffed full of similar embossed envelopes.

Mia kissed both her cheeks and pressed the envelope into her hands. "I wish you and your husband a long, happy life together. I hope this helps you two get started."

The bride, perhaps a few glasses of wine into the celebration, gripped Mia's hands. "Thank you," she said. "You do our family a great honor by attending my wedding, Signorina Scalisi."

Mia nodded and patted her hand. "I'm the one who's honored."

She stepped back to let Gloria exchange pleasantries with the young bride and surveyed the room. Seated at a round table near the back of the room, she spotted Mr. Masseria, Mr. Luciano, Frankie Yale, Charlie, and a few other men she didn't know chatting over glasses of wine.

She leaned over to Gloria. "I'd better go say hello."

Mia made her way across the room toward the table where the respected men sat. All eyes at that table swiveled to watch her with what seemed a new interest and intensity and not a little amusement. She had the feeling she'd be facing some kind of music—Mr. Masseria would likely have something to say about the fact that she had not sought his approval for her actions. That she'd known precisely what she planned to do the day they'd met at John's of 12$^{th}$ to discuss the state of things.

She squared her shoulders, making sure she took her time, indulging the people who reached out to her along the way. She would not allow any of them to think she answered to him, nor was she going to hurry over like a mindless servant.

"Signorina," a middle-aged man she did not know said, kissing her hand. His wife with whom he'd been dancing clutched her hand next.

"Signorina Scalisi," she murmured.

She shook hands with nearly everyone she passed, who all greeted her with undeniable respect in their voices. She made quiet, humble replies in return, wanting to be as gracious as possible. These people were not well-to-do, like the men she was about to speak to at the back of the room. These were the people she had decided to protect.

These were the people she'd done mass murder for, and she spoke to them all, looking each of them in the eye with the same respect they showed her.

When she'd shaken the last hand, she crossed the last few feet to Mr. Masseria's table. The men no longer looked amused.

"Don Masseria," she said quietly. "It's good to see you here. I hope you've been well."

He unfolded himself from his chair and stood, keeping his gaze on her. "Signorina Scalisi. Good to see you as well. I hear you've been busy."

"Performing does keep me busy five nights a week."

"Indeed. Sit." He glanced at one of the men she didn't know who occupied the chair next to his, grunted, and the man hurried out of the chair.

"Signorina," he murmured, gesturing to it, before stepping back to stand against the wall.

She lowered herself into the chair and glanced around the table. "Mr. Luciano, Mr. Yale." She glanced at Charlie, an unreadable but intense expression in his eyes. She hadn't spoken to him since their brief row in her dressing room last night, and she was sure he had quite a few things to say to her now. "Mr. Lazzari."

"Miss Scalisi," he said tightly.

"So," Mr. Luciano said, leaning forward. "That was some neat trick you pulled off last night."

"I'm not sure what you're talking about." Mia gave him her best impersonation of Hyman's bland smile.

He smirked. "Oh, no? You don't know nothing about those eighteen poor saps laid out on the street everybody saw this morning?"

"Totò," Mr. Masseria interrupted, holding up his hand without sparing him a glance. "All of you, take a walk. I want to speak with Miss Scalisi in private."

Frankie shrugged and stood. "I need another glass of wine, anyway."

Mr. Luciano looked less than pleased about being dismissed, but followed Frankie toward the huge wine casks.

Charlie glanced at her before stubbing out his cigarette and walking away.

Mr. Masseria faced Mia. "What you did was risky. Very risky. Theatrical."

"Well, I *am* a performer, Don Masseria."

He frowned. "This is no time for jokes. The police have been all over this place since dawn."

"I took care of all that," she said.

"What do you mean?"

"I have some friends within the New York City police department. They'll conduct an investigation, they won't get any information from anyone here, and eventually, they'll forget about the case."

"Is that what you think?" he asked, lifting a brow. "You don't think that can be traced back to you?"

"It would be quite a stretch," she replied. "But if so, I have an alibi. I was singing last night. Hundreds of people from all over Manhattan can to attest to that."

"So." Mr. Masseria leaned toward her. "You kill eighteen men for working for Morelli. But did you know some of them worked for Maranzano, too?"

"None of them were high-ranking in his organization," Mia said. "Low-level button men at best, none of them made. All of them spent more time doing Morelli's bidding than earning any money for Maranzano."

"So why didn't you kill Morelli?" he asked softly. "You'll never be able to trust him again."

"I never trusted him to begin with," Mia said. "I sent him a message—to back off. Perhaps now he understands how serious I am. Someone very smart once told me blood is too expensive. It should only be shed in the direst of circumstances."

"Eighteen men," Masseria said. "That's quite an expense."

"For the people of this neighborhood being raped and murdered by those men," Mia said through her teeth, "I'd say it was worth it. They needed the help, and they certainly weren't getting it from anyone at this table."

"Careful," he said, holding up a warning finger.

She held herself rigidly for a moment. "I mean no offense."

"Look, I understand," he said. "I'm an immigrant of this country, too. I arrived here when I was sixteen years old. The year before you were born. In many ways, I grew up here like you did."

"No offense, Don Masseria," Mia said, "but you moved uptown to get away from here as soon as you could afford it."

"And you?" he said. "I suppose your lavish hotel suite is in the heart of Little Italy, eh?"

"At least I haven't forgotten this place," she said. "At least I still care. I see it as more than protection money."

"You are fortunate I have affection for you and your family," he said, a low growl curling the edges of his words. "You are an impudent young woman. That will be your downfall."

"What will be yours?"

His face reddened. He glared at her.

She stared impassively back at him.

After a long, tense moment, he huffed out a mirthless laugh and shook his head. He still looked quite irritated with her. "You are your brother's sister."

"I am a Scalisi."

"Then be like your brother and heed my words. Your problems with Morelli are not over. He's a cunning fellow."

"I didn't expect them to be over," Mia said. "But he forced my hand. What I do from here is up to him."

"You should know," Mr. Masseria said, "that he came to see me a few days ago. After you and I met."

She drew her head back. "See you about what?"

"To apologize for destroying my stock in the explosion," Mr. Masseria said smoothly. "And he paid me a handsome tribute, to cover what was lost and a bit extra to rebuild our friendship."

"So you're aligned with him now?"

He made a casual face, shrugging. "He and I are square. I don't hold you accountable for what happened, or your Jew partner. I've worked out some warehouse space with Frankie Yale. As far as I'm concerned, I have no problems with any one of you. But that's not alignment. That's peace."

"Peace?" Mia repeated. He was too smart a man to say something so foolish.

"Peace can, of course, be fleeting," he said coolly. He rose from his seat and extended a hand to help her up. "I am going to bid Signor Bagnoli farewell. I came only to fill his daughter's bridal purse and to speak with you. It was quite a sight to see you received by your people like a *riggìna*." There was nothing mocking in his voice.

She kissed both his cheeks. "It was good to see you, Don Masseria."

He tilted his head, amused. "I'm not an easy man to speak to. And you are not an easy woman to speak to. I'm not sure if that's truly *good*." He tapped the tabletop with a finger. "Take very careful next steps. My offer of help is still open, should you need it."

He bowed slightly, stepped around her, and disappeared into the crowd. His men, the ones she didn't know, followed him like shadows.

An alcove next to the window at the back of the room caught her eye. An old, battered, tufted red chair was tucked there, out of sight from the rest of the room, bathed in shades of white and cream.

She walked toward it. Disappearing, even for a few moments, appealed to her suddenly weary mind. The chair was made of velvet that might have once been soft. It smelled musty, but nonetheless, she sat down in it. The old cushion curved around her hind end as though it had been made for her. She sighed and leaned back in the chair, crossed her legs, and stared out the window for a long moment, allowing her mind to wander.

"Bang, bang."

Mia whipped her head from the window, then froze.

Jake Morelli stood a few feet away, his fingers formed like a gun pointed at her. He grinned, then blew on the tips of his fingers. "Boy. Coulda had you there. Gangsters gotta pay attention, dollface. Lesson number one. Although, you look more like a queen on her throne sitting there."

She remained seated in the chair, legs still crossed in a relaxed, casual position even though her heart had leaped into her throat and stayed there. "What the hell are *you* doing here?"

He shrugged, stepping closer to her. "It's not hard to get invited in when the people doing the inviting don't know you from Adam. A full money envelope helps, too."

"You got some goddamn nerve to show your face around here."

"So do you, after you killed my men."

"That's quite the accusation." She kept her tone deliberately cool, even though panic began to claw at her chest. She was alone and hidden, and as good as defenseless.

If Jake meant her harm—which, she assumed, was a certainty—he had her right where he wanted. She could be dead before she was even able to utter a scream for Paolo.

He cocked his head. "Ain't we past playing coy?"

"Why don't you tell me? I don't believe you've stopped."

He smirked, then reached into the inner breast pocket of his suit coat. Mia tensed, gripping the arms of the chair, but he removed what looked like a small card and held it up.

It *was* a card—the ace of hearts from their poker game. The red lipstick print was slightly smudged.

He tossed it in her lap with a flick of his wrist. "Believe you left your calling card behind."

Her heart thundered, but her hands were steady as she plucked the card from her lap and tucked it into her clutch. She forced a smirk up at him. "Didn't want to keep it? I'm hurt."

Jake's dark eyes gleamed down at her, and she wanted to recoil at the violence she saw in them. Instead, she crossed her

legs and leaned back in the chair. She would die before she let
him get a whiff of her fear.

She supposed she'd done a bang-up job of drawing him out
—it was a shame she was completely unprepared for it.

The band shifted into their next song, a Sicilian mazurka, to
cheers from the crowd. They loved to dance, and would go as
long as the band held out.

"Hear that?" Jake lifted a finger in the air, then held out a
hand. "What do you say?"

She stared at his hand as though it were a spider. "You must
be out of your mind if you think I'll let you touch me."

"Look." He unbuttoned his jacket and held it open. "No
guns, no knives. I just wanna dance with the most beautiful
woman I've ever seen. Come on, it's a wedding, for Christ's
sake."

He would likely not let her be unless she danced with him.
He didn't seem to have any weapons on him, and if he tried
anything in front of this crowd—where Paolo and Charlie could
see her—it'd turn out as badly for him as it would for her if he
managed to land a blow of some kind.

She sighed and reluctantly stood, ignoring his outstretched
hand. They received a few curious and surprised glances when
Jake, grinning, wound an arm about her waist and hauled her in
close.

From a corner where he stood chatting with Frankie Yale,
Charlie watched them, eyes burning. She shook her head at him
ever so slightly.

Seemingly oblivious to the scrutiny, Jake swept her into a
surprisingly elegant waltz step. His confidence was disarming,
along with how closely he held her.

Mia stumbled a little, but quickly caught her footing. "This
isn't how you dance a mazurka."

"I know, but I wanted a reason to hold you close." He held
her fast to his body as he swept her around the floor, causing
other couples to stumble out of their way. The crowd, unaware
of the murderous tension between them, burst into applause.

Surely they thought her and Jake a handsome couple, and he was as gifted a dancer as she was. She did her best to smile as they whirled around.

Jake did the same, nodded and flashing charming grins to the women who cheered them on. His hand drifted to the small of her back as he held her tightly and placed his lips against her ear like a lover, eliciting more excited shrieks from the women, including the bride.

To everyone watching, it appeared a romantic overture was happening between them, that the handsome man must be professing his love to her.

"That was quite the fucking stunt you pulled, you bitch."

Mia's smile turned wintry. "Ah, finally. The truth emerges."

The hand at her waist tightened from a possessive hold to a painful grip. "You think you're real smart, huh?"

"Smarter than you. Certainly."

"Why?" His voice shook slightly, but his steps remained as smooth as ever as they glided around the floor. The mazurka ended and a true waltz began.

This time, she leaned up to murmur into his ear, her cheek against his. "The mother of the young boy your men killed wants to know the same thing. As does the mother of the girl your men raped. And the father of the young woman who overdosed on your poison and died calling *your* name."

"Some of those men worked for Maranzano," Jake hissed. "They just peddled for me as a side hustle. I got him up my ass now."

"That's not my problem."

"How long do you think you can keep this up, dollface?"

She drew back to stare up into his face. "As long as you want, Mr. Morelli."

"Until one of us ends up dead?"

"Yes," she said grimly, glaring at him. "One of us. And most of my partners want that to be you."

His Adam's apple bobbed as his face lost its usual sneer. "I thought we were partners."

"Partners don't try to have each other killed," she growled. "They don't burn each other's shops to the ground."

"I just... I got sore, all right?" he said, sounding like a petulant child. "I never took well to no broad telling me what to do, and I lost my temper. Look, nobody got hurt and I squared it with Masseria. All's well that ends well."

His nonchalance left her speechless.

"Not as far as the businessmen I deal with are concerned. They want you *dead*, Mr. Morelli."

"And you?"

"I can't come up with a good reason to keep you alive."

"Look. Let's call a truce," he said, waltzing her into a slow turn. "No more funny shit from me. I'll forgo vengeance of my men. They cancel everything else out. I'll even give up half of my percentage in the Madden deal, just to show you I'm a good sport. Back down to twenty percent, even. No heroin in the neighborhood—not that I got any more dealers at the moment. In exchange, you let the others know you're good with me. That they should be, too."

"Those are the original terms I presented you," she said through clenched teeth. "Not good enough."

"Fine." He spun her away, then back in and resumed the tight hold of his arm around her body as he lifted her other hand in his. "Then how about I pay for that little shop of yours? What else do you want?"

"You're out of the deal with the Cotton Club. I want my stolen trucks back with everything on them, or the money to cover the losses, plus an extra fifty grand for my partners' inconvenience. And I want thirty percent of all your books, card games, and protection business in *all* your territories."

Jake stopped dancing. "*What?*"

"And don't try to trick me, Mr. Morelli. I know where all seven of them are, all over this city. Shall I list them for you?"

His mouth tightened into an angry line. "You're out of your fuckin' mind if you think I'm agreeing to that."

She brought her mouth close to his ear. "You want me to

speak on your behalf to my partners. Tell me, how much is your life worth to you?"

His eyes darkened with fury. "If I'd wanted to, I could have killed you when I found you in that chair. It's because of *me* you're still alive. You're not untouchable."

"Neither are you." Without taking her eyes off him, she made a beckoning motion with the fingers of the hand that rested on his shoulder.

A moment later, a knife appeared at Jake's throat as Paolo emerged from the crowd like a wraith and snatched him from behind. His other hand slipped under Jake's armpit and pulled, effectively trapping the man.

Jake's eyes went wide. People in the crowd gasped, a few crying out in dismay. The music came to an abrupt halt.

The only sound in the room was Jake's harsh panting as Paolo held him fast in his brutal grip, the knife pressing lightly into his skin.

Mia ignored the room and stepped toward him until their noses nearly touched. "Kill him."

The knife pressed harder into Jake's skin, Paolo's teeth bared in silent rage. Jake made a desperate noise in the back of his throat.

Another sharp gasp came from the crowd.

She tilted her head. "That's enough, Paolo."

Paolo lowered the knife.

"What the fuck?" Jake demanded.

"I want you to see how fast it can happen," she said softly. "How quickly things can end for you. I want you to understand I'm only thing keeping you alive in this moment."

His nostrils flared as he stared at her.

She held out her hand. "I heard your terms. Now, you have mine. Do we have a deal, Mr. Morelli?"

After a moment that could have lasted sixty seconds or half an hour, Jake shook her hand, his gaze full of hate and a darkness that made her insides quiver with fear she refused to show him.

"Good. Let him go, please, Paolo," she said.

A small voice in the back of her mind whispered to her. *What have you done?*

Paolo released Jake so slowly, it was an unmistakable warning —one wrong move, and he'd be truly dead.

Jake jerked away from him and straightened his jacket. He glanced around, finding nearly every pair of eyes in the room locked on him.

All except one.

At the edge of the crowd, Charlie watched her with the same expression that had been on his face the night she'd used his pistol to shoot and kill Vincenzo Fiore, in that warehouse on that beach in Atlantic City. The expression that had made her feel like a stranger to him.

Mia looked away from him.

"What the fuck are you looking at?" Jake shouted at the room. He started for the door, giving Mia a wide berth but shoving through the crowd. The small handful of men he'd brought with him followed him out of the reception hall.

She had worn out her welcome, too, by now. Besides, it was time to prepare to head to the club.

"Paolo," she said.

He nodded, unfazed by the eyes that now watched them.

She looked at Signor Bagnoli, who stood with his shell-shocked daughter and her groom. "I apologize for making a scene," she said. "I hope you'll forgive me. Thank you so much for inviting me here to celebrate your daughter's wedding. I wish you all the happiness in the world."

"Th-thank you," she stammered.

But Signor Bagnoli had an understanding gleam in his eye. He bobbed his head. "Thank you, Miss Scalisi. We hope to see you again very soon."

"If you ever need anything," she said, patting his arm, "I hope to be the first person to receive your call."

On her way to the door, she paused in front of her family,

clustered off to the side. "I'll have Paolo come back to bring you home later, so you can stay."

Without waiting for an answer, she walked toward the door. People stepped out of her way before she could utter a simple, "Pardon me."

In the car on the way home, Mia thought of the looks on the guests' faces. Her family's faces. Gloria had said they must respect and fear her.

It seemed, today, fear had won out.

# PART III

# CHAPTER TWENTY-ONE

*June, 1926*

Summers in New York were typically hot, but that first week was unseasonably mild, with temperatures barely creeping past sixty-five. It reminded Mia of cool but balmy Sicilian nights out on the villa balcony. It seemed another life entirely that she'd been there.

Life had settled into an easy rhythm since Signor Bagnoli's daughter's wedding. For several weeks afterward, she'd stayed practically holed up in the hotel suite, only leaving to go to rehearsal, after which she stayed locked in her dressing room. Her security detail had grown from Paolo, Bobby, and Joey to a team of a dozen men, who guarded Gloria, Emilia, and Raquel nearly as closely as they guarded her. She also had eyes on the grocery at all times.

It was no way to live, but at least she was alive.

When reports reached her last month that Jake had left the city, she relaxed a little more. She had no idea who was running the handful of territories in which he'd operated across the city, but her thirty percent take showed up every week. Joey sent trusted men to collect, who went over the financial records in detail, and then brought her back what she was owed.

Though she felt she could take a deep breath again knowing Jake was out of the city, some deep warning inside her niggled at her, and that was what kept her from fully letting down her guard. Only a fool would ever do that.

The first Saturday in June, Mia rode around Midtown with Hyman, considering a number of potential new properties to rebuild the shop. Eventually, she settled on a lot at West 42$^{nd}$ Street near 7$^{th}$ Avenue. It was a block down and east of The Divine, and it was a busy, affluent area surrounded by fine restaurants and theaters. The new space was larger, and Hyman, pleased to have her indebted to him again, grudgingly agreed to give her full design control and a generous budget.

"But keep it reasonable," he added, wincing, after signing the purchase agreement with the previous owner.

"It'll be lovely." Mia turned in a circle and envisioned the empty space decorated. "No more French cathouse décor. You'll be proud to be my landlord." Now that she'd have a little more space than the last location, she'd be able to offer more goods— of both varieties.

"I'm already your landlord," he replied. "We can begin construction immediately."

"Swell. Tell those boys to get ready for me."

Hyman rolled his eyes. "Please just keep in mind, they're professionals who know their craft."

"Then they should be used to dealing with women who know what they want."

"I'm not quite sure anyone can be prepared to deal with a woman like you," he said drily, but the twinkle in his eyes took the sting out of his words.

She smirked. "I'll take that as a compliment. Anyhow, I'd like there to be an extra-large warehouse beneath the shop. Business has been picking up, especially now that our Canadian friends don't hate us."

"That was rather an unfortunate situation." Hyman sighed.

"I'm glad we were able to move past it, and that Mr. Morelli decided the climate of New York was bad for his health."

"I got all the trucks he stole back but one," Mia said. "But he sent money to cover what was lost between that truck and the booze on board." Her lips twisted into a wry smirk. "Most of that money ended up going to Frankie Yale to rent warehouse space until we find a new location in Manhattan."

"He is an enterprising young man, indeed, that Mr. Yale," Hyman said, sarcasm coating his words like honey.

They walked outside. The sun blazed high in the sky, and the warmth of it made her suspect the unseasonable coolness would be pushed out soon by normal warm summer temperatures.

Paolo stood outside her vehicle, nodding to Hyman before sweeping the block with his narrowed gaze. He waved her forward impatiently; he did not like it, she'd come to realize, when she lingered on the sidewalk.

"I'll be a little late to rehearsal this afternoon," she said to Hyman. "I have some business in the Lower East Side."

The only sign of his displeasure was a slight tightening at the corners of his mouth, but by now he knew better than to fuss at her about when she visited the old neighborhood. Moreover, she'd proven herself to him as an entertainer. In the last month, The Divine's business had tripled each weekend. Often, a cap had to be put on the number of people who tried to get into the club as there simply wasn't space to accommodate them.

Though their original agreement had stated her wages would be evaluated for an increase six months into her employment, he'd already doubled them. She'd been working on getting him to let her write her own song lyrics, but he seemed much more eager to pay her more money than to allow her that creative freedom.

Paolo drove her to Little Italy. The sight of it on a late Saturday morning in the summer made her smile. Mulberry Street was full of vendors selling a variety of fruits, vegetables, baked goods, and wares. People milled up and down the road, haggling, laughing, chatting. It was altogether a different place than it had been this spring, and her heart soared at the sight of it.

She had Paolo pull over to the curb, wishing to walk through the market. She'd heard of one vendor who sold blood oranges from Sicily and wanted to see how they compared to the ones from Carlo's grove.

People called out cheerful hellos to her, which she returned in kind. Some stepped from behind their carts or put down their produce to shake her hand and inquire about her health and happiness. She knew most of their names, their children's names, and asked questions to ensure they were not in need of anything, to see where she could be of use or help to them.

Inevitably, no matter how much she protested, vendors offered gifts at nearly every stop—fine, spicy salami, bottles of homemade wine, fresh fruit, beautiful flowers. It would be rude to refuse, but she always felt a bit guilty taking from them what they could sell. They often tried to pay cash tributes as well, but she staunchly refused those. She would not be like the other gangsters in the city, taking the money of the people she'd vowed to protect.

After she'd located the blood orange vendor, whose oranges were indeed juicy and headily sweet, she and Paolo walked to Most Precious Blood.

Father Alessio was near the front, chatting with a group of women who made up the women's Bible study. They had spent the last few weeks campaigning for Mia's presence in their group, which she had always demurred her way out of. That was made doubly hard by the fact that the group was led by Signora Cancio, who, after learning of the mass murder Mia had ordered on Morelli's men, had practically prostrated herself at Mia's feet, weeping with gratitude.

Now, it seemed, she was on a mission to save Mia's soul.

"Signorina Scalisi!" the signora called, spotting her. Several heads turned her way, including Father Alessio's. Smiling, the older woman strode to meet Mia, greeting her with a kiss on each cheek. "Have you come to join us this afternoon?"

"Oh, you're very kind, Signora Cancio." Mia patted her hand. "Sadly, I won't be able to join you ladies today. I have some business with Father Alessio, and then I have to go to rehearsal."

"Ah." The signora frowned. "You must make time to hear His Word."

"I know I do," Mia replied politely. "You're absolutely right."

"Please come next time. I'll let you know at Mass tomorrow when the next meeting is."

Mia hid a smile. It was the signora's indirect way of ensuring Mia would, in fact, be attending Mass in the morning. "Thank you, Signora Cancio. I appreciate your concern for my immortal soul."

She'd meant it in a teasing way, but the signora's face grew serious, and she put a hand on Mia's arm and leaned toward her.

"The women and I," she murmured, "we each say a rosary for you, send up prayers, and light candles. Every morning. For your soul. For…the sacrifice you made for us."

Mia swallowed. Her relationship with God made her deeply uncomfortable. It was a smudge in her mind that she couldn't wipe away, a deep-rooted fear that manifested in her dreams— the unbearable heat of hellfire and eternal torture for the lives she'd taken. Twenty-one lives now, by her count.

"*Grazie,*" she said.

The signora gave her a gentle, understanding smile. She patted Mia's cheek. "You have nothing to fear. God cannot punish someone who cares so deeply for others as you do. Who cared for the death of my son so deeply. I will never forget that, Signorina Scalisi." She took Mia's arm and led her down the aisle. "I have kept Father Alessio long enough. We'll see you all tomorrow. Good day."

The women all bid her farewell. She waved at them in return.

"Well," Father Alessio said with a smile. "How may we help one of our most wonderful benefactors?"

For the past month, Mia had given the priest a handsome sum of money—hand-delivered to him from her, not added to the offering plates, each week without fail. It wasn't done out of the kindness of her heart. She and the priest had an arrangement.

"I've come to give you my weekly offering." She handed him a thick envelope stuffed with cash. This week, it was double her usual amount.

His eyes bugged out. "May God's blessings be upon you, my child. Your generosity is not missed by our Lord and—"

"Just tell me what I need to know."

Father Alessio cleared his throat. "He has still not been to confession. As I tell you every week, Signor Morelli has not been here since the wedding."

"A week is a long time." Mia folded her arms. "Things can change fast. You haven't seen him at all? Not in the back of church, not in the neighborhood?"

The priest bowed his head. "With all due respect, I do not go many places. If you have not located him, I certainly would not be the one to do so."

She tapped an impatient finger on her arm. "What else?"

"No one has confessed to the use of any illicit substances. I have had no confessions of even drunkenness."

"No one's said anything about drugs? Using *or* selling?"

He shook his head, his gaze on the floor.

Mia felt a flash of pity for him. When she'd first approached him with a healthy sum of money a month ago and requested he answer her questions about the content of the confessions he heard, and if Jake Morelli still attended church or came just to make confession, he'd balked. Understandably, since he'd taken a vow to protect those confessions.

It seemed that Father Alessio, like most people she knew, would do anything for a price. The difference with him was that he was aware of his own corruption and greed and, strangely, it bothered him.

"I'll remind you that if that changes, you're to let me know immediately."

"Yes, of course."

"I have another favor to ask, Father."

"Yes, my child?"

"My brother, Domenico, was killed almost two years ago in Chicago. Murdered."

Father Alessio lowered his eyes but nodded. "I have heard."

"He's buried in Chicago, but he belongs here in New York with our parents. They're buried in Calvary Cemetery in Queens."

"Yes," the priest said. "I've done many funerals for our Catholic brethren who were laid to rest there."

"I'm going to bring him home, and when I do, I'd like you to perform the burial ceremony for him. And have a Mass here in his honor."

Father Alessio blanched. "B-but, my child... Your brother, he was—he was—"

"He was a murderer," she said evenly. "Yes. He was."

"I—I—"

"He killed a great many men, Father," Mia went on. "I'm not sure myself of how many. But I do know he also killed to protect his loved ones. He did things to ensure our survival. Did he make mistakes? Of course. He made more than his share. But he was a good man."

"I have no doubt," the priest said, swallowing. "But his actions—his sins. They're grave. I don't think—"

"His wife wants his sins forgiven," Mia said. "Absolved. She wants a Mass said for his soul. She wants him to have proper burial rites, and I want him to be laid to rest next to our parents."

Father Alessio lowered his voice to an urgent whisper, though Paolo was the only other person in the church. "The things he has done makes that impossible, my child. He never confessed his sins to me. Therefore I cannot absolve anything, and certainly not murder. Moreover, his sins are grounds for excommunication."

"*I've* done things that should surely get me excommunicated," Mia said, raising an eyebrow and glancing at the envelope the priest still held. "I think you know that. And so have you."

Father Alessio reddened as he followed her gaze down to the envelope.

"You're the only priest I know who would do this," she went on. "Any other priest in the city would refuse. And it's important to my sister-in-law. That the father of her child is absolved by God. Whatever *you* are, you are still a man of the cloth and you can perform the rites. The strength of his widow's prayers and the generous women of this congregation will take care of the rest."

He hesitated. "This…is a considerable request."

Mia narrowed her eyes. "What do we need to do so I get what I've asked for? And so you can continue to get a pretty chunk of money each week?"

The priest raised scandalized eyes to her. "I haven't asked—"

"No, but you've taken." A hard edge crept into her voice. "Each and every time. With a blessing on your lips. Haven't you? How much of the money I've given you has made it into the *church fund*, Father?"

His mouth parted but no words came out.

She held his gaze for several long, silent seconds. Then she said quietly, "How much more do you want to do me this favor?"

"You cannot *buy* absolution. You must confess your sins and seek forgiveness, *seek* absolution."

"My brother," she snapped, "is *dead*. He can't very well make confession, can he, Father?"

"You can," he whispered. "You can confess. To your own sins, since…they are likely to be great. Confess your sins, seek forgiveness, do your penances. Then I will grant your favor."

"You do know how absurd that is coming from you, don't you?"

Father Alessio reddened. With shame coloring his voice, he said, "Yes. I, too, am a sinner. But that does not mean that I do not fear God. That I do not believe in His Word. And though you offer money, there are still requirements that must be fulfilled before I…" He hesitated, as though seeking his courage. "Before I absolve a murderer."

She glared at him.

He handed her the envelope. "Ease your soul and your mind, my child. Make confession. For yourself, and for your brother. It is the only way."

She stared at the envelope. "Is this supposed to make me think you're a changed man all of a sudden?"

"When a man's soul is on the line, even I cannot accept money."

A few moments later, she entered the confessional and knelt. Through the latticed opening, she could make out Father Alessio, who crossed himself. She did the same.

"In the name of the Father, the Son, and the Holy Spirit," she said woodenly. "Forgive me, Father, for I have sinned. My last confession was…" She blinked. She could not remember when her last confession was. "It has been many years since my last confession."

"Go on, my child," came the soft reply. "Tell me your sins. Unburden yourself."

Where should she start? "I have lied and stolen, when I was a child. I stole to survive. To eat. To stay warm. I've lied to get my way. I've lied to my brother's wife about his adultery. Many times. Lied to mislead others into having a good opinion of me." She glanced up at him. "I've bribed people."

He cleared his throat. "Go on, my child."

"I've turned a blind eye to the misdeeds of others," she said. She thought of the old days in Chicago. Thought of their friends still there. "I've knowingly broken the law. Many laws. The Prohibition law."

"Go on, my child."

She thought back to the night of Sal's birthday party. It felt like a lifetime ago, but it had hardly been two years. "I watched my brother murder a man in front of me," she said. "A man who tried to assault me. I watched my brother beat his face in until he was dead because he had dared to touch me. And I was glad for it."

"Go on, my child."

Suddenly, it was hard to speak, as though the words expanded and congealed in her throat. "I sought vengeance when my brother was murdered. I hunted down and executed the men responsible for his death. One of them...I killed with my own hand. I felt no remorse. And I still don't."

There was a brief pause. Then, "Go on."

Mia tightened her jaw. She drew in a deep breath. When she spoke, her voice trembled. "I ordered the executions of the eighteen men found on Mulberry Street last month. I had them all killed."

It was the first time she'd spoken those words out loud. Strange, the way they made her feel. It was one thing to know she'd done it, to have planned it all so meticulously. But it was another to utter them aloud in no uncertain terms.

The small voice in her mind, the one that represented the innocent girl she'd once been, screamed at the horror of it. *How could you how could you how could how could*—

"Those are indeed grave sins," Father Alessio said finally. His voice was steady and gave nothing away. "And it is right that you make confession to seek forgiveness from our Blessed Lord. Your penance is that you must say a rosary for each of the lives you have taken and pray for their salvation, as well as your own, and your brother's."

*That's it?*

"I...will do that."

"And," he added, "you must never commit murder again."

The next silence stretched on so long, the priest's head turned toward her behind the screen, as if checking to see if she were still awake.

"I won't," she said quietly.

"By our Lord Jesus Christ, I absolve you from every bond of excommunication so far as my power allows." He made the sign of the cross, and she did the same. "I absolve you from your sins, in the name of the Father, the Son, and the Holy Spirit. Amen."

How should she feel, now that she'd been absolved? Not

merely forgiven. *Absolved.* Should she feel lighter? More at ease? *Peaceful?*

She felt nothing at all.

Father Alessio emerged from the booth. He placed a hand on her shoulder and gave her a kind smile. "I will see to it your brother is buried with proper rites and a Mass is said for his soul now that he is absolved of his sins."

"Thank you, Father," she said. "I'll see to it you continue to receive my *offerings* each week."

His smile dropped off his face. "Yes. The...church is most appreciative."

"I'm certain it is."

"You may receive Holy Communion tomorrow," Father Alessio added hastily. "You've been receiving only blessings since you've been attending with your family, but now that you've confessed to your sins and been forgiven, you may partake of the Eucharist."

"Thank you," she said, because she didn't know what else to say to that. "Well, I've kept you long enough, Father. I should be going." She turned to leave, then stopped.

"My child?"

Mia faced him. "I have one more sin to confess."

He raised his eyebrows. "Of course, my child."

She gestured to the confessional. "It's just us. We don't have to go back in there, do we?"

Father Alessio spread his hands and smiled. "We are in the sight and hearing of God. Please, unburden yourself."

She glanced down for a moment, then met his gaze. "I lied to a priest," she said softly.

He blinked.

She didn't wait to hear his suggestion for penance. Didn't wait to hear him offer his absolution.

Mia strode out of the church.

SATURDAY NIGHT AT THE DIVINE BROUGHT ITS NORMAL LARGE crowd. Mia's habit was to sing a few lowkey numbers while people ate their meals. Afterward, she'd step it up—literally, with a few dance numbers featuring The Divine Angels. Then there'd be a short intermission, where she'd get to sit in her dressing room and ease her feet out of her constricting heels, talk with Raquel as she touched up her face, and find a few moments of peace. When that was done—always too quickly—she'd wrap up her set with a handful of popular songs with a couple of originals thrown in.

It was a strange thing, to have two personas she could shut off and turn on as seamlessly as throwing a switch.

Her popularity now seemed to have exceeded the popularity she'd had in Chicago. No matter where she went in the city, she was recognized. People flocked to meet her and shake her hand. It made Paolo dreadfully uneasy, but in those moments, she threw her switch and became the Mia Scalisi who filled one of the classiest clubs in town, that performed at high-class social gatherings, who attended dinners and parties with Hyman Goldberg.

How surprised everyone would be if they knew the other Mia Scalisi—bootlegger and murderess.

When she finished her set that night, she took a few moments to make pleasant small talk with some of the guests, as Hyman had ordered her to do. He said it made them feel special, and when they felt special, they came back. So it became her job to make them feel very, very special.

She sighed inwardly when she spotted a table with two men who were regulars, accompanied by two young women. The men's dates changed most nights they came to the club. The two ladies tonight were fresh-faced flappers she'd never seen before.

One of the men, a red-faced ginger called Clyde whom she'd never seen completely sober and who campaigned fiercely to get her into his bed every time he saw her, reached out a hand to snatch her wrist.

"Miss Scalisi," he said, rising to his feet. "You were, as always, *divine* tonight." He cackled at his joke.

*What a boob.* "Why, thanks, Clyde," she said with as much warmth as she could muster. She tilted a friendly chin at the two dates. "And who are these two Shebas?"

The young women, a platinum-blonde and a brunette, exchanged a wide-eyed look. The blonde shot to her feet. "Violet Bates, how do you do?" she said in a rush, sticking out her hand.

Mia shook her hand. "Charmed, I'm sure."

"This is Lil," Violet said, thumbing toward her friend, who hastened to shake Mia's hand. "She's a dancer too, you know."

"Oh?" Mia gave her a polite smile. "And where have you danced?"

"Small theaters, mostly," Lil said breathlessly. "Nothing like here. I'd love a chance for an audition. Do you think I could?"

Mia pointed across the room where Hyman schmoozed with a table of distinguished-looking older men. "That's the fella who'll need some convincing," she said. "I don't call the shots here. I just sing the songs."

The two girls wasted no time rushing off in his direction.

"Gee, you chased off our dates," the other man, George, said with mock disappointment.

Clyde grinned. "That's all right. I'd rather have Miss Scalisi all to myself, anyhow." He slid an arm around her waist.

Mia stiffened, but she playfully swatted him on the chest as she stepped out of his hold. "Aren't you a cad."

"Only because you're breaking my heart," he said, reaching for her again.

She stepped behind a chair, out of range of his groping paw. "Now, now, Clyde." Her patience was wearing thin, and it was becoming difficult to keep her trained smile in place.

He gave her a lascivious grin and made a show of pretending to throw the chair between them out of his way. Mia deftly stepped back, but crashed into a small group of guests who loitered near the dance floor.

"I beg your pardon," she murmured, making to slide behind them to get to her dressing room.

The woman she'd stumbled into smiled. "If I had to have my champagne spilled on me, I'm glad it was by you."

Mia glanced at the wet splotch on the front of her dress. "I'm so sorry." She flashed a big smile and winked. "How about a whole bottle on the house to make up for it?"

The woman cupped her hand around her mouth to shout at her comrades, all only inches away. "Coming through! Make way for the lady!"

Before she could step through the small gap they'd made for her, a hand closed on her elbow. Clyde tugged her back against him, this time wrapping both arms around her waist.

"No getting away from me this time," he purred in her ear.

Her temper broke.

She clawed at his hands until he yelped and released her, then whirled around to face him, fury igniting her blood.

"The next time you touch me, I'll have your goddamn hands cut off," she hissed.

His eyes widened and he retreated a step. "Gee, it was just a gag—"

A warm hand on her back made her whirl around. She relaxed slightly.

Charlie raised his eyebrows. "Problem here?" he asked in a mild tone.

"No," Clyde said, backing toward his table. "No problem at all."

"That's swell," Charlie said with a smooth smile. "Miss Scalisi, you're needed in your dressing room."

Her anger faded as she hid her smirk. Hyman had told her she must appear "available" to the male clientele, but never actually be available. And no one could know about her and Charlie, which was occasionally a good thing, because the glimmer in his eyes now as he studied Clyde let her know the man was in danger.

She allowed him to lead her out of the main room into the

service hallway, then peered up at him. "I'm needed in my dressing room, am I?"

He gave her a charming smile. "It was either this, or I break a bottle over his head."

"I already threatened to cut off his hands if he touched me again."

Charlie looped an arm about her waist. "That can still be arranged if that's what you want."

After Signor Bagnoli's daughter's wedding, they hadn't spoken for several days. Then, on one of her evenings off, he'd come by her hotel suite to speak with her. He'd told her he'd needed a few days to think about what she'd pulled off with Morelli's men, what it meant for the business and for her. She'd braced for a lecture, but he'd only offered his congratulations on her plan and the execution of it. And, he'd apologized for making her feel that he didn't trust her or her decisions.

"You were brilliant," he'd said earnestly.

"I missed you," she'd replied.

She hadn't seen much of Moritz since then, other than a few meetings about the liquor operation with Hyman, and a couple visits out to Frankie Yale's warehouse. His behavior toward her had changed slightly. He seemed stiffer around her, but always polite. He'd said nothing of what she'd done, but she'd caught him studying her with an intent expression on a few occasions, like he was trying to read her mind.

It hurt a little that the friendship they'd once had seemed to be over. But as long as he understood she wasn't some silly little girl, she could deal with the loss of his friendship. As long as he respected her.

Mia nodded at the guard outside her dressing room door. He nodded back and, acknowledging Charlie, strolled a few feet down the hall to give them some privacy.

She pushed open the door, expecting to see Raquel inside, who always beat her there after she finished her set. Raquel had come to understand without Mia saying so that she liked to leave as soon as possible, so she'd taken to packing up Mia's costumes and belongings during her last number and leaving out her street clothes for her to change into so they could leave as soon as possible.

But tonight, she wasn't there.

"That's odd," she murmured, glancing around. It was as though Raquel hadn't set foot in the room since intermission. Her things were exactly where she'd left them.

"What's odd?" Charlie leaned against the door jamb. He ticked his chin at the rack of costumes that stood on one side. "Something missing?"

"Well, yeah—Raquel." Mia frowned. "Did you see her in the main room?"

"No, but I wasn't looking for her."

"Would you do me a favor and go find her?"

Charlie nodded. "Be back in a few."

Mia shut the door and quickly changed out of her evening dress. She reached for the simple, floral-print chiffon dress she'd worn to the club and switched shoes. Then she paced. It wasn't like Raquel at all to disappear. She took her role quite seriously, and moreover, she'd understood since the wedding that she was not to go anywhere alone.

There was a knock on her door, and she flung it open expectantly. "Well?"

Charlie shook his head. "She's not in there."

Mia's hand dropped away from the edge of the door. "Where the goddamn hell could she have gone?"

"Hey, calm down," Charlie said gently. "Maybe she just went to the ladies' lounge. Or to the kitchen to grab a bite."

"Let's split up and go look." Mia turned to the guard. "You too. Go check wherever you can."

He nodded once and walked away quickly.

The ladies' lounge was halfway full, but none of the women inside were Raquel. She scanned each face carefully, ignoring the startled looks she received in return before ducking out.

There weren't many other places in the club to go. Mia passed through the kitchen to check the back alleyway—perhaps

Raquel had gone out for a smoke herself or to chat up a fellow she'd met. There was no one in the alley.

Inside the kitchen, Mia asked the staff if they'd seen her cousin. None had.

She ran into Charlie in the service hallway. "I can't find her. She's not here."

"Me neither," he said, and now a hint of worry crept into his voice.

He followed her outside where Paolo was waiting. Mia rapidly explained the situation to him. A deep line formed between his brows. He shook his head. He hadn't seen Raquel, either.

She begged him to drive around the area so they could look for her. Charlie rode with her. They drove around Midtown for nearly an hour, but there was still no sign of Raquel.

By the time they made it back to the Murray Hill Hotel, Mia was nearly in tears.

"Something's happened," she said in a trembling voice, watching Paolo set her things down beside the sofa. "I just know it."

Charlie rubbed the back of his neck as he paced in front of the large picture window that overlooked Midtown Manhattan. "Couldn't she have gone off with a fella?"

"No," Mia said fiercely. "She's not an irresponsible girl. If she were going to do that, she would've told me first. She would never deliberately let me worry about her. She knows how I am."

"Want me to wake up Glo?" Charlie asked, gesturing toward the door that joined their rooms.

"No, don't bother her. Let her sleep. We can—we can tell her in the morning if Raquel doesn't show up." She wrung her hands.

Paolo stood at the drink cart in the corner of the room and poured brandy into a cut crystal glass. When he held out the glass, she shook her head. Frowning, he picked up her hand and pressed the glass to her palm, then mimed drinking.

It was no use arguing with the mute man, so Mia reluctantly

bolted the drink. The liquor burned down her throat and settled like a warm, soothing blanket over the maelstrom of worry firing inside her.

Charlie accepted his own drink from Paolo with a nod of thanks. "All right. I'll call up a couple of my detective pals and get them on it. If anyone can find her, it's them."

It was the best she was going to get for now, so Mia nodded gratefully.

Just as Charlie reached for the telephone, it rang. It was so unexpected, Mia jumped, her heart pounding.

Eyes narrowed, Charlie scooped up the candlestick base, jamming the receiver against his ear. "Yeah."

He listened for a long moment. An unreadable expression dropped over his features as he lifted his eyes to hers. His dark gaze was blank. He slowly extended the telephone to her.

She rushed toward him, feeling like she might be sick. "Is it Raquel?"

He just shook his head and stepped back, watching her.

Mia shoved the receiver against her ear and lifted the base to her mouth. "Who is this?"

There was a brief pause, then an all-too-familiar low chuckle rolled into her ear. Her skin curdled like spoiled milk at the sound.

"Ain't it funny," Jake Morelli said, "how things work? My guys, they was supposed to grab you tonight. But they saw your cousin, and in the darkness, she looks so much like you. You're both about the same height, same build, same hair... Though if you ask me, you got way better bubs. She needs to fill out a little more. What is she, eighteen? Nineteen?"

There had been times in her recent life where the trauma of emotion had occasionally been so strong as to be completely overwhelming, threatening to crack her sanity, that her brain seemed to go into a sort of defense mechanism. Similar to the switch she threw to transition from one persona to another, a similar switch would be thrown in moments where her nerves became overwrought, and she would turn completely numb.

"These fuckin' yahoos I pay too much money snatched your goddamn *cousin*." Jake chuckled again. "Sister, when I tell you I was fuckin' pissed. I was gonna ice her right off the bat, then I got to thinking. I says to myself, 'Jakie,' I says, 'maybe this isn't a mistake. Maybe this is an opportunity.'"

"If you hurt her," Mia said with startling calm, "it will be your last act on this earth. I promise you that, Mr. Morelli."

"As friendly as always, I see," Jake replied. "You really need to loosen up, you know? You're still a young thing. Still got some good years left. You should really pull the stick out of your lovely little ass sometimes."

"I want my cousin," she said in a voice just above a whisper. "Now."

"You didn't let me finish," he went on. "Where was I? Oh, yeah. So then, I got to thinking. Your cousin alone doesn't seem to be enough leverage. Figured you'd get over her in a few months or so. So I asked myself, what would get you out in the open? What would be a surefire way to bring you to my doorstep? I got to thinking about that little niece of yours. So I sent my guys by to pick her up, too."

Mia's blood froze in her veins, her heart mid-thump.

"That little sweetie sure likes her bedtime snack, doesn't she? Which your sister-in-law so lovingly indulges. They were both getting ice cream in the dining room when my guys got there. And how could I separate mother and child?"

"You're a liar," she said.

"Am I? Why don't you go check her room? I know you have adjoining suites."

Mia pulled the phone away from her mouth. "See if Gloria's in her room," she hissed to Paolo.

He was back in a few moments, his face drawn and pale. He shook his head.

Mia's knees buckled slightly. He had Raquel. And Gloria. And Emilia.

"Thought this would be a nice way to bring you to heel," Jake continued, as though he could see what was happening on her end of the line. "All the most important people in your life. Your family. Your blood. That's the most important thing to you, isn't it?"

"You deranged, psychotic, goddamn motherfucking *bastard*," she breathed.

"Now that I got your attention, maybe you'll shut the fuck up and listen to me."

Every cell in her body shook. "What do you want?"

"I been thinking for the past month or so," he said smoothly. "About how you humiliated me at that wedding in front of the entire Lower East Side. In front of other men of respect. Made me look like a fool. Made me look weak. Forced me to agree to your highway robbery with a knife at my throat. You know, Mia, I gotta tell you, I'm a little sore at you about that."

She clenched her fists around each piece of the telephone. Her body was so rigid, it ached.

"And, well, I suppose I'm calling to let you know my terms have changed," he said, his voice as smooth as the cream she took in her coffee each morning. "Hymie Weiss wants you dead, and he wants control of your liquor deal. That probably ain't news to you. He hired me to take care of that, but I saw potential in you. I could get him to call off the hit—if I get him to see value in that. There's a way for us all to get what we want—even you. I'm assuming with this turn of events, what you want is for your family to stay alive."

She thought she might vomit. "What. Do you want."

"I want you to come see me so we can have a little business meeting," he said. "You'll come alone if you want your family back alive. No funny shit. If I get one hot hair up my ass that you're gonna double-cross me, I'll slit their throats right there."

Mia gripped the receiver, struggling to hold onto the light, numb feeling that blanketed the despair that clawed at her. There was no word that existed to describe how frightened, how enraged, how heartbroken she felt. "Where? When?"

"Tonight." Then he gave her the address of a warehouse in a part of town near the river. "Listen, you'll get your family back.

You have my word." He let silence linger for a moment before he added, "Whether you get 'em back alive or in pieces, though, is up to you."

"She's a little girl. She's just a little girl, you crazy, sadistic piece of shit." Mia hardly recognized her own voice, so thick and choked with rage and utter violence. "If you touch them, I will kill you. I will rip your spine out of your throat. I'll bury you in a hole so fucking deep, no one will hear you beg for mercy as you die a slow, agonizing death. I *promise* you I will make it hurt. She's just a *little girl!*"

Jake was quiet for a long time on the other end. Then he said, "And she can scream as good as the rest."

In the background, Mia heard a piercing scream—a child's scream.

This time, her knees gave out, and she dropped to the floor.

"You got one hour to get here," Jake said, his voice a block of ice. "If you're even thirty seconds late, they die."

He hung up with a click that seemed to shatter her eardrum.

# CHAPTER TWENTY-TWO

C harlie wouldn't let her go to the warehouse by herself, but she refused to let him or the dozen men who'd accompanied them follow her inside, even Paolo. She would not do anything to further endanger her family.

"It's a trap," Charlie had said before she'd climbed out of the car.

"You're probably right," she'd replied. "But it doesn't matter."

Now, she walked down the dark alley Jake had directed her to and stopped in front of a steel door set in the dilapidated wall of a crumbling brick building. She tried the handle, and it opened. No one stood on the other side, so she took a few cautious steps inside, ears pricked for any noise.

The door opened to a short corridor. At the end of it, light pooled into the hall from the right side, suggesting it opened to a room there. She followed it, and gradually the sound of male laughter met her ears. One laugh in particular she recognized, and it made her skin crawl.

She drew in a deep breath to fortify herself, then stepped around the end of the corridor toward the light.

A large room with windows lining the tops of each wall

spread before her. It was brightly lit from huge, overhead lights. It looked like it had once been a large garage. A stale odor of oil clung to the air, just noticeable beneath the hazy cloud of cigar smoke.

Her gaze fastened on the middle of the room, where two terrified young women and a child sat tied to chairs, handkerchiefs between their teeth and tied around their head.

Mia swallowed a sob as she looked at her niece. Emilia's face was tear-streaked and her hair was mussed, but she couldn't tell if the little girl was hurt.

Around them, men leaned on tables or milled around, swigging from numerous bottles of alcohol. Their voices were loud but indiscernible.

"Well, hell!"

A loud voice rose above the din, and from a crowd of men to her right, Jake Morelli emerged. His suit coat was off, collar undone, and he gripped a bottle of whiskey in one hand. He held his hands out toward her with a grin as if they were dear friends.

"Life of the party just showed up, huh?" he called to his men.

They all closed in on her, sliding off tables and rising from chairs to swagger toward her. She tensed her body, but kept her chin up and looked Jake straight in the eye.

"I'm here like you asked," she said in a low, steady voice. "Give me my family and we'll leave."

"I didn't ask. I told you," he said, then took a drink from the bottle. He pointed a finger at her. "And we're gonna discuss some things first before you can collect your precious family. Fellas." He snapped his fingers.

Two men—one of whom was Detective Wallace—flanked her immediately, and before she could react, they groped her freely and slid their hands up and down her body and legs.

She tried to jerk out of their grasp. "Get the hell off me!"

"She's clean," Detective Wallace said to Jake.

He nodded, then grinned at her. "Hey, don't get mad. You're known to keep pins in your dress. Just had to make sure you played by the rules, is all."

"What do you want?" she snapped.

"Ah, ah. Temper." He strolled toward her, leering. "You might've been wondering where I've been the past month. Haven't you?"

"I tend not to notice when vermin crawl back to the holes they came from," she snarled.

Jake paused in front of her, studying her with his head tilted to one side. Then, he struck her across the face with a ferocious backhand, the line of his knuckles crashing against her cheekbone.

Emilia screamed.

Mia stumbled back as pain and fire exploded in her face.

*Don't fall. Don't fall.*

The voice in her mind was a low hum beneath the roar of pain, but she held onto it, willing herself to stay on her feet even as her ankles wobbled. Her years as a dancer aided her, her legs immediately splaying for balance as her core tightened and leaned opposite from the way momentum had sent her.

On her feet but still hunched over, Mia panted through the agony. He'd hit her with the force of three men, and as she cracked open an already-swelling eye, she eyed the rings on each of his fingers. Effective as brass knuckles.

*So that's really why they call him Gems.*

As his men hooted and brayed like drunken mules, Jake walked toward her, sliding his fingers under her chin and tipping it up. He winced.

"That's gonna leave a mark," he said. "You might need to take some time off the club. But, can I be honest with you?" He leaned close, his whiskey breath brushing her face. "I've wanted to do that for *some* time. I bet no one's ever done that to you, huh? Everyone was always too scared of your brother, then scared of Paolo, then scared of Lazzari. Not me. And let me tell you, toots. You deserve that and a few more. I should hold you down and fuck you 'til you're bloody. Especially for killing my men."

He straightened and chuckled. "Hey, what am I doing?

You're a tough little broad. You can take a punch. That ain't gonna bother you nearly as much as…" He turned to the detective, who stood close to Raquel. "Abner."

"No," Mia grunted, trying to make her mouth shape the word. "No. *No!*"

The detective closed his fist and slammed it against the side of Raquel's head.

She couldn't even make a noise of pain. Her cousin simply dropped her head, lolling to the side in the chair.

Detective Wallace laughed, accepting slaps on the back from some of the other men. "I'd call that a knockout, gentlemen."

Mia lunged toward him, staggering like she was drunk because her brain was still spinning from Jake's punch.

Jake held her back with a palm to her shoulder. "Easy, tiger. Take one more step and I'll have him belt her again."

"Leave Auntie alone, you stupid dumb-dumb!" Emilia shrieked from her chair.

Mia gasped. "Emilia—you stay quiet!"

Chuckling with amusement, Jake strolled over to the little girl and knelt down, bracing his hands on his knees. "What'd you say to me, Skeezix?"

Fear flashed across Emilia's face. Then defiance filled her eyes. To Mia's shock, horror, and awe, the little girl spat—or tried to spit; nothing came out—at Jake's feet.

Gloria moaned around her gag.

Jake laughed. "How about that? This brat's really her father's daughter, ain't she?" He looked at Mia. "Or her aunt's niece. Maybe I should have Abner here belt the kid. I mention he used box on the boardwalk?"

A blow like what Raquel had received could kill Emilia—it could have very well killed Raquel. Mia froze. "If you lay a hand on her—"

"Listen to me." He cupped her face. "I don't *like* hurting kids. I don't even like hurting women. But you left me no choice. And if you keep disrespecting me, I'll have each one of them gutted and strung up by their intestines down Broadway. And I'll make you watch."

Despite every effort to hold it in, Mia could not contain a whimper.

He patted her cheeks. "Don't make me be the bad guy."

"What," she whispered, "do you want?"

He pointed at her and winked. "I'm glad you asked. The short answer? Everything."

Mia's nostrils flared. "You'll have to be more specific."

"Well, I already mentioned how Hymie wants control of your liquor operation. So that's a start."

"I got partners," she said through gritted teeth. "It's not that simple."

Jake shrugged. "Not my problem. Or Hymie's. That's up to you to straighten out, but eventually, the North Side will have control in the east." He flashed a grin. "With me running things out here, of course. I got big plans for myself."

"What else?"

"My old territories, where you have huge percentages. You'll forgo those. I retain all control."

"Fine," she ground out.

"And our favorite subject that brought us together in the first place," he said. "Heroin. I'll be selling it wherever the fuck I want. To women, to children, to whoever wants it. I'll make couriers of whoever I want. You have no say. And in fact..." He stroked his chin as if an idea had just occurred to him. "I hear you're looking for a new place to set up shop. Near Times Square. I'd sure appreciate it if you introduced a little white powder to those uppity broads you'll be catering to. Not the kind they dab on their faces, either."

She gaped at him. "You want *me* to sell drugs?"

"Hey, you can say no to anything you want," he said, spreading his hands. "But you know if you do, none of you bitches'll walk out of here alive tonight."

Her fists balled at her sides.

"Was that a yes? I couldn't hear you."

Her nails dug so hard into her palms, the skin stung. "Yes."

He nodded. "Good."

"Is that all?"

"Not quite," Jake said. "One more thing. The Lower East Side. Little Italy. You'll let everyone there know they should start paying their protection fees to me. On behalf of Mr. Maranzano. They got a new king now that their queen has abdicated her throne."

"Maranzano?" Mia spat. "*Masseria* holds that protection business. Take it up with him."

Jake smirked. "Those people are loyal to *you*. Besides… Masseria's not going to be a concern much longer, anyway."

She frowned as he started pacing in leisurely strides. Behind him, Raquel was barely conscious. Gloria stared at her with huge eyes, frozen in her chair, and Emilia wept silently.

"I don't understand," Mia said.

"I think we should get rid of that old Moustache Pete," Jake said with a smile. "And I think you can be a great help in orchestrating that."

"You…want me to help you hit Masseria?" she said in disbelief. "Did Maranzano ask for that?"

"No. But I know he's been a pain in Maranzano's ass for some time now," Jake said. "And if I took care of that little problem for him, well…think about how good that makes me look. That's something a true *caporegime* would do for his boss, ain't it?"

"You want to kill Masseria for a *promotion?*" Mia said.

"Always looking out for number one," he said with a lopsided smile. "So, how about it?"

"You make it sound like I got a choice."

"You're right." He sauntered back toward where Emilia sat and pulled his pistol out of his shoulder holster. He pressed the barrel to her temple, and the little girl nearly hyperventilated from the fear. "You don't."

Two seats down, Gloria screamed around her gag. The sound

of it, the pure terror and rage and agony it held, made Mia want to clap her hands over her ears.

"Shut her up," Jake said calmly to Detective Wallace.

The large man stalked over to Gloria. The sound of a crack pierced the air as his huge palm met the entire left side of her face. When he stepped out of the way, Mia saw blood trickling from her mouth and the enormous red handprint on her skin.

"Stop!" Mia roared. "*Stop.*"

"Do I have your cooperation?" Jake said, pushing the barrel of the gun so hard against Emilia's temple, her head tilted to the side.

Tears streamed from her niece's eyes as she stared at Mia. The confusion and panic in her wild stare shattered Mia's heart. She was just a child. She had done nothing to deserve this— except have an aunt whose choices had brought her to this moment.

"Yes," Mia muttered.

"How's that?" Jake cupped a hand around his ear. "Couldn't quite hear you."

"*Yes!*" she screamed.

"Good." He withdrew the pistol, then leaned down and kissed the top of Emilia's head. "Stop crying, sweetie."

Emilia winced away from him, trying to quiet her sobs.

Mia wanted to slice his lips off his face and shove them down his throat for touching her.

Jake tilted his head as he regarded her. "And that's that," he said. "You just stick to warbling out showtunes and prancing around in evening dresses, and leave the business to the men. That's all you're good for, anyway. You were in over your head from the first second your brother died."

"Will you let them go?" she asked in a shaking voice.

He walked over to her, tucking his pistol in the holster. "Sure. As soon as we shake on it."

He held out his hand. Mia stared at it, at everything that hand represented. At everything she would be giving up by shaking it. She'd be serving him the Lower East Side on a silver platter, and things would fall to ruin again. Families would be destroyed, and Jake would have them all under his thumb.

Then she glanced at her family, bound and gagged behind him.

She took his hand.

He yanked her toward him and pressed his mouth to hers. He gripped the back of her head and held her there when she struggled against him. After a long moment, he released her with a smack of his lips and grinned.

"And now we got ourselves a deal."

Her lips burned and she longed to scrub at them. "Untie them and let us go."

Jake grabbed the lower half of her face in one hard grip. "That's the last order you'll ever give me." He shoved her away so hard, she tumbled to the floor, but immediately jumped to her feet, barely registering the pain.

He turned and lifted a hand at his men. Three stepped forward and began untying Gloria, Raquel, and Emilia. Gloria helped Raquel stand with one arm around her waist, and held Emilia close with the other.

"Let us escort you out," Jake said.

Mia ushered her family in front of her. "We know the way."

"Oh, but I insist." He drew his pistol again and nudged it into her back, then leaned to speak into her ear. "If you think I'm stupid enough to believe you came here alone, you got another thing coming, toots. Put your hands up. Fellas, help the ladies along, yeah?"

At gunpoint, Mia and her family were led outside. Raquel could barely walk, but the man behind her pushed her every few steps. Gloria kept her hands up, but her eyes on her daughter. Detective Wallace propelled Emilia forward with his gun pressed to her shoulder.

Outside, they walked down the alley toward the street where Charlie had let her out. As soon as they stepped out of the alley, three sets of headlights turned on.

*Don't do anything stupid*, she begged.

Charlie, Moritz, Paolo, Bobby, Joey, and all their men stepped out of the three cars they occupied, guns out. They outnumbered Jake and the two men with him for the moment, but the rest of Jake's men were starting to seep into the alley.

"What the fuck are you doing, Morelli?" Charlie asked, his voice deadly quiet.

"Came out so you could all say hello to your new boss," Jake replied cheerfully. "Miss Scalisi here has agreed to turn over your liquor business to me and Hymie Weiss. So there's gonna be some employee shake-ups, fellas. Maybe I'll still let you work for me."

"This is not necessary, Mr. Morelli," Moritz said. "I'm sure we can come to a better deal."

"This is the only deal," Jake said, holding his gun to Mia's neck. "Unless you want a child's blood on your hands?"

"Just let them go," Charlie said.

Jake nuzzled the side of Mia's face he'd struck. "We'll stay here to make sure you get safely on your way." He pushed her forward.

She grabbed Emilia away from the detective. He gave her an evil smile and winked.

"Walk," she ordered Gloria and Raquel quietly. "Now."

When she was halfway to the car, Mia set Emilia down. "Do you see Paolo?"

The little girl nodded, shaking.

"Run to him."

Emilia tore off. Paolo holstered his pistol in time to catch her and carry her off toward the car parked the farthest away.

Mia breathed a silent sigh of relief that Emilia was as far away from the danger as possible for the moment.

"Mia. One more thing."

She stopped and turned toward Jake.

He strolled toward her at a leisurely pace, stopping when he was an arm's length away. "You told me at that wedding I'm not untouchable. Remember that? Remember how you embarrassed me in front of all of Little Italy when you had your Sicilian pet hold a knife to my throat?"

Mia waited, saying nothing.

"Thanks for that lesson. You were right. I wasn't untouchable." In less time than it took her to blink, he whipped his arm up, the pistol aimed just to the side of her. "Neither are you."

He pulled the trigger.

The pained female scream that ripped through the night did not come from her.

She whirled around in time to see Raquel fall.

"Mia, get down!" Charlie roared.

The night exploded in gunfire.

She had barely enough time to hit the ground before bullets tore through the air over her. Raquel lay a few feet away, Gloria beside her, screaming.

Mia spared only a few seconds to determine Raquel was still alive and had been hit in the leg. "Help me move her!" she shouted to Gloria.

Her sister-in-law froze, her mouth open in a silent scream.

Mia grabbed her by the shoulders and shook her, hard. "Gloria," she snapped. "Help me, or we die!"

It seemed to do the trick. Lying as close to the ground as they could, they dragged Raquel behind Charlie's car. Metallic *tink*s sounded like hail as bullets hit the cars.

A hand closed around her ankle and yanked. Mia fell onto her back and stared up at the detective. His hand closed around her throat.

"I got paid for a job I never finished," he told her, and pressed his revolver under her chin. "All six of these rounds got your name on them, doll."

Before he could pull the trigger, another gunshot erupted from close by and he barked with pain, grabbing his shoulder. His pistol went flying.

Mia gasped for air.

"Beat it!" Charlie bellowed over his shoulder.

Her rolling eyes took in Jake as he and his men disappeared down the alley. The sound of car engines starting and tires screeching let her know they had the same idea as Charlie. Distant police sirens filled her ears as she scrambled to her feet, grabbing the detective's pistol from where it had landed a foot from her.

She caught sight of Bobby helping Gloria get Raquel into his car. "Get her to the hospital, now!"

He nodded, then immediately jumped behind the wheel.

Charlie rushed over to her. "Are you hurt?" he demanded. "Jesus—your face."

"Never mind that." She stepped around him toward the detective lying on the ground, clutching his shoulder. Blood seeped through his fingers.

"We need to leave," Charlie said, grabbing her arm.

She stared down at Detective Wallace. "The good detective is hurt."

"Please," he muttered around grunts of pain. "Get me some help, and I'll help you. I'll talk to Weiss. Tonight. We can get rid of Gems. If you let the cops come help me, I swear I'll help you. I'll put all the blame on him. I never saw none of yous tonight."

"Mia," Charlie snarled. "Time to *go*."

"Please," the detective said. "Let's make a deal. Just go, leave me here for the cops. I'll get in touch with you first thing in the morning."

The sirens grew louder, echoing off the buildings lining the next street over.

Mia looked down at the detective. She recalled the look in his eyes the first day she'd met him, when he'd tried to kill her in another alleyway. She thought about the way he'd hit Raquel with so much force, he'd knocked her out, then chuckled. The way he'd slapped Gloria bloody.

The gun he'd held to her terrified, four-year-old niece.

And now, he was begging her for help. Pledging his assistance. Pleading for his life.

Pleading for her *mercy*.

After years of feeling like everything breakable inside her had broken, something new shattered. It was almost a physical feeling, as though something in her brain had come loose and snapped in two.

Perhaps it was her empathy.

"Sorry," Mia said. "I'm fresh out of deals tonight."

She raised his gun and leveled it at the center of his face. Then she fired all six rounds into him, stopping only when the dry *click* of the empty revolver filled her ears.

# CHAPTER TWENTY-THREE

Before dawn the next morning, Raquel was out of surgery and in a heavily sedated sleep in her private hospital room.

Mia sat in a chair beside her bed, leaning against it, her head resting on her palm as she kept watch over Raquel. Paolo waited down in the car, respecting the privacy she wished to have with her cousin, although by now he was never an imposition on her privacy, with his silent, vigilant presence.

Raquel had been hit in the leg and a major artery had been nicked. Had the bullet pierced even a fraction of an inch inward, she likely would have bled out. As it was, due to some damage to the musculature and ligaments, she'd likely walk with a pronounced limp for the rest of her life.

The surgeon, who had worked on wounded soldiers during the war, cautioned Mia that although the operation to remove the bullet and repair the artery had gone well, the chance of infection was still high. Raquel would need to remain in the hospital so they could monitor her dressings and change them frequently. Infection could still kill her, even if Jake's bullet hadn't.

The surgeon had asked several curious questions about what had happened to Raquel and stared quite pointedly at the sides of both their faces where they'd been struck. Mia had offered him a hundred dollars to stop asking questions.

A nurse came in to check on Raquel and looked at Mia disapprovingly. "You really shouldn't be here. Visiting hours were over a long time ago."

Mia didn't spare her a glance. "Like I told the doctor, you want me to leave, you can come and pull me out of this chair. But I'm not leaving her side."

The nurse hesitated, as though considering that, but in the end made the smart choice and let Mia be.

She slipped in and out of sleep, resting her head on Raquel's bed. Every so often she would jerk awake, panicked that something terrible had happened while she'd been unconscious. Each time she closed her eyes, she saw the horrified gaze of the detective staring up at her, his lips moving in silent pleas to spare his life. In the blink of an eye, his face was a mess of blood and bone.

*Mercy.*

*Mercy.*

*Mercy.*

A gunshot exploded next to her ear, and she nearly leaped out of her chair.

But instead of her own brains splattered on the wall, she felt only weak, gentle fingers tugging at her hair. No one was shooting at her.

Raquel was awake, her brown eyes heavy-lidded but alert.

"Raquel," Mia said softly, reaching for her hand. "How do you feel?"

"Have you…been here…the whole time?" Raquel asked, her voice faint.

"Nowhere else for me to be," she replied, reaching up to touch her cousin's cheek. It was cool.

"Glo? Emmy?"

"Paolo took them home," Mia said. "I haven't been there yet."

"Em is probably...so scared." Raquel closed her eyes. "My head hurts. My face hurts. Yours looks like it hurts, too."

"I'm fine. Don't worry about me. You just worry about getting well, dear."

"What...will happen now?"

There were as many answers to that question as there were interpretations of the question itself. "What do you mean?"

"What happens to...Jake? He got...away...didn't he?"

"Yes," Mia said. "He got away. But I'll see him again. We have business now...for a little while, at least." She told Raquel about his terms, since the young woman had little memory of what had occurred in the warehouse.

Raquel was silent for a long time. "You gave up...everything."

"No, not everything. I still have you. Gloria. Emilia. You're the most important things."

"The people in the neighborhood," Raquel said. "They won't...understand. They'll think you...abandoned them."

Mia had the same thought, and it hurt. She'd fought so hard for them, and now she was leaving them to the wolves. No, worse. To the vultures.

"I didn't have a choice," she said softly. "He would have killed you. No one is more important to me than you all are."

"You can't let him get away with it," Raquel insisted, grasping Mia's hand. "I've seen how much the people...rely on you. How much they need you. He'll...destroy them."

Mia shook her head. "I won't risk my fam—"

"You need to...kill him," her cousin rasped.

She blinked. Raquel had, in the time she'd known her, always been a sweet young lady, if a bit naive. To hear her say this now filled Mia with shame. It wasn't that she hadn't entertained similar thoughts. But what bothered her most was that she had, perhaps, failed Raquel. Perhaps she had been a terrible influence on the young woman, when she'd only wanted to provide a better life than what she might have had in Sicily.

Mia wondered if this was what Nick might have thought of her destiny, had he been alive to see it.

"You don't know what you're saying," she said in a quiet voice.

Raquel opened wide her burning, dark eyes. "Yes, I do!"

"This has to stop," Mia murmured. "This...violence. It has to end."

"He is a violent man," Raquel said, her voice quivering. "He takes pleasure in the suffering of others. If you don't stop him, no one will."

Mia's heart clenched. "You just worry about getting well. After all, I'll need my assistant back soon." She offered a small smile, hoping to see one in return.

But Raquel swallowed and looked away. "When I am well," she said, "I...want to go home. To Catania."

Mia stared at her. "What? You do?" It was on the tip of her tongue to ask why, but she knew better. That would only be insulting to Raquel.

"I love you, Cousin," Raquel said. "And I love Gloria and especially Emilia. It will make me very sad to leave you. But...I don't belong here. Not with you. Not with your...lifestyle. I am—I am afraid. I miss the slowness of home. The quiet. The simplicity. It has been very exciting here, but...it has been terrifying. And I do not wish to live in fear."

"What about Will?" Mia said lamely. "Won't you miss him? He'll miss you. He's planning to return to New York next month, and I'm quite sure it's not to see me."

Raquel's jaw tightened and a single tear leaked from one eye. "He was...a kind man," she said. "Maybe in a different time or place, we might have become something together. But I cannot stay here." She swallowed and forced a trembling smile. "If he'd ever like to see Sicily, tell him to write me." The smile disappeared. "Please, Mia. Send me back when I am well."

A hot fissure burst along the seam of her heart. But she would honor her cousin. She had promised to do whatever she could to keep Raquel safe. She could not deny her this.

"Yes," she whispered, her throat tight. "Yes, anything you want."

"Thank you," Raquel breathed, closing her eyes.

The next time the nurse came to shoo her out, Mia went.

SHE AND PAOLO REACHED THE HOTEL AS DAWN BLOSSOMED OVER the horizon. He escorted her into the elevator and down the hall toward their suites, his head on a nonstop swivel to make sure no one got the drop on them.

She was happy to let him steer her around. The exhaustion of feeling so many things all at once—rage, heartbreak, despair, hopelessness, fear—was taking its toll. It was easier to find a warm, dark corner in her numbness and hide instead of continuing to feel the emotional agony that tore at her.

There were now three guards outside Gloria's door. They all greeted her, asking how she was. She gave them vague answers and knocked on Gloria's door.

A moment later, it opened. Gloria's gaunt, hollow-eyed face peered out. A dark bruise bloomed on the left side of her face. A look of relief washed over her weary face, and she pulled Mia inside. Paolo followed her in and shut the door.

She and Gloria embraced tightly for a long moment. Mia longed to fall apart and sob in her sister-in-law's arms, but Gloria beat her to it. Hot wetness streaked down her neck, and Mia knew she could not go to pieces now. Not when her strength—what little of it was left—was needed.

"Come," Mia said softly, leading Gloria to the sofa. "Sit."

"How is she?" Gloria asked, wiping away her tears.

"Doing as well as we could hope for," Mia replied. "She'll make a recovery, though she'll probably have a limp for the rest of her life. She awoke when I was with her. We talked for a while. She...she wants to go home when they release her."

Gloria gestured toward Raquel's room. "Where else would she go?"

"No." Mia shook her head. "She wants to go *home*. To Sicily."

"What?" Gloria looked as gutted as Mia felt. "Why?"

"Why *not?*" she demanded. "Look at what's happened to her. She was kidnapped, beaten, and nearly killed. Why would she want to stay here? She's terrified!"

She hadn't meant to practically shout at Gloria, but her own guilt burst through the dam of her self-control.

Mia jumped to her feet. "It's my fault," she blurted. "I promised Carlo I'd look out for her. I'd protect her. I promised Nick I'd do the same for you and Em. And look what happened. Because of *me* you three were nearly killed."

"Mia, calm down. None of that was your fault."

Something in Gloria's voice, something hollow and almost mechanic, made Mia whirl around. Gloria wouldn't look at her.

"You agree with me," Mia said. "You feel the same. You hold me responsible." She uttered a bitter, ugly laugh. Her feelings were hurt, but that was absurd. Gloria was agreeing with her own assessment of herself, and the way she'd mishandled everything since they'd come home. "Just say it. I need to hear it."

"Fine," Gloria said quietly, looking up at her. "Yes, I think this is your fault. You wanted so much to be involved in the business as soon as we got home. You didn't think that perhaps the men who'd been running it the entire past *year* were capable of continuing to do so. You thought that because you're a Scalisi, that entitles you to ownership. You thought you were your brother!"

Mia had braced herself, but the onslaught nearly took her off her feet. She released a pained breath, but forced herself not to look away.

*You deserve this*, she reminded herself. *You brought this on yourself.*

"You became so obsessed with having the people of the old neighborhood love you, you didn't stop to consider the repercussions of your actions," Gloria went on, rising as she gathered steam. "Your pride convinced you you're something you're not. You're not Mia Scalisi, the gangster. You're a *showgirl* who convinced herself a stage role was real life, and you nearly got us killed. You nearly got my *daughter* killed!"

Mia clenched her jaw, breathing hard through her nose.

Gloria's warm, olive skin went white as milk. "She's four years old, and a man had a goddamn gun pointed at her head!" Her voice rose to a scream and broke on the last word. "And *that* is your fault."

Mia's chin trembled and she held onto the back of the easy chair for support, but she did not look away. If she were being whipped, it would not hurt as much as this did now, to hear that she had so thoroughly let her family down when all she had ever wanted was to keep them safe. Because they were all she had.

From Gloria's bedroom, the faint sound of Emilia crying floated out to the living room.

"You know, maybe Raquel has the right idea," Gloria went on, practically hissing out the words. "To leave this city. To leave you behind. Perhaps she won't be sailing back to Sicily alone. At least my daughter will be with normal people, not violent, crazed criminals who just want to kill each other. And in case you were wondering, Mia, I *am* talking about you, too."

A tear, white-hot, cut down Mia's cheek.

Before she could say anything, another sound carried out to the living room. A low, deep, sonorous noise. A voice, humming a nameless, Southern Italian folk song.

As though sharing the same thought, both Mia and Gloria hurried toward her bedroom and froze on each side of the doorway.

Paolo crouched beside Emilia's small bed. She lay on her side, watching him with huge, wet dark eyes, holding onto his hand with one of her tiny ones. The thumb of her other hand was firmly in her mouth.

He was humming to her.

"She's been having nightmares all night," Gloria whispered.

Paolo didn't spare them a glance as he continued humming to Emilia, his gaze locked with the little girl's. Gradually, her eyes grew heavy until they finally shut. When her breathing deepened and evened, and her little hand went slack on top of his, he tucked her blanket around her and rose noiselessly to his feet.

He frowned deeply at both of them and shooed them from the room. They both backed up several feet as he pulled the door shut but not completely, leaving it an inch ajar to keep an ear tilted for sounds that Emilia had awoken again.

He pointed at them both, then swiped the flat of his hand through the air. *No more arguing.* Then he placed his hands under his head like a pillow.

Gloria tightened her jaw. "Yes. We should get some sleep. Perhaps...perhaps I was too harsh, Mia. I'm tired, to say the least." She sighed, then reached out to touch Mia's shoulder. "Get some sleep."

"But Mass..."

"Don't worry about that. Just rest." Gloria hesitated. "Dear, I'm—I'm sorry."

Perhaps she was sorry, but that didn't mean she didn't believe what she'd said.

It was the truth.

Paolo escorted Mia back to her suite. He pushed past her with his pistol drawn and made sure every possible nook and cranny of the space was clear. When he returned to the door where she waited, she looked at him, her face crumpling, unable to hold back her tears any longer.

Paolo tucked his gun in the waistband of his pants and drew her into his arms. His hands, kind and patting, made her think of her own father. She had not been embraced in such a tender, paternal fashion since he'd died so many years ago. It made her cry harder into his shoulder.

Paolo hummed to her, too.

"How are you?" Hyman asked Monday afternoon, sitting back in his seat with a cup of coffee. "Your face looks...like it hurts."

"That's an understatement," Mia replied.

She'd let a day pass before she'd worked up the nerve to look in the mirror. Her left eye socket had been sliced open, though not deeply enough to require stitches. A bruise formed around the outer corner and lower part of her eye, promising to get darker before it would get better. A lump topped with a small cut sat atop her cheekbone, and the entire left side of her face ached horribly.

She could deal with the physical discomfort. It was everything else that had her so heartsore.

After giving her Sunday to pull herself together, Hyman had called a meeting with her, Charlie, and Moritz at his Midtown penthouse to discuss the state of things and precisely what Morelli had demanded from her.

She'd known the meeting would be a necessity, and had expected Hyman's phone call when it came. Now, though, she wasn't sure where to start. The four of them sat in the comfortable sitting area by the fireplace. Today, the windows were open to let in the gentle summer breeze.

She kept her eyes on her teacup. They were waiting for her to speak, but she wasn't sure what to say to any of them. Especially Charlie—she didn't know how he'd receive the news that she'd been tasked with setting up his boss so that her family could live.

"You take all the time you need to heal," Hyman offered.

She gave him a wry smirk. "Sure. Can't very well have your headliner on stage with a busted face."

He gave her a reproving look. "No, I can't. However—I'm sure to your utter shock—I am more concerned with your well-being than your ability to perform onstage at the present moment."

Perhaps she was being too hard on him. She offered a one-sided smile. "Thank you."

"Take us through what he said, Mia," Moritz said. "What you agreed to."

"As he put it, the simple version is everything," she replied. "The liquor operation goes under his control. I give up all of the percentages I held in his territories. He expects to control all of the protection business in the old neighborhood. And he'll deal heroin wherever he pleases."

"And how the fuck does he expect to get around people like Masseria?" Charlie demanded. "Who still controls that business?"

She released a breath and met his gaze. "Because he plans to kill Masseria. As a gift to Maranzano."

"*What?*"

"He said I have to help him," Mia went on woodenly. "I'm supposed to ask Masseria to mediate a meeting between me and Morelli, because we just can't settle our differences. And at the meeting, Masseria will be assassinated. Probably me, too."

"I didn't want to be the first one to point that out," Hyman said.

"He's out of his fucking mind," Charlie said.

"That much has been clear for some time," Moritz said. He looked at Mia. "Can't we get to him first?"

She shrugged. "Your guess as to where he's hiding is as good as anybody's. He called me yesterday to go over all the things he demanded of me the other night. He wants the meeting set up for this Saturday. He gave me no hint where he was calling from."

"The only thing I despise more than someone telling me what to do is bloodshed," Hyman said mildly. "And based on the sort of man we're dealing with, I think that's a guarantee if we try to fight him. Perhaps we ought to start aligning our thinking to the possibility that he will, indeed, be controlling the majority share of the liquor operation."

It made Mia sick to think of what had once been her brother's brainchild falling into the hands of a man like Morelli. It would have made everything they'd gone through—including Nick's death—pointless.

"It all goes back to Hymie Weiss," Charlie said bitterly. "He wanted Nick's deal for himself—it's why he had him killed in the first place. We managed to hold it back from him, but now he's got a new method of attack—Morelli. He just won't let this deal go."

"The North and the South Sides have been at war over territories since Prohibition started," Moritz said wearily. "Johnny brought Al to Chicago to claim it for New York, and Hymie sent Morelli out here to claim New York for Chicago. It's just more of the same nonsense. It won't stop."

He was right. It wouldn't stop, as long as Hymie Weiss and Jake Morelli still breathed.

"Morelli will do anything to ingratiate himself with Maranzano and Weiss simultaneously," Moritz said. "He's spoken before about getting the two of them in the same room to join forces."

"Maranzano's a nobody," Charlie argued back. "Everyone knows Masseria is the boss in New York."

"Maranzano's built a strong, legitimate real estate business, Charlie," Moritz said sharply. "That doesn't make him a nobody. That makes him incredibly smart and arguably more powerful, since he's got plenty of legitimate backing. He might not have the clout Masseria has now, but that comes with time."

"So what're you suggesting?" Charlie said. "You *want* Masseria to get whacked? Take a guess who'd be next."

"Of course I don't want anything to happen to you," Moritz said. "Masseria, I can't say I care that much about, but I understand the connection. He's more powerful than Maranzano right *now*, and I guess that's what matters at the moment."

"Maranzano would never take on Masseria, not now," Charlie said with a decisive shake of his head. "He don't have the numbers. He'd get wiped out in a week."

"Does he know that?" Mia interjected quietly. "Does Maranzano know he'd get wiped out by Masseria?"

Charlie lifted a shoulder. "I can't say I've heard him say those exact words. I don't spend time with him. But he's been in this country since right after the war and he hasn't made a move against Joe yet. I have to imagine it's because he knows better. As long as he stays in Brooklyn and Joe operates in Manhattan, they can have some semblance of peace."

"So there's no real beef between their two groups," Hyman said.

Charlie nodded. "They don't like each other. But they stay out of each other's way, and everyone gets along fine. Besides, Joe don't like hardly anybody, anyway."

"And he's never talked about moving on Maranzano?" Mia said.

"Not to me," Charlie said. "What I do know is that he don't like war. He'll do what he has to do, but he had enough of that during his war with Totò D'Aquila. They shot at him point-blank, you know. He don't want to go through that again."

"You said Morelli wants the hit to go down Saturday?" Moritz asked Mia. "Did he say where?"

"He's leaving all of that to me," she said.

"Can't we arrange it with Masseria to have men there to take him out?" Moritz said.

"Morelli could be bringing an army with him," Hyman said. "Have them lie in wait, expecting that very thing. And we have to remember—Mia will be there. We can't do anything that would further risk her life more than simply going."

"Besides," Charlie added, "Jake's a made guy. We whack him, Maranzano's going to take that up with us."

"So many rules." Mia gingerly rubbed her aching left temple.

"Want to stay alive, you gotta play by them all," Charlie said.

"I think we should start considering ways of protecting our current assets before Morelli gets a hold of them," Hyman said. "And our business relationships, because I think it's a safe assumption to make that Mr. Morelli will bungle it all."

"Considering how he'll still make us do all the work," Moritz said drily, "my assumption is that they'll be safe. *We'll* just be broke."

As they discussed the future of the liquor operation, Mia lapsed into silence, her thoughts whirling. The key was getting rid of Morelli first, then Hymie, but Morelli was practically untouchable. Even if she knew someone who knew where he was, the likelihood of them giving her that information was low.

*There* is *someone who could help…*

Her first impulse was to dismiss the idea as soon as it came to mind, but it snagged on a stubborn mental hook before it could float away. There *was* someone, indeed, who might be able to help her get to Morelli, but the stakes were unimaginably high, and she would need to get two men who disliked each other to agree to work together—for her sake.

*There's no way I can pull this off. What would Nick do?*

Her brother had always loved high stakes—in poker, in business, in love, in life. The higher, the better. He'd tell her nothing ventured, nothing gained. "Go all in, or get all the way out," he'd say.

Even now, she could picture his grin as she told him her idea.

"Gentlemen," she said, interrupting whatever they'd been talking about. She had no idea.

Three sets of eyes shifted toward her.

She offered a small, lopsided smile, ignoring the pain in her left and focusing on the way her right cheek flexed, showcasing the dimple in her cheek not many had seen in a genuine way in a very, very long time.

"I think I may have an idea."

THE DREARY SKY THREATENED RAIN WHEN PAOLO PULLED UP TO the brick building Mia had been directed to on Thursday afternoon. She stepped out of the car and put her hand on his arm.

"Wait here, please," she said. "He might not appreciate extra company I didn't tell him I was bringing."

Paolo's displeasure was plain on his face, but he nodded and slid back in behind the wheel.

Mia walked up to the door and knocked on it three times.

After a moment, it opened. Frankie Yale peered out at her. "You're right on time."

"I'm a little early, actually," Mia said.

"Same difference, with him. Watch your step." He pointed down to where a bit of concrete rose up at the edge of the doorway. "No need to trip and fall."

"And further destroy my face?" she quipped, stepping inside.

The lighting in the corridor was forgivingly dim, but she could easily make out his sympathetic smile as he peered at her under her picture hat. "I wasn't going to say nothing. I was real sorry to hear about it."

"Not so sorry that you stopped doing business with him." She kept pace as he led her down the corridor.

"Hey, I gotta make money, too," Frankie said, shrugging. "If it makes any difference, I gave him a little what-for about it. Snatching women and kids, that's just twisted."

She flicked up her eyebrows. "I suppose that's one way of putting it."

Frankie stuffed his hands in his pockets. "Hey, uh, how's she doing? Gloria, I mean."

"Yes, Mr. Yale, I knew who you meant." Her voice came out sharp.

"Don't bite my head off, all right?" he said gently. "I'm really asking. She's a nice lady. Didn't deserve any of that."

Mia sighed. "She's doing a little better. As well as she can be, given the situation."

He nodded. "Give her my best, willya?"

She wouldn't. "Sure."

They walked down the hall until they reached a door that opened to a set of ascending stairs. "His office is at the top, can't miss it," Frankie said. "He asked that you go in alone."

"Thanks." Mia paused. "Does he know what I want to talk to him about?"

Frankie lifted his shoulders. "He's a very smart man, Miss Scalisi. And very well-connected here in Brooklyn. He knows more than you think." He gave her a onceover. "He appreciates you coming to ask permission. He said it shows respect."

"I do respect him. But this doesn't align me with him. I want that understood."

He spread his hands. "He knows that. Like I said, he's a smart man, Mia. Go on. He's waiting for you."

She walked up the stairs, feeling the wood shift and creak beneath her heels as she made her way toward the closed office door at the top. Light filtered in from dusty, high windows, letting in more of the dreary day that somehow, in this stairwell, seemed bright.

Mia lifted her fist to knock, but the stairs must have given her away, because a deep, melodic voice from behind the door said, "Come in."

She turned the knob and pushed the door open.

The office was small and furnished in warm, reddish wood. Beneath the window on the far-left side were a couple of chairs that faced each other over a small coffee table. Bookshelves covered the right wall. And directly before her was a sprawling desk, behind which a dark-haired man with a serious but strangely kind face sat.

"Ah," he said. "Mia Scalisi." His heavy Sicilian accent made her name a song. He gestured to one of the easy chairs in front of his desk. "Please. Sit."

She walked toward him and lowered herself into the chair. "Thank you for seeing me. I appreciate your time."

Salvatore Maranzano leaned toward her, folding his hands in front of him, a proprietary smile on his face.

"Tell me your troubles, and how I can help you."

# CHAPTER TWENTY-FOUR

On Saturday afternoon, Paolo drove Mia to Most Precious Blood. He parked in the alley and followed her inside.

She dipped her fingers in the font of holy water and crossed herself, then walked down the center aisle toward the altar. Eyes on the crucifix, she genuflected.

Then, she entered the confessional and knelt.

"In the name of the Father, the Son, and the Holy Spirit," she said to Father Alessio through the latticed screen. "Forgive me, Father, for I have sinned. It has been one week since my last confession."

"Go on, my child."

"I took a man's life."

There was a very long pause. "That…is a grave sin, indeed, my child. Sometimes we must kill in self-defense, which is not seen as a sin in God's eyes. Was it…?"

Mia pictured the detective lying on the ground beneath her. The moment she'd wrestled with her conscience—that all-too-brief moment where she had wondered if she should let him live. He'd been surrendering. He'd been pleading for mercy. For his life.

And she'd murdered him.

"No, Father," she said in a steady voice. "It was not."

Another long silence. She almost felt bad for him.

"What is to be my penance, Father?"

"Do you mock the Lord, my child?" he whispered.

"No," she replied. "I only wish to know my penance."

"I—I..."

She reached into her pocketbook for a wad of bills, folded them tightly, and forced them through one of the slats in the lattice cutout. "Perhaps I'll say a rosary and a Hail Mary for his soul. What do you think?" She wiggled the bills.

After a moment, he reached up and took them. "Yes, my child. That...that would be good. And do not do it again."

"No, Father. I will endeavor not to repeat my sin." She stood slowly. "I'll see you next week."

Perhaps it was the small booth. Perhaps it was knowing what she was about to go do. But the echo of her voice in the small space sounded ominous to her own ears. And when he spoke, Father Alessio's voice trembled slightly.

"Go in...peace, my child."

Mia stepped out of the booth and strolled toward the door, stopping to make pleasant small talk with the neighborhood people there to make their own Saturday afternoon confessions ahead of Mass the next morning.

Paolo held the door for her.

"Time for the meeting," she said, and took his arm on the way back to the car.

He gave her hand one reassuring pat.

Mr. Masseria had chosen the location—his favorite seafood restaurant, Nuova Villa Tammaro in Coney Island. The meeting was scheduled between lunch and dinner, so the only people in the restaurant would be there for the meeting.

When Paolo parked the car outside the restaurant and opened her door, she drew in a deep breath. So many things could go wrong today.

"If things go sideways, protect Gloria and Emilia," she said quietly. "Send them back to Sicily with Raquel. Glo only came back here for me, anyway. And make sure Aunt Connie and Uncle Joe are taken care of. Do what you can for the neighborhood. I don't...I don't know who will look out for them if I'm not there to."

She stepped around him, but his hand closed around her wrist. When she looked at him in surprise, a fierce sadness filled his eyes. He shook his head slowly.

Mia covered the hand on her arm with hers. "You have to stay here," she insisted. "I won't risk you when I still need you so much. My most trusted friend." She patted his cheek, giving him a fond smile.

He released her arm. She felt his stare the entire walk to the restaurant's front door, set deeply into the brick-and-stone exterior. A set of three curved windows flanked the curved doorway. Inside, the décor was minimal—pale walls, dark wainscoting, small, red-shaded deco lamps in the middle of each table to provide warmth to the cool atmosphere. She walked past the bar, where a bartender wiped down freshly washed glasses. He bobbed his head at her in greeting.

At the back of the room, Mr. Masseria and Mr. Luciano waited. A small dish of cake sat before Mr. Masseria, along with an espresso. He rose to greet her with a kiss on each cheek. Then he pulled back to examine her face, his eyes narrow.

"It looked worse a week ago," she said, lowering her eyes.

He pursed his lips. "It will fade. Then there will come a time where you hardly remember it at all."

She cast him a sidelong look. "That easy?"

"After a while. Yes."

Mia shook hands with Mr. Luciano, and he gestured to a chair. "Have a seat. I believe there's room for all of us."

"How many men is Morelli having escort him?" Mr. Masseria asked, sounding bored.

"Two."

Mia tightened her jaw. She tried to quash her anxiety before it became obvious to an onlooker that she was nervous.

A waiter came to take her order. She asked for a glass of the house wine.

He had just set it before her when the front door opened again. Jake Morelli swaggered in wearing a beautiful, dove-gray suit and looking like he didn't have a care in the world. Two men trailed him.

Mia tensed. Was his plan to open fire immediately, or to wait? He'd made her think he wanted to have an actual discussion first, to really pretend to air their grievances in front of Mr. Masseria in order to get him to lower his guard.

When he saw Mr. Luciano sitting beside him, his eyes lit up, and Mia's heart sank. It was clear—at least, to her—that he intended to take Lucky Luciano with him.

The feeling that she might not be walking out of here strengthened.

"Well, well," Jake said. "Ain't this a beautiful day for a meeting?"

"Sit down, Jacopo," Mr. Masseria said. "And your two men— I don't believe I know them."

"They're Mr. Maranzano's men," Jake said casually. "He was kind enough to send them to work for me a couple days ago. You see, I seem to be short on men lately." He cast a pointed look in Mia's direction. "Short on men, but busy as all get out. So much new business these days."

Mia lowered her eyes to the table, her fingers tightening around the stem of her wineglass.

"By the way," Jake said, leaning across the table toward her. He patted her hand. "No hard feelings about your face, right? It looks a whole lot better already. How's your cousin doing?"

He was so brash, she thought, looking up at him. So blatant. He wasn't trying to be discreet about anything at all. "She's well," Mia said, struggling to keep her voice steady. "She was released from the hospital yesterday."

"That's good news," Mr. Luciano said quietly, nodding.

"Yes," Mia said, staring at Jake. "And she'll have a limp the rest of her life. Because of you."

"Well." He shrugged. "At least she'll be alive, right? That's more than I can say for the eighteen men of mine you slaughtered in the streets."

"And what about the innocent people of the neighborhood *you've* destroyed?" she demanded. "The children you've killed?"

"Enough." Mr. Masseria lifted a hand. "How many times we gotta do this? How many times we gotta sit down so you can bicker at each other like children? Neither of you listen to any agreement you make in front of us. You just do what you please."

"*He* does what he pleases," Mia said.

"Listen, the bottom line is this," Jake said, jabbing a finger into the table. "No one's gonna tell me what to do—sure as shit not some broad. I haven't listened to a broad since I was eight years old, and that was my mama. I ain't like you fanooks who can't find your balls. This little bitch ain't gonna boss me around."

Both Mr. Masseria and Mr. Luciano glanced at her, brows raised, as if expecting her to respond in kind to that.

A memory of Jake striking her, of him ordering Abner to beat Raquel and Gloria, of him threatening to kill her niece, flashed through her mind. She said nothing.

"Perhaps you might try exercising a little respect in matters of business, Jacopo," Mr. Masseria said in a lofty tone. "Especially when dealing with women."

"You know as well as I do women don't belong in business, Joe," Jake replied. "They're good for two things. Cooking and fucking." He flashed Mia a bright smile. "Right, sweetie?"

She simply sipped her wine. It burned an acidic path down her throat to her stomach, where it soured.

He cocked his head. "I'm disappointed. You usually have so much to say. Is it because your bodyguard isn't here to protect you?"

"Do I need protecting from you?" she asked.

"Not as long as you play by my rules," he said. "And stay out of everything."

"What exactly does *everything* mean?" Mr. Luciano asked.

"What it sounds like," Jake replied. "She gives up her stake in the liquor business. She gives me full control of the Madden deal at the Cotton Club. She keeps her nose out of my territories, as well as my heroin business. I sell all over the city, wherever I want."

"Unless where you're selling is already claimed by another business," Luciano said, his voice low and deadly. "You might not be aware of this, pal, but you ain't the only one selling heroin in the city."

"Ah, forgive me," Jake said with an insincere smile. "Sometimes I get a little excited."

"Let's be clear about something." Luciano leaned forward. "If you sell liquor or drugs in *my* territories or Joe's, you won't be doing it for free. And we require very high percentages."

"Perhaps it's worth it to you to stick to your own territories," Mr. Masseria added calmly.

For once, Jake seemed to take the thinly veiled threat for what it was and sat back. "Right, sure," he said. "I'm open to talking percentages."

Of course, in his mind, he'd tell them whatever they wanted to hear, since he planned to kill them both anyway. Then their territories would become his.

"And another thing we need to be clear on," Mr. Masseria said. "Little Italy doesn't belong to you exclusively. I provide protection for several businesses in the area. You want to deal there, you do so at my percentages. You want to be a big boss, but you have the brain of a child." He flicked a hand toward Mia. "She's smarter than you."

Jake went red.

Before he could say anything, Mr. Masseria turned to her. "You agree to those terms?"

She lifted a shoulder. "What choice do I have? He's threatened the lives of my cousin, my sister-in-law, and my niece. Nothing's more important to me than my family. If I have his guarantee that he'll leave them alone...fine. He can have what he wants."

"You have my word," he said smoothly, winking at her. "Hold up your end, I'll hold up mine."

"All right, now you got things settled with her," Luciano said. "Let's revisit this territory discussion. I'm hearing in the streets you think Staten Island's yours, but you're mistaken."

Jake lifted his brows. "Am I? My apologies."

"Fuck your apologies. Get your dealers out of Staten Island or you're going to have a whole new problem."

"I'll talk to them and see what I can do." Jake seemed completely unfazed as he leaned back in his seat and smiled.

"This clown," Luciano muttered. He looked at Masseria and shook his head. "You think you can reason with him, go ahead. I'm done here." He stood abruptly and glanced at Mia. "At least you don't have to deal with his shit anymore."

She blinked up at him.

"Where you going?" Jake said, spreading his palms. "We're just having a friendly conversation, me and you. Ain't we?"

"Yeah, real friendly. I'm gonna get some air." Luciano stalked to the front of the restaurant. A moment later, the little bell over the doorway jingled.

Jake glanced at Masseria. "He's very emotional, isn't he?"

Masseria sighed. "I'll go talk to him. Don't go anywhere. Lucky, he's hotheaded." He tossed his napkin on the table and raised an eyebrow at Jake. "Not unlike you."

Jake shrugged. When the door closed behind Mr. Masseria, he gave Mia an appraising look. "You're doing real good. I thought for sure you'd let that temper get the best of you, but you're a real pro."

"Sure," she said drily, folding her arms. "I'm a real pro at being belittled in front of men who used to respect me."

"Soon, they won't be a problem, eh?" He chuckled and glanced at his two cronies, who sat slightly behind him. They both nodded and smiled. Jake turned back to her and leaned forward. "Listen, while we have a minute. Before they come back and things get crazy. You know I didn't really mean that shit I said about you in front of them, right?"

"Oh no?" she said sarcastically. "Which part? The part where I'm only good for cooking and fucking, or the part where you called me a little bitch?"

"Any of it." He shrugged. "I'm playing a part. Like you."

"What's the point of it all?" she said. "You're wasting time. Or are you just trying to see if you can get a better deal from them, better than what your...other boss offers you?"

"You can say it," he said. "Maranzano. Yeah, they work for him on paper, but they're my guys now. Right, fellas?"

"That's right, Mr. Morelli," the one on the right said.

Mia glanced at him, found him staring back at her, and looked away. "No loyalty among anyone anymore, is there?"

"Only to number one," Jake said, pointing at himself. "That's something you should never forget, by the way. I'm surprised your precious brother never taught you that."

Her fury rose inside her, swift as a panther with its claws out. "Never speak of my brother. Ever."

Jake smirked. "Ah, touchy-touchy. Forgive me. And you were right—I am feeling him out to see if there's something in it for me. Number one, remember. If I think I can get a better deal, then I'll wait to kill him until I can take what he's amassed for myself."

"You're a goddamn vulture," she said.

"You're goddamn right," Jake said. "Or did you think men in this life get what they want by asking nicely?"

"Even crooks have a little bit of honor."

Jake tossed his head back and roared with laughter. He looked at his compatriots. "Did you hear that shit?"

They chuckled. "Sure did," the one on the left said.

Jake reached out and patted her hand. "Boy, you really are a kid, aren't you? Crooks? Honor? Where'd you go to school?" He shook his head. "Lookit, I'm sorry for laughing. It's just that you never fail to surprise me. You know, I thought I had you pegged for a real smart broad, smarter than your famous brother ever was. And don't jump down my throat—I ain't talking bad about him. Truly, I would've liked to have met him. I've heard a lot about the infamous Domenico Scalisi. Meeting you was almost as good."

Mia drew a deep breath through her nose.

"Come on. Don't be sore." Jake ran his fingertips lightly up and down her forearm. "I'm paying you a compliment. You know, once we get this shit figured out with the liquor deal and the territories…you should really think about becoming my partner again."

Mia looked at him as though he'd just sprouted a second nose. "You off your nut?"

He studied her closely, a seductive smile on his lips. "Why not? You and me. We could run this town. Turn it upside down. New York would be our kingdom. You'd be my queen. You could have everything you want. Even after all you've done to hurt me, I can't stay mad at you. I'm crazy about you."

"A week ago, you kidnapped my family, beat them, beat *me*, and threatened to kill my niece," she growled. "You took everything I had in exchange for sparing their lives. Now you want me to be your *partner*?"

"I said, no hard feelings about that other shit," he said with an impatient shrug. "And what's the alternative? You got nothing but the club. Yeah, you might make a pretty penny there, but you know good and goddamn well it's *nothing* compared to what booze and drugs bring in. And even though I've thought about killing you a million times, I can never seem to do it. I gotta believe…it's because I don't really want to."

Mia tightened her jaw. "You're insane."

"Maybe I am," he said. "But I'm also a man who knows what he wants. I heard about what you did to Wallace. I wish I could've been there to see you unload an entire cylinder into his face. Just thinking about it makes me hard. I think I'm in love with you."

She drew back in disgust, but he only leaned closer, sliding his hand around her wrist. "And at that wedding. Even though I could've killed you for what you did, seeing you in that moment, issuing orders like you were waving your hanky around—it got me so very hot."

Mia glared at him. "Then go drown yourself in an ice bath."

"Aw, come on. What's Lazzari got that I ain't?"

"A heart." She yanked her wrist from his grasp.

"That hurts," he complained, then chuckled, placing a hand over his chest. "See? I got feelings, too."

"Now, if only you could find your sanity."

"Listen. All bullshit aside," he said. "I mean it. Maybe we reconsider the original plan for today. Let's finish hearing these idiots out. Then, we figure out how to take what's theirs, make it ours, and get rid of 'em all."

"I don't know how many different ways to say no to you."

"I thought you were a smart girl," he said sharply. "I thought you knew how this game really works. Maybe I was wrong."

"Or maybe you're not as smart as you think you are."

He narrowed his eyes at her, but instead of retorting, he glanced impatiently over his shoulder. "Where the fuck did they go for fresh air, the Bronx?"

"Nah," one of Maranzano's men said with a chuckle. "Definitely not the Bronx."

"My guess," Mia said coolly, crossing her legs and leaning her chin on her knuckles, "is that they went back to Manhattan. They're both busy men, after all."

"Huh?" Jake swiveled in his seat and stared at her. "What the hell are you talking about?"

"Mr. Masseria and Mr. Luciano," she said, tendrils of quiet delight unfurling low in her belly. "They're not here. They left."

His eyes blazed. "And how the fuck would you know?"

The bell over the door jingled again, but it wasn't Mr. Masseria or Lucky Luciano walking through the door. Instead, Charlie Lazzari walked in, flanked by Bobby and Joey. They all held pistols.

"Hiya, Morelli," Charlie said, his tone full of dangerous cheer. "How's tricks?"

Jake was on his feet in a flash, drawing his own gun. "That's far enough, boyo," he snapped. He swung the pistol on Mia. "Or she's dead."

Mia remained in her seat, chin propped on her hand, and glanced up at him with a raised brow.

The three men froze.

"Get your hands up," Jake added. "Now."

They raised their hands in the air.

"Take it easy," Charlie said.

Jake barked a laugh. "That's hilarious. You three fucking bastards walk in here pointing guns at me, and now you tell *me* to take it easy. That's rich, Lazzari."

"Don't make any fast moves," Charlie said.

"Who are you to tell *me* what to do?" Jake reached out and grabbed Mia by the arm, jerked her up and out of her chair, swiveled her around, and pinned her tight to his chest, her back to his front. He looped an arm around her neck and pressed the barrel of the gun to her right temple. "Maybe you didn't take me seriously. That's a big mistake, Charlie."

Mia gritted her teeth.

"Now," Jake continued. "You bastards drop your guns and keep your hands up. You're gonna stand over there by the wall, and you're not gonna move while I walk outta here with my pals. Let me do that, Mia lives. You try some funny shit, I'll splatter her brains all over you and that wall."

"I don't think you will," Charlie said.

"Stand down," came the low, harsh voice of one of Maranzano's men.

Charlie lifted his pistol again. Bobby and Joey immediately followed suit.

Jake shoved the gun against her head harder. "You deaf, Charles? He told you to back the fuck off."

"I heard him just fine." Charlie took a step toward them. "Are *you* deaf?"

"What the fu—"

Mia felt Jake's body freeze.

"Mia." Charlie beckoned her. "It's all right."

The pressure of the barrel against her temple eased. She threw off Jake's arm and walked toward Charlie. When she reached him, she pivoted on the balls of her feet like a dancer and folded her arms.

Jake stared at her, his mouth agape as Maranzano's man, the one who'd issued the order to stand down, shoved the barrel of his gun to the back of his head. The other man trained his gun on the side of Jake's head.

"Don't move," the man said. "Don't even breathe. Drop your gun."

"What is this?" Jake looked at Mia, something like a plea for help in his eyes.

She raised her chin. "The Scalisi family—my sister-in-law, my cousin, and my little niece—all wanted me to send you their love. Oh, and Don Masseria and Don Maranzano send their regards, as well."

His eyes went wide. "Bullshit."

"Me?" she went on. "I don't have any regards or love to send you."

"You fucking bitch."

"That's the last time you'll ever call me that," she said softly, and lifted her hand to motion the shooters with her fingers.

In an instant, Jake swung his pistol up. It was centered with such deadly precision on the middle of her face, she could practically see down the barrel, see the gunpowder igniting, see the bullet exploding out toward her faster than she could blink.

For half an instant, the room was silent. Then the deafening roar of multiple guns firing filled the room, filled the street, perhaps all of Staten Island.

The bullet that had been meant for her stayed trapped inside Jake's gun before he ever had the chance to pull the trigger.

Dozens of bullets flew past her on either side and caught Jake in the chest, stomach, back, head, neck, and face.

Jake had collapsed to his knees after the first few shots, then slumped over before Maranzano's two men, Charlie, Bobby, and

Joey walked toward him and kept shooting, over and over, letting up only when they reached the *click* of empty revolvers.

Mia walked toward Jake's body. He lay in a spreading pool of blood. His fading eyes rolled slowly, and his mouth opened and closed once, as if he were still trying to get the last word in.

She reached into the neckline of her dress with her index and middle fingers and withdrew his ace of hearts card from the only poker game they'd ever played, torn in the middle where his knife had gone through and smudged red with the kiss of her lips.

She flicked it onto his body with a snap of her wrist.

"Hope you have better luck in hell," she told him.

His half-lidded eyes shifted to her—and stayed there as his final breath departed his body.

She lingered for another moment, watching the light in his eyes dim, then turned on her heel and strode out of the restaurant to where Paolo waited to take her home.

# CHAPTER TWENTY-FIVE

*October, 1926*

C *hicago*, written by *Tribune* reporter Maurine Dallas Watkins, opened at the Chicago Theatre on the second Friday night in October for an unofficial, pre-debut sneak peek the marquee only announced as a "limited special engagement."

The official premiere date was set for December, but in fine-tuning the play, the director had decided to get preliminary opinions. Of course, most of the city already knew about the play, since it was based on two rather notable murders that had taken place two years prior, where a couple of well-to-do ladies had killed their husbands and been acquitted after media-circus trials. Maurine's coverage of those trials had garnered her a large fanbase, so a single, sneak-peek performance was a great way to gauge reception—and stir up anticipation.

Men and women dressed to the nines filled the lobby and the entrance area, forming a large crowd outside on the sidewalk as show-goers waited to be admitted and claim their seats.

Across the street, Mia exhaled a plume of cigarette smoke, surveying the scene. She took in the vertical, bright red sign of the theater and remembered how she'd felt the day she'd shown up for her audition—so terribly excited and full of anticipation that all her dreams were coming true. All she'd needed was her brother to watch her from the front row, to pass on his confidence in her so she could pull off the audition of a lifetime.

Inside that theater, she'd had one night of triumph. One night where all of Chicago had learned just who Mia Angela Scalisi was. She could still feel the beading on the beautiful white dress she'd worn. Could still feel the heat of the stage lights as they illuminated her. Still hear the music pounding in her ears as she and her partner, D.C. London, had whirled and leaped and Charlestoned across the vast stage. She saw the smiling faces, enthralled with their performance.

She'd brought the house down that night, and had been so sure it would be the first of many doing so.

Then her gaze roved the sidewalk. Mia pictured it empty, dark except for the lights over the entrance and the lights from the sign, illuminating a single body lying on the cold concrete as icy rain sluiced down. She couldn't help flinching, squeezing her eyes shut, trying to ignore the assault of the memories, the echo of shouts and gunfire and breaking glass from the most horrible night of her life that had set her destiny on its course.

"Ready, dear?"

Gloria, at her side, gave her a quizzical look. She had been spared the sight that night, though Mia herself had been the one to break the news. She was glad that, between them, she had been the one to witness Nick dead and not Gloria. It would have broken her beyond repair.

Mia swallowed and arranged her face into a smile. Gloria looked beautiful, in a black-and-silver number with a fur-trimmed coat and a jeweled headband. Though she had only been with them for a short time, Raquel's absence had created a hole in Mia's heart. She should have been here tonight, too. The only thing that kept deep sadness from swallowing her whole was the knowledge that Raquel was flourishing back home with her brother and his family, back in the warm, salty air tinged with the fragrant aroma of the blood orange groves. The nightmares,

Carlo had written her a couple weeks ago, were far apart now, and no longer nightly as they had been when she'd first arrived home. She sent her love, Carlo always wrote, but Raquel had yet to write herself, though Mia had sent her dozens of letters and handfuls of gifts.

"Yes," Mia replied. "I'm ready."

"Well, aren't we a pair tonight." Gloria smiled and linked her arm through Mia's. "I swear, they made the color red just for you."

Mia glanced down at her own bespoke ensemble, a velvet tube dress covered in silver-embroidered netting and embellished with a large, silver pendant that hung from the plunging neckline. She'd bought it as a birthday present to herself last month, though she'd turned twenty-three inside her hotel suite with just Gloria, Emilia, and Charlie to celebrate with her and sing her "Happy Birthday."

The velvet was so soft beneath her fingertips as she ran her hand along her flank to smooth it. Red, the color of blood. So much of that she had seen the past couple years. So much she had spilled.

Yes, it had been made for her.

They stepped off the curb, Mia waving to Paolo over her shoulder, and strolled across the street. Paolo had not been interested in attending the play, and had opted to wait in the car so he could keep an eye on who came and went.

Mia led her straight to the front to the bouncer at the door. "We're guests of Ms. Watkins," she informed him.

He scoffed. "You got any idea how many times I've heard that tonight? Everyone who's ever read any of her columns is a *guest* of hers."

Mia opened her pocketbook and fished out the two extra-special tickets labeled "Very Important Person" across the top. Beneath that were the words in flowing script: *The holder of this ticket is hereby entitled to all accommodations befitting esteemed members of the cast, crew, director, and playwright.*

The bouncer frowned as he read both tickets several times, turning them over and over.

Mia sighed. "Perhaps you want to call Ms. Watkins down here?"

"What gives? Don't you know who you're talking to?" Gloria demanded. "This is Mia Angela Scalisi. She was the Saturday Night Special in this town not too long ago, and she used to perform here, too."

Mia nudged Gloria lightly in the ribs, but bit back a smile. She sounded truly indignant.

"All right, already," said the indignant guard. "Listen, I got enough aggravation with this job, I don't need any more. Go ahead."

"Thanks, mac," Mia said with a wink. She took the tickets back, and she and Gloria glided into the theater.

In the lobby, Mia froze. She didn't care when someone stumbled into her back and snapped, "Watch where you're going!"

All she could think of was that moment here almost two years ago, when she'd been flirting with Charlie the moment before she'd heard her brother die. The front doors had burst with glass shards. She remembered how they'd cut her face, how her palms had stung when she'd hit the floor.

"Mia," Gloria said gently. There was an odd look of understanding on her face, though Mia had never told her all of the details. Gloria had never asked.

"I just—I haven't been back here since…" She swallowed. Why were her hands shaking?

"We can leave, if you want," Gloria said. "Perhaps we ought to. We could go see a flick instead."

"Maurine would be so disappointed," Mia said. "It's all right."

In the auditorium, they found Maurine Watkins near the front, speaking to a few people who might have been reporters. She wore an elegant black dress, and her luminous dark eyes shone with pride.

When she caught sight of Mia, an enormous smile split her

face. She excused herself and hurried to meet them. Mia caught her by the hands.

"Well, I'll be!" Maurine exclaimed, looking her up and down. "Every bit the Sheba I remember you as at the courthouse that day."

"It seems to me you always find the sneakiest ways of mentioning that day, Ms. Watkins," Mia said, arching a brow.

"That's because I don't want you to forget about that exclusive you promised me," she replied, then leaned closer. "How was that business in New York you asked me about? I heard from my dirty prohi friend that detective who went after you turned up dead."

"That business all got worked out," Mia said, keeping her face neutral. "I'm terribly sorry to hear about him. I wonder who he ran afoul of."

Maurine smirked. "Probably some dame in a killer evening dress. What do you think?"

Mia gave her a warning glance and cleared her throat. "Ms. Watkins, this is my sister-in-law, Mrs. Gloria Scalisi."

Gloria held out her hand. "How do you do?"

Maurine shook it. "Charmed, I'm sure. Boy, you Italian girls sure know how to put a room to shame. You could be in pictures, too, Mrs. Scalisi."

Gloria flushed and waved her hand. "Oh, go on. Mia's the one with any talent."

"Speaking of talent," Mia said, "I'm thrilled to see your play."

"I'm thrilled you're thrilled," Maurine said with a grin. "They say we're headed for the pictures next year. Say—you'd be perfect for the role of Velma Kelly. I need someone dark and vampy."

Mia returned her grin. "You don't say? I can do dark and vampy."

"Then I'll put your name in for consideration," Maurine said. "Get ready for a phone call one of these days. Of course,

I'm guessing you've got other endeavors that keep you rather busy lately, haven't you?"

Mia tipped her head back and laughed at the woman's sly expression. "Maurine, you gave up reporting to become a playwright. Will you ever step out of the newsroom? Or will you always be this nosy?"

"With a scoop like you around, who could help but be nosy?" She linked her arm with Mia's and Gloria's. "Come, ladies. I promised you the best seats in the house."

THE FOLLOWING EVENING, MIA, GLORIA, AND PAOLO ARRIVED AT the Hawthorne Inn around nine o'clock for supper with Al Capone. She hadn't been to his headquarters since he'd moved to Cicero in the spring of 1924, although Nick had been a frequent visitor before his death.

"Have you ever been here?" Gloria asked as they walked up 22nd Street.

"Not here," Mia said. "Just a couple of times when he was at the Four Deuces." She'd limited her visits after the first; she'd had her fill of cathouses from the upstairs level of Stems Club.

The Hawthorne, however, was just a new location for all of Al's favorite businesses—bootlegging, gambling, and prostitution. She sighed inwardly, steeling herself for what she'd see.

"When I saw Johnny in Sicily, he told me Al's changed," Mia said. "I guess he's kind of famous nowadays." She wondered how different he was from the man who had made her an incredible cup of coffee inside the tiny tenement apartment of a Sicilian immigrant woman.

As they neared the hotel, she paused in front of its adjoining restaurant. Less than three weeks ago, Hymie Weiss had ordered his men to shoot up the place and take Al out. He'd been unsuccessful, of course, and if he hadn't been a dead man walking before, he certainly was now.

"Looks like they got all the repairs done," Gloria said,

touching the large, plate-glass front window lightly. "You can hardly tell anything happened."

"Let's hope they used bullet-proof glass this time," Mia remarked.

Paolo held the hotel door for them. Inside, she glanced around. It wasn't quite as fancy as the Lexington Hotel, her old home, but for small Cicero, it was nice.

"I expected he and his men had taken over the place," Gloria said. "But it looks like they're keeping to themselves."

"Except for the guards," Mia murmured under her breath. She flicked her chin at a few Italian men in beautiful suits standing guard in the lobby. They were the only indication—and then, only to an insider's eye—that a man of respect, a "mobster" as Maurine would have called him, lived here.

They entered the elevator, where another well-dressed man operated the lift.

"Where to?" he asked politely.

The hotel was only a few stories, smaller than the Lexington. "Top floor, please."

The man turned to study her, his eyes narrowing. He gave her a sweeping, head-to-toe look, then Gloria, then glanced at Paolo. "What you want up there for?"

"We're friends of Mr. Capone's," Mia replied. "Mia and Gloria Scalisi."

"I've heard of you," he said. "Friends, huh?"

"Dear, family friends," she said bitingly, though Gloria hardly knew Al. "Not whores. Maybe you'd like to ask him yourself. He's expecting us."

"And him?" The man—the guard—flicked his chin at Paolo.

"Our bodyguard."

"You armed?" he asked Paolo.

"Of course he is," Mia said drily. "He wouldn't be much of a bodyguard if he weren't, now, would he?"

"What, he can't talk for himself?" the guard said.

"No," Mia replied. "He can't speak, due to an injury. But he can hear you just fine."

"Show me your piece," the guard said to Paolo.

The Sicilian bodyguard opened his suit coat to show the pistol tucked in the waistband of his pants.

"Yeah, I'll be needing that." The guard held his hand out.

Paolo buttoned his jacket.

The guard bristled. "Look, pally—"

"As I said, we're friends of Mr. Capone's," Mia said sharply. "Old friends. To ask my bodyguard to give up his pistol would be disrespectful."

"Mr. Capone should be the one to make that decision." The guard's tone was just as sharp.

Mia didn't know whether to be exasperated or impressed with him. "Fine."

When they arrived on the top floor, the elevator opened to a short hallway. A set of double doors at the end magically opened and another guard appeared in the doorway.

"Who're the dames?" he asked.

"Says she's—"

"Mia Angela Scalisi," a familiar voice said from inside the room. "The Saturday Night Special. And don't you fuckin' forget it."

The words were punctuated by a short, infectious bark of a laugh, and Mia's lips twisted into a smile as Al Capone shoved the guard aside and stepped out to greet her.

"Alphonse," she said, allowing him to embrace her with a kiss on each cheek. Gloria accepted an identical greeting from him, her cheeks flushing.

"Mia. Gloria." He leaned back, spreading his hands wide. "New York's been good to you ladies."

Mia huffed a humorless laugh, thinking back on the past several months. "I wouldn't go that far."

"You've been busy, from what I hear." He formed his thumb, index, and middle fingers into the shape of a gun and held them to his temple. "Very busy." He glanced behind her at Gloria. "Oh, ah. Beg your pardon."

"She knows everything," Mia said quietly, glancing at Gloria.

Her sister-in-law gave her a slight nod in return. "We can speak frankly in front of her."

Al raised a brow. "That so? Things have changed."

"That's an understatement," Gloria said, and he laughed.

"The bodyguard's packing, boss," the guard from the elevator said. "He wouldn't give it up."

Al stuck his hand out to Paolo. "Hey, any friend of Mia Scalisi's is a friend of mine."

To Mia's surprise, Paolo shook Al's hand and nodded in greeting.

"He's all right," Al said, clapping Paolo on the arm and gesturing them into the suite.

The door shut behind them, and Mia glanced around. It was painted in shades of cream and all of the furniture was white and cream. Several men milled about, holding drinks and cigars, laughing quietly among themselves, eyeing her and Gloria with open and frank curiosity.

"It's much quieter than I expected," she said.

Al chuckled. "Well, it's early. Plus I told them I was having guests tonight. Real fine, classy guests. They're on their best behavior—at least until you leave. Let's go back here."

He led her to a large office at the back of the room. A table had been set up with four steaks, potatoes, green beans. A simple meal, but a hearty one, and she was hungry.

They all sat down at the table. An older man she didn't recognize walked in with a bottle of wine. He poured four glasses.

"Thanks, Enzo," Al said.

"You want something stronger?" Enzo asked with a thick Sicilian accent that made Mia smile a little. He sounded like home.

Al glanced at her, holding a hand out. "Whiskey? Anisette?"

Paolo gave an approving grunt, tucking his dinner napkin into his collar.

"Paolo would like some anisette," Mia said. "Wine will do for me."

"Fine for me, also," Gloria said.

When Al's whiskey, and Paolo's anisette had been poured, they dug in. The steak was tender, flavorful, and perfectly cooked, and Mia said so.

Al smiled with pride. "From the restaurant next door. Owner's a good buddy of mine."

"How is he after what happened?" she asked. "How are *you?*"

A smile that was more of a snarl crossed his lips. "Fuckin' pissed," he said. "That fuckin' Irish Jew is gonna get what's coming to him."

"From what I understand, he's Polish and Catholic," Mia corrected gently.

Al glared at her. "I don't give a fuck if he's a giraffe and Episcopalian," he snapped. "That's the second fucking time he's come at me. You know what he did to Johnny. This time I coulda been plugged full of holes. He won't ever get over Deanie O'Banion."

"Not until you're dead," she said. "Or he is."

"Well, I ain't planning on dying any time soon," Al said. "So I guess it's his turn."

"That's part of why I wanted to come see you." Mia dabbed her lips on her napkin. "I have some business in the city still. Saw a friend's play last night. Tomorrow, Glo and I are going to go see about having Nick's body exhumed and cremated, so we can bring him home."

Al stared at her, then Gloria. "You're going to have his body *dug up?*"

"He never should have been buried here," Gloria said softly. "It's not home."

"He belongs in New York," Mia added. "Lying beside our parents."

Al shrugged. "Never heard of such a thing, but by all means, do what you need to. You need my help, let me know."

"Thank you," Mia said. "But I mentioned it because it'll probably be a couple days before we can have his body dug up. So in the meantime, we're going to visit him since it's been a while." She paused, glancing slyly at Gloria. Her face remained impassive, but her brown eyes glinted. "We thought it'd be awfully nice if we brought him some fresh flowers."

At the mention of the wreath, Al looked up from his plate, his fork halfway to his mouth. "Flowers, huh? And, uh, where would you be going for such an arrangement?"

"Why, Schofield's, of course," she said. "Best shop in the city. I heard it has a new owner, now that Dean O'Banion's gone."

He leaned back in his chair, a thoughtful look on his face. All coyness left the conversation. "I don't know how we could get him. That place has as many guards as this one does. And Hymie ain't always there."

Mia shook her head. "I'll make an order with him tomorrow to pick something up the following afternoon. When he's on his way back to the shop…"

Al's brow creased. "And how do you know he won't already be there?"

She smiled. "My playwright friend used to be a reporter for the *Tribune*. She's a very well-connected woman. Has lots of sources in the city. I'm told jury selection for the murder trial of a pal of Hymie's is tomorrow."

"Joe Saltis," Al said venomously. "Fuck that bastard."

"What have you got against him?"

"He was *my* guy for a long time, then he started getting cute with our territories. The icing was when he started dealing with the North Side behind my back."

"Well, seems Hymie wants to be there for moral support tomorrow afternoon," Mia said. "According to my friend's source, that is."

"How do you know that dope's reliable?"

"Her source is a dirty cop," she said. "Hymie asked him to provide some security for him and a couple friends."

"I'll be damned," Al murmured, staring at her with a face of impressed respect.

"If I have an order to pick up after that, he *won't* already be at the shop. He'll be out on the street."

Al set down his fork, studying her. "You've thought this through."

"I've been waiting two years for this," she said. "I've had nothing but time to think this through. I just needed to wait for the right moment."

Beside her, Gloria stiffened a little. This was new territory for them still, though after Jake's death, Mia had told her everything. It was too hard to keep things from Gloria, and in a selfish way, Mia didn't want to shoulder the burden of her deeds alone. The day of Signor Bagnoli's daughter's wedding had planted the seeds of openness between them, with Gloria acknowledging that Mia had made an irrevocable transition with the act of murdering Jake's men.

But Gloria was still good, Mia thought, discreetly nudging her sister-in-law's foot with her own under the table to reassure her. That was why these sorts of conversations, these things she'd come to know that she would never be able to *un*-know, bothered her. And Mia was glad for it. Because if they ever stopped bothering Gloria, that would mean she'd lost her soul and her humanity.

The way Mia feared she, herself, had.

"I know you got your own beef with Weiss," she said. "But he wouldn't be coming after you had Nick not been the one to kill Dean for you. And Weiss got his revenge on Nick."

"I know." Al nodded. "And you're right—it's the perfect time. I just gotta find some new guys. Weiss knows most of mine. He'll see them coming and know he's in danger."

"It just so happens I brought two of my most reliable men with me," Mia said. "Bobby Grata and Joey Giannino. If Weiss ever saw them, it was briefly and in passing, and not in the last couple of years."

"Is that right? Where are they?"

"Relaxing at the Drake. They like to take it easy before a job."

Al barked a laugh. "Look at you. All prepared. You gonna

clean up this little mess I haven't been able to in the last couple years, huh?"

Paolo glanced at her. A warning to be cautious. She understood—she was one word away from further insulting Al Capone.

"You've had your hands full," she said gently. "That attack on Johnny. His retirement. You've been in charge this whole time. Several businesses to run. It's not like you've had a lot of time to plan."

Al sniffed.

"But me?" she went on. "I spent a year in Sicily. Walking on the beach. Spending time with Don Catalano. Learning the ins and outs of this world I never wanted to be a part of—that *you* never wanted me to be a part of. Remember that conversation we had in that tenement? When I asked Johnny's permission for Sal?"

"Couldn't forget it," Al said. "I'd never seen anything like that before. A dame wanting to kill someone." He smiled a little. "Of course, you were never just some dame. Nick Scalisi's sister. The great Nick Scalisi." There was no derision in his voice.

Beside her, Gloria looked down at her plate.

"He was great," Mia said, and her throat tightened a little. "And it was because of Sal and Hymie Weiss that he died. Hymie's the fourth piece of the puzzle that killed my brother. I've been waiting a long time to finish what I started here. And don't mistake it—I take what happened to you and Johnny very personally. You've always been good to me. You were always good to Nick. You're family to me."

Al sighed. "So. All this. Wanting to have dinner. You came to get *my* permission—to take my hit?" But he didn't sound mad. He gave her a wry smirk. "I'll have some guys waiting near the shop. On Monday. Just in case your guys need the backup. What do you think?"

Mia extended her hand over the table, and he grasped it. "I think we got a deal."

THE NEXT DAY, PAOLO PULLED THE CAR TO A STOP ON STATE Street, a few doors down from Schofield's Flowers.

Mia's gaze narrowed as she focused on the door. "Wait here for me," she said to Gloria and Paolo.

"Be careful," Gloria cautioned.

"Always am," Mia replied with a smile, then reached up to straighten the short, sheer black lace veil over her eyes and nose.

They had just come from Mount Carmel Cemetery, where Nick was buried. As soon as she'd stepped foot there, she'd been assaulted with memories of his funeral—the second-worst day of her life. It had been hard to focus on her own grief, though, because Gloria had nearly crumpled.

They'd spoken with the cemetery's manager. Her request had been received with a fair amount of surprise, but a C-note pressed into his palm had halted any protests. Nick's casket would be exhumed and cremated inside of a week. Then, she and Gloria would finally be able to take him home. Just as she'd promised him that icy December day in 1924. The last time she'd visited him.

Though he would only be in Chicago for a few more days, it was now time to order a lovely wreath for him, from the newest owner of Schofield's.

The bell over the door jingled as Mia walked in. It was a quiet Sunday afternoon, and no one was at the counter presently. The glass cases were stocked with a variety of arrangements. For a moment, she was distracted by a huge bouquet of red roses. They had huge heads, as big around as danishes. Beside them was a stunning arrangement of large, pink Oriental lilies. Their fragrance was heady, almost intoxicating.

"Can I help you, ma'am?"

Mia jumped. She hadn't heard anyone walk up from the back. She examined the young man who leaned on the counter. He appeared to be in his late twenties, and had a headful of dark hair, long on the top, short on the sides. He had a thick neck, a prominent nose and ears, but he was handsome in an unusual way.

"I'd like to speak to the owner."

He stretched his lips in a brief, thin smile that didn't reach his eyes. "You're speaking to him."

"I was told Hymie Weiss owned the place now."

"Lady, I ain't chopped liver." His voice had taken on an impatient edge. He opened the cash box and started counting the money contained inside. "I got things to do. What do you need?"

She'd figured it was him, but wanted to be sure. "Well. Mr. Weiss," she said coolly. "You old so-and-so. I'd like to order a wreath. For a grave."

He grabbed an order sheet and a pencil. "Shoot."

She smirked. *Interesting choice of words.* She described a simple wreath—roses, carnations, daises, greenery.

"Sure." He scrawled on the order form. "Name on the ribbon?"

"Mine or his?" she asked, then waved her hand. "Guess it doesn't matter. It's the same name." She paused. "Scalisi."

He snapped his head up, then did a double take.

Mia lifted her veil, tucking it over the top of her hat.

His eyes widened a little, then he squinted at her. "Do I know you…gorgeous?"

So he wanted to play dumb. She stepped closer, her footsteps slow and leisurely. "Some people in this town used to call me the Saturday Night Special." She leaned against the counter. "On the South Side."

He shrugged. "I never made it to the South Side much. Ain't familiar with no Saturday-night nothing."

"No?" She tilted her head. "You should be. After all, you took something from me once. Something valuable."

Hymie smirked. "Listen, beautiful, if I knocked off your flat once or stole your purse at a speak, it wasn't nothing personal. I can't recall exactly, so I can't apologize to you the way I'd like. I get migraines real bad, see." He rapped the side of his head.

"Sometimes they make me all fuzzy. Probably why I can't remember you properly."

"Then allow me to un-fuzz it for you," she said, a solid block of ice encapsulating her tone. "My name is Mia Angela Scalisi."

Understanding, recognition, and wariness stole across his face before he coolly blinked it away.

"That right?" he said. "Yeah, I remember now. I've heard of you. You was down at the, whatsit. Sal Bellomo's old place. Before he got iced."

"I'm sure you remember my brother too."

"Yeah, yeah," Hymie said dismissively. "Nicky. Nicholas. Right?"

*Isn't he quite the actor?* "Domenico." She enunciated every syllable. "And cut the bullshit. You know his name. More importantly, I know who you are. And I know what you did to my brother."

Hymie tightened his jaw, staring down at her. "What do you want, toots? Come to scold me about your brother? Because I seem to remember something *he* took from *me.*" His brow lowered and a frightfully angry look contorted his face. "In this very shop. You could say I lost a brother, too."

"I'm not here to argue about who's more right or less wrong," Mia said. "I'm here because I wanted you to see my face. To know that I know. I wanted to see if you'd have the balls to own up to it." She opened her pocketbook and pulled out some money—twice what the wreath cost—and dropped it in front of him. Then she stepped away from the counter. "I'd like my wreath tomorrow afternoon."

He eyed the cash, then scooped up the bills. "I got some things to do during the day tomorrow. It'll be ready by four sharp."

"Aren't you a peach," she said.

Hymie looked at her impatiently. "We done here, then? You're wasting my time."

"You're all out of time," she murmured, then pulled down her veil and stormed out of the shop.

❀

DESPITE PAYING DOUBLE, MIA DID NOT SHOW UP TO COLLECT HER wreath at the appointed time the following day.

Instead, in the late afternoon, after she'd finished tea at the Drake one last time with Gloria, they'd gone up to their suite, where Gloria had lain down. Mia stood at the large window, looking out at the dreary fall afternoon, arms folded, thinking of nothing at all while she waited.

Ten minutes to five o'clock, the telephone on the small, round white stand beside her at the window rang. She answered it on the first ring. "Yeah."

"It's done," Bobby Grata told her, then hung up immediately, exactly as she'd asked.

She set the receiver back in its cradle slowly.

When Hymie Weiss's body was finally cleared off the sidewalk where he'd fallen after Bobby and Joey had opened fire on him and four of his pals, the other men of the North Side Gang would reenter Schofield's and see what she'd left for them: the funeral wreath she'd ordered on its stand in the middle of the store, facing the door, with its ribbon across the front that said in bold, simple letters: **SCALISI**.

A little calling card—as Jake Morelli had once dubbed it—for them, so they'd know. So they'd never forget a Scalisi was not to be trifled with. And a Scalisi always got his revenge.

She paused. That wasn't quite right.

A Scalisi always got *her* revenge.

A cold smile curled up her lips.

*That's better.*

# CHAPTER TWENTY-SIX

Before she left Chicago forever with her brother's ashes in an urn, there was one more thing Mia needed to do.

She wasn't sure, though, what exactly compelled her to the brownstone on a quiet, residential street on Thursday afternoon, with Gloria and Paolo waiting in the car. It was a home in which she had eaten Sunday supper a few times, along with Nick. It had been a home where she'd been received kindly and treated like a special family relative.

Perhaps it had been her earlier stop in the Levee District, where she'd wanted to see for herself what remained of what had once been Stems Club. The place where she had once been a princess, her brother a prince. All that remained was a battered **Closed** sign on the door, and a rusted chain and padlock draped across the front and looped around the handle to prevent any squatters from going in.

She had felt a curious, painful surge in her chest. It was hard to reconcile what that place had become those last weeks there with happier memories. So often, when she'd rehearse in the afternoons, Nick would stroll in with a box of freshly baked biscotti from a tenement woman he'd helped, and Sal would make coffee, and the three of them would sit around chatting about old times in New York.

The memory had soured in her mouth, replaced by a deep-rooted pain stemming from Sal's betrayal. He had brought everything that happened to him upon himself.

Now Mia stood in the middle of the street, staring at the home Maria Bellomo lived in without her husband. She wondered if Maria had ever remarried, or if she was still mourning the loss of Sal. She had never really known much about the inner workings of Sal's relationship with his wife. He certainly hadn't been faithful to her.

She commanded her feet to carry her across the street, up the drive, and to the front door. Would Maria even be home? On the few occasions Mia had met her, Maria had told her she'd been an active member in her community, attending various groups and leagues and gatherings. Perhaps she still led a women's Bible study. Perhaps this Thursday afternoon had Mrs. Bellomo out and about—anywhere but inside the home of a man Mia had ordered killed. Her heart rose with a coward's desperate hope as she lifted her finger to push the doorbell.

*Don't be home. Don't be home.*

A few moments passed, long enough that she gave up and eagerly turned to walk back to the car. But the sound of the door unlatching and then opening made her freeze halfway down the stairs. She whirled around.

Mia had always remembered Maria as a handsome woman, if prone to gaudy dress most of the time. She'd always enjoyed her rouge and lip paint, and felt there was nothing gauche about wearing diamonds from seven in the morning on.

The woman who stared at her from the doorway appeared to have aged twenty years in the past two. Her face was clean of makeup, and her dress was a severe, plain black. Her dark eyes were full of shock, as if Mia were the last person she'd expected to see on her doorstep.

They gazed at each other for what felt like a year until Mia ventured a hesitant greeting.

"Hello, Maria," she said softly. "How are you?"

Maria's mouth opened and closed several times, as if she could not find the words to make a reply.

"I've been in town on some, er, business," Mia continued. "I'm heading to the train station now to go home, but I wanted to stop by and...see you."

Another long silence passed.

Finally, Maria spoke, her voice low, trembling, and enraged. "You got some fucking nerve, you little murdering bitch."

The air left Mia's body with a heavy *whoosh*. She hadn't known what to expect from the woman, but the venom in her voice caught her completely off guard.

Maria took a step over the threshold. "After what you did, you turn up at my front door? What the hell do you want?"

Now it was Mia's turn to struggle for words as she looked away.

What could she say? She hadn't known Maria had somehow come to find out or assume Mia had been responsible for Sal's death, but now that she'd made it perfectly clear she held Mia accountable...she wouldn't deny it. She owed Maria that much, at least—owed her the respect to not insult her intelligence.

Mia raised her head to meet Maria's gaze. "I just came to see how you are. See if there's anything you need. Anything the children need."

"Their father," Maria hissed, her eyes bright with unshed tears. "They need their goddamn *father*, you lousy bitch." A sob burst out of her and she smacked her hand over her mouth, as if trying to force it back inside. "How could you? After everything he did for you? For your brother? After all those times I had you in my home, around my family? Why did you do it? *Why?*"

Mia glanced down the street, hardly seeing the oak trees lining the block with their beautiful shades of gold and orange and red as she gathered her thoughts. She looked back at Maria. The tears flowed freely now, and her face was the perfect picture of grief. For the first time since Sal's death, Mia felt a true stab of remorse, so strong it left her breathless.

The remorse was not for what she'd done. She'd kill Sal a hundred more times if she could for taking her brother from her. The remorse was for Maria. For Viola O'Banion. For Josephine Simard, Hymie Weiss's sweetheart who had surely discovered by now her lover was dead. For the wives and sweethearts of the eighteen men in New York.

For Gloria Scalisi.

Even for women like Anna Torrio and Mae Capone and Maria Masseria, whose husbands still lived, but who had been the targets of assassination attempts. And as long as their husbands stayed in the life, there would likely be more.

Her remorse was for all the women who loved the wrong men, mired in lifestyles that usually only ended in a couple of ways. Prison, or death. More often than not, the latter.

She was sorry for Maria Bellomo. But she was not sorry for what she'd done.

"I did it," Mia said softly, "because he had my brother killed. It's as simple as that."

Maria grabbed the doorframe as though all the strength had suddenly left her, groaning.

"Your husband murdered my brother, and then he got what was coming to him," Mia went on. "I'm sorry it had to be that way. I'm sorry for you, and for Stephie, and Pete. I'm sorry you have to spend the rest of your life without the man you married, and that they have to grow up without their father."

She gazed down at the older woman, unmoved as Maria wept into her hand, crouched near the ground. "But so does my sister-in-law," she finished coldly. "So does my niece. And that's because of Sal."

"Get out," Maria screamed through her tears. "*Go.*"

Mia turned slowly and started down the stairs. Across the street, Gloria's face was pressed to the window, her mouth open in shock. Paolo, behind the wheel, stared straight ahead.

But they both had to have heard it clearly when Maria Bellomo began hurling insults at Mia's back.

"You fucking bitch. You lowlife whore. Goddamn murderer.

Get off my lawn. Get off my property. You're going to wish I had called the police when I get through with you. I'll have you killed. You think you're the only one with connections? You're dead, you bitch, *you're dead.*"

Mia paused halfway down the drive and glanced over her shoulder. The hysterical woman had no idea that if she'd wanted to, Mia could simply lift a hand, and Paolo would be at Maria's throat before she could shout the next part of her tirade. She had no idea that if Mia desired, Maria could be in the last few seconds of her life right now.

She felt another flash of pity.

"Goodbye," she said to Maria, then turned her back on a fresh barrage of enraged screams that seemed to echo off the oak trees, follow her into the car, and down the street.

❀

She, Gloria, and Paolo boarded a train back to New York two hours later. Mia carried the box that contained the urn filled with Nick's ashes.

"We're finally going home," she whispered to the box as she waited for Gloria to settle into her seat. Then, she passed Nick to his wife.

She'd called Father Alessio yesterday, letting him know what time her train would arrive on Saturday afternoon, and she would be going straight to the cemetery. He should have everything ready and waiting for them so they could lay Domenico Scalisi to rest properly, and for good.

The priest, she thought wryly as she settled back in her seat, would probably find some way to convince her to make confession again. She was starting to suspect that was more for him to feel better about pocketing the money she gave him each week than a concentrated effort to save the tattered remnants of her soul.

Mia remembered the last train ride she'd made between the two cities. The last time, she'd been fleeing Chicago after killing

Sal. Even then, she'd been an entirely different girl than the woman she was now. Then, she'd been out of her mind with fear and exhilaration and grief and madness. She smiled a little at the thought that she'd had no idea back then what might await her. What she'd become. The things she'd be forced—or want—to do. Mia then would never have believed Mia now. Foolishly, she'd believed she could avenge her brother and return to a somewhat normal life back in her hometown.

But now, as then, she was struck by how being on a train with her brother again called up so many memories of their last train ride between the two cities, when they'd been coming to Chicago from New York. Leaving their home for a new one. Now, she was bringing him back home. It had been several years since he'd really been home—not on a business trip, not to make deals with Hyman Goldberg about her future in exchange for start-up money. His real home—their roots, their humble beginnings in the Lower East Side.

"Penny for your thoughts."

Mia glanced over at Gloria, seated across from her in their private car. Her sister-in-law smiled. "You look like you're thinking up a storm. Don't hurt yourself."

Mia returned her smile with a little one of her own. "I was just thinking about the last time I came home from here. I haven't ever made this train ride—from here to New York—with Nick before." She reached out to rest her hand on the box Gloria held on her lap.

Gloria glanced down at it, her eyes soft and liquid. "Neither have I."

"I keep thinking about how the only time he went back to New York was to hock Hyman Goldberg for two million dollars," Mia said. "To invest in his crazy idea for a liquor business."

Gloria chuckled a little. "Boy, he was proud when he came home."

Mia rolled her eyes. "He was *insufferable*. If you ever wondered what a bantam cock would look like if he were a human, Nick Scalisi is it."

Beside her, Paolo smiled as she and Gloria both broke up into laughter. It felt so wonderful to laugh, Mia realized. When was the last time she had really laughed? Not in a dark way or an exasperated way. A real peal of mirth. She couldn't remember.

"He was smart," Gloria said softly, shaking her head. "He was so smart. I often wonder what he would've become if he were still here. How much he would've grown. Twenty-five's still young, you know."

It struck Mia that she would outlive her brother. The glow in her chest faded.

"I wonder what he'd think of me, if he could see me," she said. "All the things I've done. Sometimes it keeps me up at night, wondering what he'd think."

Gloria leaned forward and put one hand over Mia's. "He'd be proud of you. He'd be so proud."

"Would he? What, exactly, is there to be proud of?"

Her sister-in-law tightened her hold. "That you never forgot where you came from. And that you always put blood first."

*Blood comes first.*

It was the first lesson he'd ever taught her. The importance of familial blood, and loyalty to it above everything else, was something he'd instilled in her and hounded from the first moments she'd been able to comprehend.

"I almost let him have them," Mia said.

"Let who have who?"

"Let Morelli have Little Italy, all its people." She shook her head. "I wouldn't call that never forgetting where you came from."

"You did it to save your blood," Gloria said simply. "You had no choice but the two he gave you, and you picked us. I'll never forget that, and Nick would've done the same thing."

"You're my family." Mia shrugged. "You're all I got. I couldn't let anything happen to you. I just wish…Raquel had stayed." Her heart ached from the hole her young cousin had taken with her when she'd gone. "I don't think she'll ever talk to me again."

"She doesn't hate you," Gloria said. She settled back in her seat, crossing her ankles. She linked her fingers together around the urn box. "It was a traumatizing experience for her. And I think she feels she let you down. They could never hate you, Mia. You're family."

Mia nodded. She changed the subject, because talking about Raquel hurt too much. "I was also thinking about our childhood. It's strange to me now, how I look back fondly on those times when back then, to me life was so hard. I'll never forget the bad times—going hungry, freezing in the winter, sweltering in the summer. Never knowing where our next nickel would come from, or if we'd be able to pay the landlord that month. When Nick got drafted and I had to fend for myself. But those aren't the things I think of when I look back."

"What do you think of?" Gloria's soft smile was back.

Mia shifted her gaze out the window as landscapes passed at blurring speeds. "I think of the summer nights we spent on fire escapes after it got really dark, drinking cold water that tasted funny from the ice chips off the old block the grocer used to keep the meats cold. We'd look out over all the city lights, and imagine what the fancy, rich people were doing and make up stories for their lives. Then we'd imagine what we would do if were fancy and rich. Other times, we'd go to the tenement of this immigrant couple. The husband brought his mandolin over on the boat. One of the only possessions they had that made the trip. He could really play. And sing. He had the most beautiful voice. His wife would bake sweet *taralli* and let us sit and listen until his voice gave out or we fell asleep. We could just be…children then."

"Except for all those nights you had to stay up and learn how to be a world-class poker player," Gloria teased.

Mia chuckled. "I complained so much about it then, because I was so tired. I'd fall asleep playing poker with him, and he'd nudge me awake with his foot and make me keep going. But you couldn't tell him his plans wouldn't work. Once he got me up to snuff, we were the terror of those card halls. Well, *he* was. No one knew about me."

"His secret weapon," Gloria said.

Mia sighed deeply. If only she'd known then that their time together was limited, that he would be taken from her before they'd had a chance to triumph after so much struggling. "I just wish he'd at least gotten to see what it became. All his hard work. If he hadn't died, none of this would be happening. I'd still have gone to New York to work for Hyman, because he sold me off, but he'd be king of Chicago."

"It wasn't quite like that," Gloria said. "The selling you off."

Mia snapped her head up. "You...*knew?*"

She shook her head. "Not for sure. No details. He just mentioned to me once he'd like that for you. He thought it would do you some good to be back home, because he thought for all you loved living in a luxurious hotel like the Lex, you missed being around the people. Not the showbusiness people. Real people. The ones from back home. He wanted you to be happy." She lifted a shoulder. "And if that meant he had to use some questionable tactics, maybe even underhanded, to ensure that... Well, I think if it had been you in his place and someone else you loved in yours, you wouldn't have hesitated for a second. You're like him in that way. You make snap decisions because you see the good they can do, and you deal with the fallout later. He knew you'd find out about his deal with Hyman sooner or later, and that you'd be furious. But he was prepared to discuss it with you when the time was right."

"Perhaps that's true," Mia said. "But also, he was a business-man. I don't want to shove him up on a pedestal just because he's dead. He loved me, Glo, of course I know he did. But I also made him a good amount of money. We had a two-man act, me and him, and I was the acrobat, and he was the ringmaster."

"You sounded fond before," Gloria said. "Now you sound...bitter."

"Not bitter, no. I just see things clearly now. I've made peace with it."

That was a lie. She had barely come to accept her brother's many sides. She still grappled with who he'd really been. In the end, she knew he was a different person to everyone, and perhaps she'd known the version closest to the real man. She would never know what his true intentions were. But she did know he'd loved her, and that would have to be enough for the rest of her life.

Now, she could give him something by taking him home. He would rest beside their parents for an eternity. And one day, she would join them in the small cemetery in Queens, and they would finally all be together again. She might be an old, old woman when that happened, but it would happen. She had to be sure of it, or else she'd slide beneath the waves of pain that threatened to drown her ever since the night he'd died.

Paolo reached over and lightly patted her arm with quick taps without looking at her. It was a surprisingly affectionate, reassuring gesture, and it went straight to her heart. She smiled at him.

"It'll be good for Em," Mia said after a long moment. "To have him close by where she can visit him."

"Yes." Gloria glanced down again at the box. "I hope she remembers him."

"We'll never let her forget him." Mia reached for her hand. "Ever."

WHEN THEY ARRIVED IN NEW YORK, TRUDY WAS AT THE STATION with Emilia to greet them. Gloria rushed forward to scoop her child into her arms and hug her tight.

Mia kissed Trudy's cheek. "How were things?"

"Nice and quiet, miss," Trudy said, her eyes twinkling. "Always a good thing."

"Indeed, it is," Mia said. "How's the shop?"

"We're almost ready to reopen next month, in time for Christmas shoppers," Trudy replied. "They've done a lot of work this past week. I daresay you'll be pleased. They finished the wainscoting, and the furniture arrived."

"Wonderful," Mia said with genuine pleasure.

An attendant brought their baggage to them on a cart, and led the way outside to their waiting vehicle. Joey jumped out of the driver's side, tipped the attendant, and loaded the bags in the car.

Trudy opened the car door for Gloria. "The, erm, warehouse beneath the shop is, ah, already being put to good use."

"Oh?"

"Yes." Trudy cleared her throat, her cheeks flushing. Her freckles stood out alarmingly. "Mr. Goldberg seemed to take advantage of your absence and it is, if I might use the American idiom, loaded to the goddamn gills."

"Brother," Mia muttered. She slid into the back seat beside Gloria, and Trudy climbed in next to her. Paolo rode up front next to Joey.

"Cemetery, Miss Scalisi?" Joey asked.

"Yes, please. Thank you, Joey." Then she turned to Trudy. "At least we're back up and running. That business with Morelli really threw a wrench in that. Was Mr. Goldberg pleasant to you, at least?"

"Oh yes," Trudy said. "I think the combination of so much product arriving and you not being there to boss him about lifted his spirits tremendously."

Mia hesitated. "So much product, you say? From...Iowa? When I spoke with Mr. Wyatt before I left, he made it seem like he was producing normal amounts."

"I believe there is other product besides the Iowa lot," Trudy replied. "Cuban rum."

"Cuban...rum?" This was news to Mia. Hyman had mentioned wanting to branch out and include other products, but Cuban rum had not been one of them.

"It appears it was a gift from a seller who's been courtin' him," Trudy went on. "To test the waters in New York and see if there could be a demand for it."

Her interest was piqued. Hyman couldn't be rid of her for long, and she fully intended to sit down with him and discuss this new venture—whether he wanted to or not.

"Did you try it?" Mia asked.

"I did. One of the young men who brought it by the shop fixed it for us. A bit of rum mixed with a Coca-Cola."

"Coca-Cola?" Mia repeated.

Trudy smiled. "And a twist of lime."

"How'd you like it?"

"I thought it was quite lovely," Trudy said. "A little *too* lovely."

Mia giggled, picturing a tipsy Trudy. "Well, thank you for looking after things for me. I'm certainly looking forward to a nice, long chat with Mr. Goldberg."

"And I reminded him you'd be wanting that chat as often as I could."

At Calvary Cemetery in Queens, the somewhat lighthearted mood dissipated into the air. Father Alessio waited with Charlie, who held three white roses, at the newly dug plot, small to fit the urn vault Nick was in. When their father had died in 1906, their mother had scraped together enough money from her savings and the kind tenement families to bury him in a pine box in a plot with no headstone, just a simple marker so the cemetery would know who was buried there. When she'd died five years later, Nick had hustled for days and nights to earn enough money for a sturdy wooden casket for her, as well as two lovely headstones.

Now, beside their plots, a third had been dug, and a third headstone added.

Together, she and Gloria lowered the urn vault into the ground. Gloria wept softly as they stood. "It's as though it just happened, all over again."

Throat tight, Mia wrapped an arm around her shoulder. Charlie held her hand on her other side. Hers felt clammy and too hot, but his was cool, dry, and reassuring. He gave it a squeeze.

"To you, O Lord, we commend the soul of Domenico Scalisi,

Your servant," Father Alessio intoned. "In the sight of this world, he is now dead; in Your sight, may he live forever."

Mia arched her brows, and jerked her head slightly toward Gloria.

Father Alessio cleared his throat. "Forgive whatever sins he committed through human weakness, and in Your Goodness, grant him everlasting peace." He made the sign of the cross, and everyone hastened to do the same. "Through Christ, our Lord."

"Amen," Gloria breathed.

"Amen," Mia murmured, staring down into the ground.

"Here." Charlie handed her, Gloria, and Emilia the roses. He placed a gentle hand on top of Emilia's head. "Give Papa the rose." He pointed at the urn.

Emilia, confused and overwhelmed, started to cry. "I wanna keep it."

Mia swiftly knelt and drew her niece to her. She cradled Emilia's soft cheek. "I'll get you a dozen white roses—or any color you want—every single week, darling. But I think Papa would like that rose you're holding. It'll keep you near him. Is that all right?"

Emilia hesitated, two large tears rolling down her cheeks. She nodded.

Mia brushed the tears away with her thumbs. "That's my good girl. Come, let's toss them in together."

Emilia stood between her aunt and mother at the edge of the plot. Gloria counted to three, and the three women Domenico Scalisi had loved best in life tossed in their white roses.

The cemetery's gravedigger had kept a respectable distance during the short ceremony. Now, he came forward, head bowed, and began to fill the plot with dirt.

When Emilia began to cry again, Gloria picked her up and turned away. "I'll wait in the car," she said to Mia. Joey and Paolo followed her, and after a moment, Father Alessio joined them, hands folded in front of him.

Mia stayed where she was, her feet rooted to the ground.

Charlie stood beside her and slid an arm around her waist. He drew her close and pressed his lips to the top of her head.

"This feels right," he said. "Nick being here, with your parents. It feels peaceful."

She nodded against his chest, not trusting herself to speak. She didn't want to cry anymore over her dead brother. If she started again, she wasn't sure she'd be able to stop.

"You did a good thing," he added softly.

How could anything she had done be considered good? She had surely earned herself a seat right next to her brother in the eternally burning fires of hell. It didn't matter that she'd bribed a priest for Nick's salvation. She could have bribed a thousand priests, and it wouldn't change anything. It didn't matter that he had an entire congregation in Little Italy saying masses to save his soul. He'd done what he'd done, and she had followed suit without skipping a beat.

But at the very least, she'd brought him home.

"Thanks," she said at last, because she didn't know what else to say. "Would you mind... Could I have a moment? Alone."

"Of course you can." He kissed her head again, then walked away toward the car, where everyone waited for her.

Mia knelt next to his grave, bracing herself against the headstone for balance. She touched the soft, fresh soil that filled his grave.

"Do you think he's right?" she murmured. "That I've done... good." She huffed in amusement.

Almost as though in response, a little surge of wind kissed her cheeks.

After a moment, she said, "I don't know if you heard, but Hymie Weiss is dead. I got him for you. I promised you I would."

The wind rustled the leaves in the trees.

"Everyone who plotted against you is gone now," she continued. "The revenge is done. And...nothing's changed. It still hurts. And in a way, it hurts even more." She took a deep breath that trembled slightly on the exhale. "I don't really know what to do now, other than keep your business alive. Rum, Trudy says. We're going to start selling rum, maybe."

She ran her fingers along the rough edge of his headstone. It was a bright, clean white-gray. It stood out starkly next to their parents' headstones, which time and the elements had darkened to a dull cement color.

"Tell Mama and Papa hello for me," she whispered, hoping with all of her darkened soul that he was with them. If there was a God, and if He was merciful and kind, she prayed He allowed them to be a family again.

She stood up, wobbling slightly on the uneven earth, and took a step back. She studied each headstone.

Emilio Scalisi. Francesca Scalisi. Domenico Scalisi.

The sense of aloneness that fell upon her almost knocked her off her feet.

She glanced down at her shoes, rapidly blinking to clear away the tears that gathered in her eyes. The hushed wind wove through the leaves, making them tremble and darting away before they stilled.

Mia raised her eyes to the graves of her family. "I'll come and see you again soon," she promised them. "*Mia famighhia.*"

As she turned away, she thought she heard the sound of a familiar chuckle, one she hadn't heard in almost two years. She froze in her tracks, the sound so dear and heartbreaking all at once. Then she whirled around, hoping against foolish hope she might see her dashing, dark-haired brother, leaning against his headstone, cigarette in hand and his old, sly grin on his face, as though he mocked the very idea he might be dead.

There was no one. The sound vanished into the whispering wind as it slid past her cheeks in a gentle caress.

Her hope, her foolish, foolish hope, dissipated like ashes in a breeze. Of course, he wasn't really there. Of course, she was alone.

Still, as she walked up the grassy slope to rejoin her new, handpicked family, she smiled.

# THE SCALISI FAMILY SAGA

Blood & Whiskey

Princes of the Lower East Side

Blood Comes First: The Scalisi Family Novellas

Scala Reale (Coming 2021)

# ACKNOWLEDGMENTS

To my beloved family, husband, and friends: Thank you all so much for your continued love and support.

To my best friend Sade: As always, I so appreciate your insight and wisdom into my characters. Your suggestions are invaluable, as is your support and your friendship.

To my editor, Michelle Morgan: To say you have been a blessing is an understatement. We are kindred spirits in so many ways, and I cannot thank you enough for your editorial wisdom and dedication to helping me produce the best story I could. It really makes my gut clench with happiness. :-D

To my proofer, Jenny, thank you so much for your assistance in Swiffering this book.

To my beta readers, your feedback and enthusiasm for my writing is critical in the development and refinement of these stories. You're all invested in Mia and her saga, and I cannot thank you emphatically enough for your time and attention.

To you, the reader: Saving the best for last! I hope you've enjoyed the second installment in the Scalisi Family saga. There's much more to come. I cannot thank you enough for your time, and I truly appreciate you choosing my work to relax and have a whiskey with. Thank you, and please stay tuned for more from Mia Scalisi!

# ABOUT THE AUTHOR

Meredith Allison is a native of Lincoln, Nebraska. She attended the University of Nebraska-Lincoln and then went on to receive her Master of Fine Arts in Creative Writing from Creighton University in Omaha, Nebraska, where she resides with her husband and a menagerie of pets.

Stay up to date with all her latest news including release dates, book cover reveals, exclusive excerpts, giveaways, and more by signing up at www.Meredith-Allison.com/mailing-list.

If you enjoyed this book, please, consider leaving a review. It is the best way to show an author how much you enjoyed their work, and it is deeply appreciated by authors. Thank you!

facebook.com/mallisonwrites

twitter.com/mallisonwrites

instagram.com/mallisonwrites